The Wolf and the Watchman

Niklas Natt och Dag

JOHN MURRAY

First published in Great Britain in 2019 by John Murray (Publishers)
An Hachette UK Company

First published in Swedish as *1793* by Bokförlaget Forum, Stockholm, 2017

1

© Niklas Natt och Dag 2017
Translation © Ebba Segerberg 2019

A CIP catalogue record for this title is available from the British Library

ISBN 978-1-473-68212-2
Trade Paperback ISBN 978-1-473-69213-8
Ebook ISBN 978-1-473-68213-9

Typeset in Adobe Garamond by Hewer Text UK Ltd, Edinburgh
Printed and bound by CPI Group (UK) Ltd, Croydon, CR0 4YY

John Murray policy is to use papers that are natural, renewable and recyclable products and
made from wood grown in sustainable forests. The logging and manufacturing processes
are expected to conform to the environmental regulations of the country of origin.

John Murray (Publishers)
Carmelite House
50 Victoria Embankment
London EC4Y 0DZ

www.johnmurray.co.uk

The Wolf and
the Watchman

Guile begets guile, violence begets violence.

– Thomas Thorild, 1793

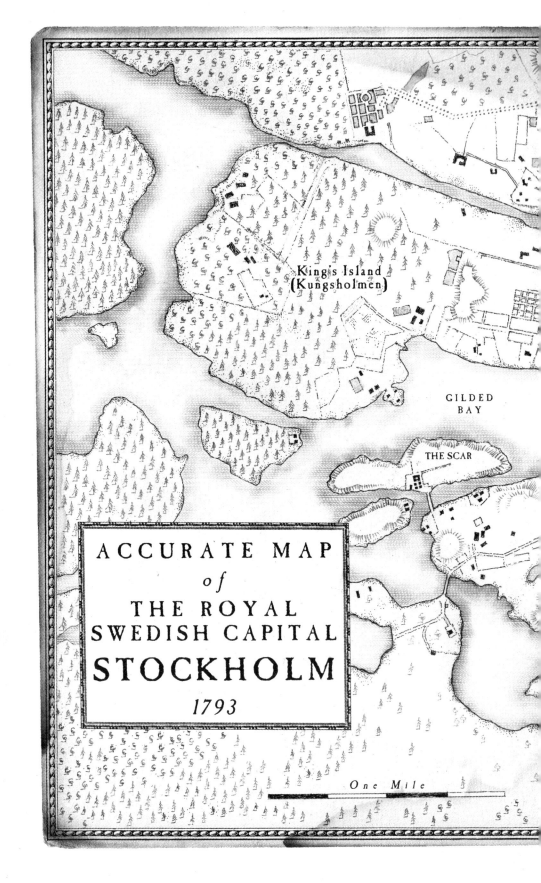

King's Island
(Kungsholmen)

GILDED
BAY

THE SCAR

ACCURATE MAP
of
THE ROYAL
SWEDISH CAPITAL
STOCKHOLM
1793

One Mile

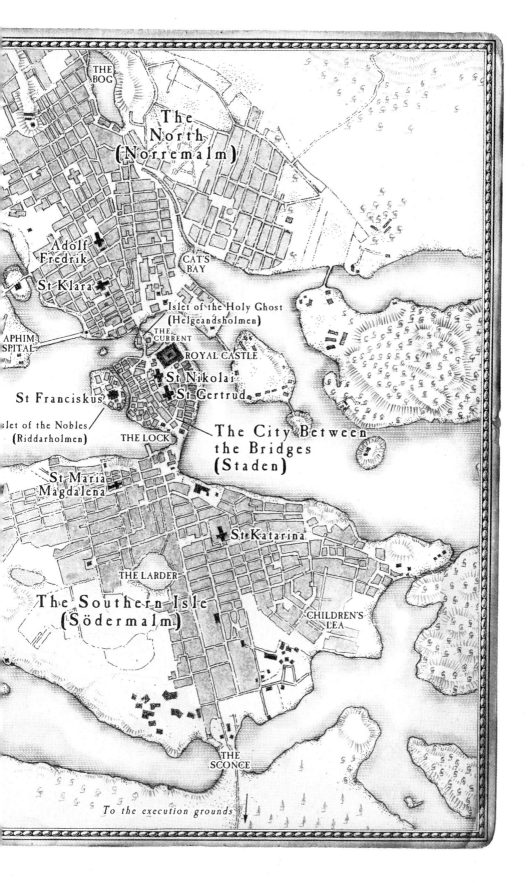

PART ONE

The Ghost of the Indebetou

Autumn 1793

A great calamity has befallen us. A thousand rumours abound, each one more preposterous than the next. It is impossible to obtain any trustworthy information, for even travellers have differing accounts and all seem to me somewhat poetical in what they relate. The atrocity of the crime, as it has been related, is too great, such that I do not know how I should think thereof.

– Carl Gustaf af Leopold, 1793

Mickel Cardell is floating in cold water. With his unobstructed right hand, he grabs Johan Hjelm by the collar: Hjelm who lies beside him, unmoving, red foam at his lips. Blood and brackish water make Hjelm's uniform slippery, and when a wave tears the last scrap of fabric from Cardell's fingers, he wants to scream, but only a whimper comes over his lips. Hjelm sinks quickly. Cardell ducks his head under, and for a moment he follows the body's journey into the depths. Shaking with cold and emotion he thinks he sees something else down there, just at the limit of what his senses are able to perceive. Mutilated bodies of sailors fall slowly by the thousands towards the gates of hell. The Angel of Death, upon whose head sits a crown fashioned from a dead man's skull, folds his wings about them. In the swirl of the current, his jaw moves up and down in mocking laughter.

1

'MICKEL! WATCHMAN MICKEL! Please wake up!'
As an agitated shaking rouses Cardell from his slumber, he feels a fleeting ache in the left arm he no longer owns. A carved wooden hand has taken the place of the missing limb. His stump rests in a hollow space inside the beechwood, attached at the elbow with the aid of leather straps. They are cutting into his flesh. He should know better by now and have loosened them before nodding off.

Reluctantly, he opens his eyes and stares out across the vast plain of the stained table. When he makes an attempt to lift his head, his cheek sticks to the wooden surface and he inadvertently pulls his wig off as he stands up. He curses and uses it to wipe his brow before tucking it inside his jacket. His hat rolls down onto the floor, its crown dented. He punches it out and then pulls it onto his head. His memory is beginning to return. He is at Cellar Hamburg and must have drunk himself senseless. A glance over his shoulder reveals others in a similar condition. The few drunks that the proprietor considered affluent enough not to toss into the gutter are sprawled over benches and across tables, until the morning when they will stagger away to receive the reproaches of those waiting at home. Not so Cardell. A crippled war veteran, he lives alone and his time is no one's but his own.

'Mickel, you've got to come! There's a dead body in the Larder!'

The two youngsters who have roused him are guttersnipes. Their faces look familiar but he is unable to recall their names. Behind them stands the Ram, the well-nourished manager who works for Widow Norström, the owner. The Ram is groggy and flushed and has positioned himself between the children and a collection of etched glass: the pride of the cellar, stored behind lock and key in a blue cabinet.

The condemned stop here at Cellar Hamburg on their way to the Sconce Tollgate and to the gallows beyond. At the steps of the Hamburg they are served their last drink, after which the glass is carefully retrieved, etched with name and date, and added to the collection. The patrons may drink from one of these only under supervision and upon payment of a fee based on the degree of infamy of the condemned. It is said to bring good fortune. Cardell has never understood the reasoning.

Cardell rubs his eyes and realizes he is still inebriated. His voice is thick when he tries it.

'What the devil is going on?'

It is the older one – a girl – who answers. The boy is harelipped, and her brother, to judge by his features. He wrinkles his nose at Cardell's breath and takes cover behind his sister.

'There is a body in the water, right at the edge.'

Her tone is a blend of terror and excitement. The veins in Cardell's forehead feel close to bursting. The pounding of his heart threatens to drown out what feeble thoughts he tries to muster.

'How's this my problem?'

'Please, Mickel, there isn't anyone else and we knew that you were here.'

He rubs his temples in a vain hope of easing the throbbing pain.

———◆———

Above the Southern Isle, the skies have not yet begun to lighten. Cardell staggers out and down the steps of the Hamburg, and follows the children along the empty street, half-heartedly listening to a story about a thirsty cow that reared up at the water's edge and took off in terror in the direction of Danto.

'Her muzzle touched the body and made it spin in a circle.'

Underfoot the stones give way to mud as they get closer to the lake. Cardell's duties have not carried him past the shores of the Larder in a long time, but he sees that nothing has changed. Nothing has come of the long-held plans to clean the shoreline and build a quay with piers, though this is hardly any cause of wonder when both city and state teeter on the brink of ruin. The fine houses around the lake have long since been repurposed into manufactories. The workshops throw their waste directly into the water, and the fenced section intended for human waste is overflowing and ignored by most. Cardell lets out a colourful phrase when his boot heel ploughs a furrow in the muck and he has to flap his healthy arm to maintain his balance.

'Your cow was frightened by an encounter with an overripe cousin. The butchers throw their scraps into the lake. You've woken me up for nothing more than a rancid side of beef or some pig's ribcage.'

'We saw a face in the water, a person's face.'

The waves lap against the shore, churning up a pale yellow froth. Something rotten – a dark lump – is floating a few metres out. Cardell's first thought is that it cannot possibly be a human being. It is too small.

'Like I said, it's butcher's scraps. An animal carcass.'

The girl insists she is not mistaken. The boy nods in agreement. Cardell snorts in surrender.

'I'm drunk, you hear? Dead drunk. Soused. You'll not forget this when someone asks about the time you tricked the watchman into taking a dip in the Larder and how he gave you both the thrashing of your lives when he came up again, soaked and enraged.'

He works his way out of his coat with the awkwardness of the one-handed. The forgotten woollen wig falls out of the lining, into the slush. Never mind. The miserable thing only cost a pittance and the fashion is on its way out. He wears it only because a more proper appearance improves the chances that someone will stand a war veteran a drink or two. Cardell casts a glance at the sky. High above, a band of distant stars shine over Årsta Bay. He closes his eyes to seal the impression of beauty inside him and steps into the lake, right leg first.

The boggy edge doesn't support his weight. He sinks down as far as his knee and feels the lake water pouring over the edge of his boot, which remains stuck in the sludge as his involuntary fall forward pulls his leg along. With something between a crawl and a doggy-paddle, he begins to make his way further out. The water is thick between his fingers, full of things that even the residents of the Southern Isle don't consider worth keeping.

His intoxication has impaired his sense of judgement. He feels a stab of panic when he no longer has the lake bottom under his feet. This water is deeper than anticipated and he finds himself back at Svensksund three years ago, terrified and tossed by the waves, with the Swedish front drawing back.

He grasps the body in the water once his kicking has carried him close enough. His first thought is that he was correct. This cannot be a human being. It is a discarded carcass, tossed here by the butcher's boys, made into a buoy as the gases of decomposition expand its innards. Then the lump rolls over and shows him its face.

It isn't rotten at all, and yet empty eye sockets stare back at him. Behind the torn lips there are no teeth. The hair alone has retained its lustre – the night and the lake have done their best to dim its colour, but it is without a doubt a mass of light blond hair. Cardell's sudden intake of breath fills his mouth with water and causes him to choke.

When his coughing fit has subsided, he floats motionless next to the corpse, studying its ravaged features. Back on the shore, the children make no sound. They await his return in silence. He grabs the body, turns around in the water and starts to kick with his bare foot to make his way back towards land.

The recovery effort becomes more laborious when he reaches the muddy embankment and the water no longer carries their weight. Cardell rolls over onto his back and kicks his way up with both legs, dragging his quarry by its ragged covering. The children do not help him. Instead, they back away cowering, holding their noses. Cardell clears his throat of the filthy pond water and spits into the mud.

'Run to the Lock and tell the Corpses.'

The children make no move to comply, as eager to keep their distance as they are to get a glimpse of Cardell's catch. Only when he tosses a handful of muck at them do they set off.

'Run to the night post and get me a fucking bluecoat, damn it!'

When their small feet are out of earshot, he leans over to the side and vomits. Stillness descends and, in his isolation, Cardell feels a cold embrace pressing all air out of his lungs, making it impossible to draw the next breath. His heart beats faster and faster, the blood throbs in the veins in his throat and he is overcome with a paralysing fear. He knows all too well what comes next. He feels the arm that is no longer his solidify out of the surrounding darkness until every part of his being tells him it is back where it once was, and with it a pain searing enough to cancel the world itself out, as a jaw with teeth of iron gnaws flesh, bone and gristle.

In a state of panic, he tears at the leather straps and lets the wooden arm fall into the mud. He grabs his stump with his right hand and massages the scarred flesh to force his senses to accept that the arm they perceive no longer exists and that the wound is long since healed.

The seizure lasts no more than a minute. Breath returns, first in shallow gasps and then in calmer, slower inhalations. The terror subsides and the world regains its familiar contours. These sudden panic attacks have plagued him for the past three years, ever since he returned from the war, one arm and one friend poorer. And yet that was all a long time ago now. He thought he had found a method to keep the nightmares at bay. Strong drink and bar brawls. Cardell looks around as if for something to soothe himself with but he and the corpse are alone. He sways side to side with his stump in a firm grasp.

2

O N THE DESK in front of him lies a piece of paper upon which lines have been drawn to form a neat grid. Cecil Winge places his pocket watch before him, unhooks it from its chain and pulls the crackling wax candle closer. His screwdrivers are lined up all in a row next to the tweezers and pliers. He holds out his hands in front of the flame. There are no noticeable tremors.

He begins his work with meticulous care. He opens the watch, loosens the bolt holding the hands in place, lifts them from the dial and places each of them within their own square on the paper. He lifts away the clock face and reveals the inner workings that can now be extracted without resistance. Slowly he undresses the mechanism, wheel by wheel, and places each piece within its enclosure of ink. Freed from its confines, the flat hairspring stretches itself out into a long spiral. Underneath is the gear train, then the spindle. Tools barely larger than sewing needles coax the tiny screws from their nests.

Deprived of his own watch, Winge is able to track the passage of time only by the tolling of the church bells. From across the Meadowland, the large bells in Hedvig Eleonora Church ring out. From the sea comes the fainter echo of the Katarina church tower from its perch on the hill. Hours hurry past.

Once he has completely dismantled the timepiece, he repeats each step in reverse order. The watch slowly takes shape again as every piece falls back into place. His thin fingers cramp up and he has to pause repeatedly in order to allow his muscles and tendons to recuperate. He opens and closes his hands, rubbing them against each other and stretching the joints against his knees. The uncomfortable working position begins to take its toll and the pain in his hip, which he has been feeling more and more often, spreads up into his lower back, forcing him constantly to shift position in the chair.

Once the hands are back in place, he fits the small key to the lock and turns it, feeling the resistance of the spring inside. As soon as he lets go, he hears the familiar ticking and for the hundredth time since summer thinks the same thought: This is how the world should function; rational and comprehensible, where every part has its given place and the effect of its trajectory can be precisely determined.

The sense of wellbeing and comfort is fleeting. It leaves him quickly once the distraction is over and the world in which time halted for a few moments takes shape around him once again. His mind begins to wander. He places a finger on his wrist and counts the beats of his heart while the smallest hand counts seconds on the dial that bears the name of its maker: Beurling, Stockholm. He makes it one hundred and forty beats a minute. He puts his tools in order and readies himself to begin the entire process again, when he perceives the smell of food, hears the maid's scratches at the door and a voice calling him to table.

———•———

A blue-patterned tureen is placed before them. His landlord, the ropemaker Olof Roselius, bows his head in brief prayer before he reaches to uncover the dish. He bites back a curse and shakes the pain from his fingertips after scalding himself on the handle.

From his seat to the right of his host, Cecil Winge pretends to stare at the grain of the table, laced with shadows from the wax candles, while the maid rushes to his aid with a tea towel. The scent of turnips and boiled meat smoothes the wrinkles from the ropemaker's brow. A lifetime of seventy years have leached all colour from his hair and beard and left him hunched in his chair. Roselius is known as a righteous man who for years has engaged himself in the running of the poorhouse at Hedvig Eleonora, and also generously shared the fortune that once was great enough to purchase Count Spens's summer house here in the outskirts of the Meadowland. His old age has been darkened by unfortunate investments in a northern mill, investments undertaken with his neighbour Ekman, a high-level official at the Chamber of Finance. Winge senses that Roselius feels himself to be ill treated and ill compensated for decades of charitable works. Now bitterness rests over the property like a bell jar.

As a tenant, Winge cannot help but feel that his very presence bears witness to unfortunate times. Tonight, Roselius appears even more lugubrious than normal and follows every bite with a sigh. By the time he clears his throat and breaks the silence, only a few spoonfuls remain at the bottom of his bowl.

'It is a hard task to give advice to the young, as one usually only receives abuse in response. And yet I wish what is best for you, Cecil. Please be kind enough to listen.'

Roselius takes a deep breath before he goes on to say what must be said.

'What you are doing is unnatural. A husband should be with his wife. Did you not swear to be with her for better and for worse? Go back to her.'

The blood rushes to Winge's face. The speed of his reaction surprises him. It does not befit a man of reason to allow his judgement to be obscured and anger to take the upper hand. He draws a deep breath, feels the beating of his heart in his ears, and concentrates on mastering his emotions. In the meantime, nothing is said. Winge knows that the years have not blunted the shrewdness that led Roselius to pre-eminence among his peers. He can almost hear his landlord's thoughts behind his forehead. The tension between them grows and then ebbs under the unbroken silence. Roselius sighs, leans back and holds out his hands in a gesture of reconciliation.

'We have broken bread together many times, you and I. You are well read, quick-witted. I know that you are neither villain nor blackguard. Quite the opposite. But you are blinded by new ideas, Cecil. You believe that everything may be solved by strength of mind, your own in particular. You are mistaken. Emotions do not allow themselves to be thus shackled. Return to your wife, for both your sakes, and if you have wronged her in some way, beg her forgiveness.'

'What I did was for her own good. It was carefully considered.'

'Cecil, whatever you may have wished to achieve, the result has been another.'

Winge cannot stop his hands from trembling and puts down his spoon in order to conceal his agitation. To his frustration, he hears his own voice emerge no louder than a hoarse whisper.

'It should have worked.'

Even to his own ears, his reply sounds like the excuses of an obstinate child. When Roselius responds, his voice is milder than before.

'I saw her today, Cecil. Your wife. At the fishmonger's, next to Cats' Bay. She is with child. Far enough gone that there is no disguising her belly.'

Winge starts in his chair and for the first time looks Roselius straight in the face.

'Was she alone?'

Roselius nods and reaches to place his hand on Winge's arm, but Winge swiftly moves it out of reach. The instinctive reaction surprises even him.

Winge closes his eyes in order to regain control of himself, and for a moment he finds himself transported to the library he carries within, where rows of books are arranged in an orderly manner and subjected to a reign of absolute silence. He selects a volume by Ovid and reads a few words at random: '*Omnia mutantur, nihil inherit.*'

Everything changes, but nothing is truly ever lost. There he finds the consolation he seeks.

When he opens his eyes again, they betray no emotion of any kind. With some effort, he musters control over his trembling hands and carefully returns his spoon to its proper place, pushes his chair back and rises from the table.

'I thank you for both the soup and your concern, but I believe I will take supper in my room from now on.'

Roselius's voice follows him out.

'If your mind says one thing and reality another, it must be the thought that is in error. How can this not be evident to you, with all the benefits of a classical education?'

Winge has no answer, but the growing distance between them allows him to pretend he does not hear.

———— • ————

Cecil Winge staggers out into the corridor on unsteady legs, and on up the stairs to the room he has been renting from the rope-maker since summer. He quickly finds himself out of breath and is forced to stop and steady himself at the doorpost.

Outside his window, the garden is still. The sun has gone down. On the slopes leading down to the shore, there is a sprawling orchard. Behind the trees, he sees the lights from the shipyard out on its island, where sailors hurry to complete their work in the hopes of putting walls and a roof between themselves and the night. In the distance, there is the tower of Katarina Church. The evening breeze is blowing.

Every day it is as if the city takes a breath, drawing in the air each morning from the sea, exhaling the same evening with a force that twists every weathervane back towards the shore. Close by, the old windmill groans in protest against the ropes that bind her sails. Further inland, one of her sisters replies in the same language.

Winge sees his reflection in the windowpane. He is not yet thirty. His dark hair is gathered with a ribbon at the neck, its colour in sharp contrast to his pale face. White cloth covers his neck in tight folds. He can no longer see where the horizon ends and where the heavens begin. Only higher up do the emerging stars betray the sky. And such is the world itself: so much darkness, so little light. His peripheral vision catches a star shooting past the upper corner of his window, a line of light that speeds across the sky in the blink of an eye.

Down by the linden trees in the garden, he sees a lantern, although no visitor is expected. He hears his name called. He wraps his coat around him and when he gets nearer he can see that there are two waiting. Roselius's maid is holding the lantern, and beside her is a short figure, bent at the waist, hands on its knees, panting, and with a string of saliva hanging from its lips. When he gets closer, the maid puts the lantern into his hand.

'The visitor is for you. I'm not going to let that one over my threshold in the condition he's in.'

She turns on her heel and marches staunchly back into the main house, shaking her head at the folly of the world. The boy is young. He still has a light voice and smooth cheeks under the dirt.

'Well?'

'Are you Winge, the one at the Inbeto?'

'To be precise, the Chamber of Police is based at Indebetou House. But I am in fact Cecil Winge.'

The boy peers up at him under dirty blond hair, unwilling to take him at his word without proof.

'At Castle Hill they said that the one who could get here the fastest would get a reward.'

'Oh?'

The boy chews on a strand of hair that has escaped from under his hat.

'I ran faster than the others. Now I have a cramp in my side and can taste blood in my mouth and will have to sleep outside in wet clothes. I'd like a farthing for my troubles.'

The boy holds his breath as if his own daring has put a choke-hold on him. Winge gives him a sharp look.

'You have already said that there are others on their way here on the same errand. I only need to wait a while and then we can begin taking bids.'

He can hear the boy gnash his teeth and curse his mistake. Winge opens his purse and takes out the requested coin. He holds it between his thumb and index finger.

'Tonight you are in luck. I do not count patience among my virtues.'

The boy smiles faintly. His missing front teeth leave a gap through which his tongue laps up the mucus running down from his nose.

'The police chief is the one looking for you, sir. And he wants you right away, in Axesmith's Alley.'

Winge nods to himself and holds out the hand with the coin. The boy takes a few steps closer and grabs his reward. He turns abruptly, takes off and clears the low wall with a jump that almost causes him to lose his balance. Winge calls out to him.

'Let it be used for bread, and not drink.'

The boy pauses and in response he lowers his trousers, shows Winge his pale behind and gives each cheek a loud slap as he calls back over his shoulder.

'A few more errands of this kind and I'll be rich enough not to have to choose.'

The boy laughs in triumph and disappears across the Meadowland, quickly swallowed by the shadows.

———•———

For months, Police Chief Johan Gustaf Norlin has been promised official housing but nothing has come of it. He still lives with his family in the same block of flats, three streets away from the Exchange. It is late when Winge catches his breath after a laborious climb up to the third floor. He can hear that an earlier visitor has managed not only to rouse the chief but also his family. Somewhere inside the rooms, a woman is soothing a worried child. Norlin is waiting for him in the antechamber, without his wig and with a corner of his nightshirt visible between the coat and breeches of his office.

'Cecil, thank you for coming at such short notice.'

Winge nods, and obeys a welcoming gesture to sit down in a chair that Norlin has placed by the tiled stove for this occasion.

'Katarina has put some coffee on the stove. It will be ready soon.'

Somewhat ill at ease, the police chief sits down across from him and clears his throat, as if to help him get to the reason for the summons.

'A corpse has been found tonight, Cecil, in Larder Lake on the Southern Isle. A couple of children managed to convince a drunken watchman to pull it out of the water. Its condition . . . The man who told me about it has been a policeman for ten years and during this time he must have had the opportunity to bear witness to all the harm that one man could do to another. And yet there he was, on the doorstep, bent over and panting so as not to lose his dinner, when he described the state of the body to me.'

'Knowing his kind, it could just as well have been the drink.'

Neither of them smiles, and Winge rubs his tired eyes.

'Johan Gustaf, it was agreed that the last task I helped you with was to be my last. I have provided the Chamber of Police with assistance over many years, but as you know, the time has come for me to see to my own affairs.'

'No one could be more grateful for all you have done than I, Cecil. I cannot think of a single time when you have not exceeded my expectations. In view of how much you've improved the department's tally since last winter, it would be obvious to anyone what a great service you have rendered me. But correct me if I am wrong, Cecil: is it not also a service that I have done for you?'

Over the rim of his cup, Norlin's gaze searches in vain for Winge's. The police chief sighs and puts down his coffee.

'We were young once, Cecil. Newly graduated from law school and eager to make our names known in the courts. You were always the idealist, the one who stood up most strongly for his conviction. Whatever the price, you were prepared to pay. Not much has changed in your case, while I have allowed the world to dull my edges. It is my willingness to compromise that has seen me to my office. For once, we appear to be cast in opposite roles and now I am the one saying to you: how often have we been placed before a wrong of a magnitude truly worth making right, that has also been in our power to correct? Few of those matters to which you have devoted yourself have been worthy of your attention. Embezzlers who can't spell, wife killers who can't even be bothered to wipe the blood from the hammer, all manner of perpetrators of violence and ruffians lured into fits of rage by strong spirits and their after-effects. But this is something else, something of an order neither you nor I have seen before. If there was anyone else I could entrust with this thing, I would not hesitate. But there is no one and somewhere out there is a monster in a human guise. The corpse has been carried to the churchyard at Saint Mary. Do me this favour and I will never ask you for anything ever again.'

Winge raises his eyes and this time it is the police chief who cannot meet his gaze.

3

CARDELL CLIMBS DOWN Miller's Hill and spits a brown slug of tobacco into the gutter. He is as clean as he has been able to make himself at a friend's well and has changed into a borrowed shirt. Past the whitewashed buildings perched on the slopes towards Gilded Bay, he can faintly make out the city on its island, a dark colossus rising out of the water, pierced by occasional points of light.

He has barely managed to leave the neighbourhood when he catches sight of a man, his face scarred by smallpox, and with the silver shield of the police authorities in a chain around his neck, heading in the direction of Polhem's Lock.

'Excuse me, do you happen to know what has happened with the corpse from the Larder? My name is Cardell. I was the one who fished it out an hour or so ago.'

'I heard about that. You're a watchman, isn't that right? The body is in the charnel house at Maria Church for now. A damnable business – I have never seen anything worse. In view of how you met, I would have thought your dealings together had come to a close, but now you know. As for me, I have to return to Indebetou House to make my report before dawn.'

They part, and Cardell begins to make his way down the hill through the dew-damp filth of Maria parish. At the bottom of the hill, he soon encounters the church wall. Maria is a cripple, just like Cardell. In the very year that he was born, a spark from a baker's cottage ignited a firestorm that laid waste to the entire hillside. Tessin's tower tumbled down through the domed plaster ceiling and even now, three decades later, the spire has not yet been replaced.

The churchyard awaits him on the other side of a gate. The graves appear to observe him in silence but an unpleasant noise disturbs the peace of the place and in the dim light it takes Carnell a moment to understand what it is that he hears, and that its source is human. It sounds like a dog barking below ground but then he notices a shadow, and on the gravel yard in front of the church stables and the gravedigger's quarters, he sees a lone figure coughing into a handkerchief.

Cardell doesn't know what to do next until the unknown figure concludes his fit, spits onto the ground and turns around. From the buildings behind him, light spills out of a window opening, and while this light robs Cardell of his night vision it gives the other a chance to spot his presence. He breaks the silence with a voice that is hardly more than a hoarse whisper, but which grows stronger with each word.

'You are the one who found the dead man. Cardell.'

Cardell nods.

'The officer didn't know, but of course Cardell is not the whole name.'

Cardell slips his damp hat from his head and makes a stiff little bow.

'If only it were. Jean Michael Cardell. When my father laid eyes on his first born, he was filled with a certain measure of pretension. Aspirations of which weren't fulfilled, as you can see. I'm known as Mickel.'

'Modesty is also a virtue. If your father did not see that, I will count it his loss.'

The shadowy figure steps out into the light.

'My name is Cecil Winge.'

Cardell scrutinizes the man and realizes that he is younger than his hoarse voice would suggest. His clothes are very proper, although of an old-fashioned style: a black coat, slim about the waist, tails ribbed with inlays of horsehair and with a high collar. A discreetly embroidered waistcoat peeks out. Black velvet breeches with buckles at each knee. A white cravat, wrapped several times around the neck. The hair is long and jet black, tied at the nape with a red band. The skin is so white it is almost incandescent.

Winge is of slender build, unnaturally slim even. He could not be more different to Cardell – a man of the kind who is seen everywhere on the streets of Stockholm, deprived of his youth by famine and war, used up before his time. Cardell must be twice as wide across the shoulders, with a soldier's broad back that stretches his coat in unbecoming lines, legs like timber, his right fist as large as a ham. The protruding ears have stopped enough blows to have accumulated scarred lumps along the edges.

Cardell clears his throat self-consciously under the gaze of the other, who gives the impression of inspecting him from top to toe without ever shifting attention from his pockmarked face. Cardell instinctively turns to the left to conceal his handicap. The uncomfortable silence that Winge appears to embrace without discomfort pushes the words over Cardell's lips.

'I met the petty constable back up on the hill. Are you also from Indebetou House, from the Chamber of Police?'

'Yes and no. You could call me an additional resource, perhaps. The police chief sent for me. And you, Jean Michael? What business do you have at the Maria charnel house in the middle of the night? One might have thought you had done the dead man service enough already.'

Cardell spits a non-existent wad of tobacco on the ground to gain some time, realizing he lacks a reasonable answer to the question.

'My purse is missing. It may have fallen out onto the body when I carried it ashore. There wasn't much in it, I'll grant you, but enough to make a night-time walk worth the trouble.'

Winge pauses before answering.

'As for me, I am here to examine the body. In the last hour it will have been cleaned. I was just going to speak with the gravedigger. Follow me, Jean Michael, and we'll see if there is any purse to be found.'

———— • ————

The gravedigger answers the knock on his door in the building next to the wall. He is old, short and bow-legged, with a crooked back and a hint of a hump on one shoulder. His speech bears a trace of German.

'Mr Winge?'

'Yes.'

'My name is Dieter Schwalbe. You have come for the body? You have the rest of the night at your disposal. The priest will read over him before morning Mass.'

'Be so good as to show us the way.'

'Just a moment.'

Schwalbe lights two lanterns with a long match that he waves in the air to extinguish. On a nearby table, there is well-fed cat washing its face with a freshly licked paw. Schwalbe hands one lantern to Cardell, closes his door and skips haltingly out in front of them. On the other side of the yard is a low stone building.

Schwalbe puts his hand to his mouth and makes a loud noise before he unlocks the door.

'For the rats,' he explains. 'I prefer to frighten them than the other way around.'

Objects are piled in all corners of the room. Spikes and spades, coffin materials both old and new, pieces of headstones splintered by winter frost. The body lies under its wrappings on a low bench. The room is cool but the smell of death unmistakable.

The gravedigger gestures at a hook and Cardell hangs his lantern on it. Schwalbe bows his head and clasps his hands as if in prayer, shifting his weight from foot to foot, clearly ill at ease. Winge turns to him.

'Is there anything else? We have much to do and time is of the essence.'

Schwalbe stares straight down into the floor.

'No one can dig graves for as long as I have without seeing things that others haven't. The dead may not have voices of their own but they have other ways of speaking. The one lying here is angry. I've never felt the likes of him. It's as if the plaster in the stone walls around us is crumbling away at his rage.'

Cardell can't help feeling disturbed by this superstitious talk. He begins to make the sign of the cross but stops when he sees the sceptical look Winge gives Schwalbe.

'The dead are defined by the absence of life. All consciousness takes leave of the body and where it now resides I cannot say, but let us hope it is in a better place than the one he has forfeited. What remains can feel neither rain nor sun, and there is nothing we could do that would disturb this man now.'

Schwalbe's objections are clear from his furrowed face. He draws his bushy eyebrows together and makes no sign of leaving.

'He should not go into his grave without a name. Plant a body nameless and a revenant is sown. Until you learn his real name, would you not consider giving him another?'

Winge considers this for a while and Cardell assumes that the answer will be the result of a calculation over the quickest way to get rid of the gravedigger.

'Perhaps we also may draw some benefit from having something to call him. Any suggestions, Jean Michael?'

Cardell hesitates, unprepared for the question. Schwalbe clears his throat in a meaningful way.

'By custom, the unbaptized are given the King's name, yes?'

Cardell shudders and spits out the name as if it had a bad taste.

'Gustav? Hasn't this poor soul suffered enough?'

Schwalbe narrows his eyes.

'One of your Karls then? There are twelve to choose from. The name means "man" in your language, if I am not mistaken, and should therefore be suitable in this case.'

Winge turns to Cardell.

'Karl?'

In the presence of death, old memories are stirred.

'Yes, Karl. Karl Johan.'

Schwalbe smiles at them both and reveals a row of brown nubs.

'Good! And now I bid you a good night, contrary to my better judgement. Mr Winge, Mr . . .?'

'Cardell.'

Schwalbe pauses on his way across the threshold and adds over his shoulder, 'Mr Karl Johan.'

———— • ————

Winge and Cardell are left alone, illuminated by the lantern. Winge turns aside a corner of the wrappings and reveals one of the legs, a stump sawn off, two handspans down the thigh. After a while he turns back to Cardell.

'Come closer and tell me what you see.'

Cardell finds the sight of the leg worse than his recollection of the corpse in its entirety, this anonymous stump that does not immediately call to mind any human form.

'A severed leg? There's not much to say about that.'

Winge nods pensively. The silence makes Cardell feel foolish and then irritated. The night seems to have gone on forever without an end in sight. Without removing his gaze from Cardell's face, Winge gestures towards his left side.

'I cannot help but notice that you are missing an arm yourself.'

Cardell knows he is good at cloaking his disability. He has practised for more hours than he can count. From a distance, the light beechwood is easy to mistake for skin and he has learned to keep the arm somewhat obscured behind his hip. Unless he waves it around, few notice his affliction before getting to know him better. Especially at night. But he sees no other choice than to confirm the observation and inclines his head.

'My condolences.'

Cardell snorts.

'I came looking for my missing coins, not pity.'

'In view of your distaste for our late King Gustav's name, I hazard that your injury occurred during the war?'

Cardell nods as Winge continues.

'I mention this only because your insights regarding amputation greatly exceed my own. Will you do me the favour of inspecting the stump one more time?'

This time, Cardell allows himself to study the area, beyond the layer of dirt that remains in spite of soap and water. When the answer comes to him, it is so self-evident that he realizes he should have seen it right away.

'This is not a fresh wound. The injury is completely healed.'

Winge nods in assent.

'Yes. Those of us who find a body in conditions such as these can generally consider the wounds either the cause of death itself or else the killer's attempts to get rid of the evidence. Neither is true in this case. It would not surprise me if we were to find that all four stumps are in a similar condition.'

On Winge's command, they go to opposite sides of the pallet, lift up the covering and fold it, corner to corner. The body gives off a sweet-sour, earthy stench that has Winge pressing his handkerchief to his nose while Cardell simply resorts to his sleeve.

Karl Johan is missing both arms and both legs, all severed as close to the body as the unimpeded work of knife and saw have found it possible to achieve. The face is also missing eyes; the eyeballs have been removed from their sockets. What remains is malnourished. The ribs stick out. The belly is distended with gases that have turned the belly button inside out, but on each side the pelvic bones are clearly visible under the skin. The chest is thin, still narrow with youth and not the full width of a grown man's. The cheeks are sunken. Of the young man who once was, it is his hair that remains in the best condition. The light blond mass of hair has been washed and combed out across the boards by the humble parishioners.

Winge lifts the lantern from its hook for a closer inspection and walks in a slow circle around the body.

'In the war, you must have seen more than your fair share of waterlogged bodies?'

Cardell nods. Yet he is unaccustomed to scenes such as this one – the analytic and dispassionate examination of a dead man – and his nervousness loosens his tongue.

'Many of those whom we lost in the Gulf of Finland came back to us in the autumn. We found them under the walls of Sveaborg Fort, beneath the batteries. Those of us who had escaped the fever were sent to pull them out. Cod fish and crabs had eaten what they could. Often they would start to move and that was the worst. Sounds came out of them, belches and moans. The bodies were full of eels that had eaten themselves fat in there and that reluctantly wriggled away across land when we interrupted their feast.'

'And how does our Karl Johan appear in comparison?'

'No similarity at all. We often salvaged our dead faster, after skirmishes the same day they had gone overboard. Pale, a little shrivelled and waterlogged, and that is what I see here too. Karl Johan did not spend much time in the lake, if I'm any judge. I would say the time should be no more than a few hours. He must've been put in the water just after nightfall.'

25

'How long did it take your arm to heal?' Winge asks thoughtfully.

Cardell stares back at him before he comes to a decision.

'Let's do this properly, so that we will be on more or less the same ground.'

Winge helps to roll back the sleeve on Cardell's outstretched left arm, until the cloth is pulled back over the straps that hold the wooden limb attached to the elbow. Cardell loosens them with practised ease and pulls his arm out. Cardell holds his stump to the light.

'Have you ever seen a man's flesh being cut before?'

'Never a live subject. I visited a public dissection at the anatomical theatre once when the surgeons were working on a the body of a deceased woman.'

'My own operation was hardly a case study for the textbooks. It was at the clumsy hands of a seaman's dirk, right under the elbow. Once I was brought to the surgeon, he had to carve away even more to save the arm from gangrene. You restrain the patient with chains clad in leather so he won't be able to ruin the operation by lunging or convulsions. The soft flesh is cut with a knife, the bone with a saw. The lucky ones are given enough alcohol to render them senseless but in the haste of the moment I was granted a sober experience. The large veins must be closed quickly. If the clamps slip, have seen fountains of blood can spray long distances. Men lose their strength and grow white in only a few moments. If all goes well, a flap of skin large enough to fold back over the stump is saved and its edges are sewn with needle and thread. See here, you can trace the scar all round and still see the marks of the needle. If the limb escapes any onset of rot, all you have to do is wait for it to grow out again.'

He smiles humourlessly at Winge, who is listening attentively.

'You have seen every stage of healing far closer than anyone would wish. Can you attempt to date the amputation of Karl Johan's limbs for me?'

'Hand me the lantern, then.'

It is Cardell's turn to circle the dead man. He bends over at each corner of the body and studies the stumps one by one. With his healthy arm occupied by holding the lantern, he is unable to cover his nose. He breathes through his mouth and exhales the pungent air in small puffs.

'As far as I can tell, he lost the right arm first. Then the left leg, the left arm and the right leg. I'd say that the right arm is three months gone, provided Karl Johan has healed at the same pace as myself. The right leg? A month, perhaps.'

'So this man has had his arms and legs shorn away in turn. Each wound has been dressed and allowed to heal, whereafter the next limb has been removed. The eyes were intentionally blinded. None of the teeth are left, incidentally, nor the tongue. To judge by the state of the injuries, the process of turning him into what we see today began last summer and was completed a few weeks ago. Death came to him only yesterday or the day before that.'

Cardell feels the hairs on his neck stand up at the full implications of what Winge is saying. Winge knocks pensively on his front teeth with his thumbnail before adding, 'I imagine it was welcome.'

He stops in the middle of replacing the coverings, carefully rubbing the cloth between his fingers.

'I thank you for all of your help, Jean Michael. Unfortunately, you have overestimated Karl Johan's skill as a pickpocket. Your purse is still in its place underneath your jacket. The bulge is clearly visible and if that were not enough, the purse in question revealed itself when you bent over with the lantern. But you knew this already, since the intoxicants you allowed yourself last night have not remained in your system quite as long as you would have me believe.'

Cardell flinches and inwardly curses the impulse that has betrayed his lie. Anger overtakes him now that his drunkenness is steadily being replaced by nausea. Winge's cold-blooded attitude to the dead man, in contrast to his own – he has seen more death than he would wish upon his worst enemy – disturbs him. He spits over his shoulder, as if to ward off evil.

'You are a cold one, Cecil Winge. No wonder you're so at ease in the presence of the dead. Let me return your powers of observation with some of my own: You don't eat enough. If I were you, I would try to spend more time at the dinner table and less on the latrine.'

Winge pays no attention to the insult.

'Something else brought you here this evening. Exactly what, we can leave unsaid. But would you continue what you have begun? Would you see this man avenged in hallowed ground? I can provide certain resources on behalf of the police authorities. I would be grateful for your assistance and am prepared to compensate you for it.'

Winge looks at Cardell with his large eyes. Something is alight in them that was not there before. It both frightens and confuses Cardell, but he feels the fatigue spreading throughout his body and just stands there until Winge goes on:

'You don't have to give me your answer immediately. I will now proceed to the Indebetou in order to listen to the morning briefings. I already know what I will hear. The petty constable will give his report. The responsibility will fall on the procurator fiscal who is already occupied with affairs that are far simpler and promise more glory than this one. At best he will urge the petty constables of Maria parish to consult their neighbourhood officers as to whether local rumours may shed light on the matter. I nurture little hope of any progress there. This broken body will remain deprived of its true name, and at the city's expense will be laid into a pit on the north side of the graveyard where we now stand. There will be no one to mourn his passing. The police chief has asked me to do what I can. On my own, I fear that it will not be enough.'

More than this is required in order to calm Cardell once his temper has been lost. He has already turned away to leave, ripe with conflicting emotions. Winge's hoarse voice follows him out.

'If you wish to help me, Jean Michael Cardell, come to see me again. I rent a room from Roselius at Spens Manor.'

4

As ever, the break of dawn brings chaos and tumult to Indebetou House in its perch at the top of Castle Hill. Winge rubs his eyes, trying to forget about his lack of sleep and wondering if there might be a pot of coffee with a few drops left for him somewhere in one of these rooms.

The stairwell is full of people on their way out or in and by others who are simply waiting here in lieu of a better place. The police authority staff are still struggling to adapt to their new premises and their new master. No one has yet managed to pair the right room with the purpose for which it would be best suited.

Barely a year has gone by since the move to Indebetou House and, according to mean-spirited rumours, the only reason for the upheaval from Garden Street was to save the city's face after the former owner of the house managed to gain access to the death bed of King Gustav and came away with a barely legible royal signature on a deed which promised him twenty-five thousand daler in exchange for a draughty and decrepit building that had long stood abandoned. Too warm in summer, too cold in winter.

The house is strangely asymmetrical, leaning into the hill where it stands between the cathedral and the empty lot where the ruins of the recently demolished Great Tennis Court are still strewn about.

In the dim morning light, familiar faces are mixed with strangers. With displeasure, Winge picks out Teuchler and Nystedt, two thugs in the agency's employ who are half carrying a man whose blackened eyes and split lip bears witness to the fact that he has just confessed to whatever it is he has been accused of. Secretary Blom passes Winge in the crowd at that moment and rolls his eyes when their eyes briefly meet. More than two decades have gone by since such methods were outlawed but Teuchler and Nystedt remain children of another time.

Those who know Winge's name and appearance without being more closely acquainted with him turn their faces to the floor at his approach. He can feel their eyes on his back once he has passed them by. On his way up the stairs he notes that no one has yet removed the former police chief's coat of arms from the wall: yet another sign of the lack of order that has plagued the agency since King Gustav joined his fathers.

———•———

Almost two years have gone by since Anckarström's shot rang out in the masquerade ball, but at the police agency it is as if the report echoes still. With the Crown Prince only thirteen years old and not yet of age, the conflict over power broke out even before the monarch lost his long struggle with death. The former police chief Nils Henric Aschan Liljensparre, a favourite of King Gustav, who had built the police agency from the ground up and had himself led its operations for almost three decades, was one of the powerful men who saw his opportunity and showed his ambitions openly: to make the King's weak-minded brother, Duke Karl, appointed to rule as the Prince's guardian, a puppet regent.

Instead, this thirst for power became Liljensparre's undoing. Baron Reuterholm took the place that Liljensparre had selected for himself, and while the Baron rules the country in the Duke's name, Liljensparre has been dispatched to Swedish Pomerania. At the beginning of the year, Reuterholm gave the office of police chief to crown attorney Johan Gustaf Norlin, an appointment it is said that the Baron has already had reason to regret. Like others who are able to see things clearly, Winge knows the reason: Norlin is a righteous man.

———•———

Up on the third floor, chairs have been placed along the walls of the corridor. Winge hugs himself and slaps his shoulders in order to force the blood out into his frozen fingertips. The damp, cold air tickles his throat and he has to take shallow breaths in order to keep his cough at bay. He is forced to wait another quarter of an hour in the draught from the leaky windows before the door to Norlin's quarters is opened and he is shown in.

Like the rest of the house, Norlin's office is in disarray. The elegant desk is barely visible under the piles of papers with which it is covered. Norlin is standing by the window. Norlin is not much older than Winge, but the year has been filled with sleepless nights that have aged him beyond his thirty years. Along the collar of his formal coat, his skin is red and chafed where his fingernails have tried repeatedly to scratch an itch. A speckled cat is perched on the windowsill, purring as Norlin strokes its neck.

'One of the few inhabitants of this house that is still of sound mind and has reasonable priorities.'

He gently pushes the cat down onto the floor, leans his back against the windowsill and crosses his arms.

'Well, was your examination satisfactory?'

'It was ill-advised of me to imply that the officer had been drinking. His reaction was completely justified. It is a very unusual crime.'

'Apart from your competence, there is another reason that I have asked you to handle this affair, Cecil. You are not formally a part of the agency and you can work in the dark. Reuterholm has his eyes on me and there are few things that rile the Baron more

32

than discovering me doing actual police work. The Baron would rather have me implementing his censorship regulations than making the city safe for the general public. Have a look.'

Norlin holds up a folded paper with a freshly broken seal.

'This is a letter signed by Gustaf Adolf Reuterholm, in which he demands to know why no progress has been made in the investigation he demanded regarding a rumour that he has tried to poison the Crown Prince. The same rumour claims that his hunger for power can be traced back to impotence and a long list of perverse tendencies. The Baron feels that he has waited long enough to see those responsible taste the rod, and now demands that I provide him with a full account of my efforts.'

'And will you send him one?'

'Since I haven't done anything, it would probably be best not to. The man is out of his mind. Reuterholm is nothing but a despot, without friends or family to provide a sense of stability. He's trying to get the fortune teller Arvidsson to speak with the dead on his behalf. Vain, testy, and resentful to boot, just like King Gustav himself as time went on. Fear of revolution and betrayal is a pestilence that spreads to all whose posteriors come too close to the throne. His Majesty asked my predecessor to recruit a cadre of informants to report on gossip and conspiracies among the people. The problem is not that people are unhappy. The problem is that Liljensparre's informants were asked to look for discontent in the wrong places. While King Gustav had nightmares of the revolution in France spreading to the far north, and did everything in his power to eavesdrop on republican chatter in the coffee houses, his killers were sneaking around among members of his own court. He was so afraid of the commoners he never met that he believed the nobles – right in front of his face – were harmless.'

Norlin gestures at his desk.

'Even if I do my best to ignore Liljensparre's gossips, I still have to receive their reports, the one more preposterous than the next:

there is an Ödman who complains that someone called Nilsson has sung the Marseillaise during a night of heavy drinking in Strängnäs. A cavalry officer with doubtful sympathies is said to have praised the notorious schemer Juhlin for his tie pin. Kullmer and Ågren wore long trousers to church, to the delight of Weinås and Falk. Carlén is hiding writings by Thorild under his pillow. And so forth. While I am distracted by this, important matters suffer. But Liljensparre, that old tyrant, felt that these things were of the highest level of interest. No doubt you've heard the nickname the men of the agency gave him? "The Arse", from his middle name, Aschan.'

Winge regards the pile of letters, takes one and gives it an indifferent glance before he puts it back. Norlin lifts up his wig and throws it on top of the piles as he scratches his hair.

'By way of the rumour mill, I understand that Reuterholm is already looking for my replacement.'

'Do you know who?'

'I have heard that the question has been put to Magnus Ullholm. A name that you know only all too well.'

'Do you know how long you will last?'

'No. But when the Baron sets his mind to something, things tend to happen quickly. Ullholm will not allow your assignments to continue. So this is a matter of urgency, Cecil.'

Winge brings his hand up to the bridge of his nose and massages his swollen eyes. His drowsiness causes blurred points of lights to dance across his field of vision.

'I am the last person you need to remind what is urgent.'

***

Norlin invites Winge to sit in an empty chair. He opens the door a crack and calls out into the corridor for some coffee, an order that is swiftly obeyed by whoever happens to be closest. With a heavy sigh, Norlin sits down across from Winge.

'Well, let us return to that corpse that was fished out of the lake. What hopes do you have of finding the person responsible?'

'I have reason to believe that the body was put in the water only a few hours before he was found. I plan to look for witnesses who may have been in the neighbourhood shortly before nightfall.'

'That seems to me a thoroughly hopeless undertaking. Is that all?'

'There is one more thing. The body was naked but partially wrapped in a black cloth of a kind that I have not seen before. It seems too costly a fabric to be discarded in such a way. Experts in these matters may know more.'

Norlin appears lost in thought and is nodding to himself.

'Keep things that you do discreet, and not only because of Reuterholm. There is discontent festering out there. We had an agitated mob at the castle gates earlier this year, howling for blood, and all because a nobleman had managed to scratch a burgher with his rapier. Every act of violence has to be handled with the utmost care. Do me that favour.'

A maid knocks at the door and enters bearing a coffee pot and tin cups. Norlin pours and Winge puts his thin lips to the rim of the cup to meet the life-giving brew. While the cat unselfconsciously jumps up in anticipation of curling up on Norlin's lap, Norlin gazes over at Winge with concern.

'I'm sorry to say it, Cecil, especially since I know that I am not entirely innocent of the cause, but damn it, you look awful.'

5

THE NAME OF the pub is the Perdition. A thick layer of soot coats the walls but anyone who strains a little can make out the mural. It is the dance of death. Peasants and burghers, noblemen and priests, join hands around a skeleton who is playing a fiddle as black as tar. The painting makes many ill at ease and the few customers can be easily counted until the hour is late and the level of intoxication has stripped all decorations of their relevance. The innkeeper Gedda has opposed all attempts at persuasion to whitewash his walls. The mural is painted by Hoffbro himself, he snarls, and a masterpiece at that.

Cardell loathes it, especially since his agreement with Gedda means he has to keep himself reasonably sober. Cardell is here as a hired muscle, employed to turn away troublemakers for a shilling or so a week and extra commission for each successful eviction. His watchman's salary is nothing to live on and this additional income is welcome. From his place on the bench by the door, he feels the presence of the skeleton for the hundredth time, its empty eye sockets searching out his gaze. Cardell shudders and stuffs his mouth full of tobacco.

He senses that this night will bring nothing good, a feeling not without a measure of anticipation. A troubled atmosphere has been brewing ever since sundown. Drinking buddies are bickering over their beer and aquavit. In the crowd, jostling quickly leads to hard words. Time and again he has to get up from his chair and break things up, trying to reason with men who neither hear nor understand until he grabs them by the neck, lifts them up until their heels swing free of the floorboards, and throws them out on the street.

A group of sailors presses in through the doors, all of them at once, arm in arm until the weakest have to break the chain and give way to the delighted mockery of the others. They are bellowing out a vulgar song at the top of their lungs. Between the lines of nonsense and drivel, Cardell hears boasting about conquering maidenheads, and now he knows for certain that the evening will end badly.

Young men, brash and drunk, in a crowd that finds honour in having each other's back. He knows them well. He was once like them. He loves them and he hates them. From his place by the door he studies them like a wolf watches a flock of rabbits and knows that it is only a matter of time until they are his.

———•———

It does not take long. A short man with a pot belly trips over his own shoe buckle and pours his drink over the back of a sailor. In a few seconds, they have the sinner lifted onto a table and they force the poor sod to dance, while they surround him on all sides and tilt the surface of the table until the wood groans. One of their number has pulled out his knife and is hunting the man's toes with its point.

Cardell meets Gedda's gaze from the other side of the establishment. Gedda doesn't care if guests spill or bleed but the furniture costs money. Without even having to think about it, Cardell's one hand goes to fasten the leather straps that hold his left arm in place.

War has taught Cardell that there is no honour in battle. And yet there is a ritual to be observed, as predictable as it is meaningless. He follows it like a familiar routine. A hand on a sailor's shoulder, mimed diplomacy in the clamour. Calming gestures. Close to his ear, someone yells at him to go to hell. Someone else spits in his face. He feels his heart beating like a drum in his ear as the world turns red. And still he controls himself. He lets his shoulders sink in submission before their triumphant grins.

When the first blow lands, they don't understand what is happening. The left hand comes up from waist height and since the hand has been carved as if the palm were open, it almost looks as if he is caressing the face of the closest man. Teeth fly through the air in a cascade of red. Cardell carries the force of the arm's momentum into the next punch, and the next, feels an arm snap, the bridge of a nose crack, a ribcage give way, an eye fly from its socket. Each hit translates into an explosion in his stump and the pain only fuels his rage.

They flee head over heels. The last one has to crawl snivelling on all fours, and manages to win the threshold only with the assistance of Cardell's boot. When Cardell turns back, their erstwhile victim is still standing on top of the table, clapping, a smile from ear to ear.

His gratitude knows no bounds. He insists on celebrating his saviour with a jug of Rhenish wine and toast upon toast. Cardell, for his part, determines that the evening's altercation is enough to secure the peace at the Perdition until the doors are locked for the night. The floor runs red and the pattern leads straight back to himself, a sign of warning for all to read. He ignores Gedda's disapproving looks and drinks long and hard. Fights are one of the few things that he finds enlivening. He used to actively seek them out, savouring after each victory the fleeting feeling that he was in control of his life. The effect has dimmed over the years. His arm hurts. He feels old, too old for a life like this. Wine is a comfort. The man introduces himself as Isak Reinhold Blom.

'I am a poet. At your service.'

Cardell raises an eyebrow as the man clears his throat.

'O Hero! We shiver at your victory, your opposition is all fled. You tread the corpses of your brethren, stain'd in deepest red!'

'Is this how you make your living?'

Blom purses his lips and lights his clay pipe on the candle.

'Such is the curse of the poet; everyone's a critic. But as it happens, no. Until the light fails I sit in the Indebetou House, up by the Castle. I serve with the Chamber of Police. As secretary, in fact, since this January.'

Cardell hasn't given any thought to Cecil Winge and his parting words until now.

'Would you happen to know a Winge, Cecil Winge?'

Blom looks curiously at Cardell and exhales a plume of smoke.

'Once you've met that man, he's hard to forget.'

'Who is he? Can you tell me anything about him?'

'He started prowling around the Indebetou at the same time as Norlin was appointed police chief earlier this year. They have an agreement of sorts. Winge has a free hand to do as he pleases, within the bounds of reason. He takes an interest in some crimes but not in others.'

Cardell nods thoughtfully. Blom draws deeply on his pipe with a gurgling sound. Then he continues:

'It so happened that we were both studying Law in Uppsala at the same time, me and Winge, although I was a few years older and never moved in the same circles. He always had his nose stuck in his Rousseau. Winge was a prodigy of a kind that hasn't been seen since Rudbeck. The man has a memory such that he can produce each word he has read as if he's got the book in front of him. Maybe that's where things went wrong. Certain people read too much and get strange notions in their head. During his early career, he made himself a nuisance by insisting on questioning the accused, something one normally avoids as far as possible. All of his cases were presented in excruciating and endless detail. Though no one in their right mind could ever doubt the

39

guilt or innocence of someone processed by Winge, he never succeeded in winning the appreciation of his peers. Most of those appointed to the lower courts want to see justice served as quickly as possible, to the extent that they even concern themselves about such things, but they were hard put to stop him since Winge was a master of logical argumentation. They resorted to scorn and ridicule instead, only to find both rolling off Winge like water off a duck's back. Since he has combined forces with Norlin, there is a rich treasury of anecdotes about everything he has managed to accomplish in the service of the agency during in the past year. Other men make mistakes, are absent-minded and if their attention span isn't lacking, their diligence often is. Not so Winge.'

Blom waves the shaft of his pipe in order to underscore his words. When he pauses long enough to take his next puff, his pipe has gone out. He puts it down with a little shrug.

'If I am to say something less flattering about him, it would be that the man has never had much in the way of charm.'

'That much was clear.'

'I met his wife at the Opera last year and when I heard her name and realized who her husband was, I was certain I had misheard. A fantastic woman, Cardell. Beautiful, of course, but also warm, tender, witty and exuberant, and these words are among the last I would employ in order to describe her husband. She must have had lines of suitors going out the door. Why she chose Winge, I will never understand. And therefore it is an irony of fate that it is he who has chosen to leave her, and not, as one would have expected, the other way around . . .'

Blom falls silent and all at once it is as if his good mood has been extinguished, like his pipe. The din of the pub fills the silence. In a corner, a man in a patched coat and with a beggar's bowl on the table before him begins to play a mournful melody in triple metre with a simple wooden recorder.

'Yes, there we have it, Cardell. I should probably have mentioned this from the first but I'm feeling the wine. Cecil Winge is dying of consumption. He was never a sturdy build but the illness has worn him down considerably. He's pale but hides it well, almost never coughs in public, and when he does it is discreetly into a handkerchief, which is always a dark colour so as not to show the blood. Rumour has it that he left his wife to spare her the sight of his decline. They say well-regarded experts from the Seraphim Hospital set the date of his death about a month since. Now he lives on borrowed time. There is no lack of respect for Winge among the men on Castle Hill but the staff have already dubbed him the Ghost of the Indebetou.'

Later, when Blom has long since staggered out in the Stockholm night on unsteady legs, after the tipsiness has increased and the tallow candles have been put out one after the other as the guests in turn forsake the overturned oak barrels that serve as tables, the publican places a hand on Cardell's shoulder.

'I hired you to keep order around here, not to stage a bloodbath. You are scaring away my clientele, Mickel. I can't keep you on any longer.'

At night, sometime after the stroke of midnight, Mickel Cardell wakes up in his room from shortness of breath and a racing heart. Pain rages in the arm, whose absence his senses refuse to accept. This is the second time in two days that neither spirits nor fighting has been able to afford him peace.

6

N O ONE CALLS it 'consumption' until it is clear that the illness is so far gone that no improvement can be expected. Only when all hope is gone, and death is considered inevitable, does one give the condition its proper name.

It was only a slight cough in the beginning, last spring, one that lasted week after week. As a child, he also often had a cough, but it was never anything to take notice of. Then came the night-time fever, bouts of sweating after which he would wake on drenched sheets and blankets. By summer, Cecil Winge had to disguise his cough with a handkerchief so as not to arouse attention, and one day in June the embroidered cotton fabric was mottled by red spots. He lost his breath easily and often felt a cramp in his side as if he had just been running. In his chest it felt as if a great weight had settled in, one whose domain was expanding at the expense of his lungs and curtailing each breath.

Physicians palpated the swollen nodes in his neck and called them scrofula. Their prescription was a foul-tasting concoction of elm, madder, ginger, licorice fern and star anise. He was to take half a bottle a day. When there was no change in his condition, the doctor thoughtfully polished his eyeglasses and suggested a drain in order to extract the unhealthy liquids from his body. With potash lye, the doctor seared a hole into the left side of his chest, an opening no larger than the nail of his little finger. A pea was inserted into the hole to prevent the wound from healing. In a few days, pus was flowing freely from the wound and the physician assured him this was a sign of an auspicious outcome. That was not to be the case. The burning wound kept him up at night. He alternated between freezing and sweating. His wife was always at his side with a cloth to dab his forehead, a towel to dry his gaunt body, a song to soothe him and allow him to drift away for some moments of mercy.

The year went on and winter became spring. One cure followed another. He bent over vats with vinegar and chalk, he drank unfiltered cow's milk and breathed stable air. Every morning he woke up exhausted, his skin cold and damp, and nothing could warm him. His veins were blue and swollen, his eyes bloodshot with dark circles, a constant ache was spreading in his hip. When his cough started, nothing could stop it and when it was at its worst, it brought dead tissue into his mouth. His spittle stank. When he was bled, it was found that the blood quickly congealed into a bluish crust, a sure sign that the contagion had spread. He could no longer be a husband to his wife and could not bear to share her bed when his coughing and night sweats set in and he was plagued with an anguish so consuming he thought his ribs would crack.

———◆———

A month has elapsed since Winge abandoned all curative advice from medical professionals. Every attempt to lessen his suffering had only served to worsen his condition. All he can do is call upon every ounce of self-discipline to ignore the tickles in his throat and he has found that distractions help more than anything else. Mental concentration empties his mind of thought and his body relaxes.

At night, in his lonely room in Roselius's house, he sits by a lighted candle and dismantles his pocket watch. He spreads the various parts before him until they are all sorted by rows. Then he puts them together again. One after another, the wheels are reunited, fixed at their centre and fitted into each other. Tiny screws hook into their grooves and are tightened. From a collection of parts all individually worthless, a clockwork is formed that functions anew.

Winge steers towards death by the same compass that has shown his way his entire life: reason. He tells himself that all men will die and that all are dying. This helps. But when the night sweats come and his thoughts race wildly, it is rather the particulars of his own demise that haunt him and not the general principle. All the clinical details of phthisis. Will the infection spread to all joints and bone as sometimes happens? Will he pass silently in his sleep or in spasms and paroxysms? What flavour of agony awaits to be his? When nothing else helps, he tells himself that most of him already died the last time he saw his wife. But this is also little comfort, as that part of him that has gone on living seems the one that most clearly perceives the pain.

—•—

Evening falls and Winge is dressing to go out. The mirror in the room is so narrow that he has to step far back in the room in order to see even half of his body. The clothes he is wearing are the only ones he owns. The shirt and his long socks are washed regularly according to a schedule he has arranged with the maids. A few strokes of the brush is enough for the rest. The fabric is starting to wear out and neither coat nor waistcoat are still *à la mode*, but they serve. The clothes he has chosen to keep are the same as he wore in his service in the lower courts, and their purpose was never vanity but propriety, intended to convey to an observer a feeling of indifference in the face of anything other than what is of the utmost importance.

He winds the cravat around his neck and ties it, puts his arms through his coat and lifts his walking stick from its corner, the one that was once only for show and that he now depends on more frequently. Winge walks slowly down the stairs, quietly, so as not to encounter any of the people of the house.

He walks down the slopes towards the sea with a handkerchief held to his mouth to ward off the dampness of the air. Down by the shipyard it does not take him long to find a man willing to row him into the city for a couple of coins. Far away he hears the faint roar of the current, but out here the water is still, only disturbed by the groans of the oarlock and the sound of the oars as they dip in the water.

They pass underneath the arch of the shipyard bridge and, with regular glances over his shoulder, the rower finds a path through the labyrinth of ships anchored outside the Quayside. Anchor cables as thick as men's thighs straighten and slack around them. Under the predominant smell of tar, there are other more subtle scents of arrack, cinnamon, coffee and tobacco.

After half an hour's trip, Winge accepts the assistance of a steady hand to take the step over to land at the Stairs of the Master of Revenue. From there, the walk to Bagge's Row is short.

———•———

The alley is lively as always. Here the brothels are stacked on top of each other, and clients in various states of inebriation mill about either on their way to or from a visit. Cheerful songs in praise of Venus echo between the buildings, mixed with bragging about deeds that have either been or soon will be performed. Others are more discreet. Many married men choose to hold a handkerchief up to their noses, as Winge does.

He finds the right entrance and walks in. The woman who has inherited this business from the late Captain Ahlström has a face as inscrutable as it is ancient and she does not betray any sign of recognition other than a curt nod.

'Is she available?'

The madam shakes her head. Winge sets his cane down and sits heavily in a chair.

'I'll wait. And fresh bedlinen, if you please. A tidy room.'

The woman gives him a look that is difficult to interpret and leaves him. Others come and go without him paying any attention. Almost an hour goes by until she returns and waves him up the stairs. He finds her door without guidance, knocks and enters.

The one they call the Flower of Finland is waiting for him perched on the edge of the bed, her legs temptingly crossed. She wasn't easy to find. He has searched for someone close to his own age, and three decades is more than most in her line of work will see. But she has remained remarkably untouched by this underground world, whose inhabitants appear to live their lives at twice the pace of others. Recognition registers in her face in the same moment that their eyes meet. Her body language changes instantly. Her shoulders sink, and the back that had arched, the better to display her charms, relaxes.

'It is you. The old bat could have told me.'

Her eastern accent is pleasant. The vowels sing. Winge nods in response and looks around the room in order to ensure that it has been prepared according to his instructions. He hands her the little cloth purse he has prepared with a sum they both know from before. She gestures for him to lay it on the dresser.

'You will stay the night, as usual?'

'Yes, Johanna. I hope the money will suffice.'

She laughs.

'Even if there hadn't been enough, I am prepared to give you a discount. You are my best customer. You pay well and ask very little, which is the opposite of what I am used to. Or is there anything else you are looking for this time?'

Winge shakes his head.

'No. Just the usual.'

He hangs up his coat and unties his cravat. From his waistcoat pocket, he takes out the little bottle and hands it to her with great care. She pulls out the stopper and splashes a few drops over her throat and décolletage. He folds his shirt and breeches over the back of a chair while she also removes the few pieces of clothing she is wearing and together they crawl into the bed.

———•———

He turns his back to her and she puts her arm around him in the same way that he has shown her. Every rib can be felt under her hand and his breaths are so shallow they are almost imperceptible. She resembles his wife, with the same long hair and the same colour of her eyes. Now she smells the same and the warmth of her arm is the same.

She blows out the candle next to the bed and feels his pulse beating weakly and his breathing slow as sleep overcomes him. Several times he becomes agitated without waking fully and she strokes his forehead with the movements he has shown her, humming the words she has been instructed.

———•———

He wakes at dawn, and as usual he does not know if he should count it as a blessing or a curse, these brief moments between sleep and consciousness where his as yet dormant reason allows him to relive what once was. He climbs out of bed and puts on his clothes. Johanna stays in bed and does not wake up until Winge turns the key to unlock the door.

'Tonight was the last time.'

She stretches and rubs the sleep from her eyes.

'Have you grown tired of our arrangement?'

'No. Not at all. But these coins are the last I have.'

She shrugs with a little smile. Winge pulls his coat over his shoulders and notes that the fabric is starting to wear thin at the elbows, thin enough to see through. No matter. He is confident all his garments will last him the rest of his life.

7

CARDELL HEARS THE church bells of Hedvig Eleonora and Jakob ring two in the afternoon as he trudges over New Bridge in the rain. The masts of the islanders fade into the mist behind the buildings of the shipyard and the eight-sided fort guarding the harbour inlet. The three tongues of the naval ensign ripple in the wind, drenched by the downpour. Cats' Bay roils under his feet. By comparison to the Larder, the water is less brackish here, thanks to the inflow of fresh water from the sea. Around the shores of Cats' Bay, the piles of manure from dumped latrine waste collect into a thick quagmire, fed further by the Rill pouring down from the north. Although the liquid has a hue between yellow and brown, there is a collection of washerwomen on the dock with piles of laundry. They alternate between dipping their laundry into the sludge, then driving out the dirty water by beating it with their boards. Next to them is the fish market.

He has to force his way past a man begging with deformed hands held out to gain sympathy. At the fish market stands the wooden horse with its sharp spine, over which a weeping man has been draped, weights tied to his feet. To judge by his clothes, he is a coach driver who has been caught padding his fees. A half-naked man stands tied to the pillory, howling, blood streaming out of his nose and into his mouth.

Cardell wanders past the shacks on the other side of the bridge. Here families live one on top of the other in lean-tos and huts that

48

look ready to collapse. They have good cause to fear the coming season: once winter has filled all corners of the poorhouse to bursting with the shivering bodies of the destitute, the frozen corpses of the rest will be piled high next to the graveyard until the ground thaws out.

He continues along the street all the way to the shipyard at Terra Nova, where the shore has been filled out with earth and dirt in order to make a place for dry docks and workshops. Then he turns away from the bay and walks onto higher land. Here habitation grows more sparse. The city begins to reach its end and the salty breeze has a better hope of chasing away the stink of the city. Cardell does not need to follow the street long until he glimpses Spens Manor with its semicircle of buildings gathered around a grove of linden trees. In the courtyard between the houses, Cardell is met by an old maid carrying a copper jug. He explains the nature of his visit.

'Mr Winge has a room on the second floor of the new stone house. You are welcome to wait down in the kitchen. The stove is lit there so you can dry off.'

The maid goes up the stairs to announce the visitor. Behind an entry hall with a well, there is bread being baked in a stone oven. Various domestics and servants dart back and forth, and wherever he stands, Cardell finds himself in the way. It doesn't take long until a mug of mulled beer is pushed into his hand. He shakes his head at a newly baked wheat bun because he doesn't have another hand to receive it. Presently the maid returns, and waves at him from the stairs. She doesn't have to tell him where Winge's room is. His racking cough could already be heard at the gate.

———•———

Cecil Winge's room is a grim place. Furniture that must have come with the rental agreement is arranged along the walls. Few of Winge's personal possessions can be seen. Books are piled in a stack, and there is a trunk. A simple desk stands by the window to catch the light, and spread over its surface is what looks like a partially deconstructed watch. Heat from the hearth below rises through the gaps in the floor and is the only source of warmth as the tiled stove has not yet been lit.

Someone who had lived a different life to Cardell's could easily have mistaken the smell that fills the air for iron. But he knows it all too well. It is the smell of blood, and under the bed he sees a container with red stains around the rim, recently stowed away. Embarrassed, he tears his gaze away from it as quickly as he can.

Winge is sitting on the bed, pale and still. He betrays no impulse to cough. While Cardell searches for the words he has been trying to find since yesterday, it is Winge who speaks first.

'You have spoken with someone who is familiar with my condition. You regret your last words even though you couldn't possibly have known at the time.'

Cardell nods with a sigh of relief.

'That is not important, Jean Michael. The important thing is that you are here. May I ask what persuaded you to change your mind?'

'You mentioned money, and God knows I need it.'

'And I would not have offered you any if I hadn't sensed that there was a deeper reason for your interest in this case. There were no coins to be had when you waded into the Larder and came out with Karl Johan in your arms.'

'During the war . . . I had a friend who was never far from my side. He must've saved my life a hundred times, just as I did his. When misfortune befell us, we were both pitched into the water. A beam of wood struck him over the head and I held his face above water as long as I could. He came to me in a dream the night before last, as he often does, and when I went into the lake in my drunken state, it was as if I was back in the same water. But this time no wave tore him from my grip, I kept my hold on him and delivered us both up on dry land. I've sobered up since, but the feeling remains.'

'Thank you for your confidence, Jean Michael. I do not inquire out of mere curiosity. The offer of financial compensation remains, but now I can pay you, knowing that your loyalty is not owed to the highest bidder. But what of your situation? You are a watch-man, and yet you seldom seem to be on duty.'

Cardell shudders at the thought of his colleagues at the watch, loathsome men with a wide variety of defects who prefer to have their bribes paid in kind.

'I'm a watchman in name only. My post is a favour to a crip-pled beggar who was disabled in his service to the Crown. Among those who have returned from the war, I count myself as one of the lucky ones. Others beg, offer themselves on the street or slave in a tobacco shop. The position of watchman came to me through good contacts, but the devil take me if I plan to spend my time chasing derelicts and prostitutes to the reform house. They've no more chosen their fate than I have.'

<hr>

It has grown darker. Winge lights the candle on the desk with a match. The flame incites the shadows to dance around them both. Winge returns to the bed and sits cross-legged.

'There are a few things that I wish for you to know. Firstly, I am acting by way of an agreement with Police Chief Norlin, and it is by the extension of his authority that we will seek out Karl Johan's killer. Norlin's appointment is nearing its end and he has called his probable successor by name: Magnus Ullholm. A couple of years ago, Ullholm was appointed to oversee the Church's pension fund for widows. At a subsequent audit, large sums were found to be missing and, naturally, suspicion was directed at Ullholm. At that time, I was posted at the lower courts, and I participated in prosecuting the case against him. I did not for a moment doubt his guilt, and even less so after he fled to Norway and thereby forced the case to be suspended. Baron Reuterholm has now chosen to take mercy on him, since the Baron knows well how to exploit a man who wants nothing more than to enrich himself. Ullholm is not a man to forget those who have opposed him. As soon as he becomes aware of my arrangement with Norlin, he will end it and do everything in his power to counteract our purpose.'

Winge stands up and starts to pace back and forth across the floor, his hands clasped behind his back.

'Secondly, the crime that stands before us is of a highly unusual nature. It is not the work of an ordinary perpetrator. What resources are needed in order to keep a man imprisoned long enough to dismember him and escape detection? Think also about the strength of will this implies. The determination. Who knows what will come crawling out if we overturn this stone? With every penny that you earn, you may well be buying yourself a formidable enemy. I mention this because the risk you take is greater than my own.'

Winge turns away, to the window. The smattering rain is slowly transforming into heavy flakes of snow.

'I will not survive this coming winter. Soon, I will be beyond all cause and effect. Whatever happens thereafter, you will be left to face it alone.'

Cardell looks down. He has not known Winge long but is now wondering if his attempts to heal the wounds left by Johan Hjelm will only leave a new one in its place. Nonetheless, he finds it an easy decision. Cardell slaps his hand onto the desk with a force strong enough to send the tiny parts of the watch into disarray.

'Then let's make the most of the time we have, so that you may have a chance to enjoy your fair share of this shit-storm.'

Cardell sees Winge's distorted reflection in the windowpane and wonders if what he sees there is the ghost of a smile.

8

THE ATMOSPHERE IN the Flag, a cellar close to the shore of
the bay, has grown lively. Two itinerant musicians, one
with a hurdy-gurdy in his lap and the other with a fiddle by the
hip, have both wanted to set up and play for the crowd this
evening and have turned their initial conflict into a collabora-
tion. The crowd is streaming in to hear them, and soon there are
people are lined up all the way out to the stairs. Outside the air
is raw. The evening fog is rising from the sea and groping its way
towards the city. Winge and Cardell are eating their evening
meal at a table next to the fire in order to avoid the draught
from the door.

Cardell has a hearty appetite, Winge almost none. From the
kitchen, there comes a steady stream of dishes: fishballs made of
pike; a terrine of buttered and salted carrots; a plate of pork
sausages; poached cod and fried herring; steaming turnips; crisp-
bread and cheese, with a plate of gruel with orange slices and
sugared rusks on the side. Cardell tucks in as if the meal is his
last. Winge allows Cardell to slake his thirst and satisfy his hunger
without interruption. For his part, he only pushes the food
around with his fork and soon puts down his silverware in favour
of coffee. Cardell, when he has finished eating, wrinkles up his
nose at the smell of freshly ground beans and declines the offered
cup.

'I've never seen what everyone sees in that muddy brew.'

'The taste may be a matter of habit but it clears the head immediately. Jean Michael, would you consider telling me how you
came to lose your arm?'

'That is a story I'd do much to avoid telling, but I'll grant you,
it would be best if everyone could hear what Gustav's Russian war
was like so that similar campaigns could be avoided in future. My
role was neither heroic nor meaningful. A trivial player in a game
beyond my control, destined for death, saved only by a stroke of
fate. I lost my arm but it saved my life.'

Despite his humble rank of non-commissioned officer, Cardell
began to suspect almost immediately that the war had been entered
into far too hastily. For five years, he served in the army's artillery
unit. Together with thousands of others, he was rowed across the
sea by the Stockholm fleet to the Gulf of Finland around
Midsummer 1788. At the island of Hangö, they joined the many
ships of the line which had set off from Karlskrona under the
command of the King's brother, Duke Charles. Cardell was shown
aboard *The Fatherland*, a warship of sixty guns designed by
Chapman and built in Karlskrona five years earlier.

'So you could say that we had an equal amount of experience
in the service, *The Fatherland* and I. I took it as a good sign. As it
turned out, I would be proven wrong.'

Cardell was standing on the deck of *The Fatherland* in the early
morning mist on the seventeenth of July when the front line of the
fleet signalled that the enemy had been sighted. Half an hour later,
Cardell himself saw the masts emerge from the fog to the east and
felt the first pang of terror in his gut. Both of the lines were fairly
even: seventeen Russian warships against about twenty or so Swedish.

'Hell, Winge, that was to be my first battle. At sea, everything
goes painfully slowly. At the same moment that the naval forces
sight each other, the manoeuvring starts. You wait for wind and

currents in order to get close enough and then get in formation with your battle line towards the enemy in order to give the guns room to play. On command, you shoot and shoot and shoot. All we see, we see through the gun ports when they are reloaded with fresh shot and powder. In the best case, you'll catch a glimpse of bloody waves and floating wreckage, in the worst case there is a pristine line of guns ready to rake our own decks clean. We are every bit as much of a target as our enemy. It is abominable. The balls that fail to penetrate bounce against the hull and shake the entire vessel. Splintered wood carves through flesh and bone as if they were newly churned butter. Men are shitting and pissing themselves where they stand and the excrement is mixed with the blood under our heels. Even sweat smells differently in the face of death, did you know that? Mix it all with gunsmoke and you end up with the devil's own perfume. If we had only had enough ammunition, the victory would have been ours.

'A thousand lives saw their end at Hogland, twice as many Russians as Swedes. As darkness fell, both sides were completely silent, and in the morning there was a Swedish retreat towards Helsinki, because without ammunition the battle could not continue. The Russians elected not to pursue. One ship was lost during the conflict, one taken in return: the *Vladislav*, a seventy-four-gunner.

'If we knew then what we know now, we would have sunk her on the spot. *Vladislav* nearly cost us the war all by herself. They had typhus on board, which we took with us to Sveaborg Fort. I stayed there over the winter while the ships returned to Karlskrona. We had to hack apart the pack ice with axes and pikes in order to open the harbour, and the ships carried the fever back to Sweden in their holds. That winter, Sveaborg turned into a circle of hell. The sick and dying were everywhere. We died like flies. In the beds of the infirmary, the men lay piled as high as five, with those on the bottom inevitably dead. Those who were the worst afflicted started to hallucinate. They widened their bloodshot eyes at things no living being could see, and screamed at the tops of their voices. I saw men so struck with terror that they forsook their sickbeds to run naked into the snowstorm. I myself was spared the affliction, and by summer, war returned to the Gulf of Finland. We were massacred at Svensksund, we stood no chance at Viborg. And yet the war had hardly touched a hair on my head, I was unharmed by fever, splinters or bullets. In May 1790, we had reinforcements from Åbo and I was one of those assigned to assist the newcomers. I was moved to the *Ingeborg*, a frigate. I hated her from the first. Chapman, who had built her too, had never sailed a day in his life, Winge. He was a mathematician who designed ships that were never intended for humans. She was one hundred and twenty feet long, with a dozen guns of which all but two shot twelve pounds. She leaked. The mould clung to the hull a hand-span thick and could be cut with a knife. By and by we joined the main force.'

For the second time, the Swedish ships were positioned like sheep to the slaughter in Svensksund, badly injured, pursued by the Russians and isolated from the naval fleet that was helplessly cut off at Sveaborg. Only the end remained. There was nowhere to flee and battle seemed the only alternative. And the King wanted to do battle.

'They came at us out of the dawn at around seven. It took them four hours to get within range and those four hours would have been the worst of my life if it hadn't been for those that followed. We had no doubt that death itself was coming towards us, divided into three hundred vessels. Many men had already tried to desert. Men had been left by the thousands in the breakers in the flight from Viborg, and that morning in Svensksund, many said they could hear the voices of their drowned comrades on the wind, calling out for company. When the Russians arrived, they fell into our right flank, which we defended. We worked the guns for hours.'

'The weather changed at midday: a breeze rose out of the south-west, first a mere whisper and then a roar. With it came a much rougher sea of waves with white ruffled crests under heavy storm clouds. The cannonades from the Swedish vessels, at anchor and lashed together, were far more effective than those of the Russians, who found themselves firing in vain, at the mercy of the heaving sea. A smaller group of Swedish ships broke away in order to attack the Russian flank from behind. The latter broke into panic at the sight of the Swedish attackers and beat a retreat. The left flank took the sign of the comrades' retreat as a general order and soon followed. The centre stayed put, alone. They were shot to pieces as night fell over Svensksund. One by one, the ships all sank and left their dying and their wounded floating on the tide that was now a boiling red mess. When the last remaining vessels finally tried to turn and flee it was too late. The storm took them and they were lost, one by one, on the Finnish reefs.

'And what about me? *Ingeborg* was hit by a Russian gun in the afternoon. The shot tore the twelve-pounder beside me from its carriage and continued through the hull out the other side. A score of gunners were immediately shredded into pieces. Those who were not in the path of the ball itself were crushed into a pulp when the gun barrel came rolling. Our enemies had heated their ball red hot before it was fired, and it ignited whatever wood it came into contact with. When our own guns could no longer be used for defence, I ran up on deck, where complete chaos reigned. Our only possibility to save the frigate – which was now sinking – was to pull up anchor and ride her aground. We struggled with the anchor when our gunpowder supply exploded. The entire capstan was shot away and those of us who were not mangled in that moment were thrown over the railing. I landed on a part of the deck that was still intact. The air was knocked out of me and then the anchor chain came rustling in a bow of iron and landed on my left arm. It fettered me to the deck and while my friend drowned, I was kept aloft. I was found later that night by a dinghy on its way back to join the main force. They made a tourniquet out of rope and then severed my arm below the elbow. And thus ended the war for Mickel Cardell. I convalesced at the tent camp in Lovisa. A hospital transport took me back to Stockholm, where I have lived for three years as you see me now.'

Cardell knocks on the table with his wooden limb.

'You know of course that the war lacked any purpose and that the victory did not win us anything. One thing has stayed with me in particular, Winge. In the early summer of 1790, I became acquainted with a young officer by the name of Sillén. He told me about a curious event right after our skirmish outside Fredrikshamn earlier that year. King Gustav and his retinue were on their way back to his ship, the *Amphion*. A certain Captain Virgin announced himself and gave a report regarding his failed attempt to take control of the nearby Russian shipyard. As if to emphasize his defeat, he showed the King his damaged hand and pointed to his first mate, who was sprawled on the deck of the ship in a tangle of his own intestines. The King pointed to the body that was still twitching, and jokingly told the other officers that the man's corpse reminded him of a stuffed mannequin from his own opera, *Gustav Wasa*, whereupon the King and his retinue laughed and applauded the witticism. Such was the man we fought for, and such the thanks that we got.'

Winge absorbs his words and drinks the last of his coffee. Cardell wipes his brow with his sleeve.

'So what now?'

'I have a name for you, Jean Michael, the name of a person who may lead you somewhere if luck stands on our side. I will take on the question of the fine cotton fabric in which Karl Johan was sent to his final rest. You know where my room is. Look me up when you have something to report.'

9

T HE PARTICULAR NEIGHBOURHOOD officer in Maria
parish, whom Cardell has arranged to meet through the
assistance of Winge and the police agency, has taken his breakfast
in liquid form. It is with some difficulty that he maintains his
balance as he appears on his front steps. He has the hiccups, and
smells like the floor of a pub. He is thick and broad, his nose is
crooked and has probably been shattered more than once. Under
the skin, broken blood vessels wallow like a pack of leeches.

'Henric Stubbe, at your service! They call me Stubby.'

The man restrains a burp with a small sound, and shrugs in
apology.

'Mickel Cardell, your humble servant, and many thanks for
your time.'

'Oh, not at all. Come in, come in. Not to drag this business out
more than is necessary, but for God's sake let's have a little something first. These streets of Maria and Katarina are nothing I
would wish even my worst enemy to view in a state of sobriety.'

After a dreary half an hour spent over a cask of wine that Cardell
guesses is a cheap blend of remnants from the bottoms of several
barrels, with the aftertaste drowned out by the addition of anise,
they step out on to Katarina Street again. Stubby is holding forth
about the neighbourhoods he has been entrusted to watch over.

'The shit that isn't hauled to the Larder slithers down the hill towards Gilded Bay. The newborns go the same direction but make a stop at the graveyard. Jesus Christ, Cardell, they may not have much to brag about here in Maria parish but they know how to fuck, and if you can't be bothered with your own wife there's always someone else's. There's childbirth upon childbirth from the time the maiden puts a ring on her finger until the crone gets carried out feet first with her titties trailing behind her on the ground, ten years and as many kids later. Few of them are lucky enough to grow up to be as fine a specimen of mankind as you or I. Those that survive get to be all of twenty-something before the fever takes them.'

Stubby, sweating under his hat and wig, sits down on a wooden box and places both headpieces on his lap while he blissfully rubs his scalp until the flakes go flying.

'The whoring is a crying shame. The girls have hardly learned to stand on their own two legs before they know how to spread them. They start going door to door with fruit baskets and do all in their power to tempt God-fearing men to sin. And it wears on them, you know, it's just a matter of time until they get the French disease, and no money for treatment remains after what little they've earned has been exchanged for drink. After a couple of years no reasonable person will even so much as look at them. No, those of us who are both wise and horny have to hurry before the bloom is off the rose.'

Stubby winks at Cardell.

'But you'll know that already, watchman that you are. See there, it's some of your colleagues.'

Cardell only needs to see the outlines of the two figures up ahead in order to know their names: Fischer and Tyst, watchmen like himself. They are walking along the street and stopping to open doors along the way in hopes of catching some young sinner in the act.

For his part, Cardell only performed a couple of hours of service as watchman before he returned to the commander and turned in his notice. His only visit to the women's gaol out on the Scar almost made him retch: emaciated bodies forced to perform their assigned labour, slowly dying of starvation and vulnerable to the attentions of his fellow watchmen. It occurred to him that whatever hell these poor souls were condemned to after death, it would be a welcome change from life within those walls. He even said as much aloud. They tried to change his mind but he maintained a stubborn silence until the commander shrugged, spat into the gravel, and turned on his heel.

Apparently, it was thought to be easier simply to keep Cardell on the payroll than risk bad blood with the man who had recommended him. He still collects the salary and all he does in return is wear some of the uniform he was issued, which is better than his own clothes in any case. The coat, boots and belt. The rod he cracked over his knee and tossed into the sea along with the rope. He steers Stubby into a corner in order to avoid an encounter with Fischer and Tyst, while the man prattles on.

'And the Larder, Cardell. What a sight for the devil. And you have gone in, from what I understand. Have you ever been here when we have a real wind blowing? No? It comes as a strong gust out of the bay. It gets the windmills going till the wood starts smoking . . . but when the gusts hit the Larder, it whips up quite a stew, I can tell you. Junk that has been lying on the bottom is stirred up. People flee down Miller's Hill as fast as they can, or out to Danto and the Winter Tollgate. How familiar are you with our Southern Isle anyway, Cardell?'

'Somewhat, but I have experienced it mostly through the windows of pubs.'

'Well, that won't do! I'll tell you all about it. It's home to a band of thieves. Children learn to steal in their cradles rather than risk starving to death, and the march towards the pillory and prison begins right there. Or to the gallows, if it comes to the worst. At the pub the other night, a man read out a letter to the *Stockholm Post* where a friend of decency was complaining about the ladies of the night on the City-between-the-Bridges, and how those whores were offering their services for a few shillings. We all laughed over the inflated prices. Over here on the other side of the Lock, anybody is yours for under a shilling – man, woman or child.'

Together they tour the streets around Larder Lake, block after block. White stone buildings house manufactories and families where the generations are squeezed in together. Here and there the houses are still built of timber, a kind that the city authorities have not yet been able to demolish as the fire hazard they are. The cobblestones in the streets are tumbled out of place by boot heels and wagon wheels.

They stop for a drink from the well at Maria Church. Cardell grimaces while Stubby chuckles knowingly.

'That's the sea breeze for you. The salt water is blowing in through the Lock and seeps all the way into our wells. Hence the taste. Many a brewer has seen his batch spoiled after using water without tasting it first.'

Stubby points out all the buildings, and gossips about those who live there, knocking on windows and doors, and allowing Cardell to pose his questions. The answers are vague. The poor and the powerless have learned to fear the authorities that without compunction drag those without work permits to workhouses and forced labour. Everything is routinely denied in a pattern learned from childhood: hear no evil, see no evil, speak no evil. After a few hours, Cardell starts to doubt the possibility that even the simplest of his questions will find an answer. Stubby shrugs his shoulders.

'Well, what were you expecting? Let's keep going down the hill and find ourselves something to eat.'

There's a loud clatter from the scales where workers are unloading their tacks of iron. The Muscovite buyers in the Russian Yard do what they can to make their strange words heard over the noise. At the Pelican on Headsman's Hill, just a stone's throw from the Lock, there are turnips and herring to be had with simple beer and a shot of brandy. The taproom is full of people and they squeeze onto benches at a long table, elbow to elbow with their fellow diners. Cardell hears the same disgruntlement from every mouth. Duke Charles's and Baron Reuterholm's names are interspersed with curses, while whispers lament the appalling state of the economy, the incompetent management of the nation, and the urgent need for change.

'May I ask, Mickel Cardell, if you'll allow me: what is it you are doing here, anyway? Isn't there enough to concern oneself with in this city as it is? I have heard of Cecil Winge, and even laid eyes on him, and it is easy to see that all is not right there. The man looks like a corpse who has escaped the grave. It goes against nature to be clambering so to life. He should have sense enough to make peace with his fate. But you, Cardell? A real man of flesh and blood, with your future before you – why waste your time on a fruitless affair such as this?'

Cardell knows how to control himself. He is used to it. His rage has percolated for so many years that every moment has been a chance to practise for situations like this. Had he been drunk, the temptation to hammer Stubby's crooked nose straight again would have been too strong. Instead he draws a deep breath and turns his gaze to the crowds in the square outside.

'We'll learn in due course if the investigation bears any fruit, Stubby. You will have to take me at my word when I assure you that I am not exactly keeping a long line of rich benefactors waiting in the meantime. Do you have any memories of that night yourself?'

Stubby drinks some of his beer as he considers the question, and then chortles.

'It was certainly a strange night, Cardell. I woke up in the middle of the night and had to take a piss – that seems to happen more and more often lately – and since the chamber pot looked ready to overflow, I walked out into the courtyard. It took me a while but as I stood there minding my business, my eyes became accustomed to the dark and it looked like there was something strange about where I was standing, as if the wall had moved. When I groped my way over there – still with my manhood dangling, you understand – I felt that there was something hard and angular in front of me. I couldn't think of anything better to do than go back and fetch a lantern, and when I came back I saw . . . a sedan chair, Cardell, a covered litter with tiny windows and curtains, and one of the handles broken off. You should know that I very seldom receive any visitors by sedan chair these days, even though I become less concerned with covering my member with each passing year.'

Stubby pauses for a moment to laugh delightedly at his own wit.

'In any case it was empty, broken and abandoned. No one was around. It was not there when I woke up in the morning and that was just as well, or it would have become the playhouse of every tot in the neighbourhood until some pauper decided to decorate it and move in permanently. I assume that the owner encountered some form of trouble during the evening, stored the damaged chair in the nearest quiet area and arranged another form of trans-port, after which their servants came back before dawn with rope or tools and were able to retrieve it.'

'What did it look like?'

'Green with gold decorations. Expensive but worn – not surprising, of course. You don't see sedan chairs on every street corner these days. Not like a few years ago.'

'Was there anyone else in your household who may have seen anything else?'

'I enjoy my own company so much that I rarely share it with anyone else. I asked around a bit for the sake of my own curiosity, but no one seemed to know anything about it.'

'From one thing to another, what do you do, apart from your post as neighbourhood officer?'

'Well, my friend, a hangover is not the only aftermath of strong spirits like aquavit. My business is the pulp. When the drink has finished brewing, there is still some detritus left, mostly berries and fruit peels. This pulp still contains some nutrients and can be used for animal feed. I collect it from the breweries, and even sometimes at the bigger households, and then sell it to the farms and stables. If you were ever offered a scoop of the stuff, I couldn't honestly recommend it, but pigs, cows and geese can't seem to ever get their fill.'

'I see. Me, I am an old artilleryman at heart and the blows and explosions have taken their toll. If you stand next to a thirty-six-pounder when it goes off, it feels like a fist in the face and if you have any snot in your nose it'll go flying through the air. But Stubby, being that you are a sensible man, with your mind still intact, do you think you could assist me in my deductions? Can you think of any mode of transportation that would serve to carry a dead body across town without being discovered?'

Stubby wrinkles his brow and chews on his lower lip.

'Well, I'd say you'd need some kind of covered wagon for that, I think.'

Cardell cocks his head in partial agreement.

'It's hard to make your way easily in a big wagon. It's also noisy with hooves clattering on the cobblestones, and the creaking wheels, and some diligent customs officer could suddenly decide to check the cargo even within the city limits.'

'Something that is both quiet and discreet, is what you're getting at, Cardell. I can't imagine what that would be?'

'What was it you said just now about the discovery in your yard, which as it happens is located not far from the Larder?'

'A sedan chair? You don't mean that the body was carried in a sedan chair?'

'Not *a* sedan chair, you fucking nitwit. *That* sedan chair. You've dragged me around half of the Southern Isle to no avail, while all the while the very thing I'd hardly dared hope for was standing for hours right at your own door. My one consolation is that I believe the walk was even less appealing for you than for me. Someone carried the body behind drawn curtains, covered in a sack, and had to leave the chair behind and then come back for it as soon as they could. It may be in a workshop somewhere as we speak. Attend me well now, Stubby. If you want even the slightest hope of retaining your office in this godforsaken shithole, you'll run straight home and speak personally with each and every person who lives in your house, from the oldest biddy to the youngest babe. If anyone has seen the chair and can describe it in more detail, or those that came to get it, you'll tell me before the street lights are lit.'

<hr />

On his way back across the Lock, Cardell talks to himself, in low excited tones accompanied by the murmur of the current.

'Well now, Karl Johan, I have you by your collar in a grip that will be hard to shake. All I need to do is find a green sedan chair with gilded decorations and a newly repaired handle.'

He glances up at the truncated tower of Maria Church and adds:

'And smelling of piss.'

10

ALL OF WINGE'S day has been spent tracing the cotton fabric. This has taken some time. The merchants have outdone themselves in their effusiveness in speaking to him about wares that are their own rather than someone else's. The best piece of information he has received sent him to an English trader who may or may not have left Stockholm yet. Where the ship was located, no one could tell him, and Winge's only option for an answer is to look through the registers himself.

The lower floors of the Customs House are a flurry of various goods and languages. Officials scurry back and forth, pursued by clerks with pencils and ledgers. Merchants, shipowners and ship's captains are negotiating their tax obligation, questioning the accuracy of the scales and integrity of their operators. Those who are not able to make themselves understood simply repeat themselves at a higher volume. It takes Winge hours before he can slip a small sum to one of the customs officers to see the lists of the ships that have arrived in the harbour. The ship in question is called the *Sophie* and its home base is Southampton. She has been assigned a docking spot alongside the Orpheus quarter, close to Castle Hill. Her departure status is noted as awaiting the right wind to carry her out.

It is starting to get dark when Winge leaves the Customs House and hurries along the quay past the stairs that lead down to the water. The Quayside is still marked by the traces of the Michaelmas autumn market, strewn with litter. He looks anxiously out at the sea but no ships appear to be on their way out. It is already too late in the day and the wind hardly manages to flutter the pennants strung on the mast.

He feels a cough in his throat, irritated by the dampness of the sea and his exertions. The cramp in his side feels like a tiepin lodged between his ribs. Reluctantly he has to slow down and when he has to place more of his weight on the silver-tipped cane, the bowing of the wood reminds him that it was carved more for decoration than support.

Winge sighs with relief when he reads the name *Sophie* on the stern of a ship. She, a schooner, her foremast shorter than her mainmast, is still tied with her starboard side to the quay. There is no activity that he can see. Evening *flâneurs* are visiting coffee houses and wine cellars, loaders and quay labourers have returned home, the sailors have disappeared up the Stadsholmen alleys in search of company and entertainment. He walks by the gangway. Only one man can be seen on deck. With a look of concentration, he is lowering a lead weight into an ironclad casket.

'Joseph Satcher?'

The man replies in French. He has a powerful build, dressed in a reinforced seaman's coat, three-cornered hat, sturdy boots, and a beard that reaches far down onto his waistcoated chest.

'My name is Thatcher. It is as poorly suited to trade with Sweden as my goods. I assume that you do not speak my language?'

Winge speaks excellent French, good German, has a working knowledge of Greek, and reads Latin with ease, but he lacks a deeper grasp of English. Thatcher nods without surprise.

'My Swedish is also not what it should be. So, French then. What is your business with me?'

'My name is Cecil Winge. You are said to be an authority on fabrics made of cotton.'

Thatcher sits down on his casket and indicates to Winge where he can sit on a deck hatch. Winge hands him the black cloth. Thatcher studies it in silence.

'My fingers already tell me a great deal, but to say anything definitive I need to fetch my lantern. But first, will you share with me the reason for asking?'

'This cloth was found wrapped around the body of mutilated and drowned man whose fate I am trying to discern.'

Thatcher stares back at him for a while, then leaves and returns from the cabin with a lighted lantern. He examines the fabric again in all of its seams and corners while Winge waits quietly. Finally, Thatcher picks up a simple wooden pipe and lights it on the lantern before he speaks.

'Tell me, Mr Winge, does the expression *homo homini lupus est* mean anything to you?'

'Plautus wrote it during the Punic Wars: *Like a wolf is man to other men.*'

'Forgive a simple merchant who has not had the benefit of a classical education. I know the words from Voltaire, but with a mind to the meaning of them, it doesn't surprise me that they are older than that. And what is your view on the matter? Are we wolves to one another, always on the lookout for the least sign of weakness before we choose our moment of attack?'

'We have laws and rules to contain such urges in those who nurture them.'

Thatcher laughs from his cloud of smoke.

'The system is working poorly in that case, Mr Winge. I myself am a good example. Your country is bankrupt, Mr Winge, and if tidings could only be carried more swiftly, I would perhaps have become aware of this in time to avert my doom. Here no one wants my wares, and in order to avoid having to return home with unfinished business, I have had to part with my goods at a loss. Add to that the greedy palms of the customs officers, where many a ducat stick, then the cleverness of my competitors and my debt to my creditors, and I am lost, Mr Winge. Did you happen to see what I was doing before you interrupted me?'

'Yes, you were loading weights into a case that appears to be your strongbox.'

'And can you guess why I would do something like that?'

Winge nods and averts his gaze. He wonders if death has a smell or another characteristic that makes it so easy for him to perceive its presence, and if his sensitivity is a result of the work that he does or of his own condition.

'You are going to throw it overboard. Since a man's papers are often worth more than his life, I imagine that you are planning to hold it in your arms and accompany it over the railing, and that the additional weight was intended as a means to shorten your suffering.'

Thatcher blows a beautiful ring of smoke over the water where it dissolves in a gust of wind.

'I am personally responsible for my goods. All that I own is mortgaged. The fine gentlemen who invested money in me in hopes of a return will tear me into pieces. Everything will be taken from me upon my return. I can achieve the same thing before I leave Stockholm and be spared a tiring journey and more troubles. My journey will be shortened to twenty feet and ends in the mud under the *Sophie*'s hull. With my papers in my arms, I lessen the risk that my debts will be inherited.'

Thatcher puffs on his pipe. Something mean-spirited appears in his eyes when he calmly fastens his eyes on Winge through the whirling smoke.

'Why should I aid you? Why should I, as my last act in this life, once again vainly place obstacles in the way of the one who has already shown himself to be the better of two wolves? If only I had been a better wolf myself, this hour would not be my last. What kind of wolf are you, then, Mr Winge? A good wolf? A skilled hunter?'

'No wolf at all, I'm afraid. What I do, I do not undertake in order to satisfy my bloodlust. Nonetheless, I will succeed in my endeavours whether you decide to help me or not.'

Thatcher suddenly shivers and rubs his arms, the pipe still hanging from his mouth. In that frame of mind in which he has already made his fateful decision, he seems halfway to another world.

'You are unnaturally pale and thin, Mr Winge. What ails you?'

'My lungs. I have consumption. I will not survive you by any significant margin.'

Thatcher laughs loudly, a thundering cheerful sound that rolls out over the railing towards the sea.

'Why didn't you say so at once? What would the world be if us dying sods couldn't stick together? There is something I can do for you, because it may be that the cloth you have shown me in fact does contain the secret for which you hope.'

He signals to Winge to come closer and holds the fabric under the lantern's light.

'See here. The cotton has been sewn in a double layer. This seam tells me something very clearly, especially since it has been ripped out along one side: someone has turned this thing inside out. Let's see.'

Thatcher reaches his rough hand through the hole where the seam has been removed, grabs the opposite side and turns the black cloth inside out as if it were a large bag.

'*Voilà!* There's something you don't see every day.'

Along the edge of the cloth there is a wide border printed in a gold colour that the water of the Larder has not managed to erase. The pattern depicts human figures in groups of four, entwined in poses depicting pleasures of the flesh. The men's members are grotesquely enlarged, as are the women's bosoms. Ecstasy is on their faces. The quartet is repeated again and again up and down the edge of the cloth.

'As an expert, I can add that both the fabric and printing are of the finest quality, even if I have to admit that I hope the artist has exercised a certain freedom and has not been using actual models. Well, not that it makes any difference now. My own exploits in that area lie behind me. May my children do better than I have, though I doubt it. Naive as I was, I raised them to become good men, and I expect them to be as easy a prey for others as I have been.'

Thatcher starts to dig the ashes from his pipe but then stops and throws it overboard. He brings his heavy body to his feet and lifts the lid of the casket in which the lead weight is resting on a pile of papers. There is room for more.

'So, Mr Winge, if you will excuse me, I have things yet to pack before my journey. Now I have helped you pick up the scent, all you have to do is follow it out into the forest to find your mark. I see how your expression has changed. You can't fool me! You are indeed a wolf after all. I've seen enough to know and, even if I am wrong, you will soon become one. No one can run with the wolf pack without accepting its terms. You have both the fangs and the glint of the predator in your eye. You deny your blood thirst but it rises around you like a stench. One day your teeth will be stained red and then you'll know with certainty how right I was. Your bite will be deep. Maybe you will prove the better wolf, Mr Winge, and on that note I bid you goodnight.'

11

CARDELL WAKES UP in a cold sweat. The straw from the mattress is poking into his back and his body is itching from lice. On the other side of the wooden planks of the wall, a child is screaming and soon it is joined by a companion of the same age further down in the labyrinth of rooms. The alcohol from last night is still in his blood, when he celebrated his deductions regarding Stubby's sedan chair. He lurches alarmingly as he pulls on the strings of the breeches he fell asleep in and urinates into the chamber pot. He opens the window and, with a well-practised flick, tosses the contents of the pot into the courtyard below. Outside the clouds are so low that the church spire of Stockholm Cathedral is obscured and ghostlike. The face of its clock, only readable when he squints until his headache grows stronger, shows a little after nine in the morning. He needs a drink.

Outside the room that Cardell has rented for over half a year, some whispering women are cooking porridge. He does not know their names but bids them good morning, asks for some sips of the well water from the bucket and continues down the stairs and out onto Goose Alley. He steers towards the Southern Square, where he can drink on credit. Out of old habit, he holds his breath when he passes the Flies' Meet, the giant mound of excrement amassed by the city, next to the harbour granaries. The Red Lock bridge is raised in order to allow a small vessel to pass upstream. The newly built drawbridge on the side of the sea, already called the Blue Lock, has only been ready for a couple of weeks and is still regarded with suspicion. It looks thin and fragile compared to Polhem's massive construction. Many still wait for the Red rather than risk their lives on the Blue. Not Cardell. If it is because his courage is greater or because he values his life less, he does not know.

Something is up. A large horde has gathered on the square, streaming their way up Mason's Pass. Passively, Cardell allows himself to be drawn along. To judge by the throng outside Cellar Hamburg, it must be an execution day. Idle folk have gathered there to gape at the condemned man who will shortly arrive by cart to receive the customary drink.

Cardell takes a quick one himself at the pub next door and then follows the flow of people along Gothic Lane and down Postmaster's Street where the buildings grow ever more scarce. The batteries of the Sconce Tollgate loom up on both sides of the road, and behind the ridge the road continues up Hammarby Hill. At its top, the three-legged gallows make an outline against a stormy sky: three upright pillars of stone connected by cross-beams to form a lethal triangle. A mob, forty men deep, surrounds the scaffold, kept at a distance by a row of watchmen that form a living fence, connected by poles they carry in their arms. The bailiff climbs up to read the sentence. Cardell notices that it is not the noose that is to be used today. This is not a matter of a thief to be hanged, but the murderer of a woman, and, as such, some-one who is destined for the block.

The cart has not yet appeared. Its arrival is announced by the clamour of the flock of street urchins and halfwits who run behind the fated man and throw whatever dreck and debris they find at his back. He is young, certainly not yet twenty, apprehended after he has strangled his betrothed over a stolen hen – he wanted to still his hunger immediately, she wanted to spare the animal for its eggs.

When he has been pushed inside the execution area, he starts to shake all over his body and a dark stain spreads down the knee breeches of his left leg. The assemblage is brimming with excitement. Two whores that Cardell knows by appearance, if not by name, are screaming insinuations about the convict's manhood. Behind them, a man whose nose has been made into a rotten crater by the French disease laughs so hard his snot goes flying. The bailiff leaves the area with as much dignity as he can muster. He is already drinking from a silver flask and is setting his feet down with care so as to save his fine shoes from the mud.

A hush falls over the crowd when the door to the executioner's house opens and the headsman shows himself. His name is Mårten Höss and he enjoys a strange mixture of notoriety, respect and revulsion. The hood that befits his profession is pushed back on his neck. While many of his predecessors have preferred to obscure their faces, he is unabashed. His face is lined but unremarkable, the black eyes devoid of expression. He himself was sentenced after having knocked the jawbone off a drinking buddy with a tankard at a time when the executioner's post had just become vacant. He was granted a stay of his punishment in return for accepting the position himself. With each stroke of the axe or sword, his own fate draws closer, and for each executed sentence, his hand appears to tremble a little more and his state of intoxication becomes more marked.

Rumour has it that Höss has tried to take his life three times already, but after his courage deserted him when trying to throw himself into the waters of Årsta, he has decided to flee the axe by drinking himself to death. This does not make him less popular: his drunkenness adds another element of entertainment to the show.

Jubilation rises as the guards step aside and Höss enters the area. He is unsteady on his feet and almost falls backwards as he tries to take an exaggerated bow before his audience. The enthusiasm of the spectators inspires him. 'Master' Höss – so-called as a nod to his incompetence – grabs the axe by its straight edge from one of executioner's assistants and swings it through the air. He slips in the mud when he makes a run towards the condemned man as if he were planning to behead him on the spot. The crowd howls with delight and clap hands.

The block is brought out. It is a simple piece of wood, scarred with gashes and stains. The convict is forced to kneel until his head is resting on it. One of the assistants places his foot between his shoulder blades while another pulls a strap around his right hand and ties it to the block. It will be severed first to ensure that the condemned prisoner does not pass into the other world devoid of suffering. The executioner takes his place and as the axe is raised another hush falls. A joker in the back rows is shushed after having taken advantage of the silence to call out the name of a sexual organ. With a roar, Höss lets the axe fall but stops it barely a foot above the trembling arm.

Höss is proud of his showmanship. He wipes imaginary sweat from his brow, clasps both hands behind his back and pretends to stretch as if having carried a heavy load. The appreciation of his viewing public is enough for him to repeat his stunt three times. The condemned man has started to cry. Although he is no longer restrained, he doesn't try to shift out of position, but the sobs that rack his body are plain for all to see.

Despite his stupor, Höss is experienced enough to know he now has to finish the job or face the wrath of the mob. The sobs escalate into a howl that causes even the excited crowd to simmer down. The atmosphere shifts to anticipation.

Again, the assistants take up their positions and restrain the condemned. Höss spits into his fists, raises the axe and lets it fall onto the man's wrist with a wet thud. Accompanied by the man's scream of anguish, an assistant picks the severed limb out of the mud and tosses it out into the crowd. The fingers and hand of an executed criminal bring good luck – the thumb in particular promises protection from the law when a theft is undertaken, and thieves are both numerous and superstitious. The hand will be cut up and sold by the street urchin who managed to wriggle out of the grasp of his competitors.

Höss staggers out to deliver the death blow as the young man is screaming himself hoarse. It is no longer a human sound but something that reaches the public from another world, like an echo that issues from behind the curtains of hell.

It takes Master Höss several attempts to cleave the head from the body. The first blow lands across the shoulder, the second flays the scalp on the back of his head resulting in a large section with one ear hanging loose. It is not easy to tell if Höss is laughing or crying when he starts to swing the axe more wildly and to yell at the top of his lungs: 'As punishment for your deeds and a warning unto others! As punishment for your deeds and a warning unto others!'

Only after the fifth blow do both voices stop, both that of the condemned and the executioner.

It is Master Höss's most blundered execution to date, the connoisseurs concur. They agree that he could have drunk a little less out of respect for his profession; it doesn't seem likely that he can get away with many more displays like this before a more capable man will be spared and Höss himself tied to the block.

When the guards march away, old women stream forward to collect the blood pooled on the ground. Nothing is as efficacious in treating the falling sickness. The executioner's assistants have turned the corpse on its back and lift its legs so that as much as possible will drain into the mud and less onto themselves when they drag it to its freshly dug grave behind the structure.

Mickel Cardell turns away. When he lifts his head he sees the thin, dark outline of Cecil Winge on a knoll next to the road. The serendipitous meeting causes Cardell to hesitate, and he stands a long time observing Winge without trying to get his attention. The pale face does not betray any emotion, gives no sign that its owner has been affected in any way by the actions just witnessed. Only when Cardell comes closer does he notice that his slender fingers are squeezing his cane so tightly that his knuckles whiten and his entire arm is shaking.

Winge is lost in thought, still turned towards the scaffold. He only breaks his gaze and greets Cardell when the latter has come quite close. A light rain starts to fall over the execution grounds.

'Good afternoon, Jean Michael. I have not seen the executioner in action for some time. I came here to see justice served in light of the murder we ourselves are investigating. This is the fate that awaits our perpetrator if we are successful in our cause.'

'And?'

'I have never seen much logic in the Crown trying to combat murder by taking the lives of its citizens, and in a manner more bestial than the original crimes. But my greatest objection is this: the law makes no attempt to understand those sentenced. How can anyone hope to prevent the crimes of tomorrow without trying to understand the ones committed today? The answer, Jean Michael, is that the very thought has never occurred to those in charge. They believe it is their task to judge and punish. Many of those I myself have tried have seen their lives ended on this hill. My only consolation is that not one of them was carted away without being questioned, and that I placed all of my efforts into proving beyond a shadow of a doubt that the accused was guilty, and that each and every one was given the opportunity to speak in their own defence.'

'The mob will never hear reason, however much you try to understand them. Without the fear of the axe and the rope, Stockholm would go up in flames overnight.'

Winge does not reply and Cardell goes on.

'My meeting with Stubby may have brought us one step closer to solving this. I'll say more when I have better information but I can at least tell you that I am looking for a green sedan chair that may have been used to furnish Karl Johan with his final journey.'

They turn their backs on the gallows and the red stain that is now all that remains of the man who was brought here to die. Together they start to walk back on the road towards the Sconce Tollgate. Winge breaks the silence once they are at the bottom of the hill.

'You told me about King Gustav and the war, Jean Michael, and it was impossible to mistake your emotions over having lost so much in an affair that was entered into on a false premise. Therefore, I wish for you to understand something about me that not many know but that nonetheless is the truth. You have inquired about me and I know the rumours say that I left my wife out of regard for her well-being.'

Cardell feels uncomfortable, ill accustomed to hearing confidences. He stares down at his boots as they trudge through what is quickly becoming a muddy mess.

'As my cough grew worse, I grew more ill, more thin and weak, and started to fade away before her eyes. I could no longer offer her anything, and could not be all that a husband should be.'

Winge's hoarse voice is a flat monotone and there is no hint of feeling, almost as if he were reading a passage from the Holy Book. Cardell perceives the control behind the words holding them steady, almost like the pressure of a storm before the breaking point.

'I understood what was happening, of course. That is the consequence of a life in the service of the law. Small details that indicate a falsehood – my senses were never sharper than in my attention to these. I found unknown items in our home. She would go out to visit with friends that I later realized she never met. But most of all I noticed it in her. She looked happy. Her cheeks were pink and there was a sparkle in her eyes where there once had only been the prescience of death.'

Winge turns to Cardell. His face is still, as with someone who has been paralysed.

'For the first time in months, she resembled the woman that I had fallen in love with.'

He lingers on this thought for a while before he continues.

'I came upon them finally, in the act, in a moment of weakness. I had done my utmost to avoid it, but I was weak and absent-minded. My coughing masked the sounds of their lovemaking and vice versa. He was a young officer with a sword and baldric, with blackened moustaches and his future before him. I could not blame her. I prepared my departure to Roselius that same evening. I have not seen her since.'

Cardell opens his mouth to offer his condolences but Winge stops him, his face turned towards Hammarby Lake, the waves of which the wind has now begun to whip.

'There is no need for you to say anything. Just as you yourself said at our first meeting, it is not pity that I seek. My confidence is not intended as an invitation to friendship but because I have a sense that we will both profit from knowing one another's strengths and weaknesses during the tribulations that await us. Nothing is more important now. I crave no words of comfort. Do not become my friend, Jean Michael. The time is too short. Grief would be the only reward for your troubles.'

They part at the tollgate where Winge signals for a horse-drawn carriage.

'Meet me tomorrow at nine at the Small Exchange. Your sedan chair sounds promising, I nurture good hope with regard to Karl Johan's epitaph.'

12

TRAVELLING BY SEDAN chair is no longer in fashion; that much Cardell is able to conclude only a few hours after having left the horrors of the execution ground behind him. He has mixed feelings about this. It should simplify the matter of locating Stubby's green sedan chair, but is complicated by the fact that the industry lacks robust organization. There is no guild to oversee the bearers, and the old litters that he used to see everywhere as a child have either gone up in smoke in one of the new tiled ovens or been bought by independents who stand on street corners in hopes of attracting customers.

After further questioning, Cardell finds his way to a stable near Children's Lea in Katarina parish. But no one there knows anything either. A bearded purveyor in a horsehair wig sneezes between rounds of snuff and curses the modern era that has robbed him of his livelihood. When the century was young, no gentleman hesitated to let himself be carried through the city by a pair of stout men. At the end of the seventies, he himself had no less than two dozen chairs in circulation. Now that figure is reduced to a third and the prices are in free fall. Bearers who once wore livery have to be content with a festoon in the pattern of the stable. The colours of his chairs? The old man shakes his head bitterly at the fact that his colours – black on white – are no longer generally known. Cardell leaves Children's Lea no closer to finding his answer.

At sundown, men begin to climb ladders or reach up with long torches in order to light the street lamps. The stink of burning oil is everywhere, although the diligence of the city watch in making sure every block maintains proper street lighting declines, the further from the City-between-the-Bridges he gets.

In the falling dusk, Cardell has made his way to the opposite end of town, a godforsaken part of the Meadowland in the area around the Northern Tollgate. He follows the Rill, the foul-smelling waterway that runs in brown curves between the houses, north, with the steep Brunke's Ridge on his left and with the shores of the Bog to the right. The water stinks to high heaven but it is still no match for the Larder. A certain measure of running water and a larger overall volume is better suited to bear the constant influx of latrine and household waste.

Past the Bog, stone houses give way to wooden ones and the stone pavement ends in packed clay. The house Cardell seeks is close to the Sourwell and is said to be the quarters of a certain carpenter who still occupies himself with the repair and new construction of sedan chairs. Between the buildings in the court-yard, it is dark. Cardell is surprised to see that people are out even though the chill of October is intensified by the night. There is a man on a set of stairs under the front door, and in the shadows of the building a short distance away is a large figure who can't seem to decide which foot to stand on.

The seated man greets him with a wave. He is as wide across the shoulders as Cardell, but heavier, with a rounded belly that strains the buttons of his coat. His body signals both raw strength and laziness. His skull is as round as a ball, and the bullish neck so wide that his head looks as if it has been placed directly on his shoulders. The mouth is wide and the lips thick, his gaze marked by a squint and a wandering eye. He is chewing tobacco and with regular intervals he shoots a well-aimed stream of spittle out of the side of his mouth. Cardell responds to his wave with a slight bow.

'Mickel Cardell is my name. I beg pardon for the lateness of the hour, but I am looking for a carpenter by the name of Vries.'

'And you've found him. That is my name and no one else's. Sit down and let me offer you some tobacco.'

Cardell remains standing but helps himself to a wad of tobacco from the pouch that is offered to him. When he comes closer he sees that the waddling figure is a young man, even though he is as large as a giant. Next to him, both Cardell and the carpenter look a little close to the ground. Cardell also sees that the youth must be an imbecile. His mouth hangs open and a long strand of saliva glitters on his chin. His eyes remind him of a cow's, mild and vacuous. Around his throat there is a leather strap, the other end of which restrains him to the wooden railing.

'And Mr Vries, how is it that you are spending the evening on your own stoop?'

'Isn't the evening air a balm for the soul? How about you, then? What brings you to me, Master Carpenter Pieter de Vries, all the way out by the Bog, on an evening such as this?'

A mocking smile appears on his lips, as tobacco juice runs out of both corners of his mouth.

'I'm on the trail of a certain sedan chair, a green one with a cracked handle. A street urchin down at Cats' Bay claims to have seen something along those lines bound for your workshop not more than four days ago.'

Vries gets a worried wrinkle between his eyes.

'Oh no, fine sir. I fail to recall anything of the sort. It pains me that you've trudged all the way out here for nothing more than a little tobacco. Maybe this chair was on its way to some other tradesman in the area?'

Cardell nods in thought.

'As a matter of fact, you've no competitors out here. And I also learned that Master Carpenter de Vries could be difficult to understand, since he hails from Rotterdam and speaks such mangled Swedish that it's a wonder he had any clients at all, capable as he his.'

The man neighs with laughter, then stands up, straightens his back with a crack and brushes the seat of his pants clean.

'I see! Well then. At least Jöns Kuling is man enough to fess up when he has been caught out in an untruth.'

Cardell tilts his head in the direction of the young man next to them, still absorbed in his world.

'Who's he?'

'That would be my brother, Måns. As you can see, he doesn't have his full wits about him. You see, Cardell, our father and mother don't come from the big city like you. They came from a village so small that a good match was hard to find and when my father came of age, he had no choice but to take his own sister as his wife. Such violations of the laws of Our Lord come at a price, and that price received the name of Måns. He took our mother's life on his way out of her, the largest infant the midwife had ever seen. He's not a great thinker but if you want someone who can hold up the bow of a sedan chair for hours without complaining, then Måns is the man for you.'

'And you take the front, I presume.'

'You are a shrewd fellow indeed, Cardell. Yes, had our roles been reversed, Måns would have steered straight to hell before our poor passenger knew any better. And here we sit waiting for better times. The carpenter asked us to come again tomorrow, but the chair is our only livelihood and we don't leave it unattended. Even less so as our greatest benefactor let slip that our performance hasn't been completely to satisfaction recently, and that if anyone were to come asking about a green chair and where it had been these past days, things would not go well for us. That is, if the situation couldn't be contained on the spot. So here we are, you, me and Måns.'

84

Jöns unties the strap that keeps Måns fettered. He takes a few steps out into the courtyard, tilts his head side to side to warm up the stiff muscles and snorts the mucus from each nostril. He gives a sinister smile and raises his fists, each as big as a bucket. His shoulders and thighs bulge with years under the weight of the chair.

'You shouldn't have come sniffing around, Cardell, for here you find the end of the road, my friend. Come now and take a round with me and we'll see what you're made of.'

Cardell circles to the left in order to keep both Jöns and Måns in his sight. The large youth appears sensitive to changes in mood and he has started to jump up and down, making small eager noises. A member as large as an arm swells along his thigh under the tight knee breeches. After having exchanged a couple of feints, Cardell lands the first blow. The left hand catches Jöns Kuling hard in the side and causes him to bend over. An expression of astonishment is changed to laughter after he feels his side and looks down at blood on his hand.

'Damn it, Cardell! That blow sure hit the spot. My chest feels like the bottom of a kettle. What an iron fist!'

'Only wood, I'm afraid.'

'You fight dirty, Cardell. A man after my own taste. But we can't have that, now can we? This fight needs to be fair. Måns!'

The brother has only been waiting for his command and his sudden attack is so direct and without finesse that it takes Cardell completely by surprise. Måns throws himself at him to wrap his arms around him in an embrace that Cardell does not have time to escape and he falls hard with the youth's entire weight on top of him. Måns straddles his chest and the blows rain down. Cardell feels his nose break, an eyebrow split and blood gushing into his eye. Jöns quickly turns up on his left and he feels fingers clawing at the straps that keep his wooden limb in place. They slip out of place, the wood glides out of his sleeve and leaves him defenceless.

85

Above the muted thuds that he knows are the sound of Måns's fists hitting against his own face he hears an almost tender whisper and sees Jöns lips near his brother's ear. The blows stop.

'Well now, Måns my dear, let's help Cardell back on his feet and see how tough he is when he's deprived of his secret weapon.'

Cardell wipes the grime from his face and blinks his sight clear. Jöns smiles mockingly at him as he tosses the wooden hand across his shoulder where it lands somewhere next to the wall. His brother Måns starts to bray with great excitement as he licks his knuckles clean. There's a ringing in Cardell's ears and the world spins round. High above him the stars are glittering. Constellations flicker and whirl. Cardell's mouth is full of tooth shards and he wonders if it is stardust he feels on his tongue.

In his mind's eye, he sees blood foaming at Johan Hjelm's mouth, hears Cecil Winge's hoarse voice and the Russian cannonades in the distance, and shivers at the toothless smile that plays on Karl Johan's rotted lips in the dim light of the crypt. He begins to stagger towards the two swaying figures as he feels his dead arm take shape at his side, raw and throbbing, ripe with pain and hate.

'Come at me then, you fucking curs.'

13

GUSTAV ADOLF SUNDBERG's establishment has just moved to Ironmonger's Square from Captain Street at Klara Church but has already received the nickname of Small Exchange as the coffee house has become the gathering place of the Quayside burghers. Many are drinking pots of hot chocolate but the majority of the guests, like Cecil Winge, prefer endless cups of the bitter Arabian coffee, especially since rumour has it that the regency is considering banning the drink entirely in an attempt to control the rampant gossiping at the coffee houses.

Here, the gossip is flowing as freely as the brew: people share tidings of the fifteen-year-old Prince Gustav's bizarre behaviour towards his courtiers; about Duke Charles, who pines for the lady-in-waiting, Miss Rudenschöld, whose heart belongs to the traitor Armfelt; about the literary scribe Thomas Thorild, who is said to have fallen from a table in Lübeck while proclaiming that his exile has granted him the immortality that his years with his tongue between Baron Reuterholm's cheeks had not accomplished. Winge decides to give Cardell one hour. When his pocket watch says half past ten, he is still alone, so he leaves the coffee house and heads north until he reaches Goose Alley where he asks around for Cardell. A shoemaker in the process of resoling a pair of cavalry boots has some information.

'The gimpy watchman? He rents a room from Widow Pihl.'

A flock of children are playing in the stairwell. The house has no masonry oven but the open hearth at the top is kept going by a thin girl with jaundiced skin. She has been sick with fever this past week and knows that Cardell left his room yesterday morning and has not been back. Winge has no option but to leave the Pihl house with nothing to show for it. The girl's voice follows him down the stairs.

'If Mickel isn't back before she comes for the rent, she'll throw him out.'

Winge takes a street up towards Old Square in order to give himself some time to think. Without Cardell's assistance, he sees his options as limited. He stops for a while at the well, where children and servants are filling their pails. When he stands up again, he steers towards the Castle and Indebetou House, with a stop on the way.

———◆———

It is late afternoon by the time he reaches Police Chief Norlin's office. Winge senses Norlin's anger through the door and assumes that he is kept waiting only because Norlin needs time to gather himself. Finally, the voice comes from the other side, whereupon the assistant steps aside and opens the door for Winge.

'Show him in.'

Norlin is sitting behind his disorderly desk, his shirt and coat unbuttoned at the throat and his wig tossed onto the papers before him. No chair has been brought forward for Winge. Norlin scratches his scalp and rubs his red eyes.

'It wasn't so long ago that we met here last, you and I. Do you remember what I said about the preconditions of this case, Cecil? Do you remember that I prevailed upon you to be discreet? Instead you choose to interrupt the gathering of the chamber with an exposition about a lewd pattern on a piece of cloth.

Didn't you see that scribbler Barfud sitting in the benches, listening with his pencil at the ready?'

'Not only did I see him, I woke him up from his drunken stupor and convinced him to accompany me to the Indebetou House where I promised that the morning assembly of the Chamber of Police would offer him a good story for printer Holmberg to include in tomorrow's *Extra Post*.'

Norlin buries his face in his hands.

'Barfud is prepared to write just about anything between his long-winded Bible passages, and Holmberg prints it without scrutiny in his disgrace of a rag, the more outrageous the better, and all of Stockholm reads it. Why, Cecil?'

'My companion, a truant watchman by the name of Cardell, appears to have been knocked off the board, and my instinct tells me that it is because he has come too close to the truth. The fabric is my last hope. It is expensive and has been in the possession of someone with means. Those who have seen the pattern can hardly mistake the description when they read about it in the paper. If someone with influence takes an interest in hushing up the affair, that person will reach out to you. They will demand my head on a platter. Perhaps also yours. And you, Johan Gustaf, will in turn give me the name of the eager one.'

'Reuterholm reads the *Extra Post* just like all the other gossip-mongers in this land. The Baron will take this as proof of my insistence on prioritizing other matters before his own affairs. This is the excuse to get rid of me that he has been waiting for. You have signed my death warrant, Cecil.'

'In view of the effect your position has had on your well-being this past year, I sense that whoever contributes to the shortening of your tenure will rather be extending your life.'

'I should have kept in mind who I was joining forces with when I first asked you for help. Cecil Winge, always willing to sacrifice any and all for his high ideals.'

Winge's eyes flash.

'Yes, it was you who asked for my help and you would have done well to remember who I am. Loyalty to you may have been enough of a reason for me to take on this case but in the same moment the decision was made, that very loyalty is transposed to the victim. He is my responsibility now, not your prestige. Only a few nights ago, I stood in the charnel house of Maria Church to examine the body. Allow me to describe him to you, who never laid eyes on him: his limbs had been severed over an extended length of time. Every wound had been given sufficient time to recover so that his body would survive the next surgery. For months, he had been kept somewhere, bound to a stretcher. He must have screamed for help, but to little avail since his tongue had been removed. He must have tried to take his own life but had not even been allowed to keep his teeth. Or his eyes. Can you imagine such a thing, Johan Gustaf? To lie alone and powerless until the day when you feel the saw on the next part of your body. I will find the one who did this. I will find out why. And you will give me the names I want as soon as you acquire them instead of complaining about Reuterholm and your honour. You call death by name, and that in my presence. Have you no shame?'

Norlin feels resignation replace the void left by anger. He misses his wife and his daughter, their scents, their laughter. From the other side of the table, Winge stares at him with pupils that have grown large in the emaciated face. Norlin sighs and places his hand on a folded piece of paper in front of him.

'I have received news from Paris this morning. My sources say that the widowed Queen is to be put before the revolutionary tribunal. You know as well as I do how it will end. Marie Antoinette will lose her head as certainly as her husband lost his. They will throw her into a pauper's grave on top of the thousands who have stood before her in line for the guillotine. These are dark times, Cecil.'

Winge's voice is soft when he replies.

'Johan, you said it yourself to me the other night: what is the reason we do what we do, if not this?'

'You are right, of course, as you always are. Don't pick a quarrel with Cecil Winge, he is always right – that was what they said at the lower courts just like they did at the university. It shall be as you wish. Leave me now so I may compose a letter to Reuterholm obsequious enough to buy a little time and lessen his fury when the newspaper lands in the bookshops.'

Winge bows.

'Thank you, Johan Gustaf.'

14

SECRETARY ISAK REINHOLD Blom hates every part of Stockholm that has made the error of spreading out past the City-between-the-Bridges, and the Meadowland is worst of them all. An early rain shower has whipped the streets into mud. Ragamuffins, paupers, vagrants and skeletal figures scurry around the corners, huddled as if to avoid the reaper's harvest that draws ever closer. Their ranks are diluted by sailors and soldiers in bedraggled uniforms.

He should have known better than to walk on foot out to the old Spens manor. The water that has collected in puddles leaks in through the seams of his boots until each step makes it sound as if he is churning butter. Blom is constantly finding reasons to curse his fate. Despite seven years in service of the Chamber of Police, he makes barely one hundred and twenty daler a year. When he stepped up from the notary service to replace old Hallquist as chamber secretary, he had been expecting a higher salary. Instead he finds his workload doubled without additional compensation.

He hears coughing in the distance. That calms him somewhat. Others have it even worse. Cecil Winge would have been able to go far with his abilities, but he will be lucky to see the new year. The hacking stops when Blom knocks at the door of his room and when it is opened a few moments later, Winge appears as unruffled as always. Nonetheless, a corner of the handkerchief that Winge has tucked into his waistcoat pocket is damp with red and Blom marvels at the force of will the effort must cost him. Blom immediately comes to the point of his visit.

'Norlin has sent me with the correspondence you requested from Indebetou House. There was no shortage of complaints.'

Blom sits in front of the masonry stove to dry out his boots as Winge receives the small bundle of papers: three letters with broken seals. Blom clears his throat and continues.

'Very likely they were written in haste after the *Extra Post* had been carried out to the bookstores. Everyone has the same errand but gives different reasons. All three give reasons that you cease your investigation. The first letter is from an exceptionally wealthy man who is worried about fluctuations in the price of cotton and its dire consequences for the finances of the kingdom. A Count Enecrona at the Chamber of Commerce wishes to warn you of the moral decay that may ensue in making ordinary people aware of matters they would never otherwise have been able to imagine. Last but not least there is a Gillis Tosse who has the considered opinion that scandalous matters by their nature support revolutionary instinct. Tosse scolds you by name as a Jacobin.'

Winge alternates the warming of the fingers of one hand in the palm of the other.

'I know Tosse. Do you also remember him? He studied at Uppsala, as we did.'

'The name doesn't sound familiar.'

'An idler without a head for books but of a family rich enough to buy him a position regardless of the outcome of his studies. I remember how he looked down on those of us who applied ourselves at our desks. I assume he saw our efforts as the very proof of our meagre inheritances. Did Police Chief Norlin tell you why he sent you all the way out here with these letters?'

'No, but he didn't need to. I'm no fool, Winge. I was taking notes when you presented your textile and I have read the article in *Extra Post*. You hope that one of these agitated gentlemen may have grounds to complain to you quite apart from the reasons they give. A connection to the body in the Larder, I imagine.'

Winge presses his lips together into a line as he closes his eyes and massages his brow.

'Just so. I have to admit I had hoped the names would provide a clearer picture but these I have never heard before, and I can't surmise what they have in common other than their fortunes.'

Blom gives him a sly smile.

'But I have. Nothing, however, comes free in this world and I demand something in return.'

'If it is in my power to give, it shall be yours, Blom.'

'The day that your health takes a turn for the worse, I would like you to inform me, and only me, as quickly as you can. There is a wager as to the date of your departure among the gentlemen of the chamber. The pot is currently three times my annual salary.'

'If the information you offer is useful, I can find no reason why someone should not be profiting from my demise. You have my word that I will send a courier in the same moment I feel the fever come creeping. Now it is your turn.'

Blom feels a quiver in his belly at the inconceivable sum that would improve the conditions of his life immeasurably and allow him to complete his great work, *The Necessity of Religion for the Welfare of Society*, not in his freezing room but in style at one of the city's better establishments over plate after heaping plate from the kitchen: hot smoked herring, mutton, ragout.

'Very well! Have you ever heard about a society by the name of the Eumenides?'

'Only in a cursory mention. If I remember correctly, they are one of the many secret orders that undertake charitable works for the city's less fortunate. They provide financial support to the poorhouses in parishes with insufficient funds.'

'That is true. The Eumenides are characterized by their great generosity, and only the wealthy can afford membership. You know that I write poetry. I was once acquainted with a Claes von der Ecken, who inherited a trade business and paid me generously to recite my poems. Ecken was a member of the Eumenides. His business took a turn for the worse, and when he wanted to suspend his charitable works in order to manage his affairs, they banded together and destroyed him. As a member, you are expected to fulfil your commitments without excuses. The bank demanded immediate repayment of his loan and suddenly no one was willing to underwrite it. One evening, there was a beggar at my door, raving about how the coins I had received for reciting my poetry were only a loan. That was Ecken, now completely impoverished. This was how my interest in the Eumenides was awakened. I was once able to cast my eyes on a membership register. My memory is almost as good as yours, Winge. All of your letter writers belong to that order.'

Winge's feet have begun to tap the floor almost imperceptibly.

'Your story is perhaps less astonishing than it would seem. Do you know where the name of this order originates, Blom?'

'The Eumenides? No, I can't say I do.'

'I once had a tutor who was infatuated with the Greek classics and who also had a refined way with a cane, resulting in my spending considerable hours poring over my Aeschylus. In our own language, the translation of this term should be "the kindly ones". In the original tale, this is how the wise refer to the furies, the gods of vengeance, in order to escape their wrath.'

Blom finds himself wishing that the visit were over and his own part in it forgotten. Only greed keeps him there.

'Another thing. I know they hold their meetings at Keyser House, next to the Red Sheds.'

Winge starts to walk back and forth across the floor as he thinks.

'I have heard that house mentioned before, as a location for one of the covert bordellos that were allowed to operate with the blessing of the Chamber of Police as long as everything was managed without any further disturbances. I find that a rather strange neighbour for an order that occupies itself with charity.'

'Oh, it gets stranger even than that, Winge. I know with confidence that the order not only has its rooms in Keyser House. They own the whole building.'

Winge turns thoughtfully to the window facing the Meadowland Tollgate with Mickel Cardell's last words in his ears. Outside in the early evening, the wind has died down and the windmill grown silent in wait for the evening breeze.

'You who know so much, Blom. Do you happen to know if Keyser House keeps its own sedan chairs and, if this is indeed the case, if they are green in colour?'

15

A T NIGHT, DISQUIETING thoughts come over him in place of sleep. The light that falls onto the desk bestows long shadows on the pieces of Cecil Winge's pocket watch. Wheels and tiny parts become insect-like figures that dance each time a draught disturbs the flame. Isak Blom had been gone a long time. The visit forced Winge to suppress the horrible coughs that have plagued him since the morning. The chamber pot with its red-stained contents remains unemptied in its place under the corner of the bed. His throat feels tight. Itching, itching.

Winge does not find it as stimulating to work with his watch-maker's tools tonight. Combining a handful of dead metal parts into a whole that contains some kind of independent life – if the maker is clever enough to place each piece exactly where it belongs – usually stills his thoughts, but he finds himself instead preoccu-pied with Mickel Cardell's path from the time that they parted ways at the Sconce Tollgate and onward to his unknown fate.

From what little he knows of Cardell's life, he imagines the man attracts violence like a magnet draws iron shavings, but he also radiates an incomparable ability to prevail in such situations. That the disappearance would be unrelated to his inquiry into the sedan chair strikes Winge as unlikely. He has relied on Occam's Razor his entire life and this tells him that Cardell came too close to a well-guarded truth. The details remain beyond his powers of deduction. Once the pocket watch is whole again, he measures his pulse at one hundred and sixty beats a minute and feels a throbbing anxiety in his chest. Sleep and peace escape him.

In the chest beside the bed, there is glass flask with doum palm, purchased from an apothecary in the Bear on Fireworker's Street across from Artillery Yard. Drops of opium in a mixture of alcohol, succinic acid and salt of hartshorn. He has had the tincture for a long time but has not yet availed himself of it. At the Bear they warned him not to exceed the recommended dose and said that it would dull not only his pain but also his senses. Tonight is the first time he is prepared to take the risk.

He counts out drop after drop of the opium solution into a cup and then drinks. Soon a warm sensation spreads throughout his body and allows a comforting hope to emerge. The itch in his throat seems to fade away on contact with the solution. Outside the window, the last rays of the sun hold on to the tip of the windmill's wings, and then it is gone. Winge loses himself in his thoughts.

———— • ————

After sunset and with his watch once more in pieces, Cecil Winge loses his sense of time. He is not aware of how many hours have gone by when he is struck by the error he has committed. Cardell appears to have been eliminated. Somewhere he has met a violent end. For his part, Winge has given himself away by revealing himself through the story in the *Extra Post*.

Would it not occur to Karl Johan's murderers now to take action against himself as well? What could be easier than to end his life? Winge's health is no secret. A consumptive who gives up the ghost after having outlived the predictions of the Seraphim Hospital's foremost experts for weeks would not come as a surprise to anyone. A visit in the night, a pillow over his face, and his end would provoke no suspicion.

Winge feels a quiver of fear run down his spine. He rises to his feet in order to peer out through the window, but only meets his own reflection, bleary-eyed and pale. He casts his coat about his shoulders, lifts the candle from its holder and shields the flame from the draught. In the hallway, he pinches the wick between his thumb and forefinger and stands still in the darkness and listens. The house is empty. The servants have their sleeping quarters elsewhere and in the kitchen the ashes have been raked over the coals for the night. Winge opens the door to the courtyard and feels the dampness in the air, the tangy steam from the fields, salted by the fog from the sea. Slowly his eyes become accustomed to the dark.

Spens Manor is quiet and without illumination. The linden trees hunch outside. No light can be percieved from the City-between-the-Bridges. The time must be well past midnight. The gate is open. On the other side, moonlight spills down over the fields and the orchard. As pastoral as the scene is in the daytime, it is ghostlike at night.

Here they buried the dead in sheer panic when the century was new and the plague came to Stockholm with a Dutch merchant. At the graveyard of Katarina Church, the bodies had been piled high, shrouded in their bedclothes, sprinkled with lime and left there for more than a week as they waited for a place to be found for them in the overflowing ground. At the Meadowland, they had been better able to deal with the remains of the epidemic. Behind the last houses, wide ditches had been dug in which to deposit the dead. Even today, the earth here is more fertile than elsewhere. The gardens of this great house stand in bloom until the first frost, but the gardeners are taught from childhood never to put their spades too deep. Winge is not alone. A shadow comes up along the road from the water, a black sliver of life that does not belong here. It approaches slowly, hunched and wary. Winge sinks back into the shadows behind the wall. Each time the moon is obscured by a cloud, the scene before him is extinguished, and when the moonbeams return, the figure has grown closer. This is not the death to which Winge has so long been trying to reconcile himself, not the predictable, creeping consumptive demise whose every detail he has been trying to steel himself in preparation for, but a violent and ignominious end in terror and ignorance, by knife's edge, cudgel or strangulation.

Now he can hear the footsteps, faint crunches. He hears his heartbeat in his ears as he strains to keep his breathing soundless. The shadow proceeds through the gate and is in the courtyard under the trees. Winge realizes that he is fighting a losing battle with an approaching coughing fit and he makes his decision. Better to let the confrontation take place here, where he can at least leave bloodstains to bear witness to a violent end. His body found under the linden trees in the morning will at the very least raise questions.

With only a couple of steps, he reaches the figure and grabs at it. Winge realizes his mistake when his hand closes on nothing. This creature lacks form. This is not a hired assassin from the city, but a phantom risen from its crypt to haunt these domains in the night. Winge feels the blood rush to his temples and flickers of light appear in his field of vision. When the apparition turns to him, its face is not human, and when Winge's forehead hits the cold ground, he is no longer conscious.

——— • ———

When he wakes again, it is in his own bed. The dawn light filters in through the dust of the window. A bunch of logs are burning in the stove and the wood crackles as it splits in the heat. It takes Winge a few moments to reorient himself. The effect of the opium has left his body and in its place the pain throbs in a bump on his head. When he speaks, his tongue feels thick.

'I grabbed your left arm, Jean Michael. The wooden stump wasn't in its place, so the sleeve was empty.'

Cardell moves the chair from the desk next to the bed.

'That may be. For my part, I felt a tug at my coat and hardly had time to turn around before you collapsed on the ground with a whimper.'

'I thought you were a ghost, that I had tried to grab a spirit. What a fool I am. In my defence, your face did not exactly help the matter. What is it that has befallen you? Where have you been?'

Both of Mickel Cardell's eyes are covered in bruises so large and blackened that he looks as if he is wearing a mask. His nose is broken, his lips split open and under them Winge glimpses several missing teeth. One of his cheekbones appears flattened, which has changed the appearance of his face. Cardell grimaces with pain as he speaks.

'I have been licking my wounds at a friend's place who lives close to the Cat's Rump Tollgate and I would have sent word to you if it hadn't been for the fact that I slept without waking for more than a day. Once I limped home, I found my room full of Polish knaves and all my possessions gathered in a sack and placed on the stairs. Without anywhere else to turn and without anywhere to sleep, I decided to come here. Hence the late hour.'

'And the sedan chair?'

'I found both the chair and its bearers. They were unwilling to answer my questions without some persuasion. The larger of the two was a relatively simple case: slow and easy to scare off for someone who knows how. His brother was a tougher nut to crack, and one who took me longer to find my way around. While the two of them were in the game, they managed to take my arm but when I found it again, I used it as a cudgel until only splinters remained. After having put up as good defence as he could, the fat one ran off in the direction of the toll, hopping on the leg I hadn't broken yet, and I doubt his brother would recognize him if they ever saw each other again. Something of the same can be said about me as well, unfortunately, and I am sorry to say I was by then in no state to prevent his escape. There's a little thing I managed to get out of him when I was fortunate enough to get his fingers under my heel: they owned a stake in the sedan chair, the rest belonging to their employer on whose behalf they perform their labour. The chair is kept not far from the Red Sheds, by the stream next to Klara Lake.'

'In Keyser House.'

'Right you are. So your investigations must also have led you there?'

'The answer is yes. Let me rest a little while yet. When I rise, we will eat. Tonight we shall put Karl Johan's murderer to answer.'

16

Dusk at the Red Sheds, and the noise of the day has died down. Among the boats delivering grain to the muddy bank, all but one has finished unloading their freight. Two dock workers, both drunk, roll a barrel ashore with difficulty. One is amusing himself and his companion by singing a vulgar ditty.

'Oh, were I in a girl's feathers, sing fal-a-dol-fal-a-dee-oh, I would line my cunt with leather . . .'

The Stream floats out on its way to the sea through the abandoned building of the great bridge. Across the water looms the imposing façade of the Hall of Nobles, with the church spire on the island just to the right. The lamps are lit on the nearby islet, in the strangely cross-hatched building with its pennant-adorned dome. The public square is empty, the laundry pier quiet. Faint voices and the clatter of wooden clogs from home-bound workers can be heard in the distance from the bridge over Klara Lake. Winge stops, turned towards the City-between-the-Bridges across the water.

'It has a beauty in spite of itself.'

Cardell nods, almost against his will.

'The city? It stinks and is full of dying people who want nothing more than to shorten each other's already cheap lifespans. But yes, in the sunset like this it is a pretty sight, and the prettier the more water that lies between it and the observer.'

Cardell spits tobacco into the current and turns to the right. Beside them, Keyser House stands menacingly with the long side of the building facing the square and the short side towards the lake. It is three storeys high with an arched entrance. The image of a setting sun adorns the pediment above their heads. A few lighted candles are burning on the second floor. Someone gives a shrill laugh. Cardell rubs his bare stump in the cold.

'And what now?'

'Unless you have brought a grappling hook or siege engine, there is only one thing we can do. We shall knock.'

—•—

The man who opens the door causes Cardell to take a step back in surprise. His skin is black and in the dim light, and the light-coloured livery, he appears headless for a brief moment. More than once, Cardell has seen King Gustav's black attendant, Badin, and the bastard he has fathered who runs about by the ships in the Quayside, but he has never seen one up close. Winge touches his hand to his hat in greeting.

'Good evening. I have come to meet with the lady of the house.'

The dark-skinned man gives him a wide smile in response, opens the door all the way and welcomes them in with a sweep of his arm. He rings a small silver bell and signals for them to proceed up a staircase that spirals upward to the right. Then he closes the oak door behind them and resumes his post on a stool under a lit sconce. On the second floor they find a door already open. A young woman is standing there, wearing a simple dress that is translucent enough to suggest her nipples. She is wearing a silk ribbon in her hair and does not seem to be wearing any make-up, with the exception of some rouge on her lips and a *mouche* at the corner of her mouth. Appearing well used to visitors, she curtsies and smiles at Winge.

'Please enter, sir. You must be one of the new initiates. Allow me to take your coat and with it lift the troubles of this world from off your shoulders. My name is Nana, and your humble servant.'

The wallpaper in the hall is covered in purple and black flowers. Red Turkish carpets cover the floor. From the ceiling hangs a chandelier holding some dozen candles. There are candelabras on tables along the wall. Winge places a coin in her hand. Her lips make a silent *o* at the weight of it.

'My name is Winge. I am here to see your mistress.'

'Of course, sir! That is how we begin all of our new acquaintances. An intimate conversation as the start of a merry relationship. Madame insists upon it. In order to better satisfy your needs, she must know all about them. You should not feel bashful. We are here to serve. I ask you only to wait here for a few moments before I show you into the salon.'

Winge nods. The girl breaks the silence after a moment with a nod at Cardell, who has remained standing by the door.

'You like to discipline your servant, Monsieur Winge? Many of our guests share that inclination and that is something we can accommodate. Simply tell Madame what you wish and it will be yours!'

'One may whip your wares?'

'Your wish is our command, sir. Certainly an overabundance of enthusiasm in that regard can affect the value of our wares in the eyes of others, but as long as you are willing to compensate our loss, all is as it should be.'

'I see.'

The clear tone of a bell sounds from the apartment within.

'Now, monsieur, if you will please follow me. Would you like your servant to remain here?'

'I prefer to keep him within arm's reach, in case my desire to whip him should overtake me.'

They follow her through the house. Outside the windows, the view of the city, is magnificent. The room they are shown into is empty. A sofa is placed across from an armchair. Winge takes his place according to the girl's instructions. She pours wine into a slender glass and hands it to him with a smile.

'Madame Sachs will soon be with you, monsieur. I hope you will not find it too forward of me if I say that I wish we will soon see you here again.'

She leaves them. Winge puts the glass down and crosses the room swiftly to an arched opening at the opposite end that is covered by a curtain. He examines a corner of the fabric which is adorned with a pattern of copulating figures.

'Jean Michael, I think we are about to hear things that are far worse than what has already been said. It will be of utmost importance for you to remain in control of yourself, for Karl Johan's sake. This Madame Sachs is our only opportunity to learn anything at all. Do you take my meaning?'

Cardell opens his mouth then closes it again without a word. He nods silently and takes up a position close to the wall. His healthy hand forms a fist in the pocket of his coat, the left sleeve of which is tied in a knot around his stump.

———•———

The age of the woman who shortly thereafter pulls the curtain aside is difficult to ascertain. It is not clear if she has aged prematurely or retained an illusion of youth in her old age. Her gown, adorned with gold embroidery on a field of carmine, is imposing. Her face is painted with a heavy lead-based white foundation that effectively covers any blemishes and wrinkles, but she has deep bags under her eyes. Her mouth smiles without warmth, flanked on either side by deep lines. Around her neck she has a scar, as if from a noose. Her welcoming expression soon stiffens into a grimace.

'You are not the guests I was expecting. Nana must have been drinking. I have nothing to discuss with you and nothing to offer. You would be wise to leave at once.'

Winge raises his hand in protest.

'You are mistaken, Madame. My name is Cecil Winge. I come from Indebetou House. I realize that you can run your establishment so openly thanks to a powerful protector, most likely with contacts in the police agency. However, systems that depend on some degree of secrecy have an inbuilt inertia, and there are enough who are unaware of your arrangement that they could easily decimate your business before your supporters have time to avert the catastrophe. I can have twenty men here within half an hour.'

Her face reveals nothing of her feelings but her voice has narrowed to a hiss.

'Do you know who you are dealing with?'

'I know that the Order of the Eumenides owns the house.'

'If you know that, then I know you are bluffing. Even if what you say is true, they would never let such an act go unavenged, and the price would be terrible.'

'I am dying of consumption. Our current police chief is about to lose his position. Neither of us has anything to lose. Try me.'

Madame Sachs snorts audibly.

'You are young and naive, my boy. Everyone has something to lose. But your little threat can only mean that I have something you want in exchange for your silence. Perhaps I will see the backs of you sooner if I give rather than take. So let's have it then. What is it you seek? A fistful each from my treasure chest? Free access to my wares to revive some memories of the extinguished glow of your marriage beds?'

'A mutilated man was taken from this house in a sedan chair and tossed into the Larder, wrapped in fabric of the same kind as that which hangs behind you. Tell me everything you know about him and his fate.'

Her eyes flit from Winge to Cardell and linger on his stump.

'Now I see. I have recently lost a chair and its carriers. The larger of the two came back the night before last, beaten and whimpering. He can't sleep at night, plagued by terrible nightmares. He has never learned to speak, but when we gave him a piece of chalk and a slate he drew a picture of a one-armed demon. I see now that reality is far less frightening than fantasy.'

Madame Sachs turns back to Winge. Cardell has seen the same expression before in dogs provoked to fight for sport. Before they engage, they measure each other's strength and weigh their chances. Successful gamblers learn from watching their eyes which they should choose to bet on. Cardell himself has played and believes himself to know the game as well as anyone. He senses her spirit. A formidable opponent. And Winge? Not much to look at but with eyes that speak a different language. No terror there. Cardell knows who will win one breath before Madame Sachs does. She laughs bitterly and throws up her hands. When she smiles with an open mouth, her teeth are blackened with rot.

'Look at the two of you! A bag of bones and a cripple in rags, and you dare to look at me in that way. What can people like you know about the desires of nobler men? Men who have grown up under the yoke of generations of wealth, waiting for their inheritance of goods, property, domains and titles. These men were raised to rule. The responsibility weighs heavily on them. They are in need of relief in a way that you cannot even imagine. They have hardly spilled their first night's seed than they order the chambermaid to take their member in her hand, then roll it between her breasts, then close her lips about it. By twelve, they have made the rounds of the household, by eighteen they have sodomized their pages. When they have tasted all that the city has to offer, they come to me. They have pissed in open mouths for their enjoyment, hit, hurt, trampled and destroyed. I can offer them better things. Whatever they desire, we obtain for them. At special soirées, I give them the unexpected, since many appreciate that which they could not have imagined. I keep a menagerie of unusual servants, some ugly in order to accentuate the beauty of others, some in order to increase the pleasure of my guests by their lowness, their humiliation, their pain or their misfortune. I have hunchbacks, dwarfs, harelips, hydrocephalics, the disfigured and deformed. Those who demand payment, we pay, as we do our other employees. Others serve us without payment. The creature in the bag was one of them. For a while it was my *pièce de résistance*. Don't you understand? Better than anything, it could remind one of the pleasures of life, of the fortunes that each and every one of its observers enjoyed. Some were content to have it in their presence while they pleasured themselves. Others chose to use it, enjoying what it had to offer, as defenceless as it was. It did not always serve willingly but it lacked teeth. They laughed as they pinched its nose while it chewed their stiff members and was forced to swallow what it received. My clientele are men who rule the world. What is the sacrifice of a half-person as weighed against their pleasure?'

Winge can feel the storm in Cardell, like magnetism in the room. He puts his arm around his shoulders before the latter takes a step. Winge nods at Madame Sachs to continue.

'Despite its grotesqueness, it retained something of its beauty. The hair was beautiful, it was young. The contrast made it popular. It made me rich without me paying a shilling for it. Why would I not be the first to mourn its passing?'

'Am I right in inferring that the Eumenides act both as your landlord and your clientele?'

'Yes. And before you set yourself in judgement over them, know that they give of their wealth to all the most vulnerable members of our society. Who are you to condemn them for what happens behind these walls, when half of the poorhouses in Stockholm would have to shut their doors without their support?'

'How did this mutilated man come into your care?'

'One night there was a knock at my door. A man who declined to give his name offered me a present: the creature. He gave no reason. He said it was in his interests that this thing live out its remaining days in my charge. He paid me for its stay and gave instructions about its care. It did not eat of its own accord so we had to pry open its jaws and feed it once a day by pouring gruel into its mouth. When its services were not needed, we kept it in a closet.'

'He was both blind and deaf?'

'It had no eyes, nor arms, legs, tongue and teeth. About its hearing I cannot say.'

'And his mind?'

'Who would be able to suffer such treatment and retain one's sanity? I assumed it was an imbecile and there was one thing that convinced me of it. I mentioned that it refused to eat. This was true with one exception: it ate its own faeces each time it defecated and somehow it always managed to do this when it was unsupervised. Who would do something like this other than one who had long since lost his senses?'

'And then? He died? You had him transported away.'

'Just so. Even though we fed it, it languished and wasted away with each day. One morning it had passed. We did not have it in the house more than four weeks.'

'Why the Larder? The Stream runs right outside.'

'My establishment has had need to dispose of sensitive waste before, with less than desirable results that way. What is laid in the water here tends to make landfall at the wharves, and poor people who don't care what the fish has grown fat on lay nets in the Bog, whereas only a dimwit would disturb the waters of the Larder.'

Cardell moves across the floor faster than Winge has time to react, until he stands with his healthy hand around the woman's neck. His fingers meet behind at the nape.

'How well do you swim yourself, Madame? Maybe we should see if you hit land at the wharf or if you continue out to sea? I have seen more than my fair share of drowned men. Heard them scream their anguish before the final plunge. Many who have never before shown a bad conscience confess their sins in such a moment. I wonder what sound you would make.'

'I am not afraid of men like you. If I counted myself among the living, I would be somewhere else, happy and free, instead of collecting coins at the edge of this vile place you dare call a city.'

She spits in his face. He lets go of her out of sheer shock and as he wipes the saliva out of his eyes, Winge stands between them. It is to him she addresses her words when she speaks again, her voice hoarse from the throttling.

'Leave now and take your one-armed beast with you. I can see that the grave awaits you with impatience. Count yourself fortunate that your dealings with the Eumenides end here, for against their might you are nothing. About the one who left me the creature in the sack, you now know as much as I do. I have never laid eyes on him before or since. I have kept my promise. Now you keep yours!'

Back outside by the Red Sheds, it is dark. No stars are to be seen. Further down, at King's Park, something is being celebrated with an illumination: every window in the Arsenal is lit up. It is Cardell who speaks first.

'When all of this is over, I'll return here and kill that woman.'

Winge answers absently, as if to prevent Cardell's voice from interrupting his train of thought.

'She saw it in your eyes just as I did, Jean Michael. If you find her here again, it will be because she has decided to welcome death. You would be doing her a favour.'

Winge wobbles as he crosses the cobblestones towards a heap of fencing material and sits on it with his face in his hands. There is a long pause before he speaks again.

'I am afraid that we have encountered a dead end. I need time to think, and of that particular resource I have very little. There is something that escapes me, something that flutters at the borders of my mind, like a moth at the windowpane. I can't see it clearly, however hard I try.'

It is Cardell's turn to reply. An invisible hand has squeezed his throat and prevents him from getting air. His heart leaps in his throat and he feels himself filled with a terror he can't explain and against which he has no defence. In the darkness, the left arm materializes by his side and sends waves of throbbing pain through his shoulder. He has to muster all his strength to keep his voice level.

'Others must know more, others whose presence we don't yet know about.'

Cardell has turned away to conceal his state. Winge's powers of observation fail him for once as he remains deep in his own thoughts.

'Yes, without them our enterprise now seems doomed to fail.'

'Are you ready to give up? Is that what you're saying?'

Winge lifts his pocket watch out of his waistcoat. He can hardly make out the hands on its face but, with his gaze fixed on the tiny indented circle where the seconds are counted, he places two fingers on the vein that beats under his jaw. For a minute, he counts the beats of his heart to one hundred and eighty before he turns back to Cardell with the answer he owes him.

'No. But time is of the essence.'

PART TWO

The Blood and Wine

Summer 1793

All things in life give us reason to drink
When you take time to consider them well.
Fate may send tidings of joy or of ill,
Both these may we with the same method quell:
Wine makes the happy one happier still,
And reduces all worries and sorrows to nil.

All times will be just what everyone makes them,
Dark thoughts won't trouble the tipsy one's mind.
Be merry with friends for as long as you have them,
Bid them adieu when their joy is declined.
Wine is the comfort that Providence gave,
From christening to wedding to dotage to grave.

— Anna Maria Lenngren, 1793

17

DEAREST SISTER!

It is my intention to write to you at every opportunity, but as I do not yet know where to send my writings, you will have to excuse the length until I am in a position to hand them to you myself.

Nonetheless it is a joy to sharpen my goose feather quill and write to you on this day that began in excellent fashion. I woke early, jumped out of bed, turned the chamber pot out from its spot under the bed, twisted the nightshirt around my waist and adopted the usual crouched position. This voiding of my bowels turned out to be of a kind that I have rarely had the pleasure, as all factors conspired to achieve the best possible result. Although my diet has been far from ideal recently, the consistency was optimal: firm enough to create a certain resistance and leave a feeling of accomplishment but also yielding enough not to present any difficulties. In the same moment that my goods were unloaded, it was as if I received a validation in the form of a fanfare from the cock in the next yard, which I did not feel was entirely unjustified. When I washed my face and dressed, it was in the best humour.

My good mood would soon come in handy. Hardly a moment after my morning ablutions, I heard from the front door the pounding which I had long feared, accompanied by stern admonitions: 'Kristofer Blix! Open the door so we may speak! Blix, you rascal!' I chose not to follow these exhortations, as I was certain they issued from the thugs in the service of a certain gentleman from whom I had recently borrowed a not insignificant sum of money. Therefore I did not waste any time, but gathered my things into my knapsack, tossed it over my shoulder and walked into the kitchen next door. At the hearth, I encountered the maid, Elsa Johanna, who rolled her eyes and frowned at me as I nabbed a loaf and opened the window to the courtyard. Six ells down was the dunghill, where the owner of the house – the widow whose lovesick nature had allowed me to live on credit – had let everything the mill horses left behind them accumulate. I climbed out and hung by my arms as far as they would let me, then closed my eyes, recited an Our Father and let go of the windowsill.

Well, you can imagine my relief when I landed in the dung without the slightest scratch. From up above I heard Elsa Johanna's farewell. 'Blix, you'll do best not to show your face here again, for Widow Beck had counted on having her bed warmed for many more nights before the debt was cleared and when the reckoning comes, your fancy hair won't count for much.' I tossed my blond curls, now long enough to reach my shoulders, waved to her while I brushed the filth from my leather breeches and walked out through the archway on the other side of the yard. I was glad that the maid had reminded me, otherwise I would surely have forgotten: I pulled my cap over my head and was careful to tuck every curl under the brim. As you well know, my blond hair has always been a source of pride for me but it is not always helpful as it makes it easy to recognize me from afar.

Oh, Stockholm, dear sister! I wish you could see the city as I do! So different from our childhood in Karlskrona. Here the houses are built out of hewn stone and the whole city shimmers like gold, especially in the morning light on a day like this. The buildings may be different but they are all painted in the same golden yellow colour. From a learned man in a striped topcoat I heard that it was the city's great architect Carlberg who issued this decree which even his disciple König followed scrupulously.

Understand this, my sister: one single man, selected for his clarity of mind, who cultivates the city for its beauty, like a garden. How much could not our own home town with its worn log cabins have benefited if subjected to such care?

My way down the Southern Isle's heights towards the Lock gave me a remarkable view of the City-between-the-Bridges and I was filled to the brim with good humour. Who can be downcast at the prospect of living in a city like this? The church spires gleamed on the island: Nikolai, Franciskus, Gertrud. The waves sparkled and shimmered. The buildings on the Quayside stand to attention against the ripples of the salty sea below, where the ships lie at anchor, and on the other side of the island lies the King's palace, a building so enormous no words of mine can do it justice.

Shortly before dinner, I passed over the Lock via the red draw-bridge, took a left along the granaries with my fingers clamped around my nostrils on account of the Flies' Meet – a heap of excrement as tall as a mountain, my sister, assembled here in preparation for transport to fields and saltpetre distilleries – and made my way through crowds of both fine folk and beggars, all of them with some detail to fascinate the eye: a gold watch on a thigh, a genuine wig, a clubfoot, or a pair of hands so deformed one wants to look away from but somehow can't. After no time at all, I found myself in the square in front of the Hall of Nobles. I had barely looked around until a cheerful voice reached my ears. 'If it isn't Master Blix, out and about in the sunshine! And on the hunt for new lodgings, to judge by the knapsack!' I turned, still alert for angry burghers and their cudgel-armed companions, but, to my great delight, saw my friend Rickard Sylvan walking across the cobblestones, dressed in a new coat with collar attached, a hideous red woollen wig, and long breeches.

'Oh, Master Sylvan, your most humble servant,' I exclaimed, 'is it possible that Your Magnificence would have any information about any fine house that may be available to rent for a manageable sum or – why not – an overlooked haystack, hopefully owned by a generous gentleman who likes to loan a coin or two to a hardworking young man on his way up in life?'

We laughed heartily and embraced.

'Unfortunately, Kristofer, I have trouble enough finding a mattress for myself, and least of all one that doesn't wander off on thousands of little lice legs in the night and leave me in an entirely different place than the one where I fell asleep. But all is not lost, my brother. I have a few shillings in my pocket and that should be enough to buy us a meal and some Danziger to wash it down.'

'Praised be Providence,' I said. 'I knew when I got up this morning that it was going to be a lucky day!' We walked arm in arm back into town to get us some nourishment.

———•———

At the the Golden Peace, the publican scowled threateningly as soon as Sylvan and I darkened his doorstep. Sylvan was forced into negotiations before we were allowed to sit down. The shillings he had in his pocket were closely examined and at first the owner wanted to confiscate the entire purse as payment for the many tankards he had downed on credit, but he was talked down into accepting an instalment with the assurance that we intended to spend the entirety on his wares. We sat down at a table and indulged in freshly fried herring and beer to our hearts' content.

After a couple of drinks, I confessed to Sylvan those troubles which weighed on me: I owed more to Jonas Silfver than I could pay. To allow myself to be whipped by his collectors would simply be a foretaste of debtors' prison, where my beauty and youth would go to waste. I was bewildered when Sylvan burst into laughter.

'Kristofer Blix, do you know nothing of the anatomy of debt?' Sylvan laid his arm around my shoulders. 'Listen, Kristofer, and I will teach you a thing or two about life in the big city, the ignorance of which you as a new arrival may be forgiven.'

My eyes grew wider as he spoke. What Rickard explained was a foolproof method of not only keeping oneself alive but even achieving a measure of enjoyment. As you know, dear sister, it is only a matter of time before one who is penniless and in debt is reported to the lower courts by those from whom he has borrowed money, whereupon all possessions of the hapless wretch are seized as payment. If these possessions do not add up to the amount of the debt, the poor bastard is thrown in prison and must wither away there until his nearest and dearest have managed to scrape together adequate funds to set him free.

'The trick,' Sylvan whispered, 'is never to borrow too much from any one lender! Let us say that you have received two dalers from Jonas Silfver. Naturally, you cannot pay them back as they have since been used to pay for life's necessities in the form of wine, women and song. You now go to another acquaintance, you borrow four dalers from this person and then set up a meeting with Silfver in order to come to an agreement about repayment. You pay him one daler with assurances about more to come before long, and how much, Blix, does that leave you to enjoy yourself with?'

'Three dalers!' I breathed.

'Just so, Kristofer, and you repeat this formula. As long as you surround yourself with generous company, everything will go well, since new loans are always used in part to pay off old debt.' Sylvan blinked and kissed me playfully on the cheek. 'That is how it is done in the big city, brother Blix! Cheers for the new friends whose acquaintance we may make even tonight and whose generosity will quickly free you from Silfver's thugs!'

'Master Sylvan's health!' I cried, louder than I had intended, to the frowns of the other patrons, and emptied my glass.

———•———

We must have stayed at the Peace a long time, but how long exactly I don't recall. It was already dusk when we staggered out onto the street, steadying each other for balance. The square and alleyways lay in shadow, but the sky was a flaming scarlet over the rooftops and lighted our way. We met a group of like-minded fellows at the well and joined them as these gentlemen were on their way to a ball up on Castle Hill. It took a little longer to negotiate our entry than we anticipated, time I used to rid myself of some of what I had drunk that night.

'*Sic transit gloria mundi!*' Sylvan cried heartily as I wiped the sick from my mouth. Once inside, I found the ballroom wondrously beautiful, dear sister, the ceilings as tall as the church back home, with galleries halfway up, where members of society drank burgundy from fine crystal and raised their glasses to us down below. If one coaxed and pleaded, they could be persuaded to empty their glasses while we tried to catch the contents with our mouths. Sylvan's wig suffered greatly due to his master's inability to move his mouth quickly enough to catch the anticipated rain, and the wet wool started to stink. But what did that matter when everything was done in the best of spirits! The entire party was entertained by our antics. By this point, the room was spinning even without the dancing and I abandoned my attempts to tackle a minuet after I almost turned over an entire table.

I sat down for a while and must have fallen asleep against the wall, for a short while later a man in livery shook me awake and chased me out.

The clock was approaching ten, when the event must draw to a close or risk the displeasure of the bluecoats. Out on Old Square, people lingered and talked, although the lanterns in the corners did little more than illuminate the ground directly underneath. Where Sylvan and the rest had gone to, I had no idea. Without anything else to do, I joined the company of a gentleman on the stairs outside the Exchange. The man didn't want to talk about anything except the music that had been performed at the ball. I was not eager to make myself appear a fool from the countryside, so I took a critical stance as this seemed to me the easiest way to make myself appear an expert. To my delight, my objections appeared to be of some interest and I maintained that the musicians seemed to have been having trouble following the notes and that their sense of pitch left much to be desired. As the man seemed very concerned with the French horn's role in the orchestra, I wasted no time in singling this out for particular scorn, an instrument that dislikes allowing itself to be drowned out even when surrounded by far more capable virtuosos. By now my eyes had adjusted to the light and I noticed that the man was sitting on a comfortable box. I looked around but there were no similar seats to be had, and as we talked it occurred to me that in certain ways the box had the funnel-like contours of a French horn. I had hardly thought that this was a remarkable coincidence in view of our topic of conversation when I received a terrible slap that caught me right above the lip.

'You little bitch's merkin!' the man screamed, who when standing on his feet rose up above me by a whole ell. 'I'll get you to sing and then we can hear how well you keep pitch yourself!' I sprinted away and even if I had clearly struck a raw nerve in my observations, the man made up for what he lacked in musicality with sheer stubbornness, because I heard the clatter of his footsteps as far as New Street, now and again followed by threatening howls.

As I had managed to steal a few winks at the ball, I did not feel the need to find a place of rest for the night. I strolled across the Lock towards Katarina parish to wait for the sunrise. I ate the bread I had left, and, leaning up against a gravestone in the sweet-smelling grass, I write this all to you, dear sister, with ink mixed in the heel of my shoe from a piece of coal and a little water. Now the sun is rising and it does not disappoint – the spires are already catching the light, cocks and crosses gleaming, once again she dresses Stockholm in its golden suit and shame on him who lets himself be bothered by a split lip!

121

18

D EAR SISTER, SOME days have gone by since I last had the opportunity to write. As I no longer dare show myself at Widow Beck's, I have spent my nights out wherever has seemed most suitable and have thereby been able to enjoy the resplendent weather of the early summer. Often one can also steal a few hours of sleep at the pub but if the owner is too watchful there are many other places that are not as demanding. A bracing walk away there are barns and haystacks, fields and beds of herbs. Who can ask for more than to lay one's head in nature's lap with leaves for a pillow and a canopy of stars? In the morning, the church bells wake the city with their clear peals and I return in across the bridges to get something to eat and help myself to drink at the well. It is from one of our many coffee houses that I write to you, strengthened by a morning cup and a piece of bread while I dip my pen in the grounds.

My friend Rickard Sylvan and I have joined a group of young men whose fathers are all engaged in trade along the Quayside. These gentlemen have money in excess and since they seem to find the exploits of Sylvan and myself tremendously amusing, they are often tempted into generosity. Sylvan and I compete in who can stand the most of what is offered. The one who manages to stand on one leg for a whole minute is crowned the winner and given the title of the majesty of the night, with a soup terrine placed on his head. The gentlemen laugh until they weep. These are golden nights, my sister! The joy seems never to end and neither does the drink. Punch and aquavit flow freely, but it is the wine that I love most, dear sister, wet and red, like sunlight itself tempted into glass and bottle. The pubs are impossible to count. They are lined up side by side, and the light of their candles spill out into the alleys, transforming night into day. We go from one to the other, our arms around each other's shoulders, happily chatting until one by one we all peel away and wander home. Rickard Sylvan, born in the city as he is, does not share my fondness for the open air, and he sleeps curled up by the stove at his cousin's somewhere past New Bridge.

———•———

When we were busy quenching our thirst in a cellar by the docks, a great commotion suddenly broke out. Someone threw a glass mug that missed me by a hair's breadth and smashed to pieces on the wall behind us. A group of foreign sailors were screaming at each other in some alien tongue and before we knew what was happening, a fight had broken out. I took cover under the table. When one of the men crashed to the floor, the rest decided to flee and from my hiding place I could see that the fallen one had been wounded. Blood was spurting out of his wrist like a firehose, from putting his hand directly on a broken wine bottle When the immediate danger seemed to have passed, I crept over to the man and took a look at his injuries.

The wrist seemed to me to be the biggest problem and of a type that I was fairly accustomed to from my years in Karlskrona. I did what I had been taught and applied pressure across the wound, over which I then placed a bandage of linen cloth that I had torn from the sailor's sleeve. Over that I wrapped the rest of his sleeve and bound it with a knot, after which the bleeding ceased. During this whole time, the sailor paid no attention to me. He sat hunched over on the floor, rocking from side to side. He muttered, downcast, in his own language.

'His friends called his wife a whore and did not appear ground-less in their reasoning,' said a gentleman with a red nose who was observing the events with interest. 'And she'll be no less tempted to continue her whoring when her husband returns with a broken face.' He laughed at his own wit.

'Let's have a drink for this poor man and give a cheer for the physician. Hail to the doctor!'

And then I received the approbation of the patrons. They drank and then each and every one seemed to want to buy me a drink and make a toast. The injured man himself stayed until a carpenter's apprentice helped him up on his legs, after which he staggered out into the night, his gaze vacant and not saying a word. The episode reminded me of my original purpose in coming to Stockholm but I have to admit that everyone who toasted me as quickly led me to other thoughts.

Bolstered by my popularity, I decided to try to put Sylvan's formula into practice. I shared a pipe with one of the gentlemen in whose company we had arrived and I asked him for a loan of twenty shillings in order to help me arrange better lodgings. His reaction was not the one I had expected. He turned pale and seemed somewhat embarrassed. He excused himself from the table without reply. I was bewildered since it was hardly a large sum to ask in view of the nonchalance with which this company normally handled their currency. My head was spinning with all of the drinks and I thought no more of it. The crowds around the tables started to thin out as the evening wore on and when I no longer saw any of my friends, I decided that it was time to find a place for the night.

Out on the street, Rickard Sylvan was waiting for me. I had hardly put my arm around his shoulder when he grabbed me by the collar and pushed me up against the wall so that I hit my head against the bricks.

'Blix, you fool! Is it true that you went to Wallin and asked for a loan of twenty shillings so that you didn't have to sleep under the open sky tonight?' I could hardly deny this. Sylvan let go of me with a loud moan. He sank down with his back to the wall and covered his face with his hands. I stood frozen without knowing what to say until he turned to me again and saw my confused expression. With resignation, he signed for me to sit down and he laid his arm around me.

'Kristofer,' he said. 'When you ask for such a small sum, Wallin realizes that you are destitute. I have led him to believe that we are both kept on a very tight leash by our families whose property we will one day inherit. You, on the other hand, have left no doubts at all that we are in fact two insignificant charlatans who barely have a penny to our name.'

'But what should I have done? We are completely broke!'

Sylvan sighed and rolled his eyes.

'What you should have done, Kristofer, is invent a reason why you needed a bigger loan – say a new wig or a pearl necklace for your mother – as your pocket money has already been used for other trinkets, and present your request as if it were the most natural thing in the world. From these gentlemen, it is easier to borrow three or even five dalers than to try to avail oneself of a couple of shillings.'

'But our clothes? We are dressed in rags! How could anyone take us for burghers' sons?'

'You need only to make the gentlemen want to believe your lies. It takes two in order to tell a good lie; one to speak untruth and one to listen willingly!' I had no answer to this and stood there with my mouth agape until Sylvan couldn't help but laugh.

'You may be a damned imbecile, Kristofer Blix, but you are at least an honest one. And that is something we shall soon be able to remedy. In future, you will speak with me before you try to borrow anything from our friends.' Sylvan, who now seemed to have regained his cheerful disposition, reached inside his waistcoat and pulled out a bulging purse. 'While you were exposing us to Wallin, I at least managed to relieve Montell of a tidy sum, that I said I needed in order to buy a walking stick with a silver top, a transaction that I was in a rush to conclude as I had seen a lieutenant colonel cast desiring glances at the same, and that my own father whose good graces such a purchase would normally depend on is visiting with de Geer in Finspång.'

'But I thought your father was . . .' I said, stopping when I perceived Sylvan's slow head shake through the haze of alcohol. 'Kristofer Blix, sometimes I fear for your future.' He gave me a disapproving look before he took my arm. 'The hour is early rather than late. Let us go to the well to wash and then to the coffee house for some breakfast.'

19

MY DEAR SISTER, today I was surprised by a burst of inclement weather that brought with it a cold I had not felt since early April. Rain water was pooling and streaming into my little nest and I was roused when a rivulet licked me on the cheek. My clothes were already waterlogged and I shivered. To regain some warmth, I jumped up and starting marching in place, my arms flapping. A few crumbs of bread and a hard piece of cheese had to serve as breakfast. I waited for the sun, only to realize that it could not manage any light or warmth through the thick clouds. Luckily the rain started to abate and I saw no sense in waiting any longer so I began walking towards town. The weather has always affected my mood, as you surely remember. In an attitude of thoughtful reflection, I decided to face what I had all too long pushed off into the future.

A quick walk brought me to a pastoral landscape and into the Meadowland with its draughty houses where the gaps in the planks were sometimes wide enough to put your hand through and touch those who were sleeping inside. The neighbourhoods were still deserted but down at Artillery Yard there was already bustle and movement. Soldiers were running to and fro or marching in formation under the command of stern provosts.

From the fish market I saw the laundry women down at the pier at Cats' Bay, where they were scrubbing the dirty linen white and beating it as dry as possible in the wet air. The sight made me think of my own appearance, covered in soot and dirt. At the Seraphim Hospital, which was where I was planning to go, a more spruced-up look would be in my favour, which spurred me to leap out onto the pier with the purpose of talking one of the women into turning her attention to my shirt. Most of them were too busy to pay me any attention and the ones who did only snarled at me. At the shore, one of them was watching a flock of children, the smallest one very little and carried in her arms, and she sang to it as she offered it her breast. The melody was melancholy and the words I heard were a tad serious for a lullaby:

'So our destinies are cast and so our years pass by, the next breath drawn may be our last, then on the bier we'll lie.'

When I stopped to listen, I noticed that one of the women on the pier had paused in her work and that tears were running down her cheeks. She looked at me without saying a word but then stretched out her hand. Maybe she had lost a son and maybe I looked like him. I quickly wriggled out of my coat, pulled my shirt over my head and held it out to her. She submerged it in her soapy tub, gave it a quick scrubbing, rinsed it at the edge of the dock and handed it back to me after a couple of beatings with her stick. I bowed in thanks and pulled the shirt back on, now clean and white.

Straight through the shallow Klara Lake, a jetty has been built, dressed with planks and some thousand ells long in order to allow the citizens of the town stay dry on their walk to King's Isle. For a long time, I hesitated at the railing by the Red Sheds. Out in the water, white peaks were forming and waves heaved up the stone walls and drenched the wooden railings. A woman holding a muddy pig by a leash laughed as she walked past. 'Watch yourself now, boy! If you hold on, you should be able to cross over without the selkies sinking their teeth into you and dragging you down into the depths!' I swallowed heavily and, with whitened knuckles around the rope that had been fastened along each side, I started to cross to the far shore.

Once I was back on land, I found myself almost immediately at my destination: a handsome door set in an archway that rose to a point at the top. Over the door could be read the words 'Royal Hospital' and two lions held a golden coat of arms between them. Next to this, a beautiful chestnut tree was in full bloom. I stepped inside, walked through the archway but soon had to stop and gaze in awe. The main building rises to four floors, flanked by two side buildings. This is the Seraphim Surgical Hospital, the Seraph as everyone in town calls it. Behind its front doors I found a large entry hall and I excused myself for getting in the way of a young man hurrying across the stone floor on his way to some urgent matter. I told him who I was looking for. 'Professor Martin,' the young man replied, 'has not been seen here at the Seraph since the year of Our Lord 1788 and that is something for which we should be grateful since that was also the year of his passing.' I was rendered speechless. The man gave me a sympathetic look. 'Is it Roland Martin personally that you were after or will his replacement do? In that case, you'll find Professor Hagström in the north anatomical theatre.' I didn't know what else to do other than nod. 'One floor up and then to the right.'

Halfway up the stairs I was confronted with a smell that I know well and will never forget: the smell of the dead. A door stood ajar and through the gap I was greeted by a macabre sight. On the table was the body of a man, cut open from his head to the end of his torso. The skin had been curled back in sections and revealed his innards. The chest had been prised open with strong hooks. Of his face, only half was left since the cranium and the facial muscle structure had been revealed. Two milky white orbs stared up at the ceiling. Only now did I notice the man who stood next to the stretcher.

'Are you looking for me?' he asked as he resumed his excavation of the dead man's chest.

'I am looking for Professor Hagström,' I said, and noted that my voice trembled a little, less due to the presence of the corpse than to that of the professor. I estimated that he was around forty, and looked to be in excellent health, with only a waistcoat over his shirt, the sleeves rolled up, and with a leather apron wrapped around his middle.

'At your service. Please feel free to come in as long as this scene does not upset you too much.'

He put down his knife and started to wash his hands in a porcelain bowl.

'How may I help you?'

'My name is Johan Kristofer Blix,' I said, and slipped my cap from my head. 'I was in Karlskrona in eighty-eight, apprenticed as a navy surgeon under Master Hoffman.'

'Emmanuel Hoffman?'

'Yes, Professor.'

'Then it's no wonder that you are so little affected by a sight that has caused many a visitor to pale and lean out the window,' Hagström said. 'If you spent the war years in Karlskrona, then it is you who are the professor and I the student, at least when it comes to the sight of death and corruption.'

Professor Hagström asked me to sit down and politely asked me about my experiences in Karlskrona while he rang for a pot of coffee which was carried in after a few minutes by a woman in white. The words poured out of my mouth. I have never told anyone about the terrible years of the war, not even to you, my dear sister, and so it is high time that I tell my tale.

———◆———

The naval fleet returned from across the Baltic in the winter of 1788 with a ship taken from the Russians at Hogland. Her name was *Vladislav*, a line ship of seventy-four guns. The fleet had hardly arrived into their home harbour than the ice came, and from the *Vladislav* men emerged with a kind of ship's sickness that had not been seen before. Those that fell ill quickly developed fever and chills. Their skin yellowed, and blemishes appeared on their arms and legs. In some, the illness went into their lungs and they coughed until their lips turned blue. The fever disappeared as quickly as it had appeared, only to return half a week later with renewed strength. I saw the strongest men survive some ten cycles of this before they succumbed, then as old men with hunched backs and empty gazes. It was a harsh winter and every board became someone's bed. More and more fell ill, not only sailors but the citizens in our town, until the naval hospital was overflowing. I became an errand boy and later, around the turn of the new year, an apprentice to Master Hoffman until his death, after which I remained at the hospital for another three years.

The Master hoped that the epidemic would wane in the spring but, if anything, it grew even worse. Thousands died while, from other parts of the country, new recruits streamed in to take their place, only to grow sick in turn.

The professor interrupted me.

'Was it the recurring fever that took Hoffman? I only know him by reputation.'

'No,' I answered. 'It was a Russian thirty-six-pounder who became my Master's bane.'

In June, the fleet sailed east in order to continue the Russian campaign and Hoffman went with them. Since there was a shortage of field medics, I was allowed to accompany them, aboard the *Courage*, built by Chapman in Karlskrona to bear sixty-four guns. We met the Russians south of Öland and exchanged fire before the enemy decided to flee with the wind at their back. I had climbed up into the rigging as I had never witnessed a battle at sea before and could not resist the temptation. I had helped the

Master spread sawdust on the floor to soak up the blood and prevent us from slipping as we attended to the injured, and I seized my opportunity in a moment of inattention. I was so high up that I could observe the *Courage* in her entirety and I saw the cannonball come flying across the water. It struck us high on the broadside and, after impact, I saw a ravaged body fly straight out on the other side in a cloud of burning sawdust.

Thus was Hoffman's end and both I and the ship's crew were grateful that the battle ended with that single exchange because I would not have been much of a surgeon for an entire ship without the Master's instructions.

The fleet returned to Karlskrona and I remained there for the rest of the war. The fever grew even worse. A tent city was created from the sails of the ships, large enough for five thousand men, and we thanked God that the autumn of eighty-nine was so cold that we could store the dead outside. That spring we saw fewer cases and the worst of it seemed over. I remained there to help as long as it was needed. When the corpses of the winter had been buried, we could go from house to house and gather the dead from their beds where they had been lying since the sickness took them.

———— • ◆ • ————

Professor Hagström observed me with a steady gaze when I was finished with my story.

'And then you came to Stockholm. Am I right in thinking that you have come to me in hopes that you may continue your career in medicine?'

'I can't deny it.'

Hagström sighed.

'We see many like you, Blix. All too many. During the war years the need was great and anyone with a pair of hands was better as a sawbones than none at all. But that is not the case any longer.

Look at our hospital here! We have wrested medicine and surgery out of the hands of the craftsmen and turned it into a science.'

The professor stood up, fired up by his own speech, and placed himself next to the body.

'Blix, can you tell me the name of this bone?'

I was forced to admit I could not.

'Where is the best place to bleed the artery that runs along here?'

Again, I could only shake my head.

'Did Emanuel Hoffman ever tell you what he believed in regard to the origin of the fever?'

At this question, I brightened as I finally had something to say for myself.

'The Master told me that it was caused by fumes emanating from stagnant pools and marshy land.'

Hagström smiled but his eyes remained sad.

'Such was his understanding. Today we have another explanation. I am afraid that your master was of the old school, capable of using his knife to sever limbs from their unfortunate owners but hardly anything else.'

Hagström looked around and, from a shelf, lifted a thick leather-bound book that he handed to me.

'Do you understand anything of this?'

The letters were familiar but they did not form any words from which I could derive any meaning. I told him as much and Hagström's shoulders sank at this answer.

'I am afraid there is not much I can do for you at the moment, Blix.' But then, his eyebrows still drawn together in a frown, he appeared to remember something and his expression lifted.

'Wait here a little while,' he said, turning and leaving me with the dead man.

In that moment I took something, sister. I admit it and I regretted it in the same moment in which it was done, but just as I reached back into my knapsack to restore the stolen object, I heard Hagström in the corridor and the moment was lost. In he came with a small pamphlet written in a language I could understand.

'Worse men than you have become capable surgeons without being able to read French,' he said, and put the pamphlet in my hand. 'This summary is something I have written on my own initiative in order to help the studies of my students. If you apply yourself, you may be able to qualify to begin your studies next year, even if I cannot promise anything.'

Hagström scrutinized me again with a look of concentration on his intelligent, open face. 'You have blood on your jacket, Blix. Is it yours?' I shook my head. Hagström took a step closer and leaned towards me. 'Your eyes have a yellow tint where they should be white. How are you living, Blix? Are you drinking strong spirits?' I felt myself blushing, which gave Hagström the answer that he needed. 'Come over here, Blix, and see this.' He lifted a flap of skin on the dead man's body and revealed a stinking clump, covered in lumpy growths. 'This is the man's liver, and it is what has ended his life. Had he had the sense to drink in greater moderation he would still be among us. Organs in this state of destruction are hidden in all too many bellies in this city and it drags men to their graves like a magnet. Let this be a lesson to you in the virtues of temperance.'

The consternation must have been easy to read in my face, as his eyes took on a look of sympathy. From a waistcoat pocket he pulled out an embroidered purse and counted out coin after coin on the table before he seemed to change his mind and simply emptied out the contents. 'Take this, Blix, and see that you take care of yourself so I will have the pleasure of seeing you in my lecture hall next spring.' I had no words. There must have been almost twenty dalers on the table! It was a treasure beyond my wildest dreams. I gathered up the coins and put them in my pockets, bowing again and again. The tears burned on my cheeks, in part from gratitude but mainly out of shame in having stolen from this Samaritan, this kindly gentleman whose goodwill I had already repaid so ill. I even saw that his eyes grew shiny in response to my emotions. He held out his hand which I took in my own, and kissed it.

When I was almost out of the door, he posed a final question in a quavering voice. 'One last thing, Johan Kristofer. How old are you?'

'This winter I will be seventeen, God willing,' I answered in the same unsteady voice.

20

DEAR SISTER, HERE come some wonderful days and nights of abundance and joy! I bade farewell to my nights under the trees in the Meadowland and among the graves under Katarina tower and for a small portion of Hagström's coins I rented a chamber in the Pomona quarter at Tailor's Alley. The view took my breath away. From the attic windows, the rooftops of copper and tile extended in all directions and gleamed like burnished gold in the sun, as far as the eye could see. At the very top of this golden city, I now had my bed, to which the sun's rays reached long after the alleys were cast in shadow. At night, the street lights blinked up at me from their deep chasms and when I raised my gaze the stars felt far closer than before. For Sylvan, I had a place by the tile stove. Over a bottle, we discussed our new circumstances and how best we could put it to use until I was ready to begin my studies at the Seraph. We talked over each other and laughed heartily as we patted each other's backs and drank toasts.

We soon arrived at an understanding of how best to manage our wealth – my twenty dalers and the four that Rickard had managed to borrow from Clemens Montell. This was not enough to last us forever. Each and every daler had to multiply.

'In order to earn more, we must first give the impression of being exactly that which we are not: two sons from wealthy families, mistreated by miserly fathers but in a position to inherit a fortune. Young men of a kind, in other words, for which each loan appears as a wise investment for the future.' With these words, Sylvan took me by the arm and we headed to a nearby clothier. We took a handful of money and the remainder we carefully hid in my straw mattress. The proprietor was curt with us at first but this attitude turned to fawning when we clinked the coins in our purse. We searched exhaustively through cupboards and drawers for clothes of the finest quality, but with enough experience to emphasize a reasonable price. Trying on these clothes was a pleasure I will not soon forget. We posed as two young noblemen, clapping our hands and pretending to compliment each other in French as we strutted in front of the mirror.

'Magnificent, monshoor Blix!'

'No more than you, Sylvan Your Highness.' We selected waistcoats with embroidery in scarlet and purple, a jacket each with gold cuffs, new shirts and knee breeches in soft leather, long socks and leather shoes with showy buckles. Sylvan found a horsehair wig in far better condition than his red one while I preferred to continue wearing my blond hair in a long tail, albeit now carefully smoothed with a horn comb and a silk ribbon at the nape of my neck. Standing side by side before the mirror, we could hardly believe our eyes. We embraced in the heightened mood of the moment. Sylvan bargained for a long time on the outrageous price we were given, after which we counted out the sum on his table and left.

Farewell not only to dirty rags and sleeping under the stars but also to the kind of establishments that we had frequented before, where drunks and riff-raff vomited over each other, infected each other with the French disease by swapping whores and took to their fists at the slightest provocation. Instead we went to the Exchange, most renowned of the city's cellars, and to balls held at the palaces. It is funny how everyone seems to want to help those who need none, while they take long paths to avoid the need that is evident. We quickly became on intimate terms with the sons of counts, burgher princes and guild members, addressing them as brothers would, and made an effort to always be pleasant, witty and entertaining. Sister, do you remember how I told you about the first ball on Castle Hill, where we happily allowed ourselves to be stained with the wine from the society people up in the gallery? To the latter, we now had full access and could, like our acquaintances, exclaim with horror at how easily the rabble on the stone floor could be led to humiliate themselves for a taste of wine. We promised ourselves never to pay a penny for whatever we ate or drank and sought out the company of those who found honour in treating us.

In this way, we passed many a summer night and when we had made ourselves a feature at the heart of these functions, eagerly sought after whenever our absence was detected, we began to borrow. We often wrote promissory notes for the loans, signed with signatures we had practised at the same table and with the same mangled quill with which I am writing now. None of our new-found friends showed the slightest hesitation. For them, money lacked value, though our friendship and society was appreciated all the more. In the evenings, we could turn out our pockets over the mattress at Tailor's Alley and see our twenty-four dalers turn to thirty, then forty, then double. We wrote a record of our debts and set aside a portion of the evening's profits in order to pay off the old loans. In a short while, we enjoyed even more trust, and if anyone seemed the least bit hesitant, we could easily wave to an earlier benefactor to vouch for us. In this way, the coins in the mattress multiplied: fifty became seventy, and seventy became ninety.

'Dear Kristofer Blix, beloved brother and highly esteemed friend,' said Sylvan one day when he returned from a stroll in the sun along the Quayside. 'Tell me, have you ever heard of ombre?'

'Of course,' I replied. 'It is a card game, isn't it? Like pharo?'

'Yes and no. Pharo is a game where luck selects the winner. In ombre – or l'hombre, to give it its proper name – skill determines the outcome and Lady Fortune has no voice.'

'Why this interest in games, Rickard?' I asked as I lay on my bed, basking in the warmth like a barn cat.

Then he proceeded to tell me that many gentlemen were obsessed with ombre and that great sums of money exchanged hands each evening in salons where the police authorities had no access. I immediately objected to the idea of setting our money at risk, as the likelihood of losing seemed far greater than any chances of winning.

'Wait, Kristofer, you are rushing to conclusions!' Sylvan protested. 'There are games and then there are games. I met Block at the Windy Courtyard – you remember him from the opera last week, I'm sure? He told me about a particular event that his friend Carsten Vikare hosts. Vikare invites guests from far and wide according to three criteria: riches, poor tolerance for alcohol, and a gullible nature. There are five players at the table but four are in cahoots against the guest who therefore has no chance but to lose all his money. They call this poor bastard the Rabbit, with the understanding that the rest are the hunting dogs. One communicates wordlessly by way of gestures and signs. Those in the know divvy up the pot with the host, who gets twice the share.'

'Well, and what does this have to do with us?' I said but I could not deny that my interest had been awakened.

'Kristofer, a place at the table is free and I have been offered that place. The risk is minimal and Block assured me that my understanding of the game only has to be rudimentary. If the

Rabbit is fat enough, we could probably double our fortune in one night, Kristofer. Two hundred dalers!'

It was as if my belly was suddenly filled with a swarm of bees. I sat up in bed so quickly that I became dizzy. I reached for a bottle of wine and two glasses, filling them both. We toasted and clinked our glasses.

'To Sylvan and Blix!' I exclaimed. 'Young, handsome, and soon to be richer than ever!'

'To Sylvan and Blix!' he responded. 'And for two hundred or more!'

We went to purchase a deck of cards the same day and played game after game of ombre according to the rules that Carl Gustaf Block had hastily described to Rickard, until it was time to dress in our finery and walk up to Old Square and the evening's amusements. The game did not appear particularly difficult. Of forty cards, eight are given to each player. In turn, one makes a bet based on a prediction of how many rounds of eight one anticipates winning. The boldest selects which suit will be trumps.

'As in life itself,' Sylvan said and emptied his glass.

21

THAT EVENING, A Thursday, we made ourselves ready with powder in our hair and a new cravat each. We inspected each other critically and brushed stray hairs and flakes from collar and lapels, and then emptied the mattress of its treasure. At seven, the players were to assemble in a room that Carsten Vikare had reserved behind Terra Nova in Forked Pass that had once been a regular pub but that was now only open to seafarers and certain invited guests. The bell tower of Nikolai Church rang a quarter to seven as we stepped out onto the cobblestones of Tailor's Alley. The heat was oppressive and the air shimmered. We carried our hearts in our throats on account of Sylvan's burden. A strike from the shadows would reward the criminal with the windfall of a lifetime.

We worried for nothing. The walk past Ironmonger's Square and on towards the palace went without a hitch. At Terra Nova, Block bade us welcome and introduced us to Vikare. Block couldn't help but wink knowingly to Sylvan and, with a tilt of his head indicate the Rabbit, who appeared to be a German in an expensive outfit and a gold chain in his waistcoat. We were offered wine as the tables were prepared and, after having drunk to each other's health, we were shown into the room by a curtsying woman. Just as I was about to step across the threshold, I felt a hand on my chest and found when I looked up in surprise that it was Carl Gustaf Block, shaking his head. He whispered in my ear:

'Only players, if you please. We do not want to frighten our prey by reading his cards from over his shoulder.' I caught Rickard's gaze. He was already in the room, about to sit in the appointed chair.

'Don't worry, Kristofer. Wait for me at the Sanctuary. I'll come to you once the game is at an end.' He gave me a few shillings. I couldn't do anything but shrug, wish the players the best of luck and turn around.

———————

At the Sanctuary, across from the bank building, the festivities were in full swing. A corpulent man with a dark red nose was waving his red bow over a violoncello, accompanied by a bald man fingering a long flute. The instruments sang nicely together. I sat down at a table and found that I did not lack for company. The music was more than enough. I pushed a twelve-shilling piece across the table, asked for Danziger beer, and asked the barmaid to keep an eye on my pitcher and refill it as soon as she saw the bottom.

I found myself in a strange mood. When I drink, my joy tends to overflow and I become giddy as in a whirling dance. This time it was different. I remember the growths that Professor Hagström had showed me in the dead man's belly and looked around at my drinking brothers and sisters, now neither beautiful nor funny. They smiled to reveal the brown stumps of their teeth, cross-eyed with greed and lechery. In the mirror behind a sconce on the wall, I saw my own appearance, still young, hardly full grown, with white skin and fine limbs. I was not yet of their number but in that moment it struck me that I would probably become one of them. No spell had been cast over me to protect me from the corruption of the flesh. My nose would also swell like a cluster of grapes, my belly begin to protrude and strain over some lethal growth, nurtured by strong spirits.

I swore then that this fate would not be mine. I would take my portion of the two hundred daler and put them to another use. The money would be enough to repay what Hagström had given me, enough to keep a humble roof over my head until the spring and longer, enough for a tutor to teach me French, which would allow me to delve into the mysteries of the medical textbooks, and enough to support my fellow students with dinner and drinks as we together strove to master the inheritance from Linné, Scheele and Acrel. I would dedicate my life to help both high and low; the poor and outcast without demanding payment for my services. When the war came next to our shores, my brothers and I would keep the epidemics and death itself at bay. No more would orphans have to dig pits in the icy ground and fill them with their own kind. As I became older I would take a wife and bring children into the world. I would be a good father, not curt and indifferent, not drunk and threatening, never hit, never whip. My children shall grow up wanting for nothing.

I was roused from my daydream when a group that had started a line dance fell onto my table. I must have sat there longer than I thought, for much of the clientele had already left. I asked the time from a man with a police badge hanging from his watch chain who slurred that it was midnight. No Sylvan yet. Maybe he had returned to Tailor's Alley, thinking that I would long since have grown tired and gone home. No Rickard Sylvan was to be found at home in Tailor's Alley. I opened the window wide and leaned out in the hopes of catching a breeze. Over the bay, the moon shone in awesome majesty with the stardusts for a court, all perfectly reflected in the still water. I sank onto the bed, staring at this wonderful sight until no amount of effort could keep my eyes open any longer.

I woke up drenched in sweat and as thirsty as a shipwrecked sailor. I had no way to determine the hour but the moon had reached far on its journey. I listened in the darkness for Rickard's breath and felt with my foot along the floor, but I was alone. I stood up to find the water pail in the stairs and lit a candle stump so I would not fall headlong as I walked to the next floor. It was once I was in the stairwell that I heard the sounds and I could not make out if it was a person or an animal. Only when I reached the bottom did I see Rickard Sylvan's shaking back. He was weeping uncontrollably with his face in his hands. When he turned, I saw that the tears had created streaks in the powder. The hairs of the wig were standing on end and the beautiful clothes were covered in dirt. It took me a long time to get him to talk to me and I only managed it after I had placed the candle on the floor, put my arms around him and rocked him until the shaking stopped and his sobbing subsided. 'It was me, Kristofer,' he whispered. 'I was the Rabbit.'

They swindled us, my sister. Carsten Vikare, Carl Block, their companions and the German, who was just as much a Stockholmer as any of the rest of us. They swindled us because they were just like us. In the midst of all the cunning with which we took on the world, we had allowed ourselves in our own way to become susceptible and believe that we were the only ones who could trick our way to unearned gold. The card players were not the wealthy burgher sons that they had made themselves out to be. They were like us, born of the gutter and just as the sharp-toothed pike swallows the greedy perch, we and our hundred dalers proved a juicy morsel. They led Rickard to gamble our money away as he believed it was part of the swindle, but when the playing was over it was his money they divided up under mocking laughter. When he protested, they hit him and tossed him out onto the street.

'Kristofer,' Sylvan said as he laid his forehead against my shoulder. 'This time we are lost. When the promissory notes become due, they will throw us in debtors' prison forever. We won't see freedom again until we are old men. There will be the workhouse and the rest of our lives we will be chained to the manufactory bench with welts from the foreman's belt across our necks.'

I remained quiet. Deep inside me, my entire being was screaming. When the candle stump went out, my imagination made its own light in the darkness and I saw as in the dream at the Sanctuary how the fog closed in around the promised land of my future.

22

WE REMAINED ON the stairs until dawn. With the morning light, the spell of hopeless calm that had descended over us was broken and we hurried up to our chamber. We hurriedly gathered those papers on which we had written our debts and found the reading ominous. Many of the promissory notes that bore our signatures were close to falling due. If we didn't repay them at least in part, anger would spread among our debtors. They would begin to talk among each other and draw the conclusion that we were swindlers who had finally collected enough in order to abscond with the money. One or more would march down to the courts, display the notes and demand the assistance of the authorities to collect the debt. The cases would multiply, the total sum would become known and we would be searched for with increasing urgency.

'We must leave, Kristofer,' Sylvan whispered with his eyes full of tears. 'And soon, before our location becomes known.'

'But where should we go?'

'We have to separate and go in different directions. Both the guardsmen on the street and the men from the police will be keeping an eye out for us in our fine clothing. If we separate, we'll have a better chance of escaping discovery.'

'And what then? We can't stay away forever.'

'We have to leave the city, Kristofer. You understand that, don't you?'

I thought with a heavy heart of everything I had sacrificed in order to come here from Karlskrona, of the highways that had worn down my soles, of the rides on wagons and carts that I paid for with services I had rather not engaged in. Sylvan, who had lived here all of his days and been given his life in the city as a gift of fate, might be ready to leave Stockholm, but for me such a flight meant the breaking of a dream for which I had been fighting my entire life. Rickard had not seen the poverty of the countryside and its small-minded misery. I told him as much but he did not want to listen. 'I'll leave by way of the Sconce Tollgate and go on to Fredrikshald, and God willing I will make it there before the summer is over.'

We packed up our few belongings, me in the same knapsack with which I had arrived, Sylvan in a bag that he improvised from a shirt. Before the cock crowed and the sun was fully up, we were standing in the alley. Neither one of us found it easy to put our feelings into words. We embraced one last time, both moved to tears, before we went our separate ways; Sylvan to the north, to try to get a few shillings from his cousin for his trip, while I turned towards the sea in order to meet with the clothing merchant in Ferk's Close. He did not turn up before mid-morning and pretended not to recognize me or the clothes that I wore. In a merchant's way, he seemed to have a sixth sense for a customer's desperation and quickly realized that I was not in a frame of mind to negotiate. I exchanged the finery we had bought for more modest items: a rough jerkin as befitting a farmhand, a woollen jacket with patched elbows, a pair of trousers and shoes constructed for lifelong wear. A knitted cap was traded for the hat. He acted surprised when I asked him how much he would pay for the difference between the items.

'Money for these stained rags? Young man, you must be joking.' In the end, he paid me a handful of shillings just to be rid of me.

I pulled the cap down over my ears to conceal my hair, stepped out on to the Quayside and looked around.

Where would I go now? I could no longer show my face in the City-between-the-Bridges. An unfortunate encounter in a narrow alley and my tale would be over. I had even spent too much time wandering around the Meadowland. The Southern Isle seemed my only viable alternative, with a crowd in which I would hardly be alone in my misery. I followed the harbour's straight line towards the Lock, past the four great mill wheels that tamed the current rushing under the street and on towards the drawbridges.

———•———

Despite what I had thought, life as a penniless vagrant was worse in the Southern Isle than elsewhere in the city, not in spite of the fact that there were so many outcasts and indigents everywhere, but because of them. At the pubs and cellars the staff had developed a keen sense of who lacked the ability to pay. They knew immediately who had found their way into the warm pub in order to help themselves to crumbs and dregs and try to steal a few moments of rest in a corner. I was mercilessly driven from some places, and denied entry to others if I could not show coin at the entrance. This meant that every nook and cranny was filled at night, and around haystacks and barns, servants had been sent out to keep watch. I came to spend my nights under the trees in Danto or around the Winter Tollgate. The coins I had received from the clothing merchant were enough for kitchen scraps and stale bread that I could soften in water and slurp up. No one could demand money for the water in the bay. I could wash my face and hands in its waves and when I needed somewhere cool to rest, I made myself a sleeping spot in the branches of those willow trees that leaned thirstily out into the bay.

———•———

They came for me one evening, dear sister, when I had already fallen asleep. As so often, I saw your face in my dream, only to see it transform into a mocking grin of someone staring down at me. A heavy boot had been shoved into my shoulder and kept me helplessly pinned to the ground. A lantern was held in my face and the cap ripped from my head.

'Well, if it isn't Kristofer Blix! I bid you a good evening, because now your rest is over.' I tried to squirm out from under the boot without success.

'I haven't heard of any Blix. My name is David Jansson, I must have got lost on my way back from the Last Shilling and lain here to wait for the morning.'

'Oh, is that so. And what is your father's name?'

'Jan Davidsson, a journeyman brass maker in Hedvig Eleonora parish, and my mother is Elsa Fredrika, born Gudmundsdotter.' I mentioned the most distant church I could think of in the hopes of being taken at my word without the facts being checked. I was mistaken.

'Well, what do you know. And where is your parents' home?'

'Out past Bog Hill, right next to the mills.'

'I'm sure they'll be happy to hear you have had an escort through such dangerous neighbourhoods.'

I was held tightly under the arms and placed with my feet on the ground, still restrained and unable to slip away into the bushes. My captors were three men. The one who had spoken was heavy set with stubby legs, his mouth full of tobacco, and with facial features that were not so easy to discern under the dirt. He walked in front with the lantern while his two companions, both silent, led me between them. I could not see them clearly as I was dealt a stinging slap on the neck with an open hand each time I attempted to turn in any direction. When I stumbled, one of them would pinch me with fingers like pincers. Their breath made me want to retch as they hissed in my ear: 'Keep pace, you little pansy, or I'll wring your neck.' We had hardly passed the Larder when I realized that the game was up and that I would pay with blows if we made it all the way to Bog Hill before I was forced to admit that I didn't know anyone there, least of all any parents.

'Stay a while. I lied. I am the one you are looking for.'

The man with the lantern turned around.

'You are the last of a dozen ragamuffins of the same age that we have had to drag through town on the same business this past week, so that is definitely welcome news.' He gave a sign, whereupon a terrible pain exploded before my eyes and my cheek hit a cobblestone on the street. As I fell, I heard laughter as if from a neighing horse and glimpsed a bloodied cudgel before my consciousness fluttered and went out.

———————

I woke from a sharp jolt of smelling salts under my nose. I was sitting in a chair and the fists that had been holding me upright let go of my shoulders when I could manage to keep my balance. My head was throbbing and a wound at the back of my head burned when I touched it. The room emerged as my sight cleared. Tapestries were hanging on the stone walls, beautiful carpets were laid on the wooden floor. There were no windows. The chair was in the centre of the room in front of an elegant desk with curved legs. On the other side of the desk, there was a gentleman sitting in an armchair. With growing unease, I started to realize that my chair had not been placed directly on the rug but on a stained piece of fabric that was spread out under me. The man noticed my gaze and said, 'You are wondering about the sheet. It is to spare my Turkish carpets from being sullied by various impurities. Many guests that sit where you are sitting now, Kristofer Blix, cannot contain themselves. Those who don't bleed, lose fluids in other ways.'

He smiled derisively when I pulled back in alarm.

'You look alarmed, Blix, and that is understandable, but your fate now lies partly in your own hands. Keep that in mind when you answer me. If not for your sake, then for the sake of my carpet.' He was dressed in expensive clothes, the stubble on his face as short as the hair on his head that formed a deep widow's peak on his high forehead. His eyes were icy blue. I would have guessed his age to be over forty. His voice was hoarse.

'My name is Dülitz. Do you know who I am?'

I shook my head. Dülitz reached for a carafe across his desk and poured himself a drink in a seltzer glass – water, to judge by its colour.

'You were raving for a while, Blix, and I thought I could hear from your accent that you are not from Stockholm. Where is your parental home?'

'In Karlskrona.'

He nodded.

'Then we have one thing in common, which is that we are both far from the place of our birth.' He drank his water. Thirsty, all I could do was watch.

'During my childhood in Poland, I worked with glass, Blix.' He said my name as if it had a bad taste. 'I made dragons, lions, kings, chimeras and dancers rise out of the embers and cool into works of art. I came here in order to find refuge when my home became a puppet state of the Russians only to find out that people like me were forbidden here from practising their craft. The King himself had made this decree, doubtless to make himself more popular with the artisans' guilds. How the poor bastards who cut panes for windows could think that I was trespassing on their territory is beyond me. Luckily, I was already wealthy and as I was in the midst of thinking about my options, there came a knock on my door one late evening. I opened and there was a young man, not unlike yourself. I bade him come in, I gave him bread and wine and finally he presented his question. – "I need a loan," he said. I was taken aback. – "I do have some coins I could spare, but why did you come to me?" – "Well, you are a Jew, are you not?" In your language, Blix, for hundreds of years, a Jew is someone who loans out money for profit. That I had never before in my life either indebted myself or others, was of no consequence to the young man. I was a Jew, therefore any and all could come to me to loan money, and this without any show of gratitude, for lending at a profit was said to be part of my nature.' As Dülitz spoke, he took a pipe out of a drawer, packed it with tobacco and lit it on a candle. 'My guest, quick to enter into debt, was not as eager to repay the loan that I had given him out of pity. I realized that I had found my new profession.'

A shadow drew over his face. 'I am no simple bean counter who drives my business by way of interest rates, Kristofer Blix. I trade in other commodities. When the young man's debt became considerable, I realized that I owned him and that I could do whatever I wanted with him as long as the fate that I selected for him was to be preferred to being tossed into the cold and damp cells of the debtors' prison. Once I formed glass into the shapes that pleased me. Today I shape your lives in the same way.'

With these words, he laid the fading pipe aside, and from another drawer he took out a leather folio which he opened before him and the contents of which he slowly started to divulge, although he did not for a single moment avert his gaze from mine.

'Do you recognize these, Blix?'

It was the promissory notes, each one that I had signed with my own name and whose collected value was over fifty daler. 'I have purchased your debts and now I also own you, Kristofer Blix, both body and soul.'

It took me a good while to find my voice again. 'What are you going to do with me?' I asked. He answered with studied indifference.

'What can you do? What are your abilities and skills? Establishing this is the goal of our first conversation. Your value, for me.'

I told him everything. What else could I do? I told him about the years in Karlskrona, I recited everything that I had learned and everything I knew, and hoped that it would be enough. Dülitz dipped a shining white feather into an inkwell and wrote down some of the words that were apparently worth noting.

'Is that all?' he asked when I did not have more to say. 'So. At the stroke of midnight every night you will appear on my doorstep. This will go on until I have decided how best to make use of you.' I experienced such relief that I had never felt before at the thought of being able to leave this abominable room, even if only temporarily, and breathe fresh air, wash the panic from my gullet and feel the wind on my face.

'The thought of escaping from me will be the first one that comes to you and therefore I want to underscore that I will find you and that . . . Let us leave it at that, since you have managed to keep the cloth unsullied until now. Rask! Please show Blix out.'

I was grabbed by the scruff of my neck and lifted onto my feet. The man had to hold on since my legs did not support me, and he kept his hold on me until I staggered out the door. Nonetheless, I managed to get a final question out over my shoulder. 'What has happened to my friend, Rickard Sylvan?'

Dülitz did not change his expression when he answered.

'We found him much earlier than you. Many of the stains on this cloth are his. Our conversation was of little interest despite my efforts, and I finally determined that his value did not exceed that of his debts. I have given him twenty days to pay me what he owes, and after that I will leave him to the courts, to a decade or two at the workhouse and to a slow death by way of the manufactory.'

Outside Dülitz's house, after my knapsack was tossed out after me, I knelt down on all fours in the dirt and vomited in the gutter until my bile ran yellow.

23

I REMEMBER THAT DAY with great regret, my dear sister. Outside in the street where I emptied the contents of my stomach, I lifted my head and wiped my mouth clean and could see that Dülitz's house was close to the Southern Square and that his henchmen had not had far to carry me from the place where they clubbed me.

I did not know what to do once this terrible night was over and yet another morning would dawn over Stockholm. I could not then know what fate Dülitz would choose for me and I found myself aimlessly walking down Horn's Street to the outskirts of the city until Ansgar's Mound stood in my way. The street was empty. The occasional drunk or lady of the evening slunk along walls after the night's adventures in the Carpenter's Garden. My route brought me around the foot of the hill and I now stood before the cliffs that rise up over Skinner's Cove. I started to climb as if from a desire to get away from all human habitation. From the top of the cliff, Stockholm spread out at my feet. When I followed the line of the city over the Islet of the Holy Ghost to the north and on to the bridge to King's Isle, I felt pangs of guilt at the sight of the walls of the Seraph. It was too much and I sank down on the rock and ended up sitting there with my arms around my knees and my forehead pressing against them.

The past week had been warm and it seemed now as if the pressure built up by the heat was in the process of dissipating. Dark clouds appeared from the archipelago. I heard thunder far away, in rumbling calls that echoed over the landscape.

The item I had stolen from Professor Hagström was still in my bag. I undid my sack, took out my loot and held it up against the early morning light. It was a small flask of clear glass. A lizard was suspended in liquid with its tail resting on the bottom. Hoffman had also had such things in his possession and he guarded them carefully, as their contents were spared from decomposition by being drenched in spirits. Master may have kept his bottles under close guard but this one was now mine. The lizard was of a sort I'd never laid eyes on before. Its body was thick, black and slimy, with an open mouth and lolling tongue. Along its back there were pale yellow spots in an intricate pattern. Its black eyes, round and still as pebbles, seemed to study me maliciously from the other side of the glass with a challenge.

'*You are a wretched coward, Kristofer Blix. You stole me for no reason, because you don't dare do anything with me.*'

I broke the wax that sealed the bottle, unwound the coils of thread that kept the lid in place and finally opened it. It had a familiar smell. The medicinal stink of the alcohol, but there was also something else, something both sharp and sweet. With my fingers, I fished out the lizard, slick and uncooperative. I shivered at the touch of the dead skin, which was completely smooth and lacked scales. I threw it off the side of the cliff, put the bottle to my mouth and drank until nothing was left.

* * *

The rush of intoxication flowed through my veins. I am no stranger to drinking, my sister, and never more so than in these months that have gone by since I set foot in the capital, but it now affected me in a way that I had never felt before. As if for the first time, my eyes were opened and gazed upon another world, concealed behind our own. It was not the morning light that was reflected in the bay! The city sat in a puddle of blood and more ran along the streets. Before my eyes the dead awoke. There was hardly an inch in the city that had not at one time been used for executions, as a plague pit or for the wide ditches where mauled soldiers were disposed of in the aftermath of battle. The hands of the dead, some clean and bone white, others worm-eaten or waterlogged as after a drowning, reached up between the cobblestones like weeds. They groped blindly after the feet of the living.

At that moment, the storm broke above me. Heavy raindrops fell over Stockholm and hammered against rooftops, bay and hills. The bolts of thunder were deafening. When the flashes of lightning came most rapidly, they caused the thunderhead over the city to resemble a giant beetle with a humped back. The creature picked its way among the houses with limbs of icy blue fire. Perhaps it was searching its way through the houses the way I had gone door to door in Karlskrona with a handkerchief over my nose in the spring of 1790, when the victims of the fever were starting to thaw in their cottages and I could follow the stench to the sleeping quarters where distended bodies were waiting in their beds, where the rats in their hundreds had lost their fear of humans and hissed to defend their treasures.

I saw in a state of dizziness how screaming women with pregnant bellies thronged Stockholm's graveyards, giving birth to tiny pale corpses that slithered from their wombs straight into the graves, so quickly that the umbilical cords pulled their mothers with them underground. From the palace at the Quayside and from the fine houses the gentlemen came in their finest clothes, with their teeth sharpened into cruel points. Laughing, they hunted down the paupers, the beggars, the orphans, spinning women, servants and maids, ripped them into pieces and feasted on their flesh until their bellies split open like over-ripened pustules.

It was not the rising sun that now burned over the roofs of the city, it was the blaze of hell itself. I saw Emanuel Hoffman come staggering out of the flame, a hole from the cannon ball through his middle, his intestines dragging behind him and his head tilted on a broken neck. He fumbled blindly in the air. 'Where are my tongs, Kristofer? Where's my saw? Come here so I can whip you until your piss runs red so that you will never again forget.'

I woke up dizzy and feverish in a ditch to the sound of my own voice and with the rain in my face. I was calling your name over and over again.

24

THE THIRD TIME I returned to Dülitz's door I was shown inside. On the two earlier nights, the door had only opened a sliver, a face briefly shown to shake its head, the bright light behind it obscuring all features, and then the door closed, leaving me to find lodgings where I could. I still felt the after-effects of the alcohol I had consumed. The lizard must have excreted some kind of substance with the power to affect the mind. When I looked up at the starry sky, I felt a sense of vertigo as if I were not looking up but down into an abyss where the stars formed strange and disturbing images.

For the third time, I went back to the house at Hawker's Street and this time what I had been fearful of finally occurred. The door opened wide, the brute in the hall stepped aside and waved at me to enter. Soon I found myself in the same windowless cellar room as before. Neither chair nor sheet was in sight, which gave me small comfort. Dülitz was sitting at his desk as if he had not moved at all since we last met. He raised his gaze from a ledger when I stepped into the room. When shadows fell across his face, I thought I could glimpse fangs between his lips and a forehead bulging with two small horns, each finger ending in a claw. I rubbed my eyes to coax back reality.

'Young Master Blix. You are expected.'

'What will happen to me?' I asked in a trembling voice and with the beating of my heart sounding in my ears like a kettle-drum. Dülitz gave me a look of indifference.

'You have been sold, Blix. Your debts are now in your buyer's hands, as is your life.'

'Who has bought them? What do they want with me?'

'Does the baker ask his customers what they want with his loaves, or the butcher what will become of his sausage? They are consumed. They fulfil their purpose. The buyer is free to do whatever he wants with the goods he has purchased. Just as in your case, Kristofer Blix.' Dülitz closed the ledger. 'Our last moments together are fast approaching and I must admit I do not find that lamentable since your nights in the field have made your presence a provocation both for nose and eyes. I know no more than you what fate has in store for you next, but do us both a favour and do not come into my presence again should you ever regain your freedom.'

A gentleman came down the stairs and I did not know then if it was still Hagström's lizard that was playing tricks on me but the very sight of him made my hair stand on end. I do not know how best to describe him. He was neither tall nor short, nor old or young. He wore clothes that had once been beautiful but that had suffered from their owner's disinterest. The cuffs of the coat were frayed and some threads from his embroidery hung loose. Several of the mother-of-pearl buttons that once decorated his waistcoat were missing. He did not wear a wig and his hair was wispy and thin. Even though he made no threatening gesture, I was quickly filled with a terror I couldn't explain.

Something was amiss with him, this I felt with all of my being. There was such a sense of emptiness around him, an absence, as if he were not a man but a thing long dead that had chosen to disregard its condition for reasons of its own. Or something terrible that had taken the guise of a human being but that could not fully perform the part. His face lacked expression, as if the muscles and tendons that controlled his features had been severed and left his visage in paralysis. Dülitz greeted the man with a nod and gestured to me.

When the man turned his head towards me, it was as if he did not see. He regarded me as if only air filled my place, as if I were a piece of furniture or a spot on the wallpaper behind me. When he spoke, it was with a toneless voice that did not betray any emotion or anticipation. Its only distinctive characteristic was a kind of stammer. It was as if certain sounds did not want to cross his lips but lodged in his mouth and forced him to pause in order to select a word better suited.

'The entire sum in bank notes, to be redeemed wherever you see fit.' The man handed an envelope to Dülitz, who broke the seal and checked the contents. He must have found them to his satisfaction because he nodded and then handed over in turn a package that must have contained the past due promissory notes that now steered my fate. The man tucked them into his coat pocket. Without a word, he turned to leave and gestured to me to walk in front of him up the stairs. I pulled my cap off my head and stopped in front of him.

'My name is Johan Kristofer Blix . . .'

He turned to me and looked straight at me for the first time and that was enough to silence me. In his pale eyes, which seemed to me to be too large and wide for the face in which they were placed, there was no pity, no compassion, only a repressed hatred of a kind I have never before experienced. A hate such as a desert landscape might feel towards the living travellers who have been foolish enough to test its dunes, as vanquishing and tenacious as eternity itself. I averted my gaze but felt his continue to sear my face. He took a step closer, enough that I felt his breath on my forehead, and even if I had wanted to back away, I did not dare move from my spot. After a long time he broke the silence.

'Someone has emptied their chamber pot in the alley outside. The lanterns did not light the cobblestones sufficiently until I perceived the smell of dung. Would you be so good as to clean my shoe?' Silence fell between us as I hesitated. Somewhere in the background, Dülitz and his goon were watching this scene but the man paid them no attention. When my uncertain gaze found its way back to his face, I was met only by the same dead eyes. He waited until I awkwardly fell to my knees and rolled my sleeve over my hand to use it as a rag. He shook his head.

'No, not like that.'

At first I did not understand what he meant. Each time I made an attempt to reach for the closer of his feet to brush away the dung, he corrected me in the same way, with the same impassive voice. When all other possibilities were exhausted, I lowered my face to the dirtied leather and stretched out my tongue, and for the first time he had no objection. He did not move in any way, did not shift his foot an inch to assist me in my work, and while I struggled not to vomit at the revolting taste, I had to crawl around to reach. I was weeping quietly and he did not betray any pleasure or distaste at my sobs or retching. It was as if I had stopped existing. When I was done, I stood on shaky legs. He stopped me.

'That wasn't the shoe I meant.' And afterwards, when I was done, he repeated his gesture towards the door without a word. I walked unsteadily up the stairs.

In the alley, there was a stage coach drawn by four horses. It had a covered top and openings on the side that could be pulled shut with leather coverings fastened along the frame. The driver had climbed down from his place and walked over to feed the horses from a haversack. The man who now owned my debts signalled to me to climb aboard. Even to the driver he was curt.

'Back.'

'All the way? Good sir, it's a long way, don't you wish to stay somewhere to rest?'

'No. All the way, with no stopping at inn or roadhouse.'

The driver muttered a reply which I did not catch. I heard the clinking of coins exchanging hands before the man sat down inside opposite me. A smack of the tongue and a flick of the reins set the coach in motion. We drove down the hill towards the water, over the drawbridge at the Lock and on along the Quayside.

The city went by and I recognized it from my waking dream on the hilltop above Skinner's Cove when blood ran in the gutters; a hunting ground where the strong pursued all who crossed their path. In the light from a lantern, I glimpsed Rickard Sylvan. He was leaning against a wall in the alley where men and boys go to sell themselves. He did not see me. In his eyes, I could glimpse nothing of that which had once set them alight, no roguish glint, no joy, not his infectious enthusiasm nor shrewd ingenuity. They had all gone out and all that remained were two dark wells of despair. It was the gaze of someone whose life flame had been extinguished, although the body staggered on and the lungs still pumped. My heart wanted to break in two.

We arrived at the Northern Tollgate by the Stablemaster's Inn after less than an hour's journey, and the driver made a stop at the customs buildings there. Above us was an ornate gateway with an arched door, large enough to let the carriages through. A groggy officer knocked on the side of the coach and tilted his lantern to cast light into our cabin.

'Good evening,' he said in a thick voice. 'Travelling late, are we?' He smothered a yawn. 'Might I trouble you for your papers?' The gentleman took a piece of paper out of his pocket. For my part, my dear sister, I had no passport as I did not enter the city with one. I had used untruths to be let in and had not dared show myself around the tollgates ever since. When I did not present any documents and simply sat there, the customs officer must have assumed that the man was my guardian and therefore directed his question to him rather than me. 'And the young sir's?' The gentleman's empty eyes turned for the first time and bored straight into the customs officer's, and he spoke with that dead voice, sounding like someone imitating the language of human beings without having heard it properly spoken.

'Tell me your name and that of your superior.'

'I am Johan Olof Karlsson, sir, and my superior officer's name is Anders Fris.'

'As you can see, Johan Olof, I am quite alone in this coach. There is no one else here.'

The officer met his gaze for a moment but then quickly looked down. He shot me a glance as I sat there, pale, blotchy and afraid, and I sensed a feeling of pity that turned the blood in my veins to ice. Without saying anything, the officer handed the passport back to the gentleman, turned away from us and thumped the side of the coach as a sign to the driver. It took me a while to realize what had disturbed me the most and it was this: I had not heard any cadence of dissembling in my host's speech, and sensed that from his perspective he had spoken the truth. I was nothing to him. But what was he going to do with me? This exceeded my understanding. I was filled with terrible thoughts and a foreboding that I had never felt before. Even during the war years in Karlskrona, death and terror went abroad so clothed that they were easy to recognize.

The rocking of the coach in the summer night made me drowsy and although I fought the impulse to fall asleep, I nodded off. It was impossible to tell for how long. I was awakened with a start when the wheels skidded in the tracks. You have never travelled beyond the borders of our home town, my sister, and never found yourself far from matches and embers as night falls, but I have, and out here is a kind of darkness that swallows everything and makes the world unrecognizable. Existence seems erased, the seeing is made blind. Not even the starlight has any power to bestow on the land any shape but a formless mass. As we drove, I could discern the outlines of spruces and pine trees in countless rows, a wide stretch of forest devoid of any points of light.

He did not move. He sat there with his blank face, staring out into the darkness through which we rode, his gaze pausing on nothing.

25

W E MUST HAVE continued through the night in the same rutted tracks as the milestones went by, for when I woke up it was light and when the coach made a stop I was almost thrown from the bench. The day that was dawning was grey. The summer heat seemed to have dissipated overnight. The gentleman was sitting straight across from me, as if fatigue could find no dominion over him. Wordlessly, he opened the door of the coach and stepped out. I followed.

'Is there a barn here where I can water my horses and a haystack for a wink of sleep?' the driver asked with a drained expression.

'There is nothing here for you or your horses,' the gentleman replied, digging a coin out of his pocket and tossing it to him. Our driver seemed satisfied with that, turned the coach around and disappeared along the same road that we had come.

We were standing on a gravel courtyard. In the centre, there was a fountain with a statue of a sitting woman surrounded by naiads and dolphins. No water flowed there anymore, but it was slowly seeping out of the openings and providing nourishment for a brown moss. It looked as if the stone itself was weeping, down into a pool so murky that the bottom was no longer visible. On the far side of the courtyard, there was a tall house with wings on either side. Around us was a dismal spruce forest and fields left fallow with crops rotting back into the earth. The house that had surely once been stately was now in decay.

Cracked plaster had fallen from the façade. Weeds were growing tall between the stones in the yard. There was no sign of life from the many outer buildings. Somewhere a dog was barking. I was overcome with terror and melancholy. Some calamity must have struck this place and left the grounds a blight on the landscape. It had surely once been beautiful. But no longer. The words were out of my mouth before I could stop myself.

'Where have we come? What is this place?'

I jumped back from his cane when I realized that I had spoken unbidden but my host surprised me instead by answering where he stood in the courtyard, turning to me as if waiting for my reaction, his eyes full of melancholy.

'This is the seat of my ancestors. No birds sing here any longer.'

I did not understand what he meant but had no intention of asking.

He waved to me to follow, but not to the big house. Instead we walked to the cluster of low buildings to the left, at the edge of the fields. He lifted a crossbar and let me in. My eyes had trouble adjusting to the dark but then I became aware of a presence, the feeling of being observed by someone waiting inside who did not wish me well. There was a stench of stale air and I took a step back when I heard a low growl in front of me. Then I saw it: an enormous shape, walking to and fro. It was a grotesque dog, the largest I had ever laid eyes on. I guessed that its withers must reach up to my chest and that its weight exceeded my own by far. Under the fur, muscles knotted up like lengths of anchor warp. I saw slime drip from its mouth and my death glitter in its eyes. The moment before its jaws would have closed on my throat, however, it was halted in mid-air and the clang of wood and metal on metal let me know that it was tethered. When my eyes had grown more accustomed to the light, I saw that rusty chains had been wrapped in a noose around its broad neck, with the other end attached to a wooden beam. My knees buckled and hit the boards and I crawled backwards while my eyes teared up at its smell and my face was spattered with the drool that flew from the beast with every breath.

'This is Magnus,' a voice said behind me. I felt my cap lifted from my head and I saw it thrown into the dark where the beast snapped at it. 'You will grow tired of my hospitality in time,' my host continued, 'and if you decide to leave this place of your own accord, you should know that the bolts holding Magnus fettered will be loosened. He will never forget your scent. He can feel the smell of your fear and the piss running down your leg and he will find you, alone out under the trees where there is no one to protect you. He will tear you to pieces and leave the remains for the ravens.' My host stepped past me and out of the building. I followed him.

———— • ————

As the exterior of the house had indicated, dear sister, its insides were in a state of dilapidation. Many windowpanes were cracked, and of many of the roof tiles only shards remained. It smelled strongly of mould and mildew; water must pour down inside from the trusses when the heavens opened. Wallpaper was warped with the humidity which had distorted their pattern so they tricked the eye. The wood floors were uneven and squeaked terribly with each step, the rooms were empty and unlit, the fabric in armchairs and sofas had become fragile and torn so that the filling was spilling out. In the large hall, my host gave me a few words over his shoulder before he turned his back to me and walked out again. 'Tomorrow our work begins.' I heard his steps cross the courtyard and found myself left to my own devices.

As I had not been assigned any sleeping quarters, I saw no option but to seek one out myself.

The expansive entry level of the building had been built for entertaining. There was a large room intended for dancing that stood empty and dark, with chairs stacked in a heap. The long table in the dining room had space for at least twenty, but the top had split down the middle and left a crack into the wood from end to end. Over the fireplace hung an oil painting but someone had disfigured it. To judge from the clothing, it depicted a man, turned towards the viewer, standing proudly in front of a fertile landscape. His hands were clad with rings and around his neck hung a medal suspended from a silk ribbon. His face was no longer discernible, my sister. Someone had cut it from the canvas. Above the shoulders there was now simply a hole with frayed edges. Much later I would find the remains of the portrait in the ashes below.

Above the stairs waited bedchamber after bedchamber, all empty. I selected one for myself. The mattress was damp and the bedframe decrepit so I decided instead to sleep on the floor with my knapsack as my pillow, as far from the door as possible and with my back to a corner.

I carried on my exploring, and at the far ends of the building were the larger chambers, surely once reserved for the masters of the house. On the west side there was another portrait, this time of a woman. She was wearing an old-fashioned dress. Her arms were raised in a gesture of invitation, as if to welcome the viewer into the painting. Her face had also been removed but more delicately than the angry slashes that had ruined the painting in the dining room. It did not take me long to find the missing piece of canvas. In the large bed that stood against the wall, some bundles of cloth had been placed in the shape of a woman's body as if lying on her back under the covers, and the face from the portrait had been carefully placed on the head. The mannequin's face smiled warmly but there was something else also, something that seemed to indicate other emotions. Whether this was a flaw in the subject herself or whether the artist had failed to do her justice, I could not tell. In the bed next to this strange figure there was a depression in the mattress and I realized that it was here that my host must spend his nights, lying on his side with one arm around the construction. My suspicion was to be confirmed during the nights that followed, for I could hear him through the closed doors of the room. He spoke with the doll at night, but I was never able to make out the actual words. Sometimes there were other sounds; I don't know if he was laughing or crying.

I returned to my chamber disturbed by what I had seen. I set a chair before the door, crept over to my corner, pulled my knees up under my chin and lay shaking with cold and agitation under I finally drifted off to sleep. At night, the house was full of rumours, my sister, as if the halls themselves were haunted by those who once lived here. I slept only in short increments. Dreams were mixed with memories as is so often the case in the borderlands between sleep and wakefulness, and I thought I heard shuffled footsteps in the corridor, screams of lust and pain and prayers for mercy, giggles, echoes of festivities which had long since faded away; believed I caught glimpses of men and women dressed in odd masks playing hide-and-seek among the rooms. Outside a dismal wind howled throughout the night and in the witching hour it began to rain, whereupon the air inside the house grew cold and damp and I heard the water pour straight onto the attic floor, two floors above me.

26

I WOKE UP IN response to the ethereal weight that can some-times be bestowed by a gaze wandering over the observed. When I opened my eyes, I found my host sitting on the bed that I had declined in favour of the floor.

'The hour is at hand,' he said to me. Once I had rubbed the grime out of my eyes, I hurried to my feet. I followed him out of the room, down the stairs and across the courtyard towards that set of buildings where Magnus was already greeting the morning with his deafening bark. I feared another encounter with the beast but we walked past his crooked shed to a small stone hut. My host opened the door with a large iron key and showed me in.

Behind the hall, in a large room with a sooty and extinguished fireplace, there was a table. Outstretched on the table was a man who could hardly have been older than I was. His hands and feet were bound with rope that had been tied under the table and that prevented him from moving. A stick had been jammed between his teeth and fastened with straps around his head. Behind this, one could glimpse the strip of fabric that had been pressed into his mouth to keep him silent. A rag was wound across his eyes. He was not awake. Next to the table there were a number of bottles with the sour smell of wine, as well as a funnel, and I presumed he must have been administered so much that he lost consciousness. He features were symmetrical and handsome, his hair shoulder length and – just as my own

– as blond as spun gold. I had hardly had time to absorb this alarming scene before the toneless voice behind my shoulder said: 'I have been told that you served as a surgeon's apprentice. Tell me, how many limbs have you severed in order to save the lives of the injured?'

'I have only used the saw and knife myself on a couple of occasions, but I was present countless times when my master performed these operations,' I answered with trepidation.

My host nodded.

'This is your patient now, Kristofer Blix. It is my wish that all of his limbs be separated from his body as if they had been savaged by grapeshot or bayonet. Both legs, both arms. In addition, I would like for him to be blinded. I want his tongue removed. I would like him deafened. This is the task that I give you in order to pay off your debt. His life is in your hands and if you lose it, whether from pity or inadequate care, then his fate will appear merciful next to yours. All tools and resources that you require will be made available to you. Is there any part of what I have said that you do not understand?'

My head was spinning. I could not believe what I had just heard. It was as if the nightmare scenes from Skinner's Cove had returned to torment me. My consternation caused me to forget my apprehension and leave all caution aside.

'No! I will not do this for any price, not even for my own freedom! Send me back to Stockholm and the courts and the gaol. I'd rather live twenty years in the workhouse than this!'

He shook his head.

'That is no longer an option. If you defy me in this, I will give you to the dog, alive and feet first.'

'But what has he done, tell me no? None can be deserving of a fate such as this!'

The man stood quietly for a while before he said, 'Make your choice.'

Through my sobs, I heard his slow breaths and I wiped my face on my sleeve. He did not need to wait for my answer as we both knew what it would be. He spoke again.

'He is sedated with wine and will remain so until the evening. By the time the sun sets, I would like to see his tongue removed. From there you may proceed in the order you find best. The pace should be as quick as possible without endangering his life. Under the table you will find a wooden case of the sort that naval surgeons use, all tools sharpened and in good condition. Anything else that you may need I would like to have announced at the moment it occurs to you.'

I could not stop crying but, with tears and snot running down my chin, I remembered Emanuel Hoffman's constant admonishments and the things he swore by in order to drive away those swamp gases that constantly threatened to spread putrefaction in the wounds of injured men. 'Juniper branches to smoke the room with,' I said. 'And spruce fir to spread on the floor. And vinegar.'

27

I WAS LEFT ALONE in the room with the bound man. My chest heaved to get more air and only after the several minutes it took to regain my breath, did I hear his. Thoughts of the horrific acts I was about to perpetrate on this young man who could have been my brother unleashed a panic in me, and I rushed out of the stone cottage. My host was nowhere to be seen. I had told him the truth. I had seen Emanuel Hoffman peel the skin and muscles back with a sure hand until the bone was revealed, fasten clamps around the arteries, steady himself by placing his knee on the injured man's shoulder, and after a couple of pulls of the saw have the damaged limb on the ground, whereupon the wound could be dressed. Far from everyone survived this intervention, and others pined during their convalescence. Rot found its way in between the stitches and caused the stump to blacken and smell, and death followed in the throes of fever thereafter. Hoffman had never let me perform this operation himself. We were both satisfied with me simply handing him the tools that he could not reach himself. How would I manage this?

I took the road past the shed where the monstrous Magnus was chained. The wall was so decrepit and dry that the logs had shrunk from one another and left gaps. I cupped my hands and stared into the darkness. Soon I could see him. He slowly rose to his feet when some animal sense alerted him that he was being watched. It seemed to me that he looked straight at me and met my gaze with hungry eyes. He was breathing through an open jaw, and before long saliva started to drip from between his yellow fangs. I saw myself on the ground with him over me; my feet between his chops, bite by bite up along my shins, crunching through my kneecaps like chestnuts. I started to cry again, dear sister, when I realized that it was not courage I needed to dismember another human being, just the cowardice of saving my own life at any price. It came to me all too quickly.

By the fountain, I remembered the pamphlet that Hagström had given me. I hurried up to my room, turned the knapsack inside out and started to read as quickly as I could. Here was help in the form of instruction and pictures of many procedures, including amputation and the tools necessary. Maybe the professor's thoughtfulness would once again become my salvation. But the tongue? Nowhere was such a thing described. It seemed I would be left to my own devices. The biggest challenge seemed to me the staunching of the blood flow. To bleed someone was beneficial in order to keep a person's fluids at a healthy balance, but only up to a point.

Since Hagström's text could not avail me, I chose to follow what Hoffman had taught me. He called it miasma, those invisible gases that rise from impurities deep underground and grope their way into the lungs of the healthy and the wounds of the injured. He was always dispatching me to find the things that helped the most and so now I went to look for a pantry. There was nothing to be found that smelled like vinegar, but beyond the empty shelves there was a door and behind that were some stairs leading down into a cellar. I found a small number of torch sticks to light my way underground and when I raised the flame above my head, I saw rows upon rows of dusty bottles. This was a wine cellar and, although it was vinegar I had asked for, I had many times set out bowls of wine to sour into vinegar in closed rooms for Hoffman. I gathered as many bottles as I could carry.

I found spruces in the forest as well as juniper. I did not have to go far. The spruce fir I spread on the floor around the bound man and the juniper branches I lit until they smouldered and gave off a thick white smoke. I waited until the smoke filled the room before I stamped out the glowing embers.

In the chest under the table I found all of the tools that I knew from Hoffman, even if these were cleaner and did not look as if they had ever been put to use. Here were the tongs, the saw, the knives. I tested their edges against my left thumbnail and found them sharp.

I now intended to take out his tongue, dear sister. I undid the strap that kept the stick wedged between his teeth, lifted out the wet ball of cloth that had been pressed in behind it and loosened the binding that had been tied around his eyes. I made a small fire in the hearth and placed an iron poker in it so that it was licked by the flames. It slowly took on a glowing red hue, fading to white as the heat increased. I carved a wedge that I pressed in between his teeth to keep his jaws open. Then I tilted his head to the side so that the blood would not run down his throat. When I lifted the knife, my hands were shaking so much that I despaired. I poked my fingers into his mouth, warm and wet, and felt around, but found it impossible to form a secure grip on the tongue. Again and again, the slippery point slipped from between my thumb and forefinger. I thought back to the feeling of trying to grip the lizard in its glass container. I gave up, put the knife down and walked out of the room. I took one of the wine bottles, a Tokay, smashed the neck in the absence of a better way to remove the cork, and drank it down until my throat burned and my white linen shirt was stained.

The sun was on its way down. It wasn't evening yet but close. I sat with my arms drawn around my knees, rocking back and forth. Only then did I hear him behind me, only a few slurred words through the considerable state of intoxication he had been forced into. He was speaking in his sleep, mumbling: 'We are indebted to . . .'

I would hardly be able to manage the task I had been assigned with my patient unconscious. If he were awake, I would have no chance. I flew up from my seat, invigorated by the wine. The glowing poker filled the room with its smell, distinct even through the heavy scent of juniper. In a mood of hopelessness, I turned over the medical chest and started to root through the various instruments. In my foolishness, I actually managed to help myself. I soon saw the tools I should have been using. Here were both pliers and scissors. I grabbed them and held the tongue fast, only to realize that the root of the tongue was still beyond the reach of the scissors. I ran back to the tools, picked up a small hammer and a chisel with a flat end. What I was now preparing to do was something I had seen Hoffman perform on some of his unfortunate patients, even though my stomach had turned at the sight. I turned the man's head so that the jawbone was positioned closely against the table, placed the tip of the chisel on the teeth along the jaw and struck with the hammer until I heard the roots give way. I moved the chisel and struck again and again. Finally only the lacerated gums and craters filled with pale shards remained where his teeth had just been. Now the scissors had room to manoeuvre. I cut his tongue as close to the root as I could manage. When I reached for the poker, I wasn't thinking straight and grabbed it with my bare hand and, for the first time since Karlskrona, smelled the stench of singed flesh. I swore, wrapped my sleeve around the end and placed the glowing white end of the heated metal into the stream of blood issuing from the bound man's mouth.

It was only then that he screamed, my sister. And that wasn't the worst of it. The worst was when he opened his eyes and looked straight at me.

That look will follow me to my grave.

28

I HAVE A GREAT deal of time to write now, my dear sister, as summer draws to a close. The assignment I have been given leaves me with many hours of leisure a day. The wounds need time to heal and I have to be attentive to my patient's ability to regain his strength. My duties are often limited to his daily care. I feed him gruel, I wash him and see to all of his needs. Often when he becomes unsettled and starts howling, I give him wine, which he does not always want and then I have to use the funnel. I can't bear to listen to him. He grows calmer as the alcohol takes effect.

The same can be said of me. I make frequent visits to the wine cellar to fetch new bottles and drink as much and as often as I dare. What I do in this spare time does not seem to bother my host. He has seen me trip in the corridors as I stagger between the cellar and my room but has never said a word. There is no joy in my drunkenness, but it is still to be preferred to the state of sobriety. At least it makes the images that stream in my mind's eye a little more blurry. Can you fathom the horror of placing the blade of a knife against an eye and applying pressure until you reach a place in all the white where something is forever lost? Scenes like these play in my head over and over again as I close my eyes.

When I remove a new part, I give it to Magnus. I see fingers and toes disappear in his red maw, listen to how he cracks bones between his jaws to expose the marrow. He stares at me from his corner as if he is trying to tell me something: '*You next.*'

———•———

The continuous effects of the wine make it hard to tell dream from reality. The patterns in the wallpaper sway and appear to move like tentacles when I pass, ready to snare me if I come too close. Down in the cellar, when I went down late one night to fetch more wine, I saw a rat king in the light of the candle, a swarm of screeching vermin with their tails tied together in a knot. Or did I dream it? It crawled along the wall with a terrible noise and disappeared in a corner. It is said to be an omen. I drink excessively before bed, both to help me sleep and to avoid waking up sober.

———•———

One night I was awakened by a sound close to me and became aware of my host, who had entered my chamber, rifled through my things, and was now sitting on the bed and reading what I have written for you, my sister. These unsent letters that are intended for you and for no one else. If this was not also a dream, I heard him laughing.

———•———

Hagstrom's pamphlet is of great assistance in my work. There are drawings that show how a limb is best separated from the body, where the cut is to be made and how to spare a flap of skin to fold back over the stump. First, I apply a tourniquet that I have fashioned from a leather bridle I have taken from one of the stables and cut to size. I treat the leather with lard to make it supple and strong so it will not break when I pull it as tight as I can muster.

———•———

I don't have much of an appetite, dear sister, which is good since I have to dig for my rations in the distended fields. What keeps my host alive, I don't know. Maybe he has stores of food that only he knows about. My shirt hangs and I have trouble keeping my breeches from sliding down. Lately I have had to use a piece of string to keep them on my hips. The portrait in the dining room haunts me. My host has told me it is his father. He says he hates him. In my dreams, I see a man in fine clothing fumble his way around the rooms of the house, an absence where his head should be. He is searching for his son in order to lock him in either stranglehold or embrace, I don't know which.

Yesterday, I made preparations to separate the left arm from its shoulder. Only it and the leg on the opposite side remain. After this day, I must find a new way to keep my patient bound to the table as hardly any limbs remain to which I can fasten leather-bound chains. I sharpened my knife and tested each tooth of the saw. I splashed vinegar onto the floor and walls, brought in fresh spruce fir and smoked the room until the air was cleansed. I had just made a noose of my leather bridle and inserted a piece of wood in order to wind it as hard as I could when I noticed something. The sun fell in and something glimmered on his finger. It was a ring, my sister, on the smallest finger of the left hand. I must have glimpsed it before but not paid it any mind until now. I bent down in order to inspect it more closely. The ring was made of gold with an oval setting. I spat on the hand and twisted it off the finger – the hand clawed at me with its dirty nails but I was quick enough to avoid being scratched. In the centre of the ring, there was a dark stone with a coat of arms carefully etched into its surface. My head spun as if something had physically struck me. I let the bridle hang and walked out to sit down on the stone step of the front door.

Far away I could hear a raven cawing, in the highest branches of a birch tree. I sat there for a long time, staring at the ring. It was of a kind that noblemen wear with a coat of arms to represent the

179

ancestral line. Even though I had never learned his name, it could be ascertained by someone capable of reading the heraldry.

I began to tremble while my thoughts whirled. Fate had given me this chance to do a single tiny kindness to the nameless one that I had sinned against more abhorrently than anyone could against their worst enemy. But how? I began to walk to and fro outside the cottage. The wine I had consumed made it hard for me to think. When I heard a voice behind me, I thought I would have a stroke and fall dead on the spot.

'How goes it with the left arm? I see your shirt is yet unstained. Why the delay?'

My host was standing right behind me. He could move in almost total silence. I felt the hairs on my neck stand up and heard the lie in my voice when I answered, as I tightened my grip on the little circlet of metal. 'No reason, sir. I was just about to begin.'

As usual, his expression betrayed nothing, his eyes as impassive as a dark tarn under the night sky.

'What are you holding so tightly in your hand? Your knuckles are white. Show me.'

I bent my head, stretched my hands out in front of me and then opened the palms. Both empty. Familiar as I was with his unnatural sense for everything one tried to conceal from him, I had dropped my secret in the grass behind me.

He stared at me for a long time as I stood there with two shaking hands stretched in the air.

'Stop wasting time. You are getting thinner by the day and you will be no good to me if you starve before your assignment is completed.'

With these words, he turned and left. When I heard his footsteps on the courtyard I threw myself down for the ring. His parting words had given me an idea which I had not previously had the power to conceive.

Back inside, I put my hand on the patient's cheek. His face was still beautiful, although there were empty sockets behind his wrappings and his cheeks were sunken where his teeth were missing. I had never touched him in this way before and it appeared to calm him. I took the ring between my thumb and forefinger and held it to his lips. Once he had felt its shape, I laid it in his mouth and fetched a glass of water. I let him drink and listened to his deep sips. I parted his lips and looked. No glint of gold could be seen. He had swallowed it.

My host had a plan for this wretch. This deliberate maiming must be part of that plan. But my patient will now carry evidence of his name and origin in his belly. How I do not yet know, now that I will soon have removed all of his remaining limbs and robbed him of his ability to manage in the world, but perhaps someone will find it and trace it back here, to the monster who is responsible for this abomination.

I do not know if my patient can still hear. On the third day, on the explicit orders of my host, I pushed a stick into my patient's ear as far as it would go and my host himself tested his hearing by clapping loudly and without reaction. Nonetheless I bent down and put my mouth close to one ear and said: 'If the ring comes out, I will give it to you again to swallow after I have cleaned it off. When the two of us part ways, you will have to take over this responsibility if you wish to keep it. How you should do this, I cannot say.'

He gave no sign that he understood. Then I cut away his left arm, carried it over in a bucket to Magnus's shed and then on to the wine cellar to drink myself senseless. I still could not sleep. As has been my practice for a long time, I mix my ink from soot and water, dip my nib and write to you, dear sister, my only friend.

Do you remember, my dear sister, how we would talk of a world beyond this one, during the spring nights when I knelt by your bed until the birdsong started and the first rays of the sun shone in through the window? How we would imagine a peaceful meadow beyond this valley of misery, where we planned one day to run hand in hand through the summer flowers without worries or fears, a place where no sorrow or strife could ever reach us? When our legs would tire, we would seek the shade under the trees, soothed by the breeze. We would drink sweet water from a spring and eat our fill of apples and wild raspberries. We would laugh together, far, far away from fever-plagued Karlskrona, where the rowboats came in every day from the fleet's winter moorings, their decks covered with blue-black corpses to unload at the shoreline. We would be as happy together as only a brother and sister can be.

I dream of meadows and wild raspberries no longer, dear sister. They are forever ruined for me. It is said that innocence, once lost, can never be regained, and this summer has stolen my dreams from me. How could I ever feel happiness or joy again after what I have seen and done?

Almost four years have gone by since the fever took you from me, my sister, and your heart stopped beating, and the sheet that I had just washed lay still across your chest and I realized that you drew breath no more, and that there was nothing else for me to do except dig your grave and bind a wreath of spring blooms to place on the earth, and fashion two branches into a cross to raise over your final resting place.

I no longer pray that you are waiting for me in the shade under that tree, with roses on your cheeks and in the white linen dress Mother gave you on the birthday that would be your last. Instead I pray that you lie still in the earth where I left you and that no Elysian field awaits us after death where you can ever learn of the things I've done. And that I myself will soon find solace in a pit just as dark, where only oblivion remains and nothing more.

PART THREE

The Moth and the Flame

Spring 1793

Feeling! Life! Where did you go?
In this abyss through which I fall,
Now shadows force me to recall
Times that long ago did flow.
This darkened path that is my fate,
These clouds that cover me of late,
These veils which all my thoughts deprave,
This cold that chills my every vein,
This weakness – all serve to explain
That I'm already in the grave.

– Johan Henric Kellgren, 1793

29

ANNA STINA KNOWS that fire is a game of angles and space. That whatever is to burn must be carefully arranged, given enough room for the flame to take hold. It is like a living thing, fire, and like everything else it must breathe. Those fires of carefully split wood that she lights in the hearth in Katarina parish are more challenging than what now stands before her. The stack is composed of bundles of kindling and firewood that will burst into flames the moment it is put to the torch. The officiant is waiting for the stroke of seven. When the watchman in the Katarina tower calls the hour, this bonfire will be lit for Saint Walpurga.

Anna Stina used to be afraid of fire. In the tales of her childhood, it was always the monster, described by those who had seen the wooden houses of the city reduced to cinder with their own eyes. But Anna Stina is a child of another time, raised in a Stockholm built of stone, not timber, and as the years go by it is harder to see the connection between that ravenous firestorm and the warming, helpful glow of the cooking fire. So also this evening, when for a few hours it is allowed to grow large, but kept tame, fed, guarded and surrounded by hose and bucket.

The evening is warm but there is a refreshing breeze from the lake. It is welcome since it puts Children's Lea upwind from the Larder, which has thawed enough that the stench is almost rendered visible by plumes of flies. Between spring and summer, the light of evening is most pleasant. Gone are the pitch black winter months when the night wanderer has to find his way down the street by feeling with outstretched arms, from the faint cat's eye of one lantern to the next, and when anything dropped is hopelessly lost in the gutter and the only hope is to ingratiate oneself with the water bearers the next morning, or simply remain standing in place to await the dawn. Of all the seasons, spring is the one Anna Stina likes the best. It is full of promises the year has not yet had a chance to break. All seems possible.

She is not alone in her rejoicing. The meadow is full of people. Children, paupers and ragamuffins from Katarina and Maria parish are sitting in the grass, right next to workers from the manufactories, those who have time and energy left over at day's end. A little further away are the fine folk, factory owners with friends from the City-between-the-Bridges, a party of noblemen and women in beautiful clothing of satin and lace. Sitting next to her is Anders Petter, the neighbour's boy. He is a few years older than her, and already in training to follow in his father's footstep and go to sea. One day he will step off the quay and walk with assurance along the gangplank, while white sails will take him out across the sea. She envies him, and feels fettered to the city by chains that, though invisible, do not bind her any the less.

The wind from the water grows stronger. She pulls her knees up under her chin, and at the same time she hears the call from up above. The torch is brought to the base of the bonfire, where the flames greedily lick at the twigs and branches. It quickly grabs hold and climbs towards the top. A tumult breaks out among those assembled when it turns out that the call did not in fact come from the church tower but from impatient guttersnipes impersonating the voice. But what is done is done. A fire guard sets off half-heartedly up the slope to hunt down the young delinquents, who in practised fashion disperse in all directions under hails of laughter, but the officiants shrug their shoulders. The joy spreads. Bottles of brandy go from hand to hand. Dusk grows ever deeper. The fire, now a luminous claw grabbing at the stars, makes it hard to make out anything but silhouettes. One of them is unmistakeable: an overzealous figure caught in a policeman's catchpole and kept helplessly at a distance by a long handle, while the jaws have sprung shut around his throat. He flails and tries to run in this direction and then in that. His colourful language and feisty character have won him a following of laughing observers. Only when the group has passed by does Anna Stina notice that Anders Petter has put his hand over hers.

Anna Stina has always known that this day was coming. She is not naive. Anders Petter had been a good companion as they played together but now they have grown older and his interest has long since extended past friendship. She has nothing against him – he is agreeable in nature and easy on the eye, with his dark hair and blue eyes – but she does not feel ready for the step that he wants to take. She has no longing for togetherness, no more than her mother, Maja, who has managed by herself all of her days. Another evening, perhaps, and maybe not even that far in the future, but not tonight. She has been expecting a moment like this one, has lain awake at night and wondered how she should submit her rejection without hurting their friendship. It surprises her that her reaction comes of its own accord, faster than she can control it. She pulls away her hand. In the silence that follows, she does not know what to say. She is grateful that the darkness is thick enough to conceal her blushing. Instead it is Anders Petter who speaks.

'You know that I am fond of you, Anna. I always have been.'

Words fail her.

'You will soon be of marriageable age, Anna. Your mother doesn't have her health. When she is gone, you will have no one. We can go to the priest, Anna, and have the banns read for us . . .'

His voice fades away until nothing is left. She still does not know what to say. She hates herself for it, feels his wound deepen with her silence. It is as if she were a slab of marble, dropped among the grassy tufts of Children's Lea on its way towards the great Sergel's chisel.

———•———

It is his sobbing that rouses her. She can't see him any longer but she hears the same boy she has comforted over skinned elbows or the blue-black bruises he had from a father who knew how to wield a hazel switch. As a child, Katarina parish was not the decrepit shanty town that they learned to see only with age, but a fantastic land of adventures and fun. The ideas were hers but without him they would not have been possible. She made the roof of a shed into the deck of a ship bound for China and India, while stones and woodchips were the porcelain and jade that would make their fortune. When summer rains brought torrents of water that gushed from the paths down the mountainside, they fought fire side by side. Anna Stina described the flames that only she could see while Anders Petter struggled and laughed with a leaky bucket. With her imagination, she reshaped their days. For a long time, she thought that was why he liked her so.

Once more her reaction comes straight from the heart, without thought or calculation. She turns around and embraces him, wrapping her small arms around his shaking frame, and feels how he has hidden his face in his hands. She rocks him back and forth as she has always done. He answers, wrapping his arms around her and laying his face against her neck while she strokes his hair. It is a cathartic embrace and Anna Stina has time to think that all will be well before his lips seek out hers. He covers her mouth with his as his arms hold her tight. When she pulls away, he follows and together they fall onto the grass. He changes position over her, pressing her onto the ground with heavy hips and when she wants to protest, his tongue is in her mouth.

Anna Stina feels a confusion as if from a misunderstanding. Fear follows closely. Anders Petter knows that he has been told no. Maybe he hopes that in the heat of the kissing he will get her into a different mindset, that a becoming modesty and thoughts of her honour were the only reasons to reject him, that she is actually grateful for this persistence so that she can pretend the responsibility is his alone. Whatever sounds Anna Stina makes are smothered by Anders Petter's mouth – first the attempts to talk to him, then her calls for help. Now she feels panic, and Anders Petter's chest and shoulders pin her to the ground while with his knees he is trying to pry her thighs apart. Something is about to be taken from her that she has not wanted to give and she can't do anything about it.

No. She sucks on his lower lip and lets her teeth bite down as hard as they can, tasting a hot saltiness as if from liquid metal. When he pulls away she manages to hit him, one slap, then two. The arms that have been pinning her on her back are suddenly needed to stop the flow of blood, the pressure that has been over her is eased and Anders Petter rolls off her and into the grass.

Both of them are crying. Anna Stina is the one who stops first. She stretches out a hand to touch Anders Petter again, as a friend, as if to say that what has happened can be forgiven, but it is as if her hand sears his shoulder. He pulls away with a jerk, gets to his feet and starts to run up the slope.

Afterwards Anna Stina can remember how much she managed to think about during the brief time it took. The conflicted feelings. Part of her whispered that the fault was her own, that what was happening was something natural, that advances like this should have been welcome. They have known each other their entire lives. Why not also in this way? One sees this everywhere in the slums of Katarina parish, how the relationships of childhood ripen into something more serious. How many are not begun with scenes like this, where the boy who has become a man knows best and the girl who has become a woman has to be forced to see reason?

Anna Stina waits a while before she gets up. Down by the shore, the fire is a glowing heap that will soon be reduced to ash. A toothless old man with his hat tilted and tangles in his beard is sitting close by above her and grinning at her, with one hand in his trousers, which are stained with dirt and vomit. He has been sitting there the whole time. He sends a streak of tobacco juice shooting out between a gap in his front teeth.

'I'd been hoping for a better show, but I'm sure you'll soon find a partner with a little more gumption and then I'd appreciate it if you sent word to a poor wretch who would be happy to pay a shilling to watch.'

He slaps his thigh and laughs at his own words. She shivers with distaste, brushes the grass from her clothing and takes the same way as Anders Petter, back towards Katarina parish.

30

WITH SPRING COMES warmer weather, and with warmer weather comes the fever. It quickly spreads and even though it takes both old and young, rich and poor, it strikes hardest among the weak. As long as Anna Stina can remember, her mother Maja has laboured as a washerwoman on Children's Lea, her back bent over wool and linen, shoulder to shoulder with other women. Every spring she falls ill. It has always been that way. The fever seems to gain easy access to the manufacturing houses even though they keep the windows closed to the unhealthy fumes of the city, and Maja Knapp is always among those affected. It starts as a soreness in the throat with swelling along both sides of the jaw. During the night she grows hot, kicks off the blankets and sweats copiously. Come morning, she stays in bed. She alternates between freezing and burning up and Anna Stina, who shares the same blanket, has to accept being in turn embraced or pushed away. Maja does not want to eat anything and hardly drinks. Every bite must be coaxed down.

Sometimes she raves. Her speech comes in a steady gush, as if she can't help it, sometimes with words that no one can understand, sometimes with a clarity as if she were awake and in full possession of her senses. Tonight, while Anna Stina tries to ease her lips open for spoonfuls of mild soup, she talks about the fire. She, like many other old people from the area, names it the Red Rooster, the calamity that consumed almost all of

Maria parish in the year 1759, when Maja Knapp was no more than a few years out of her mother's belly. Anna Stina has heard the story more times than she can remember but never like tonight. In the grip of her chills, Maja speaks without inhibitions and the details come as clearly as if she were seeing them in front of her very eyes. It is the story of how they came to Katarina parish.

—•—

Maja Knapp was born in Maria parish and she was in her family home that day, a summer when the warm weather had gone from blessing to drought. In the yard between the houses she was fashioning a farmstead out of pine cones and sticks, with cobblestones as buildings and pine needles as paling. Her father and mother were both out, working the fields beyond Danto, and while the neighbour's wife, too old to do anything else and lame on her left side, kept an eye on Maja between naps, she could play for hours in the shade of the linden tree.

It was already afternoon when the the Maria bells started to peal erratically. Two clear tones, repeated again and again, shortly before four o'clock. Soon the Katarina tower answered and a moment later the same signal came from all three towers on the City-between-the-Bridges. Then the same from the other side of Gilded Bay, from Klara, Jacob and Hedvig, and then the clock tower high up on Brunke's Ridge. Soon a gun answered from the shipyard with a double salute, two sharp bangs, over and over. All around town, flags were hoisted to mark the spread of the flames, their colours a warning of which direction to avoid.

The smell came after a while, a sharp odour of smoke. It stung her eyes. The forerunners of the fleeing mass started to appear in the streets, people who had loaded whatever possessions they most wanted onto carts or their backs. During the first half an hour, there were few enough of them to allow those who lived near the church a hope that the blaze would be extinguished. All hope died with the rats.

They came in a grey wave, up from cellars and storehouses and harbour warehouses, all rushing in the direction of the sea. As everyone knows: when the grey brethren flee for their lives, all is lost. In their wake came panic. An hour after the church bells had started to toll, the wind grew stronger, pushing the smoke in front of it and bathing all of Maria parish in twilight.

A young boy came running to help lead away the neighbours. He didn't give Maja so much as a look, and only as he was on his way out did his conscience make him pause.

'Girl! Run! The fire is coming from Danto and Horn's Tollgate. Run for the Lock!'

But having been sternly instructed not to enter the street on her own, she chose to wait until the smoke made her eyes water and turned every breath into a cough. Out on the street, she quickly lost her way. She had never before stepped past the threshold of her home, and the smoke erased the most memorable markers – the church spires, the windmills. The crowd frightened her. Heavy feet in wooden clogs, wagon wheels and wheel barrows. Rather than be trampled against the mud and stone, she chose to hide in the gap between two walls. Down by the ground there was still cool air to breathe and with her cheek against the earth she waited. Out of the haze in the west came terrible noises. Cows and horses that had been left tethered were broiled where they stood and howled their dying anguish. Maja Knapp was still in her hiding place four hours later when the sun went down and the stream of fleeing people had stopped. Only then did she dare to creep out, and she saw then how the sky was burning.

It was on the cobblestoned street that she caught her first glimpse of the Red Rooster. Higher than the Maria church tower, and with showers of sparks reaching far up in the heavens, he climbed the slope from the edge of the bay to the top of the hill with a thundering roar. He swallowed everything in his path. Flames burst up from the dry timber of the ramshackle wooden houses. They besieged the stone buildings of the rich from all sides, took a sooty hold of the pillars and ornamental finishes of the façades, shattered the windows and turned the interiors into an oven hot enough to incinerate furniture and tapestries. When the copper roof tops were seared long enough they shot up from the rafters, held aloft on the hot winds like red bats with torn wings. The heat of the Red Rooster's breath brought blisters to her skin. She would bear the marks that he left on her for the rest of her days.

Some distance down the street, she saw a one-legged man struggling on his crutch with the fire at his heels. When the crutch got stuck between two stones and was wrested from his grip, he tried to crawl. His clothes and wig started to smoulder as he screamed wordlessly and suddenly his wig was ablaze. His high-pitched shrieks continued for some time. That was when she finally started to run, crying and screaming, away from the inferno, her blackened face streaked with tears. Around her sparks were flying and igniteding new fires wherever they landed. It seemed to her as if she were running through a luminous autumn forest, with flames falling instead of leaves.

———•·•———

Her mother was waiting, desperate, at the Southern Square where the inhabitants had been forced down towards the Lock and packed in tight by city guards with bayonets. She never saw her father again.

The fire was still raging a day later. Maja and her mother at first subsisted on donations from the parish. Later the landowner at Danto took pity on them. Nothing remained of their home. Her father's body could not be distinguished from others'. Overnight, a generation was reduced to miserable wretches, doomed to wander the rest of their days along the city streets in rags and drunkenness, ghosts of the people they had once been. Three hundred manors and houses no longer existed. Some twenty blocks had been razed to the ground.

As she grew into adulthood, Maja Knapp saw them rise again from the ashes, but now in stone. The wooden houses of her childhood were gone. The carpenter starved while the mason grew rich. Maja Knapp and her mother were forced to move to Katarina parish, where the worn old wooden tenement buildings still stood, a mess of angles and recesses with additions built on every which way so that the landlords could make more money; one stray spark away from becoming a new death trap for the destitute. That's where she stayed, found a man, bore a daughter of her own. The father disappeared at the same moment her belly became visible.

— • —

Anna Stina lays her hand on her mother's forehead. Maja Knapp is burning up and her breath is weak. It must be the heat of the fever that makes her remember Maria parish in the grip of the Red Rooster. Anna Stina feels a lump in her throat. She doesn't want to leave her mother alone but she has no choice. She has to run for help even though she has nothing to offer in return.

When she throws her shawl around her shoulders and opens the door to dash out, she is surprised by the fact that someone is standing outside: Boman, the sexton from Katarina Church. He is young, with hopes of one day taking over as the parish shepherd. He smells so strongly of spirits that he must have helped himself to the bottle in the moments before Anna Stina opened the door. But she has not been expecting any help and wonders who asked the bell ringer to come. She has no time to waste on gratitude.

'Mother Maja has the fever. Please pray for her while I run to the apothecary.'

———•———

When Anna Stina returns half an hour later she is empty-handed. Josef Karlsson, the apothecary, is out for the evening, and his wife's opinion was that he would already be so affected by the punch that it would make no difference even if Anna Stina ran all the way out to the Royal Pasture to fetch him.

A silence has descended on the household. Even the families they share the building with stand still in their doorways when Anna Stina returns. Boman stands next to the bed with his hands folded in prayer. The sheet has been pulled over Maja's face and at first Anna Stina does not understand why. Boman clears his throat and the words he speaks sound uncomfortably ceremonial in his youthful voice.

'Anna Stina, your beloved mother Maja Knapp has left us, may God have mercy on her soul.'

He mumbles a few more words that she does not hear. Anna Stina feels her knees about to buckle under her. She loses her breath, as if she has been punched in the stomach. The injustice is more than she can bear. Maja Knapp, who has supported her only daughter on her own for so long, who has patiently borne the contempt of her fellow parishioners on account of her illegitimate child, who has worn out her body in physical labour every day – did she endure all this only to die alone and without comfort? It is too much. Anna Stina's entire body shakes. Boman struggles to find the right words as he speaks up once again.

'It was not for Mother Maja's sake that I came here tonight. I come with a message from the pastor, and Anna Stina should know that neither one of us could have known in advance what fate held in store this evening. I believe it was providence that

196

Mother Maja had a man of God by her side during her final moments.'

Boman stops and has to rub the bridge of his nose for a while before he can continue.

'We have received a letter that contains a testimony against you. You are hereby summoned before the Consistory in order to face the accusations of whoring and intent to lure the innocent into sin. The pastor would like to speak with you first.'

31

'AND HOW IS it that you earn your keep, Anna Stina?'
Elias Lysander is short and round; nearing fifty years of age, he is almost as wide as he is tall. The black cleric's coat is pulled tightly across his chest and belly, and his double chin swells over his collar. The room where he receives visitors is dimly lit, its walls clad in linen that have grown sooty and grimy the past decades. What was intended to create a serious and solemn impression has been lost amidst the clutter. Books and ledgers are stacked next to inkwells and clay pipes. Lysander receives her seated behind his desk while she stands on the floor in front of him. Anna Stina has hardly ever seen the pastor away from the pulpit. He seems both larger and strangely diminished at the same time. This close, he smells of sweat and smoke and his morning herring can still be detected on his breath At the same time, the power that he wields is more evident now that it is directed not at a multitude but at her alone. The voice is the same, a strong voice that demands attention with inherent dignity. She cannot prevent her own words from trembling when she answers him.

'I sell fruit out of a basket and am allowed to keep a portion of the profits.'

Lysander nods as if this answer confirms what he already knows. He lets some time pass before he continues and he keeps his gaze fastened on Anna Stina, who does not know if she should meet it or not.

'Sexton Boman tells me that your mother Maria Knapp has left us.'

'Maja. My mother's name is Maja.'

Anna Stina's voice is low and weak. Lysander shoots a venomous look with his bloodshot eyes at Olof Boman. The latter is standing in a corner with his hands on his back, feigning ignorance. Anna Stina straightens her back in the pregnant silence.

'Was.'

Lysander shakes off his irritation.

'The Lord giveth and the Lord taketh away, Anna Stina, and you should take comfort in the fact that your mother is now in a better place.'

Lysander appears momentarily confused about how to steer the conversation from this grief counselling to the matter at hand. He is hungover from the night before and his traditional series of breakfast drams has not managed to lessen his headache. With a measure of chagrin, he decides that in the absence of a more elegant solution he will have to get straight to the point.

'Have you given any thought to how you will support yourself in your mother's absence? Maja Knapp was unmarried, your father has never been heard from and there doesn't seem to be a fiancé in the picture although you are of age.' She has asked herself the same question and doubts that the answer that will not satisfy even herself will be enough for Elias Lysander. Barely a day has gone by since Maja was carried out of their building on a stretcher on the way to the paupers' graveyard at the church. Anna Stina has provided for her burial as best she could.

'I may be able to keep my room for a lower rent. Or else perhaps my landlord has a smaller room for me. In this way, I think I will manage room and board. I think I will be able to sell more if grocer Jansson lets me, and I am willing to work longer hours.'

Lysander and Boman exchange knowing looks.

'And what kind of fruit do you sell, Anna Stina?'

She senses the threatening undertow in his tone of voice.

'Lemons when they are in stock, or else plums and berries. Apples in late summer and in the autumn.'

Lysander regards her sternly.

'Anna Stina, do you know what is said of young women who sell fruit from baskets?'

She knows. She does not manage to meet his gaze when she answers.

'Many of them sell themselves for money and hardly carry any fruit at all.'

She has met them herself in the streets and among the courtyards, has seen girls she has worked with come out of the stairwells with hair on end, their dresses in disarray and with the same amount of fruit in their baskets as in the morning. All of them dream of finding a beau. All of them know the stories. They have always happened to the friend of a friend: once she was one of them, but now she dances among barons in jewelled necklaces, her hair curled in styles so high and magnificent that the chandeliers are set a-jingle as she passes by. Some of the girls manage their toil on the mattresses and in the stairwells better than others. Some take it in their stride, others suffer, few last very long. They disappear. Where they go, no one can say. Some of them leave their baskets behind not for the beautiful ballrooms and society affairs, but for some house of ill repute where they abandon their given names and spend days and nights on their backs while guests take turns to mount them. The alleys of the city have a name for such fallen women; they are known as 'butterflies of the night', and every night they swarm.

'Anna Stina, you and Mother Maja seem to have been living quite comfortably without a man in the house. You were both conceived in sin. It seems you must have earned a considerable amount from the goods in your basket. And now you stand here before me and say that it is your lemons that have so pleased your customers?'

Anna Stina feels the blood rush to her face. Her blushing will probably be read as another sign of her guilt. She does not know what to say. What is true appears to have been labelled a lie from the outset. Pastor Lysander leans forward, steeples his fingers and continues without waiting for her answer.

'You do well to keep quiet, my girl. Others bear witness to your sinful ways. Katarina parish may be blighted by poverty, but if you think there are no virtuous folk here ready to make a stand for that which is right and proper, then you are sorely mistaken.'

Elias Lysander finds himself wishing that he could have been left in peace this morning, alone with his tobacco in a chair carried out into the garden. He finds this process as exhausting as it is predictable. How dare the girl ply her barefaced lies on him, he who has lived and worked in Katarina parish for years and who knows this old story backwards and forwards? The daughter a harlot like her mother, generations upon generations that lead all the way back to the Fall of Man. They are of a kind that do not fear God, cannot tell right from wrong, are as susceptible to the lusts of the flesh as beasts in the field, simple heathens who only bow to Mammon, Bacchus and Venus. It has only grown worse as the century has worn on and for Lysander the burden becomes heavier every year.

The firestorm of fifty-nine plunged Maria parish into abject squalor, and when the stone houses were raised and the new rents with them, it was Katarina that had to take in the most unfortunate. Elias Lysander has to answer to God on behalf of these souls but, however much he toils, it is never enough. The sessions before the Consistory of the church, where the ever-dirty laundry of his parish is aired before priests from all parts of the city – from

Klara, Maria, Jakob, Nikolai and Hedvig Eleonora – these are the worst. He has started to fortify himself for these events with a few drams, but not even the brandy can take the edge off the humiliation he feels before colleagues who observe with malice what is plain to all: that Elias Lysander is a poor shepherd of his flock. Yet another sheep has lost its way, and he is powerless to prevent it. Outrage at the injustice of his position suddenly overwhelms him.

'Anna Stina Knapp, there is no point in lying. Natanael Lundström and his wife Klara Sofia, both God-fearing people who have contributed to the well-being of the parish through their donations and prayers, have submitted testimony in writing about how you have tried to lure their son, the sailor's apprentice Anders Petter, into corruption. With womanly guiles, you have lured him away, exposed your shame and rolled your hips, offering yourself and in all ways attempting to seduce him into breaking sacrament. Like so many other women before you, you want nothing more than to find an Adam for your Eve, to tempt him and to lead him astray. What you do with your basket is clear for all to see, and the Lundströms know it all too well. I see no reason to doubt their statements.'

Lysander stops himself. He is panting after his exhortation and feels his heart beating too rapidly. The girl stands there in her white linen skirt hoisted up around her calves to avoid it dragging in the dirt she has to walk through every day, her head bowed under the scarf she has tied around her head, quiet and pale. When Lysander speaks again, it is at a slightly lower volume and for his own reasons: let the harlots from the Meadowland and the slopes of Brunke's Ridge bring shame on their shepherd's chapter this time.

'Although your behaviour is serious, I would not like to see you before the Consistory. You are still young and with all the ignorance of youth which may count in your favour. It would be best if this problem were to find a solution within the parish. But you cannot be let go without suitable penance. Therefore I suggest the following: you repent your sins before me and the sexton here, you make reparations with Anders Petter and his family by prayers of forgiveness and promises to mend your ways, and thereafter only the church fine remains. As we realize that you do not have many coins to spare and we also don't want you to go out with the basket to sell more of what you call fruit, we will settle on a token sum. Do you understand, Anna Stina?'

———•———

Anna Stina feels the same paralysis as at Maja's deathbed. She can't breathe and she can't move. All she can do is sit still as Olof Boman squirms and Pastor Lysander's face takes on an increasingly deep shade of red.

'Have you lost your tongue? Don't you understand the trouble I have gone to in order to spare you suffering? You'll confess what you have done and do penance for your whoring!'

Perhaps it is because Anna Stina owns so little that she does what she does. It seems to her that someone who has more in terms of worldly possessions could afford to place a lower price on the truth. But before Lysander's furious gaze, it feels as if this is all she has, and she finds to her astonishment that she does not want to lose it. It is hers, and it is suddenly everything to her. Maja Knapp is dead and when Anna Stina makes the only decision she can, it is the first time she feels a sense of comfort since her mother's passing. Down in the earth, Maja lies safely out of reach of the catastrophe that Anna Stina already perceives. It is the faintest of whispers that issues from her lips.

'No.'

Anna Stina shuts her eyes and waits for the outburst. It does not come. When she opens her eyes again, all is as it was. Lysander is squeezed into his chair, his backside too wide for the cushion.

Boman is pretending not to exist. An unspoken hatred glimmers in Lysander's eyes, more frightening now that he is in control of it. He no longer raises his voice. It is almost soft.

'Get out of my sight, Anna Stina Knapp.'

She only starts to cry once her back is turned. She promises herself that these tears will be her last. She tells a lie.

32

' TWO MEN ARE asking for you!'
        Anna Stina knows the girl only as Ulla. Her surname is
unknown to everyone, possibly even to herself. It takes Anna
Stina a couple of moments to react to the lisped words. Ulla is not
completely right in the head and it is easy to disregard her random
words without paying any attention to their meaning. Like Anna
Stina, she sells wares from a basket, but further south in Maria
parish. Grocer Efraim Jansson has a system for his girls where
each and every one follows a certain route, and these become
well-guarded territories. God help anyone who tries to poach –
the one who gets caught red-handed can expect to be chased into
a corner, have her hair pulled, be beaten and scratched.

Nonetheless they sometimes meet where their routes intersect,
as is the case now. Anna Stina walks from the shores of Gilded
Bay to Ropemaker's Street in the west and to Katarina Street in
the south, Ulla around the Larder where no one else willingly sets
foot. They meet at the top of Postmaster's Hill with a view down
to the Lock and the City-between-the-Bridges. Anna Stina's
basket is almost empty. With luck, she'll be able to sell the rest on
her way back to Jansson, just down the hill, in the hope that he
will have more to give her. And if she hurries, she can do one
more round before the sun goes down.

Ulla squints at Anna Stina, her mouth hanging open. Anna
Stina doesn't know much about her. She has been working a

basket since spring, and the weeks spent outdoors have left their traces. Her skin has been tanned by sun and dirt, her back bent under the heavy, lopsided burden. She barely sells enough to keep her route and is always reprimanded at day's end when all is tallied and the wares left unsold have to be reduced in price before they are spoiled. Anna Stina has seen her come limping out of sheds and barns where men have taken advantage of her, her dress soiled and with her brightly coloured cap askew. Anna Stina's thoughts turn back to Walpurgis Night, to the field and Anders Petter, and she shivers at the thought of how many such memories Ulla's mind must host. That she is not yet with child is nothing but a divine mercy.

During the long, slow hours of the night, Anna Stina has had time to reflect on Lysander's words and tried to imagine the parts of the story that she cannot know for certain. How Anders Petter must have come home that evening, upset at his rejection and how his parents must have fretted at their son's agitation. She knows enough about Natanael and Klara Sofia Lundström to be able to guess the rest. The mother in particular has regarded Anna Stina with growing suspicion over the years as the friendship with Anders Petter has ripened, probably with fear that her son will be tempted into a poor match with a simple street girl instead of waiting for a promotion to first mate and courting some burgher's daughter. If Anders Petter had told them anything but the truth, she would not have had any trouble casting Anna Stina in the role of opportunist, trying to lure their firstborn into ruin with the one resource available to her. Leading questions would have yielded the answers she sought. Anders Petter, surely brought to tears at least once, would only have had to nod in order to confirm his mother's every fear.

Ulla snorts and snot runs out over her fleecy upper lip. Anna Stina is startled from her train of thought.

'What men?'

Ulla wipes her nose on the threadbare sleeve of her dress.

'They wore strange clothes. They were short an eye.'

'What did they want with me?'

'They asked if I knew an Anna Stina. Which one, I said, Knapp or the Andersson one? Knapp, they said. The one who hawks a basket in Maria parish.'

'When did you meet them? What did you say?'

Ulla twists her face in order to summon the concentration required to answer two questions at once.

'Earlier. Before midday, because the clock in the tower hadn't rung yet. I would've heard it clearly because I went to the church well, since I had the thirst.'

'Why didn't you go to the well by the square instead? If the Dragon had seen you near the church she would have had at you again. You know that better than anyone.'

Ulla smiles and proudly lifts her upper lip to display the gap left by the absence of the three front teeth that Karin Ersson – commonly known as the Dragon, since the city quarter with this designation is included in her daily basket route – removed by hitting her with a rock the last time Ulla strayed from her route.

'They asked me if I knew Anna Stina Knapp and if I knew where she could be found. I asked what had happened to the tall one's eye and the short one's leg and then the short one said I would do best to hold my tongue and answer their questions instead of coming up with my own. Then I said that I would try but that it's hard to hold my tongue and answer at the same time and then the tall one pulled my hair.'

Ulla lifts a corner of a cap to show Anna Stina a bare red spot behind her ear.

'It stung so badly that I dropped my basket and almost started to cry but then I thought that Anna Stina has always been so nice to me and I thought that these two probably didn't wish her well so then I told them that I do know Anna Stina, that she is a

207

large-boned girl with black hair and a hunchback who goes with a basket out past the Bear's Copse.'

The description fits poorly with Anna Stina's copper hair, straight back and western route at the Ropemaker's Quarter. On the other hand, it is not unlike Karin Ersson and her domains by the quarter of the Dragon.

———◆———

The two part ways. Anna Stina hurries down the cobblestoned streets in the decreasing light. In the grocery store, Efraim Jansson is already busy wrapping up the tasks of the day and preparing for tomorrow. Anna Stina has changed her mind about returning to her route to try to empty yet another filled basket and the grocer grumbles about his goods being returned unsold.

'I see, so the tender-footed Miss Knapp wishes to go home already and powder her face and splash her throat with rose water?'

She is all too familiar with the greedy glint in his eye as he consults the figures in his ledger.

'Your rhubarb is on its last legs and won't be able to be sold for the same price tomorrow. You know that very well. I will have to deduct the difference from your pay.'

She receives a couple of coins in return for what she has managed to sell; less than she had been hoping for. Out on Postmaster's Hill, the shadows have grown long. The sun is on its way down on the other side of the ridge and the light that remains is already shifting to the yellow-red hue of sunset. She looks around thoroughly before stepping out into the street but there are no men fitting Ulla's description either up on the slope or down towards the square and the Lock. Anna Stina walks uphill towards Katarina parish, past the graveyard and the Rutenbeck clothes manufactory. Further on lie the jumble of wooden houses, passages and alleyways whose names are known only to their inhabitants. Among these is the cottage where Anna Stina fears she can no longer stay.

She sees them in the same moment that they see her. They are waiting behind the corner of a peeling, shabby house. Their uniforms are blue, without lapels, buttoned up to their throats and with gaiters up to their knees. The shorter one is carrying a sabre and the taller one a cudgel and a piece of rope. The shorter one is smoking a clay pipe and she hears him swear when the surprise encounter causes him to break the delicate mouthpiece between his fingers. She turns and flees; both of them take off in pursuit after her without a word. Anna Stina dives in between two buildings. The slender gap grows even more narrow but finally lets her out into a small courtyard. She sees a gimp-legged old man sitting by the wall, taking advantage of the final moments of daylight to whittle something. He only manages a shout of consternation before she has reached the other side of the yard and vaulted over the fence. The street behind it is unpaved like almost all in the neighbourhood, just a layer of dusty earth. By chance she turns to the right and runs as fast as she can. Behind her comes a raised voice – 'Stop, thief!' – which is either her pursuers trying to rouse aid in their chase or the old man who has learned by experience that someone running in Katarina parish usually does so with stolen goods in their arms.

Some planks awaiting the carpenter's plane are leaned up against the side of a barn leaving space enough for her to crawl in between the wood and the wall. She waits there until darkness has fallen. When she peeks out again, the stars are lit above Katarina parish, more than anyone could count, and shining bright since few landlords in the area bother to pay for street lanterns. She must get away from here, but not without her possessions; she still has a handful of shillings saved, tied up in a pouch along with a brooch from Maja, a braided bracelet she was given on her name's day and a handful of marbles. There are also some scraps

209

of food, enough to last her a few days. Long enough to cross the Lock and disappear into the City-between-the-Bridges, or to the hills beyond Slaughterhouse Bridge.

———◆·◆———

She keeps close to the walls and makes a wide circle around the blocks in order not to return the same way that she came. The house has been given additional front doors as more inner walls have appeared to allow even more families to move in. Anna Stina follows one of the ditches that serves as a gutter and ducks in under a hole in a fence. She lies still for a while in the grass, alert for any movement. There is nothing.

The door that is used by the carpenter's apprentice Alm and his submissive wife is closed, but the latch is easy to lift with a stick. She steps into the darkness of the hallway, sneaking across the wood floor whose groans are drowned out by Alm's snoring, and reaches the door of the room that was shared by her and her mother Maja. She does not need to see in order to find what she is looking for. On her way back out she stops. In the kitchen she has a copper pot for cooking, well used but purchased for a sum that had taken them months to pay off. She reaches halfway to the hearth when the point of a rapier touches her shoulder.

'Oh, Anna Stina. We had started to think you weren't going to come home tonight. Isn't that right, Tyst?'

When her eyes have grown more accustomed to the dark, she sees that it is the shorter of the two who speaks. Tyst, the tall one, mutters inaudibly and the short one shrugs.

'The man hasn't put two words together since the Russians scared all language out of him. As for me, I answer to the name of Fischer and my ability to talk more than makes up for his silence, to the delight of all. If you would be so kind as to sit down on this bench while Tyst here lights a candle. Maybe you even have a little morsel of something to share in your little sack.'

Tyst makes sparks with a flint and steel and grunts as a spark takes hold and the flame lights the room. One of his eye sockets is a gaping hole. Fischer, short and stout, with thin hair combed across his bald pate and a little blackened moustache that cannot conceal the scar that runs straight down his lip, is rummaging around in her sack with evident disgust. He leaves his left leg with the stiff knee outstretched before him on the floor.

'Rotten fish and spoiled vegetables. Well, at least there is a handful of coffee in here. Tyst, if you could light the hearth, we can at least make ourselves something to drink.'

On the mantle, there is a dull little coffee grinder. Fischer lifts it from its place, puts it on his knee and snaps his fingers to draw Anna Stina's attention. He is holding a few coffee beans in his fist.

'I'll teach you a little lesson on the nature of things. Let these small beans here be Anna Stina Knapp and her little friends who run around the neighbourhood and spread their legs wide for a farthing.'

He points to the grinder.

'This here is Tyst and myself and, by extension, all of the authority and worldly power we represent.'

He pours some of the beans down among the teeth of the wheels. He cranks the handle and the beans crackle as they are crushed.

'This is the process that you are about to undergo. It may appear unpleasant to you at first, but look!'

Fischer pulls out the box at the bottom of the grinder and shows her the fine powder. He smells it with gusto.

'Ah! Coffee, all ready to be brewed and enjoyed by fine folk. All's well that ends well. So shall it be so for you too, Anna Stina, when you have been shown how to correct all the error of your ways.'

It takes a while before the coffee starts to boil in the pot. Anna Stina stares down at the floor. Fischer leans forward and drops the bantering tone. His gaze grows as hard as flint.

'You know who we are, no?'

Anna Stina knows. Except for Ulla, there is hardly anyone in Maria or Katarina parish who does not recognize the bluecoats, most often lame, maimed or mangled in some way that makes them unsuitable for other positions within the city watch or the military. Night and day, they chase beggars, petty thieves, vagrants and prostitutes – everyone who does not serve any purpose in the eyes of the city governance. Most of the bluecoats don't pose any danger, since every coin they earn is spent at the pub. Often they can be bribed or convinced to overlook an offence with the help of the very behaviour they are charged to curb. The City Guard corps are known as Corpses, and among the people these men too have been given a name.

'You are Pigs.'

He laughs humourlessly.

'So we are called and I have struck down wretches even more defenceless than you, little Anna Stina, for having taken that word in vain. Watchmen, if I may. It falls to us to trudge through the dregs of these detestable neighbourhoods and shuttle you on towards honour and glory. Elias Lysander has grown tired of you small-time whores who infest his flock like fleas, younger and younger each year, it seems. The pastor is done with shaming himself before the Consistory. With our help, he doesn't have to. We catch strumpets on commission and the pastor can go unblemished. We only have to wait till first light and we'll walk down the hill to the Courthouse for a brief stop on the way along Gilded Bay. You won't need to wait long, you'll see.'

Anna Stina has not dared to ask those questions that have answers she already knows, but now she can't hold them back any longer. Her voice hardly carries.

'What is it you want with me? Where will you take me?'

'We want you to better yourself. No, I tell a lie. Tyst and I want to be paid for catching you and whatever your fate turns out to be, I couldn't care less.'

Tyst makes a sound that is something between a rattle and a laugh as Fischer goes on.

'As to your destination? You, Anna Stina Knapp, will be bound with rope and led to the house of correction. You are a butterfly of the night who has just had her wings ripped off.'

33

EVERYTHING PROCEEDS AS swiftly as Fischer has said. She is
led down Katarina hill in the dewy air with a rope tied
around her right wrist and accompanied by the mocking calls
from the soil-carriers who may once have been the victim of a
similar fate. They wait at the Southern Courthouse for a hearing
that is over in a couple of minutes, after minimal testimony in the
form of a written statement already submitted by Lysander and
fleshed out by Fischer himself. With a few words of reprimand,
her destiny is sealed.

Anna Stina Knapp has been found guilty of whoring. Her
relegation to the house of correction is further justified by
the fact that she has lost her only guardian and thereby also
her support, especially since the grocer Efraim Jansson no
longer wants anything to do with her. The judge, of ruddy
complexion and a swollen, groggy face, chases a louse on his
chest under his shirt as he repeats words that flow with practised ease.

'It is the hope of the courts that the skills in the craft of spinning that Knapp will devote herself to in the house of correction
will serve her well as a basis for future employment within the
manufacturing industry. With this in mind, the sentence is to be
one and a half years long, after which she will no doubt be a spinstress of some accomplishment.'

He chuckles with satisfaction at his wit as the gavel falls. He studies the louse that he has crushed between thumb and forefinger, then wipes his hand on the hem of his robe.

Anna Stina is led away from the judge's stand before she has time to protest or ask any questions. Behind her there is a long line of watchmen, ready to parade the night's bounty before the law. They lead her quietly past rows of men and women, some so inebriated they are unable to stand, some nursing bloody welts from recent fights. Outside the Courthouse is the Russian Yard. Fischer yawns in the morning sun and stretches his stiff leg with his hands on the small of his back.

'I'll be damned if I walk all the way to the Scar. Let's hitch a ride.'

Tyst nods in response. Fischer tries in vain to relight his broken pipe but stops when he sees a wagon loaded with firewood on its way from the docks, pulled at an unhurried pace by an ox. He hurries over to speak to the driver and after a short exchange he waves to Tyst. There is a place for them at the back, above the recently felled tree trunks. Fischer takes the rope that restrains Anna Stina and ties one end to one of the beams that serves as a guard rail for the cargo.

'We're expecting one more passenger. It will only take a moment for Tyst to go and get her.'

When he emerges from the entrance to Courthouse, it is Karin Ersson who is at the other end of the rope. The Dragon. Fischer nods when he sees Anna Stina's look of recognition.

'We got her in the bargain, thanks to that imbecile of a basket girl. This one gave us less of a chase; all we had to do was follow the loud grunts of a horny potter. We were able to catch Miss Ersson in the act, as it were.'

When Tyst comes closer, Anna Stina sees the Dragon up close for the first time in a long while. Her dress is caked with dry mud. Her crooked back forms a hump at one shoulder, a silhouette all basket girls have learned to avoid from a distance. The Dragon looks the worse for wear since Anna Stina saw her last. Her body, tall and lean, has thinned out over winter. Her hair is so streaked with the filth of the streets that it looks prematurely grey, and dried blood is caked at the back of her head. Her clothes are torn, her feet bare and covered in sores. She must have been sleeping outside for weeks. Her icy blue eyes are wide open and staring. Anna Stina has seen the same look in the eyes of the tame bears that are chained and made to dance at the Royal Pasture while their masters crack their whips; a barely restrained rage, powerless and desperate but always ready to ignite like brimstone, a kind of insanity carefully constructed in order to keep fear at bay.

Tyst pushes the Dragon in front of him onto the cart. She shoots a quick, furtive glance at Anna Stina before she finds a knot in the wood to fix her stare on. The driver smacks the ox into motion and the wagon starts rolling uphill. The road goes past the debtors' prison before it makes a turn down towards the bay, past two ancient windmills. When the road meanders again she sees it for the first time: the Scar, just past Workhouse Bridge, the one she has heard called the Bridge of Sighs.

———— • ————

The island is rocky and barren. What little earth there is to cover the underlying rock is not enough to support life. At the far end of the bridge is a cluster of buildings and behind them looms the workhouse itself. Anna Stina has not seen anything like it in either Maria or Katarina parish. Closest to her rises the tower of the workhouse chapel. A lone black bell hangs under a roof topped by cross and pennant. Behind it stretch wings with barred windows. The old folk say that some places develop their own memories and their own power. Anna Stina believes it. She has felt cold shivers at the execution ground at Hammarby and near the old plague pits, has felt the residual dread lingering by the wooden horse and the pillory. She has even sensed something around the manufactories, as if the bricks are saturated with malice. When she crosses the bridge, she experiences an overwhelming surge of the same feeling. From the walls of the workhouse, a wave of old hatred washes over her, one that has been building up for decades. This is a place of torment.

From the left, she hears a sound, of the last kind she would expect from this sombre setting. Someone is singing. The voice carries well in the calm morning and you can hear that the singer was accomplished in his youth. The tones are true though the bass voice has lost much of its timbre.

'The God of Night here prepares to take his prey . . .'

The song issues from a tall manor house right next to the road, in which a window is open. The exterior of the building is the same yellow vitriol as can be seen everywhere in the City-between-the-Bridges, but it has deteriorated from its proximity to the water. Humidity and frost have thrust their fingers deep into the plaster and loosened large chunks. When the wagon nears the main building, she sees that its condition is similar. The voice fades away behind them.

'Into the depths of the abyss, is where I'll find my way . . .'

The driver halts his ox. Fischer and Tyst untie the Dragon and Anna Stina and lead them down from the back. Fischer casts quick glances on either side before he speaks to the driver.

'So, my friend, now it is time for your payment. Girls, please lift your skirts for our good man here and don't hesitate to tip generously.'

The Dragon hesitates but then shrugs her shoulders, laughs loudly and pokes her tongue out at the driver at the same time she does as she has been told. Anna Stina is filled with the same feeling that she had standing in front of Lysander, a fierce resentment of what is being taken from her, so small in the eyes of the world but of infinite importance to her. Again, she stands as if paralysed. She forms fists with her hands so tightly that her nails cut into her palms. The driver points accusingly at her and airs his displeasure.

'What about that one? This one isn't much to look at and if she were alone I would never have agreed to come all the way out here.'

Fischer gives Anna Stina a look of venom and signs wordlessly to Tyst, who loosens the cudgel at his belt. At that moment, a door behind them opens. A man in a black priest's frock comes out. He stops when he sees the small group by the wagon and surveys them quizzically. The priest is tall and thin, with grey hair that stands on end. His eyes bulge, the pupils suspended in the middle of the whites, and his eyelids blink with an uncanny regularity. He appears to sense something amiss. He walks closer and stares blinking from Fischer to Tyst with evident distaste.

'Well?'

Fischer whips off his blue hat and answers in a deferential tone.

'Fischer and Tyst, numbers twelve and twenty-five of the watch. We are here to commit two new spinning novices into the care of Inspector Björkman.'

The priest snorts and steps closer until the tip of his nose is only a finger's width from Fischer's. The latter has to dig in his heels so as not to stagger backwards.

'Inspector Björkman's care, you say? You can't possibly be referring to the same Inspector Björkman who spends his days bellowing forgotten old arias from an equally forgettable time on the opera stage, perhaps as an elegy to the monarch who placed him in his position only so the man could indulge in the gluttony he holds more dear than anything but wine and masturbation. Not that Inspector Björkman, surely.'

Fischer stands crestfallen and does not know what to do. His eyes almost well with tears in his attempt to meet the priest's gaze.

'You appear to have lost your tongue, Fischer. Allow me to enlighten you, so that you can better answer for yourself when someone next brings up Inspector Björkman. Björkman is a whoremonger, a bastard, a swine of a man who would not hesitate to step right out into the paddock and copulate with the sows until he rolls over lustily in the mud to frighten the good folk of Maria parish out of their wits with the thunder of his snoring.'

The priest's voice gets louder the longer he speaks. Spit flies from his lips each time he hits a consonant. Anna Stina realizes that it wasn't his intense gaze that made Fischer's eyes water. The stench of alcohol that emanates from him has now reached her, even though she is a couple of metres away and a light breeze is blowing in from the water.

'But perhaps you are cut from the same cloth, Fischer, judging by your belly.'

The priest has started to walk around Fischer, his hands on his back, as if he were a stern provost in the midst of an inspection.

'Well, Fischer, did you cast any longing glances at our livestock on your way here? Maybe you caught sight of the bull in a state of excitement and longed to jump the fence and take your place with your rear in the air. The beasts are not formally under my charge, and whether or not they even have souls that can be saved is a question for wiser men, but I promise you that I will not fail to cast my vote for your swift descent into hell if such is the case. In fact, that is exactly where I encourage you to go now, and to be quick about it, as soon as your goods have been transported inside the gates and registered there.'

Fischer, on whose brow efforts at self-control have drawn beads of sweat, hurries gratefully over to loosen the restraints on Anna Stina's arm. With his mouth close to her ear, he whispers his parting words.

'If we see each other again, Anna Stina Knapp, you'd do well to pray to the gods that you see me first.'

He pushes her and the Dragon inside the gates where a guard in the same blue uniform is waiting. The priest disappears behind them towards the house by the bridge, somewhat unsteady in his gait and muttering to himself as if he were still berating Fischer, who spits over his shoulder.

'So that is Pastor Neander. I have heard that the man is out of his wits. Now I know it for a fact.'

The watchman at the gate, an older man with patchy skin without hair or eyebrows, giggles maliciously.

'Sorry to hear it. A fellow who crosses paths with Neander when he is in that mood is certainly unlucky.'

'What's amiss with him?'

'Apart from a general lack of common sense, he has recently heard that our favourite basso and workhouse inspector Björkman has submitted his resignation, and intends to retire to Savolax.'

'Given the way he feels about the inspector, one would think that he would rather rejoice in their parting.'

'Oh, those two have a complicated history. The pastor has spent years composing fiery letters of protest against Björkman to every authority one could think of, including His Late Majesty, King Gustav himself, which ended with the pastor being fined twenty dalers for having taken a tone in his missive that was not fit for a regent's eyes. It is said that he toasted in champagne the same hour that he heard the King was shot. My guess is that Neander is upset that Björkman – thanks to his exit – will escape the revenge that the pastor has been brewing for so long.'

'Who will replace Björkman?'

'No one knows, but it could take as long as the autumn, maybe longer. Who the hell wants to settle down on this miserable island? Björkman, of course, has been neglecting his duties for twenty years, and that is probably the only way he retained his

220

sanity. I have barely seen him at the workhouse since the winter. Neander holds his prayers morning as well as night, usually so drunk he can't read to save his life, and in any case he wouldn't give a shit about the inmates unless they can somehow serve as ammunition in his battle with Björkman. Anyway it is Pettersson who rules this place, as you know, and that will hardly change just because we get a new inspector.'

'Damn, what a shithole this is. Lord knows I don't have many things to be grateful for, but avoiding this hornet's nest is one of them. Here you have two new spinstresses, sluts both. Best of luck, little girls.'

Fischer touches his hand to the brim of his hat, turns on his heels and limps back out of the gates.

34

THE WATCHMAN WITH the singed face calls over a younger colleague, pulls back the latch and lets all three of them into the interior courtyard, which is laid out around a well with a pump. The little square patch of sky above feels as distant as if Anna Stina were viewing it from the bottom of a shaft. Behind the windows in the wings, each one fitted with bars, shadowy figures can be glimpsed, bent over their work. The far side of the yard is taken up with an older building, akin to the manor houses that Anna Stina has seen on the outskirts of the Southern Isle, constructed more than a century ago for the enjoyment of the wealthy. It must have been here first and become a part of the workhouse with the construction of the rest. The watchmen come to a stop on the gravel. Here they must wait for the custodian.

He is in no hurry. If the Dragon is feeling the same anxiety as Anna Stina, she doesn't show it. Instead she is nagging one of the watchmen who have been set to guard them. She is jumping up and down and asking for the latrine. He shrugs his shoulders.

'You'll keep silent, if you have any sense at all between your ears. Petter Pettersson will be here shortly and you'd do best not to anger him.'

The Dragon gives him a look of fury and makes a face behind his back as soon as he turns away. They wait.

The custodian is an enormous man, his shoulders wider than Anna Stina could reach with both arms stretched out. The blue uniform does not fit him. He wears his jacket open and she doubts he would be able to button it upon even if he wanted to. Sweat pours off him in the heat. His face is large and round, split by a mouth spanning from ear to ear, with a nose that is wide and upturned so it looks like a snout, and peering eyes set deep in bloated flesh. His thick head of hair is bound at the neck into a tight knot. His skin is covered in old scars and his voice is a throaty bass.

'Welcome to our humble shed, my little chickens. Pettersson is my name and I am the custodian of this place along with my colleague, Hybinett. Your presence here has been requested in order to mend your sinful ways. Names?'

It is the young watchman who points and answers.

'Anna Stina Knapp. Karin Ersson.'

Pettersson inspects them both. Anna Stina lowers her gaze in the way she has learned that such men prefer. The Dragon stares back at him with defiance. She is swaying on the spot in order to relieve her pressing needs. Pettersson points at her with a hand that is as large as a smoked ham.

'What is the matter with Miss Ersson?'

'The girl says she needs to piss.'

'Is that so, Miss Ersson? You're of course accustomed to running around and being able to tinkle at will, free as a beast in the wild.'

The Dragon waits before she answers. Anna Stina hears the unspoken challenge that Pettersson's words carry, though he has made his voice mockingly gentle, and she prays quietly that Karin Ersson will have enough sense not to reach for the gauntlet that has been thrown. But she does. She tilts her chin and spits out her answer.

'I don't see what anyone else has to do with me emptying my bladder.'

The corners of Petter Pettersson's mouth turn up in a smile that makes Anna Stina shudder. A well-fed barn cat with a mouse in its claws. He slowly moistens his lips with the tip of his tongue as he walks closer.

'Let me have a look at you.'

He takes Karin Ersson's chin between his thumb and forefinger and turns her face up to the light.

'Oh, I've known girls like Miss Ersson. They brighten the pubs and cat-houses of the city. Do you like to dance?'

Anna Stina wants to tell her not to take the bait, to keep her mouth shut in the hopes that he will get tired of his game. But she can do nothing. The Dragon smiles with confidence.

'I can certainly take a couple of turns on the dance floor.'

Pettersson feigns admiration and turns to his colleague.

'Isn't that what I thought? I know my workhouse girls all right. Are you a skilled dancer, Miss Ersson, or do you lean on your partner like a sack of potatoes and get tired after a polonaise or two?'

The Dragon gives a spiteful laugh.

'You're looking at someone who can dance all night long while others wear out and fall to the floor!'

Pettersson nods.

'So you say! I'd like to take your word for it, but I've learned that people so often overestimate their abilities. Would you care to dance a little right here, just for me?'

The Dragon hesitates. After a while she doesn't know what else to do except take a few jumping steps on the spot. Pettersson shakes his head.

'No, no. Around the well. That's how we do it out here on the Scar. Why don't you dance around it a couple of times so that we can see how good you are?'

He offers her his arm, bends one knee as he bows and scrapes his foot. She allows herself to be led to the well where the pump leans out over a stone basin to collect any spilled water. At first, the Dragon looks unsure of herself, but then summons her resolve and with a grin places her arms around an invisible partner and starts to dance in a rapid three-beat that only she can hear. She circles the well once as she whirls around and around. Pettersson claps his hands and whistles.

'Well, how about that! It turns out Miss Ersson can dance after all. May we ask for another round, and with the same conviction?'

Her second round is much like the first. But when Pettersson asks for a third and fourth the novelty has worn off. The Dragon has tired of the game and lets her arms hang at her side as her pace starts to drag. When Pettersson claps and asks for yet another turn around the well, she slows to a stop and folds her arms across her chest.

'Now that's enough dancing. It's no fun anymore and I still need to go to the latrine or to a bush if that's all there is. Or just around the corner.'

Without his eyes leaving Karin Ersson, Pettersson snaps his fingers at the watchman who is standing next to Anna Stina. He traipses off across the courtyard and out through the front doors of one of the two wings without a word. All humour is gone from Pettersson's voice when he speaks again.

'You can piss later. Now you dance. Come on then, Miss Ersson, do another round. Soon Löf will be back and he'll bring a little surprise for us. You have time for one more round before. Two even, if you're lucky.'

Her movements no longer resemble a dance, more like a half-run with the occasional skip. When Löf, the watchman, returns he has a small sack over his shoulder and Pettersson takes a few steps closer to the Dragon. Löf hands him the sack and he holds it out to the Dragon with an arm as thick as a tree trunk.

'Master Erik is in here. In a moment, I'll introduce the two of you.'

From the sack, he takes out a long, braided leather strap with a sturdy grip. It is about two ells in length and comes to a slender point at the other end.

'You may not have seen a lash before. We don't need the help of Master Erik as long as you keep pace nicely. Do another round now and with a little more bounce, if you please.'

<hr />

The Dragon does three and a half more rounds before Pettersson strikes his first blow. She has slowed down to the point where he can match her speed with his long boot-clad strides. The crack of his whip echoes between the walls of the yard and her yell follows. The slender leather at the end of the whip has caught her above her ankle and left a red welt. She bites her lip to keep the tears back but one can hear by her distressed breathing that Karin Ersson is on the verge of crying. Pettersson has also noticed.

'Oh, but that was nothing, Miss Ersson. Master Erik can do so much worse. Keep dancing and we shall see if he'll be forced to partner you again.'

Faces have appeared in the windows around the yard, gaunt and pale. The Dragon dances five more rounds until he strikes again, now across her calf with a force that draws blood. After seven more rounds, the Dragon loses control of her bladder and dances on with a wet skirt. The salt stings her lacerations and the crying begins, at first almost imperceptibly, then with increasing volume. Soon one can barely distinguish the yowling sounds she makes when a blow strikes her from the rest of her noise. She pleads and wails, promises Pettersson one thing after another. He takes no notice. Finally she simply calls for her mother, in long drawn-out screams. All the toughness the Dragon has developed in her years on the streets of Maria parish is stripped from her by the whip, in layers, as if Pettersson is peeling one of the onions out of Anna Stina's basket. Soon a terrorized child is all that remains. After two hours she can only crawl, as Pettersson lets the blows rain down over her thighs and back. When the sun is at its zenith, the bell in the tower begins to peal. The spinners shuffle out of their rooms to be fed. Some of them point and laugh at the Dragon's dance. Most of them can't even summon the energy to look at her. While Anna Stina stands there with her eyes closed, forgotten and with legs that tremble with the effort of simply standing there for the duration, she feels something inside her take the opposite turn. A shell begins to form around her. She hears how a monster of a man torments a girl for his enjoyment and with the law at his back, without anyone moving so much as a finger in protest. Pettersson is of the same ilk as Anders Petter at Children's Lea, as Lysander in his office, as the magistrate in the courts, as Fischer and Tyst with their cudgel, rope and rapier. While the Dragon draws a circle of blood around the well, Anna Stina swears that she will never again be that defenceless girl, however she may look to the world. In thought and action, she must leave this despicable place and she must do so quickly before she loses herself and joins that shuffling flock of living dead that the spinners have become. For Karin Ersson, it is too late. Anna Stina knows that she will be a dragon no more.

Pettersson is panting so that his bellows of a chest heaves under his shirt, partly from the exertion but more, Anna Stina realizes with horror, out of arousal. He stops to wipe the sweat from his brow and catches sight of Anna Stina standing there next to Löf, who has started nodding off on his feet in the midday heat.

'Hey, Jonatan! Take that one and show her a bed, a place to eat and her spinning wheel. Bring me a bottle when you come back. Discipline is thirsty work and I have a feeling that Ersson here still has a waltz or two in her, even if you wouldn't believe it by looking at her.'

35

S HE SLOWLY LEARNS the ways of the workhouse. Spinning is what she must do, day in and day out, at a spinning wheel next to many others like it, squeaky and worn after countless hours of working the pedal and wheel. They are roused at four in the morning to gather in the chapel, presided over by the priest who greeted them at the gate. He is usually so hungover his hands shake in the pulpit. Afterwards they are given crusts of bread and small beer for breakfast in the same rooms as they do their work, where they also sleep at night in narrow beds lined up along the walls. Dinner is served at twelve and supper, after the day's work is done, at nine in the evening. Tough pieces of salted meat and spoiled herring, rounded out with soaked oats and turnips. The meals are served on old wooden trays shared by four at a time. It is not enough to satisfy the hunger of even one. She soon discovers why. A watchman is present at each meal and additional food can be ordered through him. He makes a note of the orders in a large ledger. For each completed spool of yarn, an inmate receives a small salary and with this they are expected to purchase the kind of food that is not served for free. Butter, cheese, milk, meat that has not spent months in brine. Everyone does it. The only alternative is to face a slow death by starvation.

Their work is measured in 'strings': each a full spool of finished yarn, measuring three thousand ells in length. It takes Anna Stina the whole first day to spin one thousand ells. She has always had an easier time using her left hand than her right and the movements at the spinning wheel are difficult for her to learn. The twisted fibres pulled between her fingers are either too thick or too thin. The strand breaks time and again. She has to join the breaks and do it quickly since a floor supervisor is constantly moving among them to monitor their work. By evening, she realizes that she is not learning fast enough. If she doesn't start spinning longer and better yarn, she won't get enough to eat and if she doesn't eat, she won't have the energy to spin. She is no stranger to starvation and knows well how hunger slows down both mind and body.

The other three in her eating party differ in age. One is old, so wrinkled and aged that her body seems to have wrapped around the spinning wheel as if her entire being were now devoted to this occupation and good for nothing else. She mutters to herself as she works. A milky white membrane has spread across one eye. The other stares vacantly into space. Her hands move as if by their own accord.

A woman who is the same age as Mother Maja had been seated a little further away. She is thin and jittery. Each time the watchman makes his rounds, her eyes swivel to his switch and her breath becomes quick and laboured. When he is behind her back she pulls her shoulders up around her neck to protect it from a sudden blow. Sometimes she jerks for nothing, so violently that the woollen yarn in her hand is torn in two.

The girl closest to Anna Stina can't be many years older than her, with jet black hair and eyes just as dark. She keeps her head bowed over her work but her eyes move all over. Concealed under her fringe they dart back and forth and don't miss a thing. Anna Stina felt them watching her as she was shown to her place and when she first started to spin, but the girl quickly turned her

229

attention elsewhere. When the watchman turns his back to speak with the colleague who is coming on duty, Anna Stina bends towards the girl.

'Show me how to spin.'

Without breaking pace with the foot on the pedal that powers the wheel that pulls the wool onto the spool, the girl glances at Anna Stina. The watchmen conclude their conversation and the new one walks down the room and back. When he is out of earshot, she whispers a response.

'The first string I help you with, I want the whole payment for.'

The watchman turns around. He must have heard something but can't identify the source and – after having let his eyes run up and down the twenty or so women in the room – he gives up. It takes a while before Anna Stina feels safe to answer. She has had time to think about her counter-offer.

'You can get the whole amount for the first and half of the second, but you will have to give me time before I make my first payment.'

The girl next to her looks at her sceptically. Anna Stina meets her gaze.

'If I don't eat more soon, neither one of us will get anything from me.'

The girl leans over and stretches out a hand with her thumb splayed. Anna Stina hesitates for a moment before she gives her own thumb and when their fingers meet to bind their agreement, she adds:

'If it breaks or gets knots, I will keep my payment, and the first string has to be ready by tomorrow night.'

The other girl smiles faintly and snorts.

'Agreed, but if you starve before you learn, I get your dress and everything else you leave behind.'

She gently turns her spinning wheel so that Anna Stina can see. She changes the pace of her foot on the pedal and starts to make every motion more slowly. It helps.

Later that evening, on the way to evening prayer and while it is going on, they have the opportunity to talk, whispering in the pews. The girl's name is Johanna.

'So what's your number?' she asks.

'One and a half years.'

Johanna chuckles without mirth and is silent for a moment to make sure she has not attracted the attention of the watchmen.

'You are new. Here our punishment isn't measured in years or days. It is measured in strings. With one and a half years, your councillor meant one thousand strings. It is said that we can spin seven hundred strings a year if we are diligent. Two a day, six thousand ells. Not even the Ewe, the one-eyed crone next to us, can do that and she has had her whole life to learn how.'

Anna Stina is quiet as she counts. She tries to see into her immediate future, feel the wool in her hands, how she will become better at spinning while one day gives way to the next. She thinks about her foot and hand working as quickly as they can and she tries to picture one thousand strings in time. The realization is like a punch in the gut.

'Three years! Or more, even.'

Johanna's silence is empathetic, from one who once made the same calculation herself and remembers the feeling. She shrugs.

'Maybe four or five. If you make enemies in here they will take it out on your fingers first. Then you will spin one spool a week and have to steal so you won't starve. If you are found out they'll just add to your sentence.'

Around them the other inmates try to find a few more minutes of rest before the watchmen who are patrolling the aisle find them with their long canes. The girls sit quietly in the pews as Pastor Neander reads slurred passages from his Bible, until Johanna leans over towards her ear again.

'What were you sent here for?'

'Whoring. But I am innocent. What about you?'

231

'To think that two innocents would be given spinning wheels next to each other.'

Johanna shrugs her shoulders again when she goes on.

'There are murderers and thieves here. All I did was lie with men for a farthing a piece.'

<hr>

High above the courtyard, the stars wander on their way through the pale evening. Once the watchmen have escorted the inmates from the church to their rooms, they leave and take their lanterns with them, plunging them into darkness. The doors to the rooms are locked. The spring night outside is light enough to filter in through the windows and make the bars cast a net of shadows over the floor. Anna Stina lies awake. The hay in the mattress stinks and crawls with lice. Rats scuttle along the walls to seek out the spots where crumbs have been dropped. The night relaxes that self-control the spinners manage to maintain with some difficulty while the sun is shining. Many of them can be heard moaning and crying. Others are snoring or snuffling, or talking in their sleep. Anna Stina also feels the prick of tears but remembers the promise she has made to herself and stares straight up into the ceiling. After a while, shapes and colours begin to dance before her eyes. Johanna has the bed next to her. She whispers into the darkness.

'Are you awake?'

It takes a while before she gets an answer.

'Yes. It's hard to sleep at night although the working day is long.'

'Who are the other two who eat with us?'

Johanna sighs from her bed. She is probably weighing the benefits of trying to fall asleep with the welcome idea of distracting herself by thinking about something else. It takes her some time to choose.

'One of them is Lisa. She's not right in the head. She'd been married but it's said that her husband drove her out of her mind. They found her walking along a street one morning without a stitch on her. She could just as well have been taken to the hospital in Danish Bay but they sent her here instead. She can't spin fast enough. She's thin already. There is a bet on whether she'll survive until the last leaf falls from the chestnut tree in the meadow outside. Someone suggested the same bet against the first snow, but could find no takers.'

'And the old one?'

'She is called the Ewe, on account of having a beard and because she puts small pieces of wool in her mouth and works them with her jaw all the time. She rarely speaks out, even though she is always talking to herself and to folk only she can see. She's been here longest of all. She can remember what this place looked like when it was only Ahlstedt's converted manor, before there were two wings and a chapel. They have divided us up, you know. Prossies and thieves over here, and those who have done worse over there. The Ewe was with the worst of them for years, but she is old and harmless now, and they chose to move her here. And here she'll stay until they have to carry her out.'

'Do you know what she did to end up in this place?'

'They say she dropped her children down a well.'

<hr />

They lie still for a while without saying anything else.

'Johanna, I can't stay here.'

There is no answer.

'There must be some way out.'

She hears the bitter chuckle again.

'Not lately, there hasn't been. Last year a couple of women in the south-west corner managed to pry a bar from the window. There were seven that dared to make the jump and run across the bridge. There was a scandal, and it was the only time I saw the inspector himself in the workhouse. He has a nice voice but how he screamed and shouted. They inspected each window, removing any rusty bars and putting new ones in place. They counted all the keys and we were assigned more watchmen. Anyone who so much as looked the wrong way got the lash. Since then, no one has managed to escape.'

Anna Stina feels whatever hope she still has flutter like a flame in the wind. It takes a while before Johanna whispers her final comment.

'Well, actually, there was one. Her name was Alma. Alma Gustafsdotter. She was in the same group as the Ewe before I took her place. And you know, it doesn't take long before the ones who flee end up back here anyway. All the watchmen have to do is make a couple of rounds in their old neighbourhoods, then they find us and tie a new knot around our arms and drag us back to the wheel again, our laps full of wool. But not Alma.

'No one knows how she did it.'

The mournful cry of a loon comes across the bay. Maja Knapp used to say that it was the sound drowned sailors make, calling out their longing for hallowed ground from the deep.

36

TWO WEEKS PASS before Anna Stina sees the Dragon again, but when she does it is only by chance; she could just as well have let her gaze wander across the group of convicts without recognizing her. The lanky body is now cowering and hunched over. One leg is twisted at an angle so the Dragon has to walk bandy-legged to keep her feet from hitting one another. Every bit of skin that is visible from under her dress varies from shades of blue-black to yellow among half-healed lacerations and wounds, and she does not seem to be able to stop shaking. The Dragon has been made an old woman in just a few days. When she meets Anna Stina's gaze, there is no hint of recognition. If she does not stop the trembling she won't be able to spin, and Anna Stina has already seen the results among other spinners in her own room. They begin to move more slowly until finally they sit in apathy, hardly touching the wool unless the watchmen threaten them with the cane. They spin less and less, receive no payment and are unable to augment their meals and – as the days go by – the flesh leaves their bones. In the end they collapse and are carried to the brief respite of the infirmary on their way to the grave.

Anna Stina has started carrying a bit of cheese and bread rolled into the sleeve of her dress and when she passes the Dragon out in the yard, she tries to hand her the food before the watchmen catch on. But the Dragon pulls away as if struck, signalling only confusion and anxiety. The custodian, Petter Pettersson, appears endlessly amused by how meek the brash girl he met only a couple of weeks has become. He enjoys sneaking up close, then jumping at her and shouting 'boo'. His cronies among the watchmen laugh, but still they are of another kind. Punishments are meted out every day and every one of them can swing Master Erik, but no one does it with Pettersson's frenetic energy and relish.

Johanna whispers that people have also started to make bets on Karin Ersson. She doesn't even eat the food that is served, does not defend the morsels that are hers when others steal them off her plate. If she makes it another two weeks, it will be a miracle. For Anna Stina, it confirms what she already knows. It has gone quicker for her, but Karin Ersson is simply hurrying down the path where many of them are bound. The inmates may be released once their spinning wheels have paid out the strings they have been sentenced to deliver, but very few of them leave the Scar in any true meaning of that word. Something vital shrivels up inside while the body staggers on, reformed in a manner that suits a very similar life in the manufactories outside. Perhaps the hardening she felt inside herself when the Dragon was whipped was the first phase of the process. It may help her to survive, but at a price that no one should be made to pay.

———◆———

Only at night does she dare to speak uninterrupted with Johanna in the dark room, their whispers hidden in weeping and moans. Neither of them would yet call the other a friend. Johanna knows this and Anna Stina senses it. Relationships of that sort can easily become a weakness, a gap in the shield through which danger may gain entry. Forming strong ties here likely paves a road to sorrow and betrayal. And so they are satisfied with mutual respect. Johanna recognizes another survivor, and Anna Stina has been able to buy knowledge that would otherwise have cost her far more. Simply having someone to talk to is enough, with a boundary drawn this side of deeper confidences.

'Tell me more of the girl who disappeared.'

'I don't know more than I have already told you. I can ask around if you want to know more, but that can be risky when Pettersson is on the alert and I won't do it for less than half a string.'

Anna Stina is better at spinning now, with Johanna's example to follow. She is as far from reaching her quota as the others, but skilled enough to buy butter and meat on Sundays. Even though the payment for half a string is a high price – enough to force her to go to bed hungry several nights in a row – the decision is easy.

'Then do it.'

<hr />

Anna Stina's dreams are not the same as before. She lies awake after Johanna's breathing becomes regular and deep, staring upward and seeing her thoughts take form. Mother Maja lies pale and dead in the ground. She sees Anders Petter, Lysander, the magistrate, the watchmen, the custodian, and they mock her from their heights. Sleep comes creeping. As long as she can remember, she has sometimes dreamed of the great fire, about the catastrophe that Maja Knapp has described to her from childhood, in equal parts to teach her about the dangers of fire and because Maja herself was not able to escape her memories of it. Fire found its way into Anna Stina's dreams, formerly as a source of horror. The dream is much the same now, but the roles have been reversed. Now it is she herself who is the Red Rooster. She incinerates all in her wake. The workhouse, chapel, tenements, manor and courts: she lays everything in smouldering ruin and feels a wild joy. In the roaring furnace that is her stomach, she consumes her adversaries. When she jolts awake in the darkness of the night, her heart beats with raging euphoria. The purpose of the workhouse is to teach her to spin wool and to imprint on her the city's striving towards efficiency and productivity. But more than anything else, she is taught the art of hatred.

———•———

The result of Johanna's questions takes all week. Anna Stina has grown used to the fact that the voice that whispers from the foot of the bed has no face. She prefers it that way. In her mind, she can give Johanna a face better than in real life. Healthier, rounder.

'There are some who remember Alma Gustafsdotter, even if many of those who were here then don't and some who weren't imagine that they were, just from hearing stories about her. She did her spinning in the same wing as we do, and shared meals in the same group as the Ewe. She arrived here last autumn and disappeared this March. She had the French illness and was often sent to the infirmary to bathe and in the winter she was whipped once when she was accused of theft. She was lucky enough not to get Pettersson, though.'

'And her escape?'

'Everyone is in agreement about one thing. Alma was sitting in the pews for evening chapel, she ate her supper like everyone else and she lay in her bed when the lanterns were carried out for the night. In the morning, her bed was empty. The watchmen didn't know what to think. They turned the room upside down, piling the beds up in the middle of the floor, knocked on the walls, tested the bars of the window. We could see them through the glass later that day, a long line of men who beat the bushes with canes and swords. But Alma Gustafsdotter was never found.'

Anna Stina feels a pang of disappointment. The story contains nothing that can help her, no clues to lead her to the same escape.

'Is that all?' She hears Johanna's voice take on a new tone of satisfaction when she speaks again.

'Not much to spend half a day's earning on? Calm down. There's more. I talked to the girl who has the bed closest to the door. She said she knew exactly what had happened. She's not very old but unfortunately not particularly bright either, but she says she was woken up a couple of times in the middle of the night at around the time when Alma disappeared. There was someone at the door who was rattling the lock and she assumed it was a phantom trying to get into the room to satisfy its hunger. It came back night after night while she pulled the covers over her head and gnashed her teeth. Finally it managed to unlock the door and open it up. She felt the draught. According to the girl, it snuck into the room and gobbled poor Alma right up under the cover of darkness only to return to its den under some barrow.'

'Alma was accused of stealing something, you said. What did she steal?'

'From what I heard, there was a tin spoon that was never found. as well as a couple of vials of medicine from the infirmary that she claimed to have taken because she had an aching tooth. Now you know as much as anyone does about Alma Gustafsdotter, apart of course from the hungry ghost. I know that it isn't much, but I want my payment regardless.'

There was something in all this, Anna Stina feels sure of it. The girl, the spoon, the infirmary, the toothache, the rattling at the door at night. She asked a final question.

'Have you talked to the Ewe?'

'Bah! No one has talked to the Ewe for years. She only talks to herself.'

<hr />

The following day, after the meagre breakfast, Anna Stina starts to push her spinning wheel inch by inch closer to the Ewe, who stares straight ahead with her healthy eye as she spins assuredly. Anna Stina strains to hear the steady stream of mumbled words, so low that the watchmen can't be bothered silencing her. They are easily lost in the clatter and buzz of the spinning wheels and she has to bend in close to hear. It sounds like a chant without a melody, repeated to the rhythm of the pedal.

'Three fathoms and three splashes and three decades, three decades and three thousand ells of wool a day, all good things are three.'

When the watchman leaves the room for a moment, she whispers as close to the Ewe's ear as possible.

'Do you mean your children? Three splashes?'

The Ewe pulls back a little and loses her timing. Her healthy eye swivels and lands on Anna Stina as if for the first time. After a while she furrows her brow and resumes her spinning. The chant comes back once she is working at her usual pace.

'Three fathoms and three splashes and three decades, three decades and three thousand ells of wool a day, all good things are three.'

'Have you been in here for thirty years?'

The Ewe looks distracted again and gives Anna Stina another glance.

'Do you remember Alma Gustafsdotter from last autumn and spring? The girl in your eating group?'

The Ewe appears to be weighing her options but finally she leans over with a mischievous glint in her healthy eye.

'They say that I did it because I hated them, you know, but it was the opposite. It was for love, to spare them from all the suffering the world had in store for them. Every day is worse than the day before, and for this I am happy. Each time the sun rises, it proves I did the right thing.'

Anna Stina does not know how to answer. She only nods and the Ewe winks at her when she starts to spin again.

'Three fathoms and three splashes and three decades, three decades and three thousand ells of wool a day, all good things are three.'

Anna Stina is filled with a sense of hopelessness. The Ewe is another false lead, yet another creature ground to dust under the heel of the workhouse, gone mad, now useful only as an extension of her tools. She sees no point in risking discovery by the watchmen and decides to wait until evening, so she shifts her spinning wheel back to its original chalk marks. When the Ewe starts talking to her after supper, it is the last thing she expects. It happens almost imperceptibly, to the same monotonous rhythm as her spinning chant. What she says appears to be a stream of memories from her many years at the workhouse.

'They think it is hard work to spin wool but they know nothing. They think there isn't much food, but they have no idea. In the year of seventy-two, the same year King Gustaf took his throne, they wanted to extend Ahlstedt's manor, and those of us who were here were put to work dragging and carrying, even though we had to pay for food and clothing ourselves . . . logs and hewn stone blocks, mortar and plaster in a yoke, people perished like flies but not old Maria. No, she was tough, even then . . . chewed on her fingers and had a handful of gravel when there was nothing else to eat . . . They think Pettersson is a plague, but he is not out of his mind the way that old Benedictius was . . . he and von Torken and old Johan Wik, they starved us, worked us to death as surely as if it was our own graves we were digging . . . Old Maria has outlived them all . . . the inspector was to live there but nothing came of it . . .'

The Ewe smiles at her memories. Anna Stina looks down at her clawlike hands as they move with spindle and yarn and she sees with a shiver that her fingers still bear teeth marks.

'We only managed to get as far as finishing the cellars that spring. It was a beautiful summer . . . Someone from the men's workhouse took me into the bushes and he was a fine fellow. He starved before the year was over but I remember him still . . . We carried on with the building all summer while the city celebrated with drums and gun salutes, and when the autumn came we didn't have time to finish everything, even though Benedictius roared and tore his hair . . . I had to carry away the stone I had helped to bring there. We had to make a hole in the cellar wall for the water to drain away while the house stood roofless over winter . . . It was not enough . . . Damp crept in everywhere and saturated the walls, a draught blew through the hole and neither the inspector nor the pastor wanted to move in . . . Now there are sacks of turnips there, rotting away . . .'

It takes Anna Stina a while to sift through what she hears and to realize its value. When she does, the blood rushes to her head and she has to bend closer in order to hear the Ewe's voice over the sound of her own pulse.

'Ma'am, did you tell this to Alma Gustafsdotter? The other girl who sat where I am sitting now?'

The Ewe looks surprised.

'Three fathoms and three splashes and three decades, three decades and three thousand ells of wool a day, all good things are three. He was a fine fellow . . .'

This is the solution. Somewhere there is a cellar with a tunnel through the foundation, constructed to lead away the rainwater and snowmelt while the building stood without a roof during the winter of seventy-two, and overlooked once construction was resumed. Alma Gustafsdotter knew it. All she needed was a way to take herself to the cellar under the cover of darkness, move the sacks of turnips, creep a few ells towards freedom, and disappear forever.

37

S HE CAN'T SLEEP that night. Instead Anna Stina tries to see months into the past when winter had set its claws into the Scar, when the sun barely managed to inch itself up over the horizon to polish the ice of Gilded Bay and the inmates had to work in semi-darkness. Time would have dragged, the duration between the hours of the clock grown longer and Alma Gustafsdotter feeling bored. She would have moved her wheel closer to the Ewe in order to make time pass by listening to her mumbling. There she suddenly stumbled upon a promise of liberty.

How long did it take Alma to prepare her escape? She came in the autumn and vanished in the spring. The Ewe could have told her story early on when Alma was new, but in that case Alma was clever enough to wait for the ground to thaw since the risk was otherwise great that she would find the hole in the wall blocked by ice or lidded by a snowdrift with an iron crust, tempered by the icy winds from the water. So Alma bided her time.

Anna Stina tries to imagine Alma Gustafsdotter's footsteps towards the point of disappearance, the same path that she herself now must follow. Where is the location of the cellar? Finding it, she guesses, will be the easiest part. It was part of an extension to the old manor, Brewer Ahlstedt's old house that was sold and remade into a workhouse. The new construction must be located towards the back of the grounds. The Ewe mentioned sacks of turnips and all the food that Anna Stina has seen is carried down the stairs of the old house. There must be a kitchen there, and all food supplies stored in its vicinity. On impulse, Anna Stina rises from her bed and slowly tiptoes between the silent spinning wheels to the window. She presses her cheek to the glass and tries to peer along the outside of the building towards Ahlstedt's house. She can't see beyond the corner of her wing, but just as she is about to give up, she notices the moon shadow and on the ground of the Scar it is now clearly visible: the roof of her wing appears in black, changes into the outline of the older house, and then continues as a lower wing that stretches in the opposite direction. That's where it is! Below, her freedom awaits. All she needs to do is make her way there.

———•———

The days go by and Anna Stina continues to spin, string after string, counting no longer. Instead she becomes more attentive to the routines of the watchmen as well as the customs and schedules of the workhouse. Alma's concerns and challenges have become her own. First there is the door of the workroom, which is carefully locked every night. It takes her a couple of nights of thinking before she links up everything that she already knows into a chain of events that makes sense to her. The solution is the tin spoon, the one Alma was whipped for having stolen but that was never recovered. She may have used it to shape into a key, and the many nightly visits of the phantom at the keyhole were her attempts to try her craft until she was certain of the fit.

Anna Stina has listened carefully each time the watchmen have locked them up for the night. The lock is rusty, the key on their key chain heavy, and to judge by the sounds they make, the mechanism hasn't been oiled for years. Tin is soft, and she doubts that a single spoon would be able to turn the mechanism without bending. Maybe Alma knew of a method to harden the soft metal. Maybe that was why she stole medicine for toothache during her

244

trips to the infirmary. For Anna Stina, it doesn't matter. The only spoons she has seen are of brittle wood, and she has nothing sharp to work them with and knows as little about tin as she does of locks. Nonetheless she must find a way to get herself out past the closed door at night. This is the first obstacle, the first one of four.

Will there be other locked doors along the way? If Anna Stina is right, Alma must have managed with a single key. The door to the Ahlstedt house at the top of the stairs is often left ajar to provide the watchmen with an easy way up to the floors they inhabit, without having to walk through a spinning room. If the front door of the manor is not locked even at night, then a person who managed to make their way out into the yard would be able to proceed through the old house and down into the cellar. That must have been what Alma did. Have the routines been reviewed since then, in the wake of Björkman's outrage? If so, Anna Stina sees no signs of it. And in that case, only one lock blocks her path. To make her way down into the cellar without detection, that is her second challenge.

To find the hole itself, the old drainage tunnel in the wall, and to make her way through it, is the third. The Ewe's mutterings have not revealed much about its exact location. The opening must be small enough to have been overlooked by twenty years' worth of watchmen. Even if everything goes according to plan, she will only have the remainder of that night to find her way.

The fourth and final challenge: she cannot return either to Katarina or Maria parish where she is known, and where Fischer and Tyst or their colleagues will look for her. Johanna said as much, and Anna Stina has no reason not to trust her. Those who manage to escape are soon brought back, and with more strings added to their quota. If she reaches the other side of the wall, she must make a new life for herself beyond the reach of her adversaries. How, she doesn't know.

———•———

When Sunday comes, work is set aside for the long church service. Pastor Neander, who has lately been handing the evening prayers to his assistant, is even worse for wear than usual. He forgets when psalms are to be sung and when prayers recited, when the sermon should be delivered and when the sins forgiven. With trembling hands, he helps himself to the communion wine without concern for who is watching. He reads aloud from the Bible, stuttering and blinking his eyes that are watering from the exertion. He reads from the book of Matthew about the return of Jesus to Jerusalem. They have all heard these verses before. Neander struggles along to the twenty-first chapter, where the merchants are driven from the temple.

'It is written: My house shall be called the house of prayer . . . but ye have made it a den of thieves.'

At these words, Bengt Neander pauses, suddenly thoughtful. Between bushy eyebrows and wrinkled skin, his eyes grow dark.

'My house. A den of thieves.'

He slams his Bible shut loudly enough to waken those who have clandestinely nodded off. With alarm they meet his gaze, now staring angrily into the pews. The rest of his sermon does not come from the Holy Book, but is made up as he goes along. The longer he continues, the more enraged he becomes. His voice increases in volume until he is roaring about the Pharisees and the scribes, about the merchants and the Romans, about all those who profit on the suffering of the righteous and the meek. The pastor shows his brown teeth in a mirthless grin as he segues from talking about the holy land some seventeen hundred years ago to what he sees before him on the Scar today. His attempts to cast Inspector Hans Björkman as an opponent of Jesus become increasingly less subtle. Satan's worshippers may have beautiful voices but their tongues are cloven, they have refined the art of deception and flattery on the finest of stages. When none present – even the simplest of the inmates – can mistake who is being

246

referred to, the assistant pastor feels compelled to deliver Neander from himself, and when clearing his throat in desperation turns out to have no power against the pastor's thunderous voice, he sees no other option than to begin ringing the bell early. Disrupted by the tolling, Neander regains control of himself with difficulty.

Like everyone else, Anna Stina listens at first with astonishment to the pastor's tirades. Then she realizes that he could become her lifeline, this bitter old man who has turned to drink for comfort as he sees himself robbed of his retribution. She recalls the words of the watchman on her first day on the Scar: Hans Björkman's time as inspector will soon be over, after twenty years of mismanagement. Soon he will set sail for Finland. She can hardly sit still in the pews for the remainder of the service. In order to succeed in her intention, she will need both to act quickly and to have luck on her side, for at the same moment that Amen is said, the watchmen will start herding the spinners into the courtyard and from there onward to their rooms.

It is over. They all rise in their seats and begin to shuffle out into the aisle. On wobbly legs, she pushes her way against the stream, up towards the altar where Neander is shaking the last drops of wine from the chalice into his mouth. Peter Pettersson, the custodian, is positioned at the very front, surveying the scene as the chapel is being emptied. He is as large as she remembers and he is standing directly in her path. Now he sees her, with a mixture of surprise and anger. She hardly has time to think before she feints to the left, ducking under his arms and calls out to Pastor Neander.

'What if there had been a way for Our Lord to punish the merchants for their sins before they left the temple?'

That's as far as she gets before Pettersson wraps his hand around her neck. He almost lifts her off her feet, and she closes her eyes as he raises his other hand for the blow.

'Oh for shame, put the girl down.'

Neander's voice has regained the strength of the sermon. It is enough to stop Pettersson in his tracks.

'Even the custodian must know better than to perpetrate violence in the God's house. Do you not fear the Lord?'

Pettersson has no reply. He simply narrows his eyes with disdain.

'You'd do best to drop her, Petter Pettersson. Leave a man at the door to walk her back to that part of the workhouse where she belongs. This girl is weighed down with religious concerns. As the shepherd of her soul, it falls to me to ease her mind.'

Pettersson snorts, relaxing his grip with exaggerated slowness to demonstrate the unnatural strength that extends all the way out to the tips of his fingers.

'Of course, Pastor. You know I would never raise a hand against a defenceless girl . . .'

He walks a few steps down the chapel before he turns and stares into Anna Stina's eyes.

'. . . while in the house of God.'

———— •·——

Bengt Neander waits until Pettersson's large body has exited the front doors.

'Speak quickly, my girl. I have a headache. I don't have half of Mr Pettersson's strength but if you are not worth my while I'll make sure you leave with three slaps and not just the one.'

Neander's hair is standing on end. It appears he has not washed for several weeks. Dirt is packed into every furrow of his face, prematurely aged by its constant scowl of disapproval. Under the sour whiff of spilled wine, she perceives even stronger substances. Anna Stina also senses that his patience is wearing thin. She must take the risk of getting straight to the point.

'Inspector Björkman will soon leave this place without just punishment for his sins. You wish to be an instrument of the Lord while there is still time. I know a way.'

'And what business does a fledgling spinstress have with matters that concern the inspector and myself? Out with it.'

'The inspector is already under scrutiny after the escapes last year, and as yet no one has made it out through his new security measures. If someone were to escape, he would be humiliated, perhaps enough that he would lose both his current position and his next.'

She is guessing wildly but hopes she is right. Neander gives her a look both cunning and stern. He waves her into the sacristy after gesturing to the watchman by the door to remain standing. He barely makes it inside the door before he draws a tin flask from his coat and takes a greedy gulp. The sharp smell of wormwood brings tears to her eyes as he speaks again.

'You are cleverer than age would suggest, but you overestimate my power, I'm afraid. As pastor, I have no means to sway the watchmen. No key has been placed in my trust. Even if I had one, men are posted by the main entrance at night. What you suggest is something I have already considered many times, my girl, and were it but within my reach, I would have emptied the entire building by now. What would it matter when the sluts are back at their spinning wheels within a couple of days? But Björkman – cursed be his name – is clever enough to read my intentions, and in this place he has managed to separate spiritual matters from the worldly. I hope for your sake that you have thought further than this.'

'There is a way out, another way. I am certain of it. All I need is help to unlock the door to the south-west wing.'

'You're lying. What way would this be?'

'There was a girl who escaped last spring. I know how. There is a hole through the cellar wall. Inspector Björkman must have quieted down her disappearance before the news spread, but if you are ready with a report this time, the inspector won't manage the same feat again.'

Bengt Neander studies her for a long time as he ponders. After a while he starts to rock back and forth on his heels, muttering to himself. He chews absently on a strand of his beard.

'One more escapee. After all the funds the inspector has demanded from the Board to remand the situation . . . Well, well. A single door; one key only.'

He rubs his eyes with his thumbs and spits his beard out.

'You know, I've done something similar in the past. I coaxed an inmate like yourself to bring misfortune on Björkman but the plan misfired. I sent a complaint in her name, but the Board recognized my writing. I should perhaps have learned from my mistakes.'

He chortles and toasts to himself before taking yet another sip from his flask.

'Or maybe it's the other way around. Maybe my only mistake was using a musket when a cannon would have served me better. What you suggest is not impossible. I must make inquiries. When I know more I will send for you after evening prayers. One more thing. Turn this way.'

Neander gives her the slap he prevented Pettersson from delivering. Anna Stina does not doubt he lacks Pettersson's power, but nonetheless her cheek burns and her ears ring.

'For your sins, and so that you understand that you are not to deceive me, and because this is as close as I will get to shaking the hand of a whore. And because I don't want it to be said of me that I have inappropriate dealings with the likes of you. Your red cheek will speak for itself.'

He shows her out and hands Anna Stina to the watchman who is waiting for her, and who grabs her by the arm. She hears Neander whistling to himself as she is led out to the courtyard.

38

PETTER PETTERSSON'S QUARTERS are in the north-east corner of the Ahlstedt manor house, the better of two identical rooms. Right next door is Johan Franz Hybinett, who shares Pettersson's duties. Although the window is wide open to the bluffs and the bay, the room is as hot as an oven in the summer heat which has arrived early this year. Constant sweating is never enough to cool Pettersson's large body. He has removed his jacket and shirt in order to stretch out on the bed. He stares up at the ceiling where his predecessors, or whatever trash stayed here before him, have carved their names or fantasies into the wooden beams to stave off boredom. A name and a year here, a gushing prick there. All have faded to grey over the years. The end of Pettersson's twelfth year on the Scar is fast approaching. This room has been his for the duration. He came to his post from the royal breweries in eighty-one, where he had been given a position after his dismissal from the army. Since then he has languished here among his colleagues in blue and yellow uniforms, and even if the custodian service is not formally a part of the city watch, he has found that his lack of a disability among the lame and crippled watchmen has taken on the mantle of a handicap in itself. Even Hybinett suffers from the after-effects of a mortar misfire and can barely close his right hand. Here, Pettersson must be ashamed of his healthy body. His dismissal from the military was due to other factors and he is convinced that the watchmen – who love nothing better than to gossip – have either heard or guessed his story. Pettersson was sent home because he was deemed a liability. Massive, strong, aggressive and conniving, with a taste for cruelty that time and again drove him to exploit his physical superiority to cause others pain, soon no corporal wanted to touch him with a ten-foot pole. They got rid of him on a mere technicality, arguing that it was only a matter of time until he caused real harm. Petter Pettersson was used to hearing accusations, but never before had others needed to perjure themselves just to spite him. The memory of the injustice makes his blood boil to this day. Workhouse custodian on this desolate crag. That's all he's good for.

The posting does come with certain benefits, of course. He has held on to it as if it were dear to him. In eighty-three, before he had learned to master himself, he had managed to whip one of the inmates, Löhman by name, severely enough to cost her her life. It was early morning, he was on wake-up duty, and instead of using his voice, he struck with Master Erik straight down among the beds. Even so, Löhman had refused to move and when, after a dozen blows, she was still lying down, it was as if he saw red. He struck and struck, in the end by using the fat end of the whip instead of its slender braided tongue.

Löhman never rose from her bed again. When he was forced to report her to the infirmary, she lay still, whimpering, come dinner time foam was coming out of her mouth, then she passed away. There were many who were prepared to bear witness to what had occurred. Björkman was forced to bring him in for questioning and even though Pettersson maintained that the whipping could hardly have been enough to end Löhman's life, that she must have succumbed to some weakness of the lungs she had incurred during the night, or at most an unhappy combination of both of these factors, he was given fourteen days in the lock-up on bread and water.

He remembers those days, two long weeks in a cell with hunger clawing at his belly. In the dimness he relived each blow, each welt that the whip had left on Löhman's skin, and when he once again saw the light of day and returned to his duties, he knew it had been worth it. He has learned to be more careful but he can't live without it. A pressure builds inside him that can only be relieved by way of the whip. The boundless power. His large body towering over one of the emaciated inmates, the leather in his hand. He stiffens just thinking about it and in his room he unbuttons his trousers and starts to rub his groin. It is over all too quickly, this meagre enjoyment, and, as always, it will not satisfy.

Like the other watchmen, he has gone to one of the spinners and cornered her in some remote corner of the building – it is, after all, what most of them are in here for, and many of them give themselves willingly to anyone who offers them a drink or a chunk of meat. But even that was a disappointment to him. Afterwards, when he pulled up his trousers and tucked his shirt into place, she smiled at him, the little harlot, as if this in turn had given her some measure of power over him. He turned and left, agitated for reasons he himself did not fully understand.

What the spinners are prepared to offer him willingly does not interest him as much as what he can take from them against their will. The dance around the well is something else entirely, and it takes longer – so much better than a few quick thrusts of the hips, a moment of pleasure, a sneeze of the pelvis. During the dance, he is in another world. The other watchmen all choose to look the other way. He has not danced with anyone since that girl Ersson, who all but volunteered with her big mouth and saucy attitude. That kind is his favourite: those who retain some self-confidence, who believe they still have worth. To whip the living dead is as meaningless as tenderizing meat. Ersson was a welcome interlude. Now she limps around, scared out of her wits. His groin throbs warmly each time he sees her.

Pettersson breathes heavily after his exertion. The frustration that weighs him has hardly been alleviated at all by the physical release. The pressure has begun to mount again, worse now than ever after the service with that drunkard pastor whose unpleasant grin always seems to mock him out of the corner of his eye, an old sot who dares to discipline him in front of the spinners. His chest will burst if he does not get any satisfaction soon. He knows how. He has made his selection, has found the girl, the impertinent one in the same eating group as the old hag. He has seen it in her eyes. There is a sense of pride there, a resistance. She is up to something, he knows it. Soon he will invite her to dance. Soon, but not too soon. The longer he can hold out, the greater will be his reward.

Betting is underway in the wing where there are men, those who are either too old or too young to serve elsewhere, where hard labour is the order of the day. They know Petter Pettersson, may have a measure of understanding 'man to man' about how he handles his well-known desires. It has been weeks since he thrashed that new girl and soon it will be time again. But who will be next? The one who spilled her porridge in her eagerness to reach for the extra herring tail? The one who has been the laziest and has barely spun a full string in an entire week? They observe him closely, noting which girls cause his eyes to linger, trying to read his thoughts. Those who want and can afford to bet on which wing the girl will come from, which eating group, and even – though the odds may still be high – which name.

It is Johanna who lets Anna Stina know.

'You are the favourite. They're barely paying out the betting sum if he chooses you. They say that they have seen him glaring in your direction each time we leave our room. You came with that other one, the one he danced with last time, and now they're certain you'll be next in line.'

The dance itself, being pushed to the point of exhaustion around the well and flogged to pieces by the lash, is not what frightens Anna Stina. What frightens her is that her escape can never happen after Pettersson's dance. The custodian may be skilled enough now not to kill his victims, but to claim that he leaves them alive is not true either. The Dragon is still shuffling around wide-legged on her damaged hips, defying those who have placed bets on her impending death, but she no longer speaks, flinches at shadows, can't sleep because of her nightmares and is so easily spooked that anyone can frighten her. Even if her scars and injuries should heal, her consciousness has found a refuge deep inside from whence it will never fully return. Why should Anna Stina fare any better?

Evening prayers are already over. She will have to wait until the morning before she can speak with Neander and hurry their plans along. She prays that Pettersson can keep his urges in check for just one more day. When the room is dark and locked, she can't sleep. She hears from her breathing that Johanna is also still awake.

'Johanna, if you ever managed to escape from here, what would you do to avoid being caught again?'

Johanna doesn't answer immediately.

'You're up to something. You may think I haven't noticed but I have. Don't be afraid, I won't snitch.'

'There is a way out, I think, and I'm going to take it if I have the opportunity. You can come with me.'

Johanna laughs.

'In less than a hundred strings, I will have served my time and if I keep my head down, I'll be out before summer is gone. If I've spun this much, I may as well spin the rest.'

Anna Stina can't refute her reasoning. It takes a while longer until Johanna answers her first question.

'Most of those who end up here aren't worth much. You've been a good companion, so I'm going to tell you something. I had a friend growing up. Her father ran a pub and as far as I know, he still does. It is called the Scapegrace. Not far from the Red Lock. Years ago, her parents had a disagreement that no one was able to reconcile, although the pastor in Nikolai parish himself tried. It all ended with the mother leaving, and she took my friend with her. She came from somewhere outside of the county and she must have gone home to her parents. I lost my friend but the father had it worse. It broke his heart. He's not been himself since, even though many years have gone by. He stands there behind his counter and pours drinks when his customers ask for something, but it is as if he is just going through the motions. His name is Kalle Tulip, called the Flowerman, even though most of his regulars think that the Wilted Flower would suit him better. My friend's name was Lovisa Ulrika. Kalle Tulip was so proud the day she was born that he gave her the Queen's name.'

'That's a sad story.'

'Look, I'm not trying to tuck you in. Stay quiet and listen. You and Lovisa must have been born within a year of each other. Her eyes were as green as yours, and the red hair almost the same. And if you manage to get out past these walls and away from the Scar, you will never be safe on the Southern Isle again. Instead you should go to Karl Tulip at the Scapegrace and tell him that you are his daughter, Lovisa Ulrika, the childhood friend of Johanna Ulv and that you have now returned to your beloved father after all these years.'

'Wouldn't he recognize his own daughter?'

'Of course. He's not stupid. But he will believe you because it is a lie he wishes to hear more than anything else in his life.'

<hr>

To Anna Stina's relief, Petter Pettersson is not in his usual place at morning prayers. Instead it is the same watchman who first showed her into the courtyard, the one who stood beside her while Pettersson thrashed the Dragon. Jonatan Löf is his name, younger than most of his colleagues, and there doesn't seem to be much wrong with him except a slight stiffness in his back. He is known for being mild-mannered and sells both food and alcohol without charging an exorbitant amount. Anna Stina decides to take the initiative, goes up to him in front of the pews after the prayer is over, curtsies and asks to speak to the pastor. She hardly believes her eyes when he steps aside with a little smile and lets her approach Neander, who in turn waves her into the sacristy with an irritated grunt.

'What's the matter with you, you stupid girl? Don't you understand that people will get suspicious if you come up to see me time and again? I have no key to give you yet.'

'It must be tonight. Tonight or never. At any moment, Petter Pettersson is going to drag me out to the well and make me dance. After that, I won't be able to crawl through a hole anymore.'

Neander's breathing becomes laboured, he fumbles around blindly for the back of a chair and sits down hard. He chews his beard and rubs his scalp until flakes of dry skin fly. When he starts to think aloud, she realizes that he is still drunk and must not have slept in his bed at all before prayers.

'Hell and damnation. Shall I have no reward for all my troubles? Why do you try me so, Lord? Tonight, she says, but it is too early, too early. But Björkman, that greedy bastard, that gluttonous dog, is soon beyond reach and the complaint has already been written . . . but perhaps there are other ways, just as effective . . .'

After a couple of minutes of this muttering, the pastor appears to arrive at a decision. He slams his palm onto the table.

'By the devil, little girl, listen carefully. Tonight, you say, and tonight it shall be, whatever the cost. You'll stay awake and wait for a knock at the door. Someone will open it for you. Then you disappear and whatever happens to you after that is of no concern of mine as long as you stay away long enough for Björkman to be held accountable for his mismanagement. Do you understand? All right, be gone and may Jesus Christ and Beelzebub and Odin Allfather be with you. Or else they'll have me to answer to.'

———•———

When Anna Stina comes out into the courtyard, led by Löf, the watchman, something is happening. They are all lined up, each eating party standing outside their rooms, and Petter Pettersson walks up and down between them, proud as a cock, shining like the sun. Löf gives Anna Stina a shove in the direction of her eating party and she hurries over to stand next to the Ewe, Johanna and Crazy Lisa. Petter Pettersson's booming voice echoes between the buildings.

'Ladies and gentlemen, a theft was discovered earlier this morning. And as you stand here so nicely, we are turning all the beds upside down in order to uncover the stolen goods. No one who is innocent has anything to fear. You can calmly rest your eyes on the gorgeousness before you as long as the search is in progress.'

Anna Stina feels all hope die inside her. It is too late. Pettersson has selected his victim and now all that remains is the dance. They will find whatever small item he has planted among the blood-gorged lice in her mattress, and her vehement objections will make no difference. Pettersson will send for Master Erik and mete out the punishment according to the allowable limits. She is close to tears. She bites down hard on her lower lip, a pain she herself can choose.

A few minutes later, they find the wooden knife. A triumphant watchman proudly holds it aloft and walks straight towards her, dangling his prize between thumb and forefinger. Pettersson asks him which bed it was found in. Then the watchman grabs Johanna

258

by the arm and drags her over to the well, where Pettersson's smile stretches from ear to ear.

———•———

It is half past four in the morning. When more than half the day has gone by, Johanna's screams can still be heard, fainter with every blow that falls. Anna Stina never sees her again.

39

THE BED NEXT to Anna Stina is empty. As they did with the Dragon, the watchmen must have carried Johanna's limp body to the infirmary to be patched up as best they can. The night-time sounds in the room are more alarming than usual. Whimpers and fragments of words can be heard from all corners, violent intakes of breath as inmates wake up from harrowing dreams. Most are sleeping restlessly after having been forced to listen to the screams from the courtyard until long into the afternoon. When Anna Stina walked to vespers, there was a stain around the well where Johanna dragged her body on the ground. Red marks were splashed onto the outside of the well, quickly drying to brown smudges, the origin of which no one who hasn't been there would be able to guess. Her feelings leave no place for fatigue. Terror, grief and sorrow over the fate that became Johanna's, a whispered relief that someone else has taken the place she thought would be hers, immediately followed by shame at the very thought. Inside, she also has a growing sense of panic, a feeling of having been caught up in something she cannot stop. Anna Stina needs to summon every ounce of strength she has for her escape but what has happened to Johanna has cut a deep gash from which her energy seeps out. Not tonight, God, not tonight. And yet she knows the time for choices has run out. She waits in the dark.

The knock comes as quietly as has been promised. At first Anna Stina isn't sure she has heard correctly, but when she heaves her hips over the edge of the bed and tiptoes across the floor, she hears a key turn in the lock. The door glides open a fraction. Someone is waiting on the other side and soundlessly inches the door open enough for her to pass. It is Jonatan Löf, the young watchman. He holds a finger to his mouth, puts his shoulder to the door and at the same time holds the handle so that he won't stress the hinges when he closes again. He locks and then signals for her to follow him.

They walk briskly across the yard and up the stairs towards the old building. From the upper floor, she hears voices and laughter. The watchmen are up late, carousing. Inside she hears the sounds of games and drinking: the smattering of well-thumbed cards on a tabletop and the clinking of bottles and glasses. Löf waves her into a shadow next to the door while he steps through the open half. After he has ensured the lower floor is empty, they pass through a dark kitchen where the warmth from the stove still lingers, and where Löf stops to light a small torch on the embers that he protects with his cupped hand as they continue on through a small dining room and down a corridor. She doesn't find it very easy to see as the flame blinds her rather than lights her way, but Anna Stina can tell that they are passing into the new wing, the one whose foundation the Ewe helped to build.

The ceilings grow lower and the texture of the walls ever more coarse under her hand. No gentleman has ever had these surfaces decorated with a brush and wallpaper. Behind a door without a lock there is a creaking staircase leading down into the cellar. On a hook is a lantern with a small candle that Löf lights after first having closed the door behind them. At the bottom of the stairs, he speaks to her for the first time.

'No one should be able to hear us down here, though that's no reason for us to speak louder than needed. You're in luck, you and your friend Neander. It is Pettersson's habit to treat everybody after he has had his fun with the whip, so that no one will go to

Inspector Björkman and sing a song about excessive force. By now there aren't many up there who can still walk straight.'

Anna Stina watches him and waits. He senses her question.

'Neander gave me a few dalers to unlock your door, show you down here and then keep quiet about it. He told me to wait while you do what you need to do. Take the lantern. You'll have an hour, by the look of the candle. Maybe more.'

She nods. Before he gives her the lantern, he opens the glass and lights a clay pipe already filled with tobacco. He perches on one of the steps as he hands over the lantern with a little smile.

'I wish you luck.'

When Löf has disappeared out of reach of the faint lantern, all that can be seen of him is the glow from his pipe. Each time he puffs on it, a red glow flares up in his face. It seems to her like a theatre mask suspended in a void, rather than something that belongs to a living man.

The cellar is large and walls divide the space into separate vaults, some internally partitioned with wooden boards. She hears the movement of rats, scrambling along the walls. Eyes glint and then fade away as they are caught in the light. It stinks. The whole cellar is filled with food, some of which has clearly been forgotten and left to spoil. Crates of withered apples, sacks of turnips, half-filled barrels of salted meat where the bottom has disintegrated and the brine has spilled out onto the earth floor. She guesses that it is the meat that is responsible for the worst smell, a heavy, revolting stench of decomposition. Flies and moths swarm to her lantern's allure, buzzing in her ears and flying into her face as if intoxicated by their satiation.

Methodically, with an occasional glance at the dwindling candle, she starts to make her way around the walls. It takes her longer than she had hoped. All is in a state of disorganization, with things piled on top of each other and lying heaped in the corners. Again and again, she has to lie flat on the floor and try to peer through the clutter. Each time she is greeted with the sight of the stone foundation.

Finally, all that remains are the small spaces between the wooden partitions. Here sacks and junk are piled so high that she is unable to get close and has no other option than to begin lifting things away, one by one. She places the lantern on the floor as she works. The labour is heavy. Cloth and musty wood coverings disintegrate under the weight of their contents. Before long, woodlice crawl over her arms and shoulders. Each time the flame gives a flutter, she is sure that it will go out and leave her in darkness. The stench only gets worse. But slowly she makes progress. She clears a path through the mound of forgotten objects, until she can feel the stone in front of her.

———— • ————

She jumps when she hears Löf's voice again, very close. He is sitting cross-legged next to the lantern a few steps behind her. He has moved so quietly that she didn't hear anything, occupied with her efforts in moving the debris.

'How're you doing? Not much light left in the lantern.'

She senses a gap at the place where the wall meets the floor.

'Neander left me certain instructions for how to proceed if you didn't find what you were looking for in time.'

She lies down flat on the ground and explores the gap with her hands. It is smaller than she had expected, the upper edge only a couple of hand-widths above the floor.

'The pastor was not keen on tempting fate one more time by having me lead you back across the yard. Should someone out relieving their bladder happen upon us, it'll end badly.'

She stretches her arm in as far as she can and meets empty air. It is here. Alma Gustafsdotter's way to freedom.

'If you don't find what you are looking for before it is too late,' Neander asked me to put my hands around your throat and strangle you, and leave you by the wall under a few bags of turnips.'

She turns around. He is twirling his reedy moustache between thumb and forefinger and smiling at her in the light of the lantern. In desperation and triumph, she returns his smile.

'It's here! I've found it. It's a channel for rainwater, built when the house stood without a roof in the autumn of seventy-two. It goes right under the wall.'

He tilts his head to the side.

'And I was secretly hoping you wouldn't find what you are looking for. Neander promised me a bonus for the trouble of silencing you for good, and in all honesty, I saw other benefits as well. Now it seems I'll have to satisfy myself with just one part. You'll forgive me for wanting to do it in the dark. You are so thin and dirty I prefer not to look at you.'

He blows out the tallow candle. There is no way past him as he approaches her with open arms, forces her down on the floor, tears open her white dress and takes from her what she refused Anders Petter on Children's Lea an eternity ago.

After he has finished, he leaves her there on the cellar floor. She lies outstretched on her back with eyes open, but it is so dark they might as well be closed. In the darkness she sees herself as if from above, somehow illuminated, a body that could just as well have been another's. Emaciated, naked, filthy. She doesn't recognize it. Insects crawl across her skin, and she feels nothing. They are gathering to drink the blood that has oozed out of her and collected in a clotting pool under her thighs and lower back. She does not cry. There are no feelings anymore. Her chest moves up and down and she realizes that she is still alive, but that a choice has been put before her. She no longer needs to live. It would be so simple. All she has to do is listen carefully to the shallow motion of her lungs and her weak pulse and will them to stop forever. They would obey.

She does not know where she finds the strength in this repulsive place, what hidden stores still exist inside her, but she knows she cannot let it end here. She cannot allow it. A fire still burns inside, and she makes her choice and starts to crawl towards the wall on her elbows and knees. The pain is nothing now. She feels it as if from a distance. The rough surface of the gap scrapes her shoulders as she forces herself in with her arms stretched above her head. She has to turn around and enter on her back, crawling under the earth like a caterpillar on her heels and shoulder blades. She only needs to move her head slightly to hit her forehead on the stone above her. She feels its mute mass, the whole house, sitting heavily on this foundation. Her progress is slow, inch by inch, until she is surrounded by stone on all sides.

She feels it in front of her. Something blocks her path ahead where the gap narrows. One of the stones in the ceiling appears to have slipped down and restricted the passage. The foundation, poorly built by inmates supervised by builders underbidding one another, has subsided. It is her hand that touches it first, the curious object pinned underneath and whose stench has spread throughout the cellar.

What she feels is a foot.

Alma Gustafsdotter's cold, dead foot.

Alma never left the workhouse on the Scar. She came this far but no further, pinned under a stone halfway to freedom until she perished from thirst and hunger and the rats.

Anna Stina does not know how much of the night goes by as she clears her path. It seems to her that time itself abandons her in a nightmare she will never forget, a shivering abyss full of emotions and forms and voices and sounds. The corpse is as soft as mud. It falls to pieces under her touch. Bit by bit and handful by handful, she shifts it. In the chest cavity that once was firm enough to be wedged between earth and stone, vermin have built their nest. Gnawed bones yield with minimal force and send new residents scrambling in all directions. When the way ahead is free, Anna Stina turns her head to the side to push her way past the hanging stone, slithering like a snake under a sharp point that scrapes her skin. Slowly but surely she makes it to the tightest point. She empties her lungs of air, pressing herself on, feeling mortar crumbling against her ribs. Flares light up in front of her eyes as the pressure makes the next breath impossible. How she manages to press herself along the single inch that separates life from death, she will never know. Maybe she is starved worse than Alma was. Maybe it is because the stones are now slippery with the juices left by the body. Maybe the dead girl in the cellar behind her puts her hands on the soles of her feet and gives her the one little push that is needed.

On the other side of the wall, a warm wind blows up from the bay. It is the pinpricks of light in the dark sky that she sees first, once her face is out of the tunnel. Above looms the wall of the workhouse, but beyond is a starry sky spanning from horizon to horizon. In the distance, from out over the sea, thunder comes rumbling. When she feels the first raindrops against her bare skin and sees her image reflected in the water near the Bridge of Sighs in the brief flashes of lightning, she knows that she will never be the same again; she will never again be Anna Stina Knapp.

40

WHEN SUMMER NEARS its end, her moon's blood fails to flow for the third time. The first time she paid no notice. Many of the girls at the workhouse stopped bleeding, probably because their gaunt bodies knew they had to conserve every last bit of strength. The second time, the same. She tells herself that her body needs more time to recover, even if under Karl Tulip's care she has started to reclaim the flesh stolen by hunger. She lives under his roof now and helps him with the run of the Scapegrace. Her name is Lovisa Ulrika now. If he knows that she isn't his prodigal daughter, he only shows it in the way he allows her space, careful not to crowd her with the father's love that has been rekindled in his breast. Life has returned to him. Gone is the greying old man she first met, hunched as if taking cover from the world behind his counter. The Flowerman's glory days are come again. His laughter rings out across the establishment as he jests with his customers. His mood is infectious. The Scapegrace changes colour as soiled walls are washed white, the floors are swept, the tankards scrubbed and dried. The clientele swells. Even fine folk from the square by the Hall of Nobles have been spotted among the guests when the hour grows late and thirst allows for less discrimination.

When the third time comes and goes, she knows that the good fortune that has been within her reach is doomed to be fleeting. Against her will, she is with child, Jonatan Löf's child. When she

267

first arrived, Karl Tulip took her by the hand and went up the hill to Saint Nikolai to speak with the pastor, get her name added to the books and counted into the parish once more. As her belly grows larger, she will bring dishonour to her new name and her new father.

Those who still remember Lovisa Ulrika from her childhood and who, after a couple of glasses, joke about how odd it is that cheekbones can change place in a face in a few years, and the shape of a nose be so remodelled, but who have nonetheless kept any suspicions to themselves at the sight of the Flowerman's unbridled joy, will soon speak another language. They will name her a fortune-seeker, a trollop who has engaged in acts of whoring and deception and who in her desperation is prepared to do anything in order to secure a future for herself and the bastard she bears. Even the Flowerman himself will have to listen to reason when the pastor and vicar come to him in their long black coats for a serious conversation. The girl is a tramp, they will say. Can he be certain she is really his? His regulars, concerned about his wellbeing for the first time in years, will convince him. She, Anna Stina Knapp, will be thrown out into the gutter. From there, the road back to the Scar will be all too short.

Pastor Bengt Neander is no longer anywhere to be found, she has heard. The complaint he submitted in order to condemn Hans Björkman tested the already thin patience of the Board and his account did not fit well with the bones that were found in the cellar, human remains that despite their advanced state of decomposition could only be connected with the missing inmate, Knapp. Rather than stay and invite suspicion falling his way, he has been seen boarding a ship bound for England, cursing and on unsteady legs. Björkman is also no longer in his post. He has sailed in the opposite direction, across the Baltic. But Pettersson remains, as does Master Erik. They wait patiently for her on the other side of the bay, to invite her for a last dance around the workhouse well.

———•———

She meets him for the first time one evening in September. It is time to close up, and most of the customers at the Scapegrace are not hard to convince. Even the most truculent lets himself be bribed over the threshold with the offer of one for the road. Karl Tulip has already withdrawn after a hard day's work. When she makes a final round among the upright barrels that serve as tables, she notices that one guest still remains, a man who has curled up on the floor in a corner of the room, next to the fire to warm himself. He is pale and emaciated and his age not easy to guess. He looks both young and old. His long hair is blond but so dirty that its exact hue can't be discerned. His face is a mask of congealed dirt. It isn't the first time she has laid eyes on him. He staggers between the pubs like a wraith, from their hour of opening until late at night. Now he doesn't want to move at all. His breathing is shallow and hissing, his eyes are closed and his body knotted up around whatever warmth it retains. He does not respond to her nudge and she has to get down on her knees and shake his bony shoulders. He stinks. A mere bag of bones under her touch.

'Wake up. The hour is late. You can't sleep here.'

She shakes him again, gently at first but soon harder, and only then does he open his eyes. She reads there the same emotions this past year has taught her: fear and confusion, pain of a kind that will bite for as long as the memory lingers, and she sees that he is young, younger than she would have guessed from his careworn appearance. His eyes roll back in his head and the lids close again as he glides back into his stupor and leaves her without clear options.

Anna Stina cracks open the door to the street. It is blowing hard in the alley and tonight there are teeth on the wind. The

269

light from the street lamps barely reaches the cobblestones. The year is winding to its end, with night frost expected any day. She pulls the door shut and slides the wooden latch into place, fetches some logs for the fire and blows life into embers hidden under the ashes of the hearth. She puts a copper kettle with some water and soap on the stove, and when the water is finger warm, she washes his face clean with a rag.

The crusted dirt slowly dissolves and is washed away. Under this layer, he is hardly more than a boy, no older than herself. He is slowly coming back to consciousness and although his state of intoxication hinders his ability to control his body, he does what he can to help her remove his shirt so that she can soak it and clean him up. The water in the pot clouds and blackens, and she has to put on more. She gives him well water to drink, then she grinds some coffee beans and boils a pot. She has never learned to appreciate the bitter taste herself but has heard others say it helps to sober them up. She speaks quietly to him, trying to rouse him with her questions. Slowly he wakes to the point where he begins to speak.

'My name is Johan Kristofer Blix.'

'I am . . .'

She has to stop herself.

'Lovisa Ulrika, Lovisa Ulrika Tulip.'

She does not want to tell him about a background that isn't hers and for his part, he appears equally unwilling to confide in her.

'My parental home is in Karlskrona. I served as a surgeon's apprentice there during the war. I came here to Stockholm to find my fortune, but what I found instead was . . . something else.'

They sit there together in silence. She gets a blanket and lays it across his shoulders as his shirt dries in the warmth of the stove. Unexpectedly, Anna Stina feels a sense of intimacy growing between them, and it is this that compels her to ask the question that was her first thought at the moment that he named his profession.

'They say that there are herbs, special herbs for women who are with child against their will. The kind the butterflies of the night use.'

She is unable to keep her emotions out of her face. Not grief over the child that will be unmade but anger at the thought of its father and the unclean feeling that she has never been able to scrub away. She has to wait a long time for his response. Finally he nods.

'Can you help me find some?'

His gaze wanders to her belly, concealed under the folds of the ample dress she has bartered for her old one to buy time. He blinks as if it is the first time he sees her, and Anna Stina catches a glint of something else in his eyes, something other than hopelessness and despair. Even his voice has another timbre as he gives her his answer.

'Yes. Yes. You have helped me and I will help you.'

41

KRISTOFER BLIX HAS lived his life in a haze since summer's end, never sober if he can help it. When he isn't sitting in a pub or an inn, he has been staggering around the alleys. He wakes up wherever sleep last found him, in a doorway or next to a fence or in his own vomit in a corner of the Scorched Plot, and when he wakes and finds that no wagon wheel has crushed him in the half-light, it seems that the world itself is taunting him. For a few appalling moments each morning, hungover and between sleep and consciousness, he is back in his dank bedroom, facing another day when he will wash the shrinking man in his care and pour more wine down his throat, apply a tourniquet, cut away, carry off the remains to Magnus in his shed, sit shaking in a corner and drink himself to sleep while the shadows descend on the haunted decay of the estate and the tawny owl howls from the forest. Even now, afterwards, aquavit is the only source of relief. He seeks the bottle whenever he can. His body wastes away but his core is still young and resilient. It still has power to resist the poisons he feeds it, long enough for him to meet the girl. Her name is Lovisa Ulrika and she has asked him for help. She needs it and there is no one else. Kristofer Blix understands that this is a golden thread of mercy that has been extended to him in the darkness where he lives out his final days. Providence has given him the possibility to atone, a life for a life.

The girl lets him stay at the Scapegrace until morning. His shirt is dry and the fabric so clean that it feels as if the entire item of clothing has been replaced by something better. For the first time since his return to Stockholm, it is not brandy that he sets out to find. He needs it no longer. Instead he steers his course out towards the edge of the city, over Slaughterhouse Bridge, past the fish market and north along the Rill and the Bog. He makes a circle around the Cat's Rump Tollgate and seeks what he is looking for in the Great Shade by Lill-Jans. There, the tree trunks stand quietly, the forest is empty and cold and the leaves are like flames glowing in red and gold. Soon they will fall. It is late in the season but he scans the earth around stumps and uprooted trees, all the kinds of places that Emanuel Hoffman once showed him.

— • —

He returns to her the following day with the promised herbs in his pocket. The girl, Lovisa, seems surprised and has trouble adjusting to the difference that has come over him. He declines both wine and spirits, but eats ravenously of the bread she gives him. He has bound the herbs into tiny bouquets for her to store hanging up in order to conserve their potency, and he asks her for a pot. He shows her each step and ensures that she has grasped what should be done.

'Allow the decoction to simmer until the water changes colour. Strain it through a cloth and drink it when it is cool enough. Make a fresh batch each evening.'

'How will I get more herbs when these are gone?'

'I'll gather them and bring them to you.'

Anna Stina takes her first sip, likely prepared for a taste at least as bitter as coffee or as sharp as brandy. Kristofer knows that the mixture doesn't taste strong at all and he sees the relief on her face.

'How does it work?'

'The herbs awaken a thirst in your flesh, and it is the unborn child that is consumed until nothing remains. That was how my

273

master put it when he explained it to me. But the process takes time. You will have to be patient. This method is the best and the safest.'

In the middle of October the news reaches him. In the *Extra Post* he reads that a dead man has been found and he knows it can't be anyone else. A body has been rescued from Larder Lake, without arms and legs, without eyes and teeth and tongue. His handiwork. Kristofer shudders at the reminder but takes comfort in the fact that the suffering he helped to cause is now finally relieved. He says a prayer for the dead man and knows that he is walking another path now. Every day he visits the girl to assure himself of her health, and he waits another week before he tackles what he has long prepared for. One morning, freezing as he does so, he washes his stained clothes in the stream, lets them dry in the autumn sun and makes his way to Nikolai Church to speak with the pastor. He waits until there is an appointment for him, presents himself and explains why he has come.

'I intend to take a wife.'

Kristofer leaves his name and that of Lovisa Ulrika Tulip. The pastor congratulates him and asks him about his home parish He answers that the Blix family has always belonged to Fredrik Church and the pastor promises to send a message as soon as he can so that the banns can be read there as well.

Kristofer can no longer put off the only matter that remains. He takes the hill down to the Scapegrace and waits until evening falls and the hour for his daily visit has come. As the girl is preparing her daily decoction, he stops her by placing his hand on hers. He picks out one of the leaves and holds it up before her.

'This is field horsetail. Master Hoffman told me it was good for the liver.'

He chooses a flower.

'This is Saint John's wort. It is what makes the water red.'

He picks up more and explains their beneficial effects: angelica, sweetgale, cow parsley. One he saves until the end.

'And this is chamomile. I chose it for the taste. None of them have any power to harm your child.'

She doesn't know what to say but Kristofer sees how the colour rises in her cheeks.

'You are too far along now. There is no time. You can't get rid of it anymore. The child will be born.'

He can't pick out any words in her screams. She beats him with her open hands, in the face, on his chest, wherever she can reach. At first he stands still and accepts her blows without defending himself, then she comes closer to him and he opens his arms to fold her sobbing body in an embrace. The strength drains from her, she calms down and into his ear he whispers that he is having their banns read, that the child shall bear his name. It will not arrive in the world a bastard, she will not birth it in sin.

———•———

Anna Stina Knapp no longer knows what to say or feel. She is carrying Löf's piglet, a seed planted in evil and with violence. For a long time she has imagined the unborn as she saw his face in the glow of the pipe: a malignant phantom hovering in her own dark interior with a mocking smile on its lips. Even so her feelings have evolved as time has gone by, and it is with increasing hesitation that she takes the medicine she has been given. She can feel it, the life that grows inside her, still only faintly, like the brush of a moth's wings. How could something so tiny, fruit of her own body, become like its father against her will? Now the choice has been made for her.

When she goes to Karl Tulip and tells him, he starts to cry and it takes her a while to realize that they are tears of joy. He embraces her, puts his ear to her belly and tells her that he had a dream that he was to have a grandchild and how he woke up delirious with joy. He doesn't ask who the father is. She tells him anyway. It is Kristofer Blix, the thin surgeon whose health has improved so much lately. He has proposed marriage to her. They will be wed as soon as some time can be found. Tulip flashes a knowing smile with a glint in his eye that lifts decades off his furrowed face.

'You know, I have seen the two of you together. I thought as much. There's nothing wrong with my eyes and I'd have to be blind not to see that there's something going on between the two of you.'

Something has shifted inside her. At night, Anna Stina doesn't dream the same dream about the Red Rooster, that she is the blaze – filled with roaring hatred – that decimates Stockholm and leaves it in smouldering ruins. It is the child that is the fire now, but not one that ravages. Rather, one that forges and reshapes. She will bring life into these accursed times and the child – be it girl or boy – will be hers to raise. It will not become like the others. It will grow up, grow strong and help make this world into something else, rid of injustice and malice. The child will bring children of its own into the world who will continue the struggle and the chain will endure. Such will be her vengeance on this hateful world. If it is a boy, he shall be named Karl Kristofer, after his father and grandfather. If it is a girl, she will be Anna Stina, named for someone who no longer exists but who will not be forgotten.

42

AT THE END of October, the cold strikes Stockholm with the force of a blow. One morning, Gilded Bay lies shiny and frozen. Kristofer Blix stands at its edge as the sun dips closer to the horizon on its brief way across the winter sky, under the ancient tower that has hosted kings and king-slayers alike.

He thinks about the late summer weeks before he met the girl and fate brought him to a crossroads he could never have fore-seen. In his constant state of drunkenness, he wandered the City-between-the-Bridges and sought death as if it were an old friend late for an appointment. His hope was kindled each time he spied a brawl, knives drawn in anger, or a heavy load that toppled and fell onto the quay. But still it eluded him. No one raised their hand at his meagre frame, no accident could be bothered to take his life, as if his had no worth and the lives of others were far more tempting. He wanted to end it himself but found as before that he does not dare. It is a sin, as everyone knows. If the paradise of which he dreams is a black void of forgetfulness, he assumes the hell reserved for suicides to be a place where he would be forced to remember, to relive time and time again the summer days spent with bloody hands and terror in his chest. How would he ever be able to take his life? He tried instead to find a way to shorten it, discreetly enough perhaps to avoid the Lord's attention. He starved himself until his hands became thin and cold and trem-bled at any start, but in the end hunger always got the better of him. He tried to dig himself a grave with the bottle but without success.

He has asked the girl to do him a favour. He has given her a wrapped package that he has sealed with wax. In it lie all the pages he filled, the letters he wrote over the summer to a sister who no longer exists. He knows now where they belong. He read the address in one of the newspapers at the bookstore, the same one that gave him the news of the body found in the Larder, and he finally understood the only words that ever crossed his victim's lips as he lay in his drunken doze, before his tongue was removed. 'We are indebted to,' was what he heard then. Now he knows better: 'At the Indebetou.'

Kristofer Blix sweeps his gaze across the bay. The sun shines off the day-old ice. It looks as if a road paved with glimmering gold stretches out to him where he stands. This is the path to the heaven that has been promised to him. It all became clear in the same moment the girl asked for his help. A life for a life. By saving the soul of the unborn child, he has purchased the right to dispose of his own.

He takes off his shoes and stands with bare feet on the cold ground, and lays down his jacket, shirt, trousers and jerkin beside them. The hat on top.

His body is no longer haggard and gaunt. It has regained the lustre of youth. His golden hair that reaches far down to his shoulders is no longer matted, and the sunken face has filled out. It is as if time has been rolled back and once again allowed him to look no more than the seventeen years that are his.

He takes his first steps along the golden path. Under him, the ice is so clear he can make out the stones on the bottom until the water grows too deep. He continues, step by step. Behind him, he hears how some people have gathered on the shore, calling him to turn back. But they are already in another world, while he is halfway to the next. He closes his eyes, the sun warming his skin in the frigid air, and he smiles as he walks even further out where the ice creaks at every step. And then it breaks.

PART FOUR

The Best of All Wolves

Winter 1793

Rapture tolls the world's last knell,
The Lord will hold his judgement dear;
Steadfast friends need hold no fear,
While sinners must in darkness dwell.

– Carl Michael Bellman, 1793

43

WHEN MICKEL CARDELL wakes up, he does not know where he is, but his cheeks are wet and he tastes the salt of tears in the corners of his mouth. It is dark all around. Beneath him, something cuts painfully into his side. A round, smooth shaft. As he feels with his hand along the wooden surface, he realizes he is lying on the handle of a broom. His headache is abominable, as is the taste in his mouth. When his eyes grow accustomed to the dark, he can make out the shape of a door.

He remains on his back a moment longer, in the hope that his memory will return. Frothy tankards, smoky pubs, a growing state of drunkenness, voices raised in anger, an exchange of blows. As his senses return, Cardell becomes aware of the cold. Freezing air is rising from the cracks between the floorboards and his teeth are chattering. Stockholm, as always. November now. He is inside the cupboard at the Perdition, at times used as a place to store customers who cannot be managed in any other way. And Cecil Winge is dead.

In his state between wakefulness and sleep, Cardell cannot at first tell nightmare from reality, but the memory surfaces out of the mists of inebriation and the loss hits him yet again, as mercilessly as when the message was first delivered. He loses his breath, fighting to draw in air, and his left arm flares with sudden pain. A whimper escapes him while he massages the scars left by the surgeon's knife. Lightning flickers behind his closed eyelids.

Cardell rolls over onto his stomach. The weight of his left arm is still unfamiliar. He has a new carved hand, of oak this time, and it weighs more than the one he lost. He has not had time to get used to it. Nonetheless, it serves its purpose. Oak may be harder to swing but when it hits the mark, it spreads death and destruction. The new straps fit better. Cardell does not intend to lose it again. He loosens the straps now to regain some blood flow and finds that two front teeth have become jammed between the knuckles of the wooden fist. As life returns to his left arm, he redoes his straps and bangs on the door.

'Open up and let me out, for fuck's sake.'

It takes a while before he receives an answer from the other side.

'Have you calmed down now, Cardell? I don't want any more trouble, do you hear?'

'My temper will only worsen as my patience is tried.'

Something heavy that has been placed in front of the door is dragged aside. Cardell lifts his arm to shield his eyes from the light and lurches out of the cupboard. The taproom is a mess, shards of glass and bottles strewn over the floor. Cardell slumps down on the first bench he sees and rests his face in his hands. When he looks up, Hoffbro's mural grins down at him from the wall. The scythe-wielding corpse dances with joy.

'Gedda, give me something strong. I feel as if my head is about to burst.'

The publican returns with a mug of ale.

'Hear me now, Cardell. If you're going to behave as you did last night, I can't have you here anymore, not even as a customer. You scared away my clientele, and those I employed to keep order in your stead quit on the spot rather than put themselves in your path.'

Cardell downs his drink in one swig and replies when he has regained his breath.

'Calm yourself, Hans. Bad tidings found me late last night and I took them poorly. I'm not expecting more. I have neither friends nor family left.'

Cardell turns his purse inside out on the table. Three shillings and a German farthing.

'You can add the damages I have caused to my tab and I'll settle it once I get paid. Other that that, you may consider our acquaintance at an end, unless you're willing to repaint your walls. Death has laughed in my face one time too many.'

<hr />

The alleys are twilit already. The sun has barely managed to crawl over the rooftops before it plunges downward again. Snow lies on the cobblestones and has gathered in drifts along the walls. The street lamps have not yet been lit and no light is coming from the houses either, where folk gather by the windows instead in order to take advantage of the last light of the day. It is cold and even though Cardell's heart beats like a trip hammer and sweat pours down his body to ease his hangover, he has to pull his coat around him more tightly to shield him from the wind coming off the bay. He treads his path towards the Hall of Nobles and turns right, up towards Castle Hill. If he is lucky, he will still find Isak Reinhold Blom at the Indebetou. Lost memories from last night return to him as he walks.

It was a young police assistant who said it first. The boy must have seen him in Cecil Winge's company before and stepped forward to express his condolences. At first Cardell didn't understand a thing, but others confirmed what their colleague had said. The secretary at the Chamber of Police had confirmed the news himself: the Ghost of the Indebetou was no more. The cold had worsened Cecil Winge's illness until yesterday, when he had breathed his last.

Cardell was already drunk at this point. The announcement was not unexpected but it still knocked him off balance. Deep inside, Cardell had been convinced that their time together would not end until they had shone light on Karl Johan's fate. The body in the Larder had made Cecil Winge cling to life, whatever the cost. Cardell remembered how he had drunk so much until he appeared to be suspended in a sphere of his own, separated from the din of the world, a place peaceful enough to accept the parting, when some passer-by had bumped straight into him.

Rage at the world's baseness and grief at the news of the death had lit him up like a cartouche of gunpowder. Harsh words had been exchanged, followed by blows. Finally they must have overpowered him and thrown him into the cupboard among the brooms, where he soon fell asleep. Karl Johan haunted his dreams from his lonely hole in the graveyard of Maria Church. The dead man whispered lipless accusations, his voice seething with worms.

'You were to bring me justice but you failed. The other has atoned with his life. You'll be next.'

———•———

When Cardell turns the corner of Stockholm Cathedral, he has to hang on to his hat. Out there, where the flowing lake water joins the sea, along the islands lined up in a row, snow whirls out of menacing clouds. Indebetou House lies quiet. The police cannot afford to waste money on candles and they have been forced to adjust their routines to suit the sun. He has the good fortune of running into a man on his way out who can tell him that Secretary Blom is still inside, hunched over his accounts, although – as the man adds in a lower voice – this is only so he can avoid using his own firewood at home, the wily old fox.

'Not that he has any need to be so miserly these days.'

The point of the gibe escapes Cardell, but he is happy enough to be let inside.

Blom's office is bursting with books and ledgers. As expected, a tiled stove is spreading heat in the room, to the point that Blom can sit at his desk in his shirtsleeves. Cardell does not bother to knock.

'I was told last night.'

Blom pushes the paper he has been working on inside a folder.

'My condolences, Cardell. It is a great loss to us all.'

Cardell sits down on a stool and unbuttons his coat. The brisk walk has cleared his head. For the second time since waking, he feels the familiar sense of panic coming on. It is not unexpected but no less painful. His throat narrows and each breath becomes a struggle. Dark spots dance in front of his eyes. He closes them and tries to force his heart to slow down. Blom waits quietly until Cardell is successful and feels life returning to his body.

'Anything to drink round here?'

Blom hesitates, flustered. His face takes on a tinge of colour.

'I feel the utmost compassion for you in your grief but I have my duties to attend to. Each moment counts if I am to get any sleep tonight . . .'

'Really? Let's see it then.'

Cardell deftly snatches the folder Blom has been working on. Blom tries to get it back but is not quick enough.

'Funny, Blom. This doesn't look like police business to me. Seems more like a beggar's letter to Baron Reuterholm about a position at Drottningholm Palace. "Your Excellency –" What's this? Are you sick of your secretarial post after hardly a year of service?'

Blom sinks down on his chair and dejectedly rubs his face with his hands.

'Damn it, Cardell. That's not meant for your eyes. But I'll let that go. Police Chief Norlin has finally been given the notice we've long been expecting. It certainly makes sense. Reuterholm wanted a lapdog and our Johan Gustaf Norlin went his own way, as shown in no small measure by Winge's stunt in the paper with those obscene draperies.'

'Who'll take Norlin's place?'

'Norlin will be posted up north, for his sins. His replacement will be Magnus Ullholm, who is leaving his position at Drottningholm Palace. It is his old job that I am now seeking.'

'I've heard that name before. He is the same Ullholm who was forced to flee to Norway after accusations of embezzlement. And now he will be made chief of police.'

'You have to keep in mind that the primary qualifications for the job are an unyielding loyalty to the current regime, accompanied by inclinations towards servility and flattery.'

'To judge by what I've glimpsed in your letter to the Baron, I must say that if anyone is well suited to recognizing servility and flattery, it'd be you, Blom.'

Blom's frowning face grows even redder.

'By the devil, Cardell! I only get one hundred and fifty dalers a year. That is nothing to live on. To be seen in the company of the likes of Cecil Winge and yourself will do me no favours, so if there is nothing else, I have other duties to which I must attend.'

Cardell stops at the mention of the meagre salary. What was it the young man at the door had said? Cardell squints thoughtfully at Blom, who has stood up and is holding the door open for him.

'You'll sit down and shut your trap, if you know what's good for you. There's something here that doesn't add up. I need to think it over.'

Cardell curses his sluggish mind. His current state doesn't help. On the other hand, there's never been anything wrong with his instincts. Blom is hiding something. The secretary has broken out in a sweat even though the chamber is no warmer than before. His eyes dart around the room and return time and again to a table close to the fire. Cardell follows his gaze. On top of a pile of books sits a bundle wrapped in paper and tied with string. Cardell walks over and picks it up. It is addressed to Cecil Winge, the name written in a childish handwriting and in ink so thin it is almost transparent.

'How'd you come by this, Blom?'

'A girl came and left the package at the entrance this morning. Since I am the secretary, it was brought to my attention.'

Blom casts longing looks at the door of the room. Cardell catches his eye and slowly shakes his head. He shifts his chair to block the exit. He lays the package in his lap as he loosens the strings and unwraps it. It is a bundle of mismatched sheets, wrapped in a bit of stained fabric and written in the same childish hand. He starts to read the crooked lines of text and his heart begins to beat faster. When he puts the pages down again, he fixes Isak Blom with a glare. The fog in his mind slowly dissipates.

'How did you learn of Winge's passing?'

'I don't remember exactly. Someone came with a message.'

'You spoke with this messenger yourself?'

'No, I . . .'

'That's odd. One of the police officers I spoke with last night told me that it was you who informed the agency of the exact hour of death, and of the details. Another question: a man I ran into at the door implied that you had recently come into wealth. May I be so impudent as to ask where this money came from? Perhaps a recently departed aunt?'

'Now listen, Cardell, you have to promise me you will remain calm . . .'

Cardell stands up, locks the door, and puts the key in his pocket while he and Blom begin circling the desk, the one in order to increase the distance between them, the other to narrow that gap.

'From what I hear, there's been a sweepstake here at the agency about the exact time of Cecil Winge's demise. Could that be the way that you have become so rich, brother Blom?'

'Dear Mickel . . . you have to understand my situation . . .'

'When you received this package, Cecil Winge was still alive, but you had no intention of sending it on to him. You'd already decided to consign him to the grave with your falsehood in order to line your own pockets. If you want to live out this day with only a swollen lip, you'd do well to weigh your words carefully now. Is Winge alive or is he dead?'

Cardell overturns the desk, takes several steps and grabs Blom by his collar as he readies his wooden fist for the blow. Blom's voice rises an octave.

'Be sensible, Cardell. I met ropemaker Roselius at the coffee house and heard him complain that he was about to lose such a good tenant. Winge has taken to his bed for the last time and is filling his chamber pot with bloody discharge. The doctor has abandoned him for patients in whom there is still hope to be found, and the pastor has been to see him for his last rites. What does it matter if he died yesterday or if he dies tomorrow? For me it makes the difference of almost a year's salary! Can't you understand that, Cardell?'

Down by the Quayside a few minutes later, before Cardell stretches out his left arm to catch a ride with a passing wagon, he first pauses and wipes the wood clean on some snow.

44

N O WAGON SEES him waving at them through the falling snow either at the Quayside or on Blasius Point. Cardell is not aware of the fact that he has started to run until he hears his soaked leather soles smatter against the planks of the small drawbridge that lets the fishing boats pass New Bridge on their way into Cats' Bay. He feels an intense sense of urgency, as if the burden he bears were enough to drive the sick man from his deathbed at the eleventh hour. Sharp snowflakes pour at him out of the black of night, clawing at his face. Beyond the iced-over bay, he glimpses the fish market, deserted since before the snowstorm. Before he knows it, he is up at Artillery Yard, the air turning to fire in his lungs. Music is coming from Hedvig Eleonora Church. A choir is singing 'Te Deum'. They sing badly, the congregation probably swelled by folk who have simply wanted to escape the storm. But their struggle to hold the tune does not rob their voices of meaning. There is hope and desperation in equal measure. He counts the streets until the city ends and he sees the walls of the mansions and the cluster of linden trees crouched under their burden of white.

The door is unlocked. His thighs are hurting as he runs up the stairs to Winge's room. A single candle is burning inside. Next to the bed sits a priest in black who, in the customary manner, has blurred the lines between prayer and slumber. A maid, whose face Cardell recognizes from his earlier visits, is wringing a wet cloth in a washing bowl and looks up with surprise. Cecil Winge is lying motionless in his bed. Cardell did not think that Winge had any more weight to lose, but sees now that he was mistaken. The skeletal frame reminds him of the frozen bodies at Svensksund, but the face remains uncovered. He must still be alive. Cardell turns to the maid first, once he has regained enough breath to get the words out.

'Is he conscious? Can he be woken?'

'Alas, Mr Winge's not spoken or moved since early morning. Mr Roselius has held vigil by his side and taken his farewell.'

Cardell nods mutely. The bowl next to the bed is filled with clotted slime. Next, he turns to the pastor.

'Get out. That's my chair you're sitting in. You and your scripture have done the best they can. I've another book here and we'll soon see if it can't do better.'

Cardell does not wait for a reply. He wrenches off his coat, wet from both snow and sweat. The maid comes to his aid and, as she is helping him unfasten the straps of his wooden arm, the hesitating pastor appears to reach a decision and passes them without a word on his way out and down the stairs. Cardell sits heavily on the spindle back chair and listens to Winge's shallow breathing before he turns to the maid.

'Is there any coffee? Beer? Please fetch both. I'll be staying for a while.'

She leaves them alone. Cardell studies Winge's face. His eyes are sunken and his cheekbones stand out in his fallen cheeks. The skin on his forehead is stretched so thin and white that it gives Cardell the impression of the skull beneath shining through. The long hair is fanned out, damp at the temples from his fever. The whites of his eyes appear under the eyelids. The coughing fits have left red stains on his lips and shirt collar. Cardell shudders at the sight.

'By God, Cecil Winge. I wouldn't have thought this of you. A man in his prime who gives up so easily at a little cough. Is it sympathy you're after? You don't fool anyone, I'll tell you that for free. You look the picture of health. It was said in my time as a soldier that pain is only weakness leaving the body. I'm sure that applies to consumption as well. Show some courage, damn it!'

Cardell perches the sheaf of pages on his knee and tries to balance them there as he looks through them.

'Now you listen to me. Dying is something you should have thought of earlier, when the situation was less hopeless. Because we're not done yet. Not by a long measure.'

Cardell opens Kristofer Blix's memoir, clears his throat and begins to read aloud.

'Dearest sister . . .'

One hour follows the next. The maid comes and goes, with beer and water, and later with some slices of bread and a pitcher of milk sweetened with honey. Cardell hardly notices her.

When he comes to, it is because the morning light is shining through the window directly onto his bent head. The pile of papers is gone from his lap and he feels a prick of panic at the thought of their loss. It must have slid out of his hands when he nodded off, this most valuable artefact that has come into his possession either by accident or providence. He doesn't see it on the floorboards under his feet, and it is only when he raises his eyes that he sees Blix's pages resting under Winge's thin hands. Cardell rubs the sleep out of his eyes and, as he studies Winge's sleeping face, the latter opens his eyes. First they stare at each other in silence. Cardell is the first to speak.

'So you're alive, after all. Well, you always have an answer for everything. Did these letters save your life like a spell out of a fairy tale or is it simply a great coincidence we've witnessed this night?'

Winge shrugs.

'My illness flares up from time to time, this relapse worse than ever. Everyone thought it the end, myself included. As for the reading, I will have to owe you an answer, but I would hazard to guess that the infirm are always helped by being reminded of what's left to live for.'

Winge's gaze slides over to the window. A shadow seems to fall over his face when he speaks again.

'You told me that you were close to death during the war. Did you ever see him in the eye? His shape, I mean?'

Cardell winces at the memory of *Ingeborg*'s destruction and the vision he had as Johan Hjelm's lifeless body was sucked into the depths of the Baltic.

'Yes, I saw him then. He was waiting for his tribute under the keel of the fleet, with black wings spread and the grinning face of a naked skull.'

'Perhaps death comes to us all in a different guise. I found him to be a twilit abyss, a yawning void of darkness. I knew that at his embrace I would disappear out of time and mind, never to return. As he pulled me closer, I had time to consider the life I had led. It seemed to me that I had made a choice between reason and emotion and remained faithful to the former in all of my days. In my legal profession, I took pains to make sure every defendant had his say. No one that I have defended in court, no one that I have accompanied to the defendant's bench, has been sent unheard to their fate. Even in private matters, I have . . .'

He pauses and has to begin again.

'Jean Michael, lately I have come to doubt my conviction. Not from a rational perspective but from all the pain that I have felt. In these final days of my life, I have asked myself if a path that leads to such a dark place can really be intended for human beings. But now, as the abyss awaited me with its promise of eternal solace for the misery I have experienced, I was at last able to look beyond my suffering. I have stood up for what I hold to be righteous my entire life. And suddenly it seemed to me that I carried a small flame in my hands, a tender flame to light the darkness. It was such a comfort to me that my fear vanished and I prepared to take my final steps with peace of mind. It was then that I heard your voice. I turned from the abyss. When I came to, you were snoring. I found that I had enough strength to pick up the papers. I read Kristofer Blix's narrative.'

'And now that you live again, have the pain and doubt returned?'

In Winge's eyes Cardell sees sorrow, but also something that will not yield. He presses his thin lips into a white line before he gives an answer.

'Yes. Yes, it would appear they are the constants of my existence. The best remedy for both, it seems to me, is to bring Karl Johan's murderer to justice. Help me from this bed, Jean Michael, and if any warm water remains to wash the fever from my body, I would be grateful.'

'Are you sure you're well enough to get up? It's only a few hours since the doctor left you for dead.'

'There can't be much weakness left in my body at this point, if what I think I heard you say earlier is to be believed. Let us use the remaining time to make use of the knowledge we have been given. Do you remember what Madame Sachs told us at Keyser House?'

'The less I remember, the happier I am.'

'Karl Johan had the habit of eating his own faeces when unattended. She thought this behaviour a sign that he had lost his mind. In light of what we now know, I posit the opposite. This was the only way for Karl Johan to retain the only thing he owned, an object that could lead someone to find his rightful name and thereby also his killer's. Blix gave Karl Johan the ring and he made sure to hold on to it in the only way possible. He found it and swallowed it again and again. Through everything he was made to suffer, he retained his sanity.'

Cardell feels nausea squeeze his stomach. He has to alternate between swallowing and taking deep breaths in order to keep his food down.

'Oh God. Oh damn it all.'

'I'd be hard put to give better words to my own feelings on the subject. We cannot let his plight have been in vain. If we hurry, we may be able to convince the gravedigger to put his spade in the frozen ground with enough vigour to reach the body before the sun goes down. What we need to do is best done under the cover of darkness. Surely the ring is still there. It will bear a coat of arms, and behind that is Karl Johan's true name. Let us hurry.'

45

WHEN SCHWALBE THE gravedigger appears in the gap between door and frame, he peers at them for a while before recognition dawns on his face.

'Mr Winge, yes? Mr . . . Carlén? Kardus? Caliban?'

'It's Cardell.'

Schwalbe welcomes them with a sweep of his hand. A fire is burning in the hearth and a Bible lies open on the table.

'You must forgive me, Mr Cardell. I usually have an eye for faces but yours looks as if it's been somewhat rearranged. I don't believe your nose was so far to the left and one of your eyes looks as if it has slipped to the side. And Mr Winge, are you eating well? I've been told that pallor is in fashion but when you have the snow at your back, you look as if you are nothing but a coat and breeches that have escaped their wardrobe.'

Cardell grunts as he stamps the snow from his boots.

'If we were all to go through life with a beauty such as yours, Schwalbe, the artists of this world would have to go begging for their bread.'

Schwalbe grins widely, displaying the brown stumps that are his teeth.

'You've come back for your difficult cadaver, the angry and limbless one, your Karl Johan? In fact I've been expecting you back.'

'How come?'

'There are those in the parish who have the gift of second sight, and they say his soul won't go to rest. He slithers among the gravestones like a slug, surrounded by a faint shimmer and muttering words that cannot be heard. That is why I know he has left something unfinished in life and therefore I have been awaiting your return.'

Winge and Cardell exchange looks. Cardell is comforted by the naked scepticism he finds in his companion's eyes. He himself is more uncertain. Winge takes out his purse and counts out some money on Schwalbe's table.

'We would like the grave opened as soon as possible. It is of the utmost importance that we have another opportunity to examine the body and for this we will need you to lend us your room.'

Out in the graveyard, the naked linden trees stand in a row, still young as they were planted only after the great fire cleared space for them. A listless wind coaxes snowflakes from the branches and sends them dancing through the air. Schwalbe pushes through the thick snow cover, followed by Winge and Cardell. He finds his way to the grave site by markers only he knows, sweeps the snow from the spot with a spruce branch and begins the laborious work of digging. He alternates between hoe, shovel and crowbar. He soon finds his rhythm and begins to hum a melody as he keeps pace with his instruments. Cardell watches this spectacle with a mix of excitement and concern. The cold is harsh, and their exhalations form plumes in front of their faces. Winge stands next to him, propped against his shoulder and with a handkerchief over his nose to warm his breath.

'There's no reason for you to stand out here, tempting fate. Go back inside to the warm. I'll let you know as soon as Karl Johan is out in the open.'

Winge gives a shake of his head. Cardell would most like to run on the spot and shake his arms to warm his body but Winge's hand keeps him from moving. He stays where he is and stops his teeth from chattering by sheer force of will. The time goes by until Dieter Schwalbe's thin-haired head – too sweaty for a hat – is bobbing level with their knees and he is able to free a small bundle out of the ground with a final groan.

'Will you help me get him up?'

Cardell swears at the first touch.

'I'll be damned if he isn't completely frozen as well.'

Winge nods thoughtfully and turns to Schwalbe.

'We'll need to thaw out the body.'

Schwalbe is helped out of the hole by Cardell.

'As it happens, I was anticipating this very situation and put a couple of extra logs on the fire. I'll get a sled to pull him on, then more wood. Then I'm heading down to the Lock to get myself something to eat and a few drinks. Leave him under a sheet when you're finished.'

Schwalbe's unquestioning acceptance bothers Cardell for reasons he can't explain.

'The reason that we . . .'

'*Nein*. I have some idea, but as long as you remain quiet, I can still hope I'm mistaken.'

<hr />

They pile on the firewood until the heat causes the beams in the cottage to groan and creak. They place the stiff corpse, still in its shroud, on a bench close to the fire and then wait. Cardell is amazed at the change that has come over Cecil Winge in only a few hours. It is true that he basically needed to be lifted into the wagon and that he was so weak Cardell had to not only steady him but rather carry him across Roselius's frozen garden. But already he looks different. His eyes are shining, his skin has a healthier complexion, and his hair, now combed and gathered at his neck, has regained some of its former vitality. He no longer needs to be supported. Instead he makes restless trips across the floor while the body slowly thaws. As time passes, Cardell finds he has to breathe through his mouth in order to manage.

'The stench gets worse. D'you think Karl Johan's ripe yet?'

'Yes, let us get to work.'

With sleeves rolled up and fingers and a knife for tools, they examine the soft cavity, where the worms that had settled into their winter rest are disturbed, waving their stout bodies in confusion. Then the light from the lantern catches a glint of metal that shines through in the red-brown darkness.

Winge holds the ring up to the light and inspects it closely. Cardell forces himself to remain still in his excitement. He feels the moment weigh so heavily that it is almost unbearable. How many times must Karl Johan have searched for the ring and swallowed it in hopes of a moment like this, somewhere on the other side of his passing? He feels their combined hopes like approaching thunder in the air, and holds his gaze locked on Winge's face in anticipation of reading insight and triumph there. Winge turns the ring in the light to let the shadows show its pattern.

Cardell soon senses a note of disappointment before a single word is uttered. Winge does not stop looking at the ring as he speaks, as if he is waiting for it to recast itself into a more promising shape.

'I am not without a working knowledge of heraldry. Even though I have not seen the mark of every great family and therefore cannot call all of them to mind, I am quite familiar with the conventions. The coat of arms we see here does not belong to a nobleman. The shield is divided into blue and red, with three six-pointed stars on each side accompanied by a charge: a laurel wreath and a rampant lion, the crest surmounted by a plume of pink feathers. The shield is almost ridiculous in its profusion of ornate detail, the kind of heraldry a child would draw from fantasies of knighthood and honour. Nor is the ring itself made of gold, as it usually would be. It is stained and discoloured where the gastric juices have marred the surface. The stone is surely nothing else but coloured glass.'

Only now does he put it down and rub his eyes from the exertion.

'This is less than I was hoping for, Jean Michael. It is a very perplexing ring.'

Cardell's shoulders, almost raised to his ears with anticipation, now drop as quickly as if the string holding them up had snapped. Winge is quick to continue.

'When someone is knighted, skilled penmen from the Royal Academy of Letters create the heraldry. They select emblems with a connection to the person's life and work. Take Olof af Acrel, King Gustav's physician, whose arms displayed the caduceus of the medical profession – a snake coiled around a staff – but looped through a crown, and in this way both his profession and the King's appreciation were given prominence. This design, however, came from somewhere else.'

'But where does it leave us? Is it another dead end?'

Winge leans closer to the light and loses himself again in contemplation of the design.

'It reminds me of something. It is familiar in some way.'

Cardell feels his frustration rising and it demands expression. With an oath, he lets his left fist slam into Schwalbe's tabletop, hard enough to leave a mark, and he sucks in air through clenched teeth when the blow reverberates up into his stump. Winge turns away from the ring and fixes Cardell with his gaze.

'Jean Michael, would you say that you are in full possession of your senses?'

'What kind of question is that on a night like this'

'I will take that as an affirmative. Is there something that you prefer to eat over anything else? Any dish in particular?'

If Cardell didn't know Winge so well by now, he would have thought he was being mocked, but there is no trace of humour in Winge's face. As there never has been.

'I like cabbage rolls.'

'And the worst thing you know?'

'There was a soup at Sveaborg fort that was served whenever the fleet was icebound, and guessing the contents of the swill was the best distraction to be had from day to day. I found a whisker in there on one occasion, and even though I hoped it had once been attached to a cat, I somehow highly doubt it.'

'And yet if the choice were between this unpalatable soup and the contents of your chamber pot, you would no doubt prefer the former. What I am trying to say, Jean Michael, is that Karl Johan would not have eaten his own waste for weeks on end if there was no hope that anything good would come of it. He knew that the ring would make it possible to trace his identity, even if it were to require a considerable effort.'

46

MICKEL CARDELL HAS found a new room to rent, in the same neighbourhood. His new lodgings, narrow enough to be able to touch all four walls from his bed, can hardly be distinguished from his old. The mattress is thin in places where it should be thick, worn down by generations of sleepers. But the place is warm enough and cheap enough. It'll do. Brandy helps him sleep, and he drinks more of the same for breakfast to soothe the many aches that come with dawn.

Tired as he is, Cardell is not ready for bed. Each time he shuts his eyes, images from Schwalbe's cottage await him. It's been years since Cardell could call himself a stranger to nightmares, and when evening comes without a message from Winge, it is not to bed that he steers his course but to the pubs. He has said farewell for good to the Perdition but the choices are endless. He crosses Ironmonger's Square somewhat aimlessly, and from East Street takes a side street at random towards the quay. Above the door he reads a sign that says 'Terra Nova' – the new world. The name has a familiar ring to it. A new world would suit him perfectly.

———◆———

There are more people about than he would have guessed on a weekday evening like this. The crowd seems so exhilarated, Cardell has to ask what the matter is. A smoothly shaved guardsman turns to him with an expression of disbelief.

'Have you not heard? How can you not have heard? The city hasn't talked of anything else since the news spread last night.'

A shadow crosses the guard's face.

'She's dead! They've chopped her head off.'

'Who, damn it?'

'The Queen!'

Cardell can't believe his ears. The man must have drunk himself silly.

'Sofia Magdalena? Gustav's widow? What the . . .? Did the court finally have enough of her musical soirées?'

'No, the Queen of France, you idiot. Marie Antoinette. The news came yesterday. They shoved her under the blade and threw her body into an unmarked grave. The barbarism!'

The guardsman grabs Cardell by the shoulders and puts his mouth close to his ear to whisper surreptitiously.

'And yet there are those who think that the mob has right on its side, not least here in this establishment. A word to the wise.'

The man spits on the floor with disgust and elbows his way towards the door.

———◆———

Later, with a few tankards in his belly, Cardell is well aware of how right the guardsman had been. The city appears unable to get its fill of the scandal. Everyone has heard a story of how the Queen met her fate, and they tell it eagerly, whether Cardell asks them to or not. One says that she laughed derisively at the crowd and claimed that her life of adultery and indulgence had been worth a hundred guillotines. According to another, she wept silently. A third said that her last words went to the executioner: an apology that she had happened to step on his foot on her way up the scaffold. Cardell does his best to keep the voices out. With each drink this becomes easier, but others are drinking at the same pace and get louder and louder the later it gets. The revolutionary talk grows stronger. There is a rumour that Duke Charles has made sure to have his own expensive imported art smuggled over the border in order to avoid taxation. Right should be right for high as for low, his critics maintain; the same men and women who have found it the easiest to conceal their sorrow at the French Queen's demise.

When he first sees the ring, he blames it on the alcohol. He shakes his head and rubs his eyes, convinced that the wishful thinking has made him hallucinate, but it is still there when he looks again. A young man in pantaloons and a taffeta waistcoat wears it on his left hand: gold, with a black oval-carved shield. Cardell makes his way over in order to get a better look. Similar heraldic rings are seen here and there on noble fingers, but no; the closer he gets, the more he is certain. The design is too small to see in detail but the construction is the same, the setting as if made from the same mould.

The room spins and the tobacco smoke stings Cardell's eyes. He blinks tears down his cheeks when he turns next to examining the ring's wearer. Maybe twenty. Gaudily dressed in clothes that are as expensive as they are tasteless. A bright white cravat tied at his throat, a scarlet coat and well-powdered hair. Cardell curses the tankards he has downed when he realizes that his open staring has drawn the man's attention. With silent oaths, he sits back down on a bench and steels himself to drive the alcohol from his blood as he keeps the man in his line of sight. He waits.

<hr>

It takes a while before the man's group breaks up. They all have a similar appearance, dressed like peacocks and with exaggeratedly elegant manners. Every third word is spoken in French or English. They bid each other farewell by kissing on the cheek. Cardell has started to sober up and walks out ahead of them to the alley, where he turns to a wall and pretends to have a piss. With approval, he notes that the man has a walking stick that strikes the cobblestones at every step. The sound makes it easy to follow him, even when he turns a corner.

He must have overestimated his state of sobriety. As careful as he is, he can't help kicking up some ice shards and sees the man throw a quick glance over his shoulder. Up at Parsley Pass, he starts to run. Cardell gnashes his teeth and follows as best he can, but soon notices that he is losing ground. Out on Skerry Street he can barely hear the steps, and when he reaches Merchant's Street, no one is to be seen. He leans forward with his right hand on his knee and lets himself catch his breath. When his lungs have stopped burning and he has spat the taste of iron from his mouth, it strikes him that the pursuit may not be over. Cardell knows the City-between-the-Bridges well. If his target had rushed into the nameless alley to his right, he may have learned that it ends in a snowbank piled up against a wall, as all snow that men don't have the energy to shovel as far as Old Square usually ends up there. He peers around the corner and finds the alley empty. A second look has him chortling with satisfaction.

'You breathe quietly, I'll grant you, but in this cold it matters little. A smoking chimney would have been easier to miss. Come out from behind that drift and we'll talk.'

The plumes of steam stop as the man holds his breath, but he soon realizes the futility of his actions. When he steps out, it is with shiny metal in his fist. As Cardell moves sideways to block the exit, he assesses the dagger's length at about seven inches. The young man points it at Cardell as he draws closer.

'Now that I see you up close, I'm not sure why I ran. You are fat and slow, old man.'

Cardell doesn't take his eyes off the knife.

'Cautious and seasoned, I'd say.'

The young man holds his weapon between them, its point raised. Cardell knows what he should do. The risk is considerable but it is his best chance.

'Care to dance?'

Cardell jumps forward in what looks like an embrace. He outweighs his opponent by far and sends him flying until his back hits the wall. The air goes out of him like a cracked bellows. Cardell opens his eyes and checks to make sure, but when he looks down he sees that he has succeeded in his plan. The force was strong enough to press the handle of the knife into the young man's middle and take all the fight out of him. Cardell lifts up the arm he has been holding in front of him. The knife's blade is wedged two fingers down into the wood.

'Would you look at that.'

The young man has slid down the wall, curled up in pain. Cardell brushes the gutter free from snow and sits down beside him. He waits a while until the groans have stopped.

'Melt a little snow in your mouth, boy. You'll see it'll make you feel better.'

With a sour look, the young man does as he is told.

'Right?'

He nods in response.

'There was no reason to draw arms. I've no intention of hurting you. There's only one thing I ask: that you could please show me that ring you're wearing. I won't steal it.'

The young man licks his knuckle and pulls the ring off. The design of the shield is different from Karl Johan's. At the same time, Cardell is right. All of the other elements are identical.

'Can you tell me where you came by this?'

The young man's voice is hoarse and strained as the pain forces him to keep his breathing shallow.

'It is my family's coat of arms. My father gave it me on his deathbed.'

'The hell you did. If you are a nobleman, I am Gustav Adolf himself, just returned from the front at Lützen and in perfect health. Now tell me the truth.'

He receives a churlish glare in return.

'There are a lot of easygoing goldsmiths around who make them. As long as you pay up, they'll create a coat of arms for you.'

'So you and your friends can make yourselves out to be better than you are?'

The man smiles faintly and rests his eyes on Cardell's wooden fist, the knife still stuck in its side.

'I imagine it is hard for a fine gentleman such as yourself to understand, having never had any reason to wish for a better station in life.'

Cardell can't help but laugh.

'How common are they, these false rings?'

'Lately, there's been rampant inflation in them, unfortunately, which has made the pretence harder to maintain. I see a great number of this style on evenings like this. There are simply too many of us who are prepared to pay for borrowed feathers. With the degree of your curiosity, I'm surprised that you haven't seen one until now.'

'I've only recently found an interest in other people's rings.'

Cardell fills his mouth with tobacco and passes the leather pouch to the young man, who nods his assent and stuffs a wad in his cheek.

'What's your name?'

'Carsten Norström. Here in the city I go by the name of Vikare.'

'Carsten Vikare?'

The name is one that Cardell has heard not too long ago. The last of the alcohol makes his thoughts run slow. He churns the tobacco leaves between his teeth until his tongue bathes in their juices and he has to spit a brown streak into the snow. He snaps his fingers when his memory returns.

'That's right! You and your friends are swindlers who take money from easy prey. "Rabbits", is what you call them. Do you happen to remember a Kristofer Blix? Do you know where he can be found?'

Vikare has started to sweat in the cold.

'Blix is dead. He drowned himself in Gilded Bay only days after his banns were read.'

'Is that so?'

'It was never our intention to . . . It was just for sport.'

So seventeen years is all there was to be for Kristofer Blix. Cardell had never dared to hope to meet him in life, but the news is still sad. Such a short life, filled with so much death, and now ended in despair. Blix may have been a coward but Cardell wonders how much better he himself would have done under similar circumstances.

'How much did you take from him and his friend? One hundred dalers? I grew fond of young Blix during what we may call our short acquaintance, and it strikes me now that I was not completely honest with you earlier.'

Carsten Vikare raises his eyebrows and stops in the middle of chewing.

'How so?'

'I believe I said I had no intention of hurting you.'

47

WHEN THEY MEET up later in the morning over a hot coffee pot at the Small Exchange, Cardell does not tell the whole story to Winge and also does not call Carsten Vikare by name. Nonetheless, he has rarely seen Cecil Winge in a better mood.

'I feel our luck turning, Jean Michael. This was a fortunate encounter and you could hardly have conducted yourself better. For the first time we know something definitive about Karl Johan's person. He was young, he came to Stockholm from somewhere else, he was not of a fine family, nurtured dreams of better things and sought out a goldsmith to fabricate a noble background.'

Cardell, who has had more time to process the information, has an easier time controlling himself.

'That's all well and good, but I don't really see how anything has changed. We still don't know his name, and without that we know nothing. Maybe the smith who forged the ring would remember him?'

Winge shakes his head.

'There are too many smiths out there and most of the ones who would take on this kind of work would be journeymen working outside the approval and knowledge of the guild. Their names will be as hard to find as Karl Johan's own, and even if luck were on our side I don't see why Karl Johan would have given them his name, either the one he was born with or the one he aimed to take.'

Cardell holds out his arms in a gesture of defeat.

'Then it is as I said. Things are as they were and we're no closer to a solution.'

'Yes and no. When I first saw the ring, there was something in it that I found remarkably familiar but I could not for the life of me figure out what it was. All I could say with any certainty was that the coat of arms did not belong to any noble family in Sweden. Now we have our explanation: Karl Johan drew the design himself.'

'So?'

'I don't know. I need more time to think it over.'

— • —

Back out on the square, the wind is whipping sheets of snow from out of the alleys. Cardell stretches his sore back, misjudges the surface of the road and – his arms windmilling furiously – falls backwards as the air currents tug on his coat and his heels slip on a patch of ice. He curses vehemently from the snowdrift in which he lands.

'You know, the Golden Sun inn is not that far from here. The snow and cold are making me thirsty. I know you do not have a habit of drinking alcohol but a drunk man thinks differently to a sober one. If there is anything stuck inside that great big head of yours that isn't coming out of its own accord, it's with brandy we'll shake it out.'

Winge opens his mouth as if to protest, but changes his mind and makes a slight bow in Cardell's direction before he lends him an arm to get up. Cardell pretends to make use of it to express his gratitude at the gesture, but is fully conscious of the fact that even a fraction of his true weight would have brought Winge down as easily as if he had been a small child.

At the Golden Sun, a fire is roaring in its brick den, gnawing at the logs that sputter and crack as the flames find their marrow. A loaf of rye bread and a wedge of cheese accompany two mugs of hot chocolate, and soon there is also red wine in a jug with two shallow cups. They toast, and Cardell calls out for more food. With the next jug, they get a ragout, a lean winter hare drenched in gravy. They drink cup after cup, and Cardell – who can't help but wonder what effects the alcohol will have on Cecil Winge – observes with chagrin that, if anything, he appears only more buttoned-up and melancholy, though a faint wash of colour has started to spread across the pale cheeks. It surprises Cardell that it is Winge who opens his mouth first.

'Let me present you with a problem, Jean Michael. If you love someone more than yourself, isn't it then sensible to try to do everything in your power to guarantee that person's happiness?'

Cardell frowns and shakes off a shudder.

'I know little of such things.'

'I beg to differ. It isn't possible to be a human being without in one way or another being placed in this kind of situation.'

Cardell feels a tingle in his stump and turns to the fire when he replies.

'Those kind of feelings never lead to anything good. The one you love always leaves you for some reason, and you'll end up feeling worse than you did before.'

'That is a wise answer and very relevant to my argument. Let me give you a concrete example of what I mean. Suppose that a man finds out he is dying. He knows that his love for his wife is reciprocated and that his death will mean a catastrophe for her. The thought of her life after his funeral torments him night and day; he sees a lone widow dressed in mourning, chasing all suitors away with the memory of her husband as her youth is wasted. He wonders if there is anything he can do in order to prevent this from happening, though he cannot change his fate. Have you followed me thus far, Jean Michael?'

Cardell nods. Winge reaches for the wine, empties his cup and immediately fills it up again to the brim.

'The dying man knows his wife better than anyone else. He knows what she likes and what she finds distasteful. One evening he meets a young corporal in the army, in uniform, with blackened moustaches, a handsome man with his future ahead of him. They converse and the dying man notes that the corporal not only has physical advantages but is also a sensible man with a good head and his heart in the right place, with a becomingly youthful innocence. The dying man invites the corporal to his home and quickly makes a friend out of him. He introduces him to his wife, whose melancholia in view of her husband's impending demise lends to her beauty something sublime. He notes that this does not escape the corporal. They begin to socialize more frequently, and the dying man begins to find excuses to leave the two of them alone. It takes a long time and a great deal of effort but, in the end, a mutual sympathy begins to take root. The dying man imagines how these two, who are both fond of him, will come to dry each other's tears on the day he draws his last breath, and go together towards a shared future. A marriage.'

Winge closes his eyes and throws his head back, so that his ponytail lashes against his back when he empties his glass.

'Children.'

He coughs when some of the wine goes down the wrong way. Cardell stares at him in horror.

'You did this? Are you out of your mind?'

'Yes, this I did, Jean Michael, and there is no reason it should not have worked.'

'Except that living people are not marbles on an abacus or numbers in a ledger.'

'It would have worked, Jean Michael. If my cough had not muffled the sounds of their lovemaking and if I had allowed the door to the bedchamber to remain closed, I would have maintained the charade until the end, as was my intention. But there is a difference between having planned something and seeing it with one's own eyes. I left our home the same evening and moved to Roselius's house.'

'And the child that is on its way? Are you the father or is it the corporal?'

'I don't know.'

Outside the window, shadows pass through the alley, bent over in the hill towards the square, leaning backwards and with their arms outstretched for balance. A new log is added to the fire and it sends a shower of sparks over the floor. Cardell jumps onto his feet to help the maid stamp them out.

'Damn it, girl, you should be careful. One spark is all it takes.'

Winge sits without moving. Cardell gives him a worried look and sits down again.

'And let's get another drink over here before I die of thirst. This floor isn't the only thing here that's dry as tinder.'

They drink together and the hours go by. The dining room of the Golden Sun fills and drains with the tide of visitors. The customers amble in from the cold, thaw their frozen flesh, make noise and laugh. In a separate room there is a card game, and sums of money change hands to elation and cursing. The pub owner Olof Myra, ancient and wizened as if he were made of the same stuff as his wooden beams, lets them sit undisturbed until midnight draws closer, but to no avail.

'What now, Jean Michael?'

Winge can't speak clearly any longer. Cardell feels the floorboards swaying like the deck of a ship. With a superstitious glance, he assures himself that the walls have windows and not gun ports, and that what lies beyond them is the city's paved alleys and not the waves of Svensksund.

'Now we're finished. We drink the pale draught of death and are back where we started. As wise as we were before but less sober, at least. Myra! Two tots of aquavit before you show us the door.'

They raise their glasses.

'To going in circles.'

'*Skål*, Cecil Winge. My idea was perhaps not as good as it first seemed, and given how good my ideas normally are, I should have been able to work that out with my arse. Tell me, what's going on? You look all pale all of a sudden. Did you choke on something?'

Winge stares vacantly into space, suddenly as sober as the day he was born.

'Wait, wait . . .'

The black pupils jump back and forth between things Cardell can't see. When the gaze refocuses, it is fixed on Cardell's ruddy face.

'Arse.'

'Beg your pardon?'

'The Arse! I know who he is. Karl Johan. Come with me!'

48

THEY RUN THROUGH the snowstorm, where gusts of wind strike the alleys unpredictably and where heels slip on insidious stretches of ice. The drink makes them oblivious to the cold. No one has bothered to light the lanterns along the houses, assuming that the night watch will not take its duties seriously on a night such as this. Cardell keeps his collar upturned with his healthy hand to stop the snow from creeping down his neck, on the heels of Winge, who is a blurred figure in the snowy haze in front of him. He does not need to see. The barking sounds of Winge's cough are enough to show him the way. He wants to ask his friend to slow down and catch his breath but has enough trouble simply keeping pace. A black lace headdress, torn from a head somewhere in the distance, rolls by over the frozen dung of the streets. At Castle Hill, Winge tries the handle on the front door of Indebetou House and finds it locked. Cardell's pounding eventually rouses a sleepy night guard who curses at the same moment he lays eyes on Cecil Winge, followed by a quick apology.

'It isn't that I wished death upon you, sir, but when I see you above ground like this I realize that I have a bone to pick with Secretary Blom.'

Only with a combined effort are they able to close the door behind them. With shaking hands, Winge holds the ring in front of Cardell and points at the wall in the stairwell where the coat of arms belonging to former master of police Nils Henric Aschan Liljensparre still hangs undisturbed.

'Do you see now? Aschan, alias "the Arse"?'

Cardell squints and tries to force his eyes to focus first on the design of the ring, then the richly decorated shield on the wall.

'There are certain similarities but I wouldn't say they're exactly alike.'

'Just so. And that is as it should be. If I am correct, Karl Johan has stood many times where we are right now and with his gaze directed at the same target. Karl Johan's coat of arms bears so many similarities to that of our former police chief, Liljensparre, also known as the Arse, that it can't be coincidental. He has modelled his design on Liljensparre's.

'So? That coat of arms is no well-guarded secret. It's hanging in the stairs for all to see.'

'Yes and no. Before the police department was moved to Indebetou House, it was hanging in the stairwell at Garden Lane, but none of these locations are ones to which everyone has access. One of the criminals who is led past on their way to a hearing would hardly be inclined to imitate the chief of police. Nor had Karl Johan worked for the police in any formal capacity. I know each petty constable, notary, assistant and neighbourhood officer by name and face. In neither of these groups is there anyone with the kind of blond hair that we know Karl Johan had, much less one who disappeared under mysterious circumstances. But Liljensparre also had another body under him, a corps of informers whose purpose was to spy on all those who might have wished ill on the Crown.

'And much help that did.'

'It is said that one often meets one's fate on the path one has taken to avoid it. King Gustav was no exception. Nonetheless, there were a great many informers, and men with ambition who lacked the potential to succeed through other arenas flocked to this group. It was the perfect company for the likes of Karl Johan, and since these young fortune hunters only indirectly met the police chief, they found it easier to idealize him. As Liljensparre's nickname indicates, this was seldom the case among those who took orders from him directly. But they were constantly coming to this building to dispatch their reports before Liljensparre was sent into exile, and it was a source of irritation for the more established police officers.'

'I don't understand how all this brings us any closer to discovering Karl Johan's true name.'

'What day is it today?'

Cardell has to think for a moment. Ever since the false death announcement earlier in the week, the days have run into each other, separated by a minimum of sleep. Winge turns to the night guard, who reluctantly shakes off his sleepiness and provides an answer.

'It is Saturday, Saturday the seventh.'

'And the hour?'

'We are approaching midnight.'

'Then we have no time to lose, Jean Michael. Out at the Exchange, they are celebrating Norlin as he prepares for his departure. If we are lucky, the subject of the party is still in attendance. I need to have a few words with our sacked police chief before he disappears into the north.'

———◆◆◆———

They crest the hill and reach Old Square, with the Exchange on the left. The spire of the cathedral casts its shadow through the storm high above the roof of the palace. Winge sighs audibly in relief at the sight of the illuminated building that indicates the festivities are still underway. There are candles in every window. Inside the ballroom, the tables have been pushed to the walls in order to make room for the dancing, and the heels strike so hard against the floorboards that the chandeliers have started to sway overhead. Cardell sees many familiar faces in the crowd, the size of which is at least two hundred. Even Governor Modée has joined in the dancing, his face as red as a freshly cooked crayfish, and his untied cravat hanging down his back. Familiar faces walk to and fro with champagne flutes in their hands. Cardell catches a glimpse of Trade Commissioner Cederhielm's back between two swags of drapery, where he relieves himself against the wall, laughing at something on the ceiling.

'Norlin was a popular man after all.'

Winge nods in assent.

'It is his very qualities as chief of police that has led to the termination of his employment. Do you see him?'

Cardell lets his gaze travel across the room.

'By the table of honour.'

Winge reaches Norlin in the corner. Norlin's nose and cheeks are red, and his elegant wig is dishevelled. He does a double take when he catches sight of Winge.

'Cecil, I heard you had given up the ghost. Have we celebrated so widely that we have raised the dead?'

'You can only see me because you yourself have just crossed to the other side, Johan Gustaf. Your worldly remains are lying down there on the dance floor, dead after an excess of wine and a candied almond in your windpipe. I have come to show you the way to shores of the Styx and deposit you into Charon's embrace.'

Norlin drops his glass. The blood drains out of his face and he stands without knowing what to say for several seconds, until a woman with the model of a frigate braided into her hair bumps into Winge on her way down the stairs. Norlin bursts into laughter.

'Damn it, Cecil Winge! The Ghost of the Indebetou, indeed! You're drunk. I have never seen you under the influence before, or heard you joke, and I sense a connection. Though I must say the hiccups detract a little from the overall effect.'

Norlin gestures as if to embrace all the injustice of the world.

'So my tale as police chief is at its end. If the north becomes too cold, the thought of escaping the intrigues of Stockholm will warm my heart.'

'Do you know when Ullholm's administration will assume power?'

Gravity returns to Norlin's face.

'I can't say for sure. In a week, perhaps. I'm sorry I couldn't buy you more time, Cecil.'

'I have come to put myself in even greater debt to you, Johan Gustaf. When I came to you in your office after having examined the corpse from the Larder, your desk was covered in unopened letters from Liljensparre's informers, reports that continued to stream in from all over the country although it had been almost a year since he disappeared in Pommern. Do those letters still exist? Has the office been tidied away?'

'I leave that work with full confidence in the hands of Isak Blom.'

'I have reason to believe that some explanation for the death that has occupied me and Jean Michael here this autumn will be found among these writings. Do you, Johan Gustaf, consent to providing me with access to them this very evening?'

'If that is all you ask, then it is the least I can do. Take Blom. The worthy secretary has had enough to drink.'

Norlin shoots a meaningful glance in Cardell's direction.

'But don't let him walk downstairs on his own. The other day he slipped and managed to hurt his face something terrible.'

———•———

Isak Reinhold Blom, conversing with two white-painted ladies in wide skirts, drops his goblet on the floor at the sight of Cardell, who is forced to grab him by the scruff of his neck to prevent him from hiding under the table.

'Don't hit me anymore!'

Cardell holds the little man upright, although his legs have given out. Winge places a calming hand on his shoulder. Blom allows himself to be plied with wine and regains his self-confidence with each sip. In the hall, they find his worn coat. Winge is first out the door. The few steps down to the square are occupied with guests who have stepped out to cool themselves, sufficiently warmed by the dancing and wine to laugh at the snowstorm that has decreased visibility to the point that the well and its pumps can't be seen. A woman with bare shoulders is trying to catch snowflakes on her tongue, to the laughter and applause of a collection of admiring gentlemen. One of them takes a step back just as Winge is about to pass. They collide and, when the man turns around, stand face to face. The recognition is immediate on both sides. Winge takes a step back.

'Gillis Tosse. I haven't seen you since our student days, nor have I heard your name since I saw it on a report to Norlin that called me a Jacobin.'

Tosse's cheeks are flushed with intoxication but his voice is steady.

'Cecil Winge! I wish I could say the same about you, but your name is everywhere these days.'

He pauses for dramatic effect and an unpleasant smile appears on his face.

'But not for much longer, it seems.'

'How are things with Madame Sachs these days?'

Tosse shrugs.

'Oh, there will have to be a great deal of work on her part to regain the confidence she has lost. Keyser House stands empty for the moment, but our little society does not lack resources and has other facilities to use that are just as good. You should not trouble yourself over the thought of having deprived anyone of their amusements.'

'Are you the kind who likes to watch as others exploit those who can't defend themselves, Gillis, or do you participate? From my memories of you in Uppsala, I would have to guess the former.'

Tosse takes a step closer and lowers his voice as he places a hand on Winge's shoulder.

'Cecil, I know you don't have much time left. I wish no one a death by consumption among bloody sheets but I would like it to be a comfort to you that your fate would have been far worse had you had time to continue to defy the Eumenides, and to no avail. There are things in this world that no one can change and the right of the strong is one of them, whatever your beloved Rousseau may say.'

Winge shakes off Tosse's hand.

'If Reuterholm hadn't got rid of Norlin, your days would be numbered.'

Tosse throws his head back and laughs.

'Reuterholm? Oh, Cecil, suddenly I remember it like yesterday. You were always the most remarkable mixture of cleverness and naivety.'

He downs the last of the wine in his glass, drops it nonchalantly onto the steps and turns back to his group, laughter still bubbling over his lips.

———— • ————

Winge and Cardell, with Isak Blom between them, walk along together on the more protected side of the square, hunched against the wind. They walk out onto Castle Hill and through Cellar Alley, to Indebetou House, where the guard appears to have deserted his post. Blom fumbles with his keys as Winge clears his throat.

'Isak, how long have you been with the agency? Since eighty-seven or eighty-eight?'

Blom glares down at the ground while he fights the wind opening one of the doors.

'Eighty-six.'

They stamp the snow from their feet in the entry hall. When Cardell puts his hand on the wall it is as cold as the air outside. Blom waves absently with his hand over his shoulder as he leads them further into the building. Winge follows him, his hands on his back.

'You served alongside Liljensparre for years. What do you remember of the informers that he cultivated across the city and the country?'

'King Gustav became more and more anxious as the years went by and his enemies multiplied. He was at his most relaxed at Haga, in his fantasy world under the fir trees and the rocky shores that he gave Italian names, far from the intrigues of the city. The nobility spat over their shoulders when they heard his name, the court feared his whims, his own pages told hair-raising stories – and one of them went on to become his killer. Liljensparre started his police operation during Gustav's fourth year as regent, in seventy-six, but as time went on, Gustav saw a greater need. It fell to Liljensparre to find ears for the King, to recruit a collection of men to listen to private conversations and report on matters told in confidence. During the final years, it was the situation in France that was of the greatest interest. Gustav feared the revolution would spread. Liljensparre's songbirds were sent out to look for traitors.'

Winge nods.

'Yes, that is also how I remember it. Liljensparre's resignation came a year ago, in December. News of his exile would have taken some time to reach everyone who sent him reports. We are looking for one or more unopened letters from the spring and summer.'

Blom points down the corridor.

'I took everything that was on Norlin's desk and carried it off to a box room full of papers for which no one has any interest but

321

no one will throw out. In a corner, you will find a cupboard that was already old when the police moved into the building. Everything that remains of Liljensparre's correspondence is in there. Let me find you some light.'

Blom's candle lights up a room covered in books, ledgers, folders and papers. When Cardell opens the cupboard in question, piles of documents that have been leaning against the cupboard doors tumble out onto the floor.

'Shit. If you clear the table, I'll pick all this up. Well, how should we proceed?'

Winge makes a slow circle around the papers and plucks at random among the unopened envelopes.

'We'll sort them all. Do you remember our conversation at the Maria graveyard about Karl Johan's half-healed stumps? Let us follow the wounds back in time. When do you think the first limb would have been severed from the rest of the body?'

'Sometime in July would be my guess.'

'We may then assume that all letters from Karl Johan would have stopped by July. We'll sort the letters by sender and by date. If a packet of letters from the same sender includes anything from August or later, we can rule them out. Any regular correspondence that ceases in June or July will be of interest.'

<hr>

An hour or more passes while they examine hundreds of letters. In silence, they sort them in into piles, as if involved in some arcane game of cards. Certain piles are returned to the depths of the cupboard, in Cardell's case accompanied by a curse. The collection thins until only a few remain. Winge places the remaining piles in a row while Cardell does his best to control his impatience.

'And now?'

'We open the letters that remain and see if the contents can give us any additional information.'

Cardell is not a born reader. The long rows of characters tire him and the content rarely appears worth the effort.

'Good Lord. These gentlemen would represent the highest talent in the realm if they were competing in their capacity to induce utter boredom. This one can't even spell a single word.'

'Let me see.'

'It's just a bunch of nonsense.'

Winge furrows his brow in concentration.

'Of course. But I don't think it is random nonsense. This letter is written in code, a system in which certain letters are exchanged for others.'

'Where does this leave us?'

'In ignorance of its contents. Who is the sender?'

'The letters are signed Daniel Devall.'

'And the dates?'

'The first is more than a year old, the last is dated in June.'

Winge puts his hands up and rubs his temples.

'I once learned a method for cracking codes, but those final glasses of wine at the Golden Sun appear to have banished this knowledge to the furthest reaches of my memory.'

He begins to walk to and fro across the floor in a small circle, soundlessly moving his lips and scribbling in the air. After a while he stops and returns to the table where he lifts one of the envelopes. He laughs with satisfaction.

'Jean Michael, you must pardon me. We have made it much more difficult for ourselves than necessary. You should not have let me drink so much.'

Winge holds the letter aloft and Cardell leans in. At each end there are the remains of the seal, the one he recently broke in order to open the letter. The small coat of arms, stiffened in wax, is the same as on Karl Johan's ring. It takes Cardell a while to find the words.

'Karl Johan's true name is Daniel Devall?'

'Beyond a doubt.'

'Does he list a location?'

'Yes, the last of the letters refer to an estate called Birdsong. Does that mean anything to you?'

'I've never heard of it.'

'Nor I. Let us see if Isak Blom has anything to add.'

Blom is over the desk with his face in his arms. He is snoring loudly and fights off the attempts to wake him until Cardell pokes him hard in the ribs.

'Have you had any luck?' he says with a start.

Winge nods.

'Possibly. Do you happen to know of a place called Birdsong?'

Blom rubs his face.

'Birdsong is a manor house, a hereditary estate. The lands lie by the river Saga, not far from the old royal house in Väsby. It belongs to the house of Balk, a family of counts. Their heraldry is simple, as is typical of the older houses: a white fess on a black field. As far as I know, there are not many Balks left at Birdsong. Gustav Adolf Balk was in the King's council some decades ago. I have a vague memory that he disappeared abroad. He may have had progeny. Balk was a great line at one time, and in more than one direction. But no longer. More than that, I don't know.'

Winge is already halfway out the door by the time Blom finishes.

Merchant's Street lies narrow and empty past Castle Hill. The storm has died down somewhat and a new day is dawning, though the winter darkness will linger for a couple of hours until the sun summons enough energy to rise past the horizon. Winge turns his brim down over his eyes to be able to look around for a wagon. Cardell follows closely, filled with trepidation. What recently was progressing too slowly is now happening too quickly.

'Is it wise to leave in such haste? Shouldn't we make the necessary preparations?'

Winge answers over his shoulder.

'What would you suggest?'

Cardell swears as his heel slips between two stones.

'A sabre each, knives in our boots, stilettoes up our sleeves? Pistols and muskets? A mortar pulled after the wagon in case we are refused entry? Nor do I have any papers to show the customs officers.'

Up by the Scorched Plot, there is a driver attending to a loose horseshoe. Winge waves at him while he lets Cardell catch him up.

'Don't worry about a passport. I have papers with Norlin's signature that will guarantee passage for the two of us without any questions asked. As for the rest, what few allies we had are all gone. It is only you and me now, Jean Michael. I am no man of violence. If a superior power awaits us at journey's end, we don't have much to offer in terms of resistance. Our hope must cleave to what we do have, and for me time is of the essence, not only with regard to my health but also in view of Ullholm's approach. Right now there is a gap between two administrations, that of Norlin and Ullholm, and we would do best to bring our adventure to an end before this situation is resolved. Do these conditions affect the strength of your conviction? I am getting on this wagon without much to lose. You can still turn back, and I would be the last to blame you.'

Winge heaves himself up onto the seat and gives the driver a gesture in the direction of Slaughterhouse Bridge. Cardell waves the snowflakes out of his face and snorts.

'If we could take a moment to stop for provisions at the Stablemaster's Inn before we leave the city, you will have a more cheerful travelling companion and a more pleasant journey. A quick one for the road would also do much to balance my humours.'

Winge chews thoughtfully on his cuticle.

'Agreed,' he says at last. 'Even I seem to have been blighted with the most remarkable headache.'

49

A RIDE IS TO be found at the Customs House. For a couple of weeks, wagon wheels have been replaced by sleigh blades. The Stablemaster's Inn, the last stop that separates Stockholm from the wilderness, sells bread, meat and tobacco, as well as wine to wash it down. The road is in poor condition. The mild weather of the previous week has turned to cold and the blades rattle across frozen ice formations, at times sharp and at times wavy. The horses have trouble finding purchase on the ground. Mile markers of wood, iron or stone pass slowly by. Every ten miles or so there are slumbering roadside inns and rest stops, where time becomes drawn out as tired horses are changed and the driver fills the servants in on the latest gossip from the city.

Winge knows the road well. He has beaten this path often during his student years in Uppsala and the fact that certain portions of the way are ploughed more regularly than others is no surprise to him. A distant sun rises in the east and lights the dead landscape for a couple of hours. The light wanders from one shoulder to the other and pushes long shadows in the opposite direction. The forest, ancient and indifferent, lies quietly along both sides of the road. Winge's pocket watch, his ticking Beurling, taken apart and put back together so many times, lies open on his lap until the light becomes too dim to read the position of the hands. When the stars begin to appear, Winge and Cardell pull the furs and blankets of the sled more closely around them, each lost in his own train of thought, interrupted only by the driver's utterances to his horses. The moon is new and barely large enough to cast any light.

Cecil Winge finds himself returning to the confidences he shared with Cardell only a few hours ago. He remembers how it was his wife who became furious when he came upon them in the act. As for himself, he only felt an endless grief, and that seemed to irritate her even more. Should he have demonstrated his feelings with brute force, whipped the corporal from the bed and beaten him bloody? Violence has never appealed to Winge on his path of rationality. Now he wonders if there is a place where love allows itself to be translated into violence, a place out of reach of his own. Somewhere far away, a lone howl rises towards the moon. He recalls Josef Thatcher's words of farewell and shivers.

'You are indeed a wolf after all . . . One day your teeth will be stained red and then you'll know with certainty how right I was.'

———— ◆ ————

The sled continues through the evening. One after the other and the sixty miles are put behind them. At the outskirts of Sala, built on the edge of a mine, the driver directs them into a square yard between a house and stables, pulls on the reins and turns towards his passengers.

'We won't get closer than this to your destination. For my part it's time to find a bed for the night and to feed my horses.'

Inside the warmth of the inn, there are still guests up eating their supper. A generously proportioned woman rules the establishment and snorts when asked about Birdsong.

'There is nothing for you there, much less at this time of night. No one's found it worth the trouble to visit Birdsong for a long time.'

'If there is no ride to be had, perhaps we could borrow a horse each?'

'In this cold, and to guests whose names I haven't heard before? Not for all the money in the land.'

Winge counts out some coins on the rough tabletop until the value of the horses is exceeded. The corners of the woman's mouth climb higher in her lined face until she gives Cardell and Winge a shallow curtsy that is not without humour.

'Apparently there is more money in the land than I would have guessed.'

———◆———

The two horses are broad work animals and speed is not among their virtues. The smaller roads have long since been buried in snow and will not see the light of day until spring. Cardell and Winge follow the directions that the collective wisdom of the inn has dispatched. They ride along in the moonlight, with a hill in the distance to their left and the North star straight ahead, until after what must be an hour or more a line of linden trees appears in the snow. The horses plough their own path until they reach the trees where the ground lies flat. At the far end of the pathway there are buildings, dark and quiet. The manor house looms on the other side of a courtyard with a fountain that is covered in a crust of ice. Winge pulls on the reins and forces his horse to a slow stop.

'Does this look familiar?'

Mickel Cardell, unused to the saddle and secretly happy that faster animals had not been possible to find, swings his leg across the horse's back, lowers himself onto the ground and for a while ends up with one boot stuck in an uncooperative stirrup.

'From Blix's letters? Yes, the poor bastard described the place well. But there can't have been anyone here for a long time. It's as silent as the grave, but no smoke is coming out of the chimneys, I can count at least a dozen broken windows and no signs of light or footsteps are to be seen.'

'And yet here we are. Let us not turn back until we have made sure. The house is large. We have much ground to cover.'

The front door is slightly ajar. The snow has accumulated into drifts on both sides, and they have to apply their combined weight to force one of the door halves to yield enough for them to enter. The hall is enormous and deserted. Winge stands still, listening.

'As you say, it is difficult to perceive any human presence. Let us begin from below, Jean Michael. I will take the corridor to the left, you the right, and then we will work our way up. We will meet at the stairs before we ascend to the next floor. From the placement of the chimneys, you will soon encounter the kitchen. See if you can find any lanterns or anything else to make light.'

———◆———

A door takes Cardell into the first room on the right. A drawing room, he guesses, once upon a time used by the family to greet their guests. Ice and, before that, rain and damp has run down the walls and onto the floor where the boards are swollen to the point that some of them are curved like a bow. In the dim light, every-thing has the same grey colour: the curtains that hang in rags around the windows, the furniture in which mice and rats have built their nests, the paintings with canvases buckled by the weather and wind. Further into the house, grey turns to black. He feels his way along the wall and encounters book spines in a row on a shelf and to his joy also a small candlestick holder made of brass, cold enough to stick to his palm for a moment. The wax is fragile and frozen, and the sparks from Cardell's many attempts to light the wick with his flint and steel illuminate the moulder-ing shelves in frozen moments. Finally, the fire takes. A hesitant flame flutters upward.

With his arm, he cradles the light from the draught and walks further in. Everything is quiet, dead, cold. The frost has penetrated deep into the walls. The roof must leak like a sieve. Behind an empty pantry and all kinds of storage areas, there is a staircase that goes both up to the next floor and down into a cellar. He stands without being able to make up his mind, then decides to explore the cellar. The light conjures barrels and shelves from the dark and, to his delight, Cardell sees that they are groaning with bottles. Many of them are frozen solid but the deeper he goes, the more bottles there are that have survived the neglect. Cardell selects one, breaks the neck and puts it gingerly to his lips, careful not to cut himself. Tokay! With a sigh of pleasure, he turns his back to the cellar and returns to the stairs.

A sound comes from above. A footstep on the creaking boards or a piece of furniture that has been knocked over. Cardell realizes that his adventure with the candle and bottle of wine has made him forget the time. Winge must have tired of waiting for him by the stairs after inspecting his half of the house and decided to meet him on the upper floor. He takes a few more sips and continues up. The small windows in the stairwell let in the moonlight and, together with the wine, they make him feel better about this hopeless undertaking. The light he carries in his hand has deprived him of whatever night vision he has had and blinds him just as much as it lights his way.

'Don't move.'

It isn't Cecil Winge's voice. A quiet monotone, and something else as well: a difficulty in getting the words out, perhaps because of the cold.

'Blow out the candle and turn around.'

Cardell does as he is told. In the sudden darkness it is hard to see who has spoken. His figure is outlined against a window, behind which the world is divided in two between a dark sky and a radiant field of snow.

'You may not be able to see what I am holding in my hand. It is a carbine with the barrel pointed directly at your chest.'

Cardell squints in order to see better. The man is of average height with a moth-eaten wolfskin fur thrown over his shoulders. Under this, his clothing matches the rest of the house. What was once magnificent is now falling apart. The breeches are shiny with wear, buttons are missing, seams are dissolving. The man's face is weak and appears old beyond his years.

'I can see it now. We had those in the navy. It's a handsome weapon but not exactly the latest model, I see.'

'Don't be fooled by the state of this place. It has no bearing on this piece. It served my ancestor well, from Narva to Fraustadt, and has never once failed. Have you come to steal wine? Are you alone?'

Cardell's pulse is throbbing against his eardrums. He is adept at this kind of lie and does not hesitate for a single heartbeat.

'Yes, I came in the vain hopes of finding something that can help me manage the winter. It's been a long time since I had any friends.'

The man nods.

'Parts of your clothing belong to a watchman's uniform, if I'm not mistaken. What is such a one doing so far from the city?'

'Perhaps he has left his post and tried to survive as best he can after his earnings have long since been spent on wine. I was told the house was empty and that no one would miss what was taken from here.'

'Turn around now and go back the same way you came. There's no need to look over your shoulder. I am here, beyond your reach and with the carbine pointed at your back. There is a little shed close to here, at the edge of the fields. That's where we're headed.'

Cardell gives him thoughtful look.

'That musket has quite a fickle mechanism. In the navy, it was said that the gunpowder failed to ignite at least once in every five shots you try.'

The man stands as still as Cardell for a while until his toneless voice is heard again.

'There is a dunghill not far from the place we are headed. It has been many yards deep for generations, fed by the uncleanliness of both animals and humans. Not even the winter cold manages to still its putrid warmth. It bubbles and smokes from inside. Worms older than the linden trees live there. I am not unprepared for visitors. I keep my bullets in that dungheap, and every day I go there with my carbine and exchange my bullets for fresh ones from the heap. Your death in fever and chills is assured if one of them so much as grazes you. The wound will begin to fester, then become gangrenous, and your passing follows only after hellish suffering. My gun has never failed yet. Maybe fate wants this to be the first time. The risk is yours to take.'

Cardell considers the value of his life for a few seconds before he shrugs, turns, and heads down the stairs.

———•———

They walk across the snow. The stars and the moon light their way towards the barn, the first of a number of smaller outbuildings. In front of the door there is a heavy latch.

'Lift it up and go inside.'

Cardell has trouble grabbing it with one arm but puts his shoulder under the wood and heaves it out of its socket. The door glides open. Cardell is hit by a stench so acrid he lays his sleeve over his nose.

'Jesus.'

'What is your name, anyway?'

'I am Mickel Cardell.'

'Well, Mickel Cardell. I have a proposition for you. I want you to think it over carefully before you answer. I wish I could offer you something better, but I have to stay here for a little while longer, waiting for another guest, and I don't want to risk you returning here with others in tow.'

Somewhere deep inside the shed, Cardell perceives movement. Something large is waking up in there and drawing closer. The links of a chain jangle as it is stretched to its full length. He sees the dog – impossibly huge – with eyes like glowing coals and saliva running out of the corners of its mouth.

'This is Magnus, Mickel Cardell. He will become your tomb, so to speak, once he has consumed your remains. You are a large man. I would prefer not to drag your body across the floor to him, and therefore I offer you this. Go over to the wall and then step as closely to Magnus as you can without him being able to reach you. There you will get on your knees. I will shoot you in the neck, so that you will fall forward within reach of his chain. It will be a clean death, a quick and humane end, and neither one of us will be stained with your blood. If your inclination instead is towards desperate action, I will shoot you in the stomach and leave you to the cold, the pain and the chills. Magnus is large enough to keep the shed warm. Unless the bullet lands badly, you will not freeze to death tonight. Perhaps not tomorrow either.'

The hair stands up on the back of Cardell's neck. He doesn't know how to answer. He sees a flicker before him and the dancing dots fill the darkness behind the dog with meaning. Black wings in an abyss. Death pulls closer, the same force that almost closed its bone-white fingers around him in the waters around Svensksund. With shaking legs, he places one foot in front of the other and sinks to his knees by the wall, where each knot in the wood has become an eye socket of the grim reaper.

'A little closer, if you please. Both Magnus's fur and the one I wear have seen better days, but that is no reason to soil them.'

He shuffles closer, inch by inch, on his knees. Magnus's drooling jaws and greedy predator's eyes are very close, with a breath that stinks of spoiled meat and blood. A moment later, behind Cardell's shoulders, there comes the sound of movement and the rustle of frozen clothes. When he turns his head, he sees the outline of Cecil Winge in the open door and sees that even the man in the wolfskin coat has turned around to size up the intruder. A shot is fired with a wet crash. Red is spattered around the room.

———◆———

It seems to Cardell that the shot reverberates in echo after echo, and that the silence then lingers for an impossibly long time. The smoke of the gunpowder rises towards the beams before it dissipates. He is dead, he knows that, and he understands that the reason he does not feel anything is because he is already beyond pain's domain, in the place to which he has so longed to go while the *Ingeborg*'s anchor kept him chained to life. Along his legs he feels the warm flow from the shot that must have struck him in his lower back. Yet he feels no wound, even when his fingers probe for one, and soon his nose tells him that the wet is something other than blood. Alive and unharmed, he hears Cecil Winge's voice break the silence.

'Of all things you might have shot here tonight, I would have considered the dog the least likely.'

'Magnus has served his purpose. Your name is Cecil Winge. You are the one I have been waiting for. My name is Johannes Balk. The responsibility for Daniel Devall's fate is mine. You have come to take me to Stockholm. So let us go. There is nothing here for me anymore.'

50

T HE SUN SEEMS more distant than ever as it rises to begin a
journey so short it resembles a fading ember rolling along
the horizon. The pale light shines on Cecil Winge and Johannes
Balk as they sit alone in the sled. Mickel Cardell sits in the front
next to the driver, out of earshot of the conversation, his arms
wrapped around himself to conserve heat. Down in the sled,
Winge shifts his pensive gaze from his friend's back to Balk. In
the early light of dawn, Winge has an opportunity for the first
time to have a good look at the man sitting on the furs across
from him. His age is difficult to establish at first glance. Young
but aged before his time, or old with a pronounced lack of matu-
rity in his features. Words that Kristofer Blix chose come back to
him and he finds himself in agreement: there is a remarkable
absence.

Winge's next breath catches in his throat. His thoughts are
interrupted by a sudden coughing fit and he leans over the side of
the sled and shields his mouth with a handkerchief as he spits a
red streak down towards the runners.

'How is your health, Mr Winge?'

Johannes's voice is a monotone. It is as if he has never learned
to understand the musicality of language and therefore simply
adopted one pitch. This lack reminds Winge of his younger years
in the classroom, where he and his friends were taught to read
aloud in languages they had not yet mastered and whose meaning

they did not understand. Sometimes it is as if the man's tongue is not capable of making the right sounds and forces him to stop his speech and select another word.

'Why such consideration?'

Johannes Balk looks up at Cecil Winge and their eyes meet for the first time in earnest. Balk's pupils are so large and black that the colour of his iris is not evident.

'And why should I not show care about my fellow man, Mr Winge?'

'Because you are a monster, Johannes.'

Balk allows the silence to settle between them without looking away. He nods and Winge feels goose pimples spread across his arms and chest.

'The world has made me what I am. If what you say is true, how should we then think about the world? But perhaps I have other reasons to concern myself about your health than compassion. All in due time.'

'You already know who I am?'

'I became aware of your name in the *Extra Post* when the newspapers first announced the corpse found in Larder Lake, and then I made my inquiries. I probed with interest into your legal career. You have always held fast to your ideals. You never failed to question the defendants and always allowed them to speak before the court where everyone can hear. I have to ask you, Mr Winge, if you still believe that a monster like me deserves the same right, after all that has happened and everything that you know about me.'

'Everyone is equal before the law. The right is yours regardless of your crime.'

'Will you allow me to tell you my story to you first, at my own pace? I will not hold anything back. Pose your questions and I will answer after the best of my abilities. Would that be all right, Mr Winge? I don't know how much time you have to give me.'

'I do not know myself. I wager we'll find out.'

'A prologue first, if you'll allow.'

Johannes Balk closes his eyes and takes a deep breath. When the air leaves his lungs, two plumes of steam issue from his nose. He begins.

'It is the tradition in my family to christen the oldest son after King Gustav II. King Gustavus Adolphus's war made our fortune, as it did for so many others. One hundred and fifty years ago, we laid the lands of the German prince-electors in ruins as we held the Lion of the North as hard by the tail as possible. We stood wrapped in blood and honour, we were made into counts, our strongboxes swelled from the weight of plundered gold. We built Birdsong on our ancient lands, cleared the forest and worked the land. My father was the last in a long row of Gustav Adolf Balks, fathers and sons.'

'I remember your father from my childhood. He sat in the council until King Gustav made himself omnipotent. A great man.'

Again, Johannes Balk looks into Winge's eyes and his gaze is inscrutable.

'It is said that great men are created by the challenges they overcome. No one can deny that my father encountered many. There were five generations of Balks between him and the battle-fields where our ancestors won their fortune. Each of them took from the coffers without putting so much as a shilling back. My father only inherited debts. He became aware that noble birth is not much use without capital, but he set about restoring the House of Balk to its rightful place. For a long time, he remained a bachelor. We have never been a comely family, but at my father's birth, it seemed that all of the features that had plagued us came together. His bulging eyes and potato nose made up for his lack of a chin, and he was gaunt and lanky, with sunken temples and thin hair. He had to search far and wide until he

338

found himself a bride. It was a marriage of convenience. Not far from Birdsong there are larger tracts that before my birth belonged to the House of Vide. At this time, the Vide family was at the brink of extinction. Lukas Vide, the patriarch, only had one daughter, and he and his wife were too advanced in age to bear an heir. There were no other branches of the family. What did exist, however, was an intact fortune. What the Balks had squandered, our neighbours had cultivated. One evening, my father rode over to Lukas Vide to ask for his daughter's hand. It was a stormy meeting.'

'For what reason?'

'The daughter's name was Maria Vide, Mr Winge. In these parts, she was known as the Virgin Mary. She was simple. More than three decades earlier, she had been born feet first. It was a difficult birth. A doctor saved her life but she never gained full possession of her wits. In order to eat, she had to be fed and she never left her bed. She spent her days staring at things that no one saw and if anything went on behind her dull eyes, she never let anyone know. When my father asked for her hand in marriage, Lukas Vide could not believe his ears. He became furious and wanted to throw his guest out. Gustav Adolf stood his ground and spoke for the rational merits of his proposal. By way of this marriage, a pure formality, he would inherit the Vide lands and take on stewarding them as they themselves had always done, if only for one generation longer, enough to promise a future for the peasants the Vide lands supported. In this way the property would not pass back into the King's hands only to be sold to strangers so that jewels and trinkets could be purchased for the mistresses of the court. Gustav Adolf swore to give Maria the same care that her own parents provided, now their lives were drawing to their end. After a time, Lukas Vide gave in to the logic of my father's proposal. They shook hands and the Virgin Mary was carried limply to the church and was married without a word. Only the closest members of the family were present. The dowry was grandiose with a promise of more as soon as Lukas Vide passed on. In this way, Gustav Adolf Balk saved his ancestral home. He had my mother's portrait painted not as she was but as she should have been, in a pastoral scene with Birdsong in the background. Such a mockery.'

Johannes Balk pauses. His speech flows more easily the more he talks, and the stammer he betrays from time to time becomes less marked.

'As you can understand, there was a scandal when the Virgin Mary's belly could no longer be concealed by all the quilts in Birdsong. In the agreement with Lukas Vide, it was assumed the marriage would never be consummated. Now they were forced to send for midwives and physicians from Sala for the birth. Thus I came into the world, proof that Gustav Adolf Balk had stepped into his half-dead wife's bedroom and violated her unmoving body. It is said that Lukas Vide suffered a stroke at the news. Gustav Adolf visited his father-in-law's bedside and with his silver tongue he comforted him by saying that the future of their combined estates was now assured; that what had happened should be taken as good news. Vide could hardly wish his grand-child into the grave. He lived a few more years, withdrawn, and in chagrin. They never spoke again. After his death, his estate was combined with ours, under Birdsong. Everything Gustav Adolf had pursued became reality. Thanks to him, I was born and could grow up in abundance.'

Under the sleigh, the metal scrapes against the ice, a drawn-out whisper as toneless as Balk's own voice. The angle of the light is faltering and darkens from pale yellow to the deepest red.

'He who wishes to raise a monster, Mr Winge, does well in teaching it to hate from an early age. He often hit me, my father. As the great man that he was, he exercised his power over every-one in his environment and not least his own offspring. When I grew older, I learned to distinguish between the various reasons for his beatings. Often it was for his own sake, to vent his own ill humour at some temporary setback. But he also hit me when he seemed to be in a good mood, and I became aware that he must have learned that this was how a child would be made good and obedient. He must have had memories of a childhood where he must also have been unable to sit on chairs without spilling tears, and to some extent he must have credited this rearing with his late successes. Often he demanded answers to questions as a way to test me and, afraid of giving the wrong answer, I began to trip over the words, which aggravated him more and made me, in turn, more hesitant. As you can hear, this is an impediment I have never managed to rid myself of. A monster, raised by a monster. I find it a comfort that I myself have not brought any children into this world. In this long line of villains, which surely stretches all the way back to the dawn of time, I will be the last, and even if this will count only as a footnote to my epitaph, it must be counted a blessing.'

Balk made a brief interruption as he nods to himself.

'He did other things to me as well, my father, at night, when he had drunk himself into a state, and the silence of the house must have seemed to beg for a child's tears.'

Winge can't see if anything changes in Balk's face or if it is only the shadows from the trees by the side of the road that are playing tricks on him.

'I exacted my revenge as children are wont to do, against all those who were too weak to defend themselves against me. The frogs that played in the pond. Dogs and chickens. They learned to fear my wrath as I had learned to fear my father's.'

Soon the sun is gone. Winge feels the cold intensify. Another winter's night is on its way. In the Stockholm they are drawing closer to with each passing minute, it will demand its tribute in beggars' lives, and force Dieter Schwalbe and his fellows to vain attempts at hacking a way through the frozen ground, until they give up and pile up the dead until spring.

Balk brushes the snowflakes from his shoulders and adjusts the furs around his legs.

'There's still some distance to go. Let me get to the heart of my story.'

51

THE BOY GROWS up so alone that the word loses all meaning. There are constantly people around him but he is cast in another mould, the last in a long row of noblemen, and with his father often away in Stockholm, he is the only one of his kind. Superior. When he follows the sound of laughter to the servants' quarters where children are playing with each other, they quickly grow quiet. He is met with downturned gazes and they are quickly sent out of the way on their duties while the parents mumble their excuses. He senses the hostility of the children, even though they don't show it. He grows used to empty rooms.

A steady stream of tutors teaches him all he needs to know for some future of which he is kept ignorant, and the instruction is never given with any kind of affection. They beat him as his father has done, according to instructions about the character-building nature of corporal punishment. Birdsong is a sombre place and few seem able to stand it longer than a year. Not to one single person does he become more than a necessary evil in order to make enough money to go elsewhere. In time, the boy empties the pond of frogs, and small animals learn to fear the sound of his tread.

Slowly he becomes aware of his mother. Birdsong is not big enough to hide its secrets indefinitely. There is a floor where he is not allowed to go, and a room he is not allowed to enter, where bowls of porridge are carried up and returned empty. They hold her there, as dead to the world as the day his father first brought her to this place. He starts to investigate. There is a key ring hanging on a nail in a cupboard, rusty and forgotten, covered by cobwebs. At night he tries the keys, one after another, rubbed with fat from the storehouse, frightened by every sound the lock makes in protest. After several attempts, he finds one that fits.

She is lying completely still between the sheets under a white canopy. He crosses the floor slowly so the floorboards won't creak, and he comes close enough to see her face for the first time. It resembles his own. He lays a hand on the blanket and feels the warmth of her completely motionless body. Her eyes are empty when he steps directly into her line of sight. He lies down at her side, curling up close to her and feeling comforted by her presence. He comes here every night.

Gradually a change comes over her. From having lain as still as if he were not there, she begins to move. When he looks in her eyes, there is a flash of recognition in response. She wants to lift her hand to his face and, as the nights go by, she comes closer. Soon his cheek will feel the tenderness of a mother's touch, and each dawn, as he smooths out the blanket and leaves, he thinks that it will happen when he returns.

It takes weeks. And when she finally manages it, her hand twists like a claw, and her long nails scratch the face where his father's features are as visible as her own. A hissing sound issues from her throat. Crying with shock and fear, he runs from the room. The lacerations are deep. He has to lie about how he came by them.

———•———

He does not return until he hears the floorboards groan at night and realizes she must have stood up from her bed, as if their meeting has awakened something deep inside her. At first, he peers through the keyhole. When he finally musters the courage to turn the key again, he realizes that she takes no notice of him, as long as he keeps his distance. He spends nights sitting on the floor with his back to the wall. He leaves her when it starts to get light, half an hour or so before her servants – an old couple who have accompanied her from her childhood home – lead her back to bed and tuck the bedclothes back into place. When midnight comes, she has to begin again.

It takes her almost a year before she can walk well enough to reach the window before dawn. Once there, she performs the same ritual, night after night. Slowly she lifts her hands towards the crane flies that bounce against the glass in a vain attempt to gain a freedom they can see but cannot reach. Her slowness and patience make her a formidable hunter. She catches them one at a time under a cupped hand and grips each tiny body with her thumb and forefinger. She brings them close to her face. Then she patiently pulls off the wings, and each leg, careful not to harm the life that still trembles in the slender torso. The boy sees her lips moving and realizes that she is whispering to them as she mutilates them. He has to dare to move closer before he hears that she is saying his father's name. It is the only revenge available to her. The boy is filled with a mixture of strong emotions. He does not return the following night, leaving her instead to her own devices.

———— • ————

A fever claims his mother's life later that winter. The maimed crane flies still lie in rows on the windowsill. The last one is still moving, days after Maria Vide has been buried in the ground. The boy does not grieve for her.

When the ice begins to melt in the spring, Gustav Adolf Balk's boot heel slips on the cobblestones of a Stockholm street and he breaks his femur. The royal physician himself attends to the injury and realigns the bones, but everyone knows that the spring air brings sickness. The wound is not large but it putrefies and begins to ooze pus. His father is bedridden as the gangrene digs deeper into the marrow, and the toes first redden, then grow pale, and finally blacken. In March, the boy is called to the city for the first time in order to attend his father's deathbed. Gustav Adolf is too sick to be moved. The pain in the leg that it is now too late to separate from his body is too great to manage a wagon ride, and the rot has started to spread to his pelvis and groin through darkened veins.

The boy is brusquely shown to the bedchamber, where the baskets of potpourri can no longer conceal the stench of corrupted flesh. A chair has been brought in so he can hold vigil at his father's side. For a long time he sits quiet and awestruck before the heap of blankets and coverings that quakes with each rattling breath. His father's face is pale and sweaty, his gaze anxious and confused. They are frequently left alone as the priest has other duties. It takes a long time until he finds the courage to stand up and lift his father's hand. There is no strength in it that he can perceive, and he can wave it up and across the blankets without his father being able to do more than utter faint whimpers. He pulls the covers away to reveal Gustav Adolf Balk's face, large, red and terrified, and he puts his small white hand over his father's mouth and pinches the nose closed with his thumb. He is astounded at how easy it is to stop the flow of air. Helpless teeth try to gnaw at his hand from an impossible angle. Gustav Adolf's body shakes under the covers, he turns blue, and his eyes look as if they are going to pop out of their sockets. The boy performs the same trick over and over again but doesn't have the courage to keep his hand in place long enough. Instead he always relaxes his grip and lets his father regain his breath in a long, slurped inhalation. Gustav Adolf Balk passes away alone in the night. The chambermaid who puts her soft arm around the boy's small shoulder mistakes his giggles for sobs and dries his tears of joy with a handkerchief.

His father is laid to rest under a stone in the church where his ancestors are buried and where their weapons adorn the walls in a place of honour in front of the choir, in the home county of the Balks not far from Birdsong. One night at the beginning of summer, the boy keeps himself awake until the house is asleep, walks out across the courtyard and on past the linden trees that border the road. While the darkness in his bedroom is a source of terror, this darkness is of a different order, a friend that soothes and protects.

After a while, he reaches the church and finds the front doors unlocked and the church completely empty. He feels his way across the stone floor until his fingertips spell out his father's name. He undoes the buttons of his breeches and lets them glide down as he crouches. The next morning, the cantor will find the small heap of excrement buzzing with flies, and the filth smeared straight across the letters that form the name Gustav Adolf Balk. He remains silent, cleans the floor and, for the rest of his days, lives in the belief that the devil himself passed through their sleepy region, surely on his way towards more urgent matters to the south in the big city.

For the boy, the sense of triumph quickly passes. He sleeps poorly, haunted by a nightmare that replays the sound of his father's approaching steps in the corridor outside his bedroom. In time, he also becomes aware of something he would never have been able to guess. That there are worse things than being beaten, and that loneliness is one of them.

52

IT IS MONDAY afternoon and Mickel Cardell wraps his hands around the white stoneware of a cup so as to absorb its warmth. He sees Winge again for the first time since he climbed off the sled from Birdsong at Northern Square and staggered home across the bridge to wash, and try, unsuccessfully, to get some sleep.

'So did you get anything out of the man on the way?'

Winge nods seriously.

'Some. He is sleeping now. I am not sure where the trial will take place. Until then, I have placed him in custody at the Northern Gaol, in Kastenhof, anonymously for now. We still don't know when Ullholm will turn up and I prefer to keep the whole affair as quiet as possible until my interrogation is completed and the trial can begin. I am well acquainted with the guards and can come and go incognito.'

Hours have passed since they returned to the city and went their separate ways at the Customs House. Nonetheless it seems to Cardell that the wind is still clawing at his cheeks.

'Don't believe for a moment that I'm not grateful for having been spared being shot in the stomach and fed to a dog, but why did he yield so easily? After all we have gone through, it almost feels like a discourtesy.'

'I hope to gain an answer to that very question as well as others.'

'What'll you do next?'

'I am off to Kastenhof to speak with Balk. I'll meet you here tomorrow at the same time.'

———•———

Cardell finishes his drink alone with a grimace of distaste. He has heard others say that coffee drives the fatigue out of the body when one needs to stay awake, and has decided to put up with the taste in case it actually works. He elbows his way out onto the square through the crowd of more enthusiastic coffee drinkers. It isn't often that Stockholm fills Mickel Cardell with anything but annoyance, but for once he is grateful to see the city again. Remembering the shed at Birdsong, there is a whisper of a death the terror of which he has never before imagined. It is one that has been filled to his measurements, in sharp contrast to the haphazard chaos of war, which strikes indiscriminately in every direction. He wants to sleep less than ever, and is happy that the weight hanging at his side offers a distraction. It is the purse he has helped unburden Carsten Vikare of. He has not counted out the coins, but to judge from the combined weight, it is every farthing that was cheated from Kristofer Blix, with interest. Cardell has rarely played host to such a sum, and even more rarely felt such pangs of conscience over it. Seldom has he given a thought past the notion that each treasure belongs to the one who finds it, but this is different. These coins belong to someone else.

The fresh air rasps his throat and nose and, although every inhalation stings, it serves to remind him of the life he recently thought he had lost. He has a mission and feels with each step across the snow how his new purpose increases the distance between himself, the beast Magnus, Johannes Balk's carbine, and the terrors of Birdsong. Balk is now Winge's to handle, so his own thoughts go to Kristofer Blix's writings. Isak Blom told him that a young girl had left them at the door of Indebetou House,

349

marked with Cecil Winge's name, and Carsten Vikare mentioned that Blix had left behind a young widow.

Cardell has changed his breeches, stiffened where the urine had soaked through, for the only other pair he owns, the ones that belong to the uniform he was given when he entered the night watch and that he doesn't like to wear. None of the other tenants had any hot water to share, and he had to make do with scrubbing his body with snow out in the yard. Some youngsters took advantage of his vulnerable position by bombarding him with snowballs, and his explosion of curses caused the shutters of the building to rattle on their hinges. Now, with movement, warmth has started to return to his body and his mood follows pace. He walks along West Street and turns right up the hill until he reaches Stockholm Cathedral.

Inside the vastness of the building it is hardly warmer than outside. The pastor is said to be at home with a cold, but at Cardell's insistence, a frozen chaplain finally appears who can be persuaded to consult the church records. Yes, there is an entry for Johan Kristofer Blix in connection with a recent declaration of marriage, and then there is a cross next to his name to mark his death. After a coin has been placed in the clergyman's trembling hand, he manages to remember more about the remarkable affair.

The young man passed away in an accident not long after the young couple had become engaged. The bride was already expecting. The chaplain rolls his eyes, not without equanimity. That children are born so soon after the wedding as to reveal their parents' youthful enthusiasm is more the rule than the exception. He and his colleagues took pity on the young woman and have maintained that the wedding actually took place before Blix's passing. In this way, the unborn child will be spared the label of bastard and, instead of being taunted as a whore, the mother will gain the status of widow. The chaplain nods to himself. He knows they have broken the sacrament but cannot see how the Lord could possibly object.

'And the name of the widow?'

'Lovisa Ulrika Blix, born Tulip. Her father runs a pub by the name of the Scapegrace.'

'You are unusually well informed for a clergyman.'

The chaplain smiles and rolls his eyes again.

'This is a thirsty parish and after communion the chalice is sometimes so dry that we clergymen are forced to seek the sacrament elsewhere.'

———•———

The walk is hardly a stone's throw back along the way he came. The Scapegrace is a modest establishment where the tables consist of barrels turned on their side in rows. An older man with watery eyes comes to meet him and lays aside the drinking mugs he has been drying clean with a dampened cloth.

'Excuse me, but we haven't opened yet and there's no hot food to be had. If it's a meal you're looking for, it'll have to be cold cuts.'

'That doesn't matter. I'm not here for any provisions. I've come here to find a Lovisa Ulrika. You wouldn't happen to know where she is, would you?'

The owner warily looks him up and down.

'Lovisa is my daughter.'

'And is she home?'

Karl Tulip shakes his head.

'Unfortunately not. She is an industrious young woman, of the kind one often despairs of seeing in the younger generation. And yet it pains me how much my business lays claim on her time. If she isn't at the well she'll be at the market, and if you don't want a long wait, I suggest you come back on another occasion.'

Cardell doesn't know what to say and stamps his boots to rid himself of the snow.

351

'Is there any message you would like me to pass along to her?'

Cardell hesitates, weighing the purse in his hand inside his jacket.

'No, this is a matter that can't be relayed by others. I'll come back another time.'

'Much obliged, and better luck next time.'

53

THE SPRING WAS warm, as was the end of the summer. The snow is already thick now, and those who claim to be able to read all the patterns in aching joints or other omens have long said that it will be the worst winter in living memory.

Anna Stina Knapp believes it. The nights have already begun to claim their share of those who sleep outside from drunkenness or poverty, and with the ground frozen solid it is impossible to bury them until the weather turns. Rigid corpses are piled on top of each other in graveyard sheds and, when they are filled, still more bodies are stored outside the building wrapped in their shrouds. On her way from the fish market, Anna Stina has seen the snow bank outside Jakob Church, where frozen hands and feet stick out of the snow cover. At the top, the frost has been scraped clean from a corpse's blue-black face, and in its mouth witty gutter-snipes have stuck a broken clay pipe and signed their work with piss.

During the day Anna Stina answers to the name of Lovisa Tulip, and her work at and around the Scapegrace takes all of her time. Her day begins early, and she learns to dress quickly and greet the workers who empty the barrel under the outhouse at the Scapegrace in order to shuttle the contents away on their wagon. It is one of the many tasks she has taken responsibility for after having noticed how others were taking advantage of the Flowerman's inattention by demanding payment every week without performing any services in return. She carries water until the pumps by the well on the square freeze up. She washes dishes and tankards by rubbing them with snow, she carries wood up from the timber rafts down by the quay, and every morning and evening she sweeps the floors and scrubs them as needed. These labours ease the pangs of conscience she feels when she meets Karl Tulip's blue-green eyes in a face where his eyes and wrinkles are lifted into a smile each time he sees her, and every time he tenderly puts a hand on her growing belly. She knows that he already sees her as his daughter, and wishes she could also see him as her father.

In her dreams, she is no longer haunted by the Red Rooster, but the future will still not leave her in peace. When she wakes, her blanket is wet with sweat although her room is draughty and cool. It is as if her child has lit an ember inside and keeps her warm despite the cold. She grows larger day by day. When she can't sleep, she lights a candle and studies her reflection in the buckled glass of the window facing the alley. She imagines that her face is getting rounder, both from the food she now receives and the life burgeoning inside her. The starving girl of the work-house is not so easy to recognize. But this transformation is not enough. Not even what Kristofer Blix – whose name she now carries – has done for her will be enough.

Stockholm is so terribly small. Everyone throngs on the same streets, in the same places. When Anna Stina leaves the Scapegrace, she ties a kerchief over her red hair and lets the front hang down over her forehead. She stays north of the Lock, away from the territory where Tyst and Fischer hunt for sinners, but there are also watchmen in the City-between-the-Bridges and each time she catches sight of their blue coats and white belts, her heart skips a beat in her chest.

In her dreams, the same scene plays over and over: she is busying herself with something in the pantry behind the main room of the Scapegrace and, as she steps back across the threshold, she

354

meets his gaze and drops what she has been holding in her arms without hearing it hit the floor. Petter Pettersson is standing there, leaning against a barrel and with a sarcastic smile on his face. He bows and calls her by her true name. She stands frozen in place when he closes the distance between them and takes her hand in his.

'Miss, I believe you owe me a dance.'

The customers at the Scapegrace, whom she is starting to count among her friends, point and whisper, and Kalle Tulip breaks down into sobs when the extent of her deception dawns on him. Petter Pettersson ties a rope around her wrist as if it were a mark of affection and leads her out on the street to a wagon, ready to take her back where she belongs, to the workhouse and the Scar, where Master Erik awaits, where she will be forced to dance enough circles around the courtyard well to obliterate what she is and leave behind only shards of humanity. The child she is carrying will be lost. In the hope of saving her own life, her body will repel all excess, and leave the one who is still unformed as a red spot in the gravel next to the well, something she will have to walk past again and again as terror and insanity make her their own.

———•———

It is afternoon when Anna Stina Knapp returns to the Scapegrace with the groceries she has bought with the Flowerman's money: a couple of freshly trapped rabbits in their winter pelts; some fish clubbed on the ice; bread. The sun has already dipped back below the horizon, and in the alleys the whirling snow makes the few still moving around outside hurry along in the wind by the side of the buildings to find a roof over their heads. Kalle Tulip has some spiced wine on the stove and a cup set aside for her. He embraces her and rubs her shoulders with his large hands to warm her up.

'There was a man here asking for you.'

'Did he say what he wanted?'

'No. He said that he would be back.'

'What did he look like?'

'He was a large fellow, with a hideous face. Does that sound familiar?'

Anna Stina shakes her head at his mildly quizzical gaze.

'Oh, and he was wearing a uniform. He was dressed like a watchman.'

The word is like a slap and she has to turn away so he won't see how the blood rushes to her cheeks.

She is not safe. She owns nothing. Her new name and the world that has just been given to her is subject to the goodwill of others. The watchmen will return and they know her face belongs to Anna Stina Knapp and not Lovisa Ulrika Blix. Unyielding reality will topple her lie, and the nightmare must come to pass. The child that she at first wanted nothing more than to get rid of is now a furnace of tenderness within her, and if they find her again it is doomed before it has even taken its first breath. When evening comes, she sits in her room, studying her reflection in the window and cursing her pale features. Anna Stina spends the rest of the night with her arms around her slender shoulders, rocking back and forth on a squeaky stool, lost in thought over how best to rid herself of the face that Maja Knapp has given her.

54

CECIL WINGE PULLS the scarf tightly around his neck to protect the sliver between coat and neck from the falling snow. He leaves the City-between-the-Bridges at the Royal Mint and takes a route across the frozen timber at the bridge by the timber yard, crosses the Islet of the Holy Ghost out of the wind by the royal stables and Per Brahe's house, to struggle on into the wind again by Slaughterhouse Bridge. To his right, out of the gushing lake water, rise the stone pillars of the half-finished North Bridge, each surrounded by a stranglehold of icy shelves. The unfinished ends of the foundation fumble in vain for the support of the arches to bind them together.

The lower court building, still called Kastenhof after the brewer who ran the cellar pub there over a hundred years ago, sits on one side of Northern Square. Five steps take him up to the entrance, above which the royal monogram has been carved in resplendent sandstone. Winge is recognized at the door. He addresses the guard on duty by name and is shown to the gaol, a corridor where a row of doors lead to walled-in cells, all lit by narrow window slits. The room has spartan furnishings: a bed hardly tall enough to hide the chamber pot; a dresser; a stool.

Johannes Balk sits in the dimly lit cell. He is staring into space before Winge's arrival wakes him from his reflections. Behind them, the door is bolted, and the sound of the guard's boots on the stone die away as he leaves.

Winge nods at him in greeting.

'Good morning. Have you everything you need? Food, blankets, tobacco?'

'I need nothing. I've never smoked. The fish and pork are sufficient. The cold doesn't bother me anymore.'

Something about Balk reminds Winge of a spider, unmoving and patient in its web, tauntingly passive. A plate with the remains of a meal stands on the chest: porridge, and what looks like boiled pike. Balk rubs his eyes while Winge sits down on the stool.

'Do you know, Winge, that I am several years younger than you, though we look as if we were born the same year? Perhaps life carves our faces with the experiences that we suffer through, and perhaps it is my actions that have aged me prematurely. Where were we? Oh, the middle of the second act. I was just preparing to leave the country.'

The water in the pitcher that stands next to the bed has already formed a layer of ice at the top. Balk cracks it with his index finger before pouring himself a mug. He clears his throat and drinks, stopping for a while as if to find the place where he left the story, and then he begins again.

***

In time, the boy becomes a young man, but without a father or a mother he is doomed in many ways to remain a boy. As long as he is too young, Birdsong is under the control of a board of trustees, a collection of stern gentlemen in Stockholm who have assisted Gustav Adolf Balk in his affairs, and whom the young man only acquaints himself with through the letters he receives, which are written in a style so formal, their content is not so easy to surmise. Twice a year, a proxy is sent out to Birdsong to oversee the management of the estate and to ensure that the young man's education continues according to his father's wishes.

On his seventeenth birthday, he receives a communiqué with unexpected information: according to the terms of Gustav Adolf

Balk's last will and testament, a fund has been set aside for an educational tour of the continent. A particular route has been outlined, with the addresses of bankers who, forewarned of his arrival, are prepared to pay out travel funds in practical currencies in exchange for the notarized bills included in his instructions. His journey begins by sea, from Stockholm to Reval, then south to Paris, Florence and Rome. For the second time he leaves Birdsong, and sees the sombre buildings disappear behind the end of the linden trees.

───────•───────

It is in Paris that he departs from the itinerary. He has read about the city, the scene of novels and stories, home to thinkers and visionaries. He has always longed to see it with his own eyes and finds that art has not done justice to reality. There is something in the air here. At each coffee house and restaurant, people discuss the conditions and rights of humankind. Slavery is unanimously condemned. Many go even further, comparing the submission of the slave with the fate of the people under their monarch. Beneath the beautiful ideals he catches a glimpse of the feeling that he, more than anyone else, is familiar with: fear.

As if by some sixth sense, he already feels surrounded by the bloodlust that mercilessly follows in fear's wake, and when the day of departure draws near he finds he does not want to leave the city. Something is coming and, whatever it is, he wants to witness it with his own eyes. During the first few months, he spends every waking moment on the city's streets and public squares. He listens to the discourse in a language he has learned by way of books and the caning of his tutors, but quickly understands it better and better. With a few dispatches to his home he can secure credit with French bankers, and rents a room in the Latin quarter.

There is life and movement everywhere. The city is seething with revolt, fomented by the poor harvest of the year before.

At the beginning of May, there is a convocation of the Estates-General, the first in almost two hundred years. The National Assembly is proclaimed, the Bastille is stormed, and by the summer of eighty-nine, Paris is under self-rule by grace of the city council and the newly formed National Guard. In the rest of the country, peasants cast off the yoke of oppression. Feudal lords are forced to flee or relinquish their ancient rights. He stands in the middle of all of this, a passive but enthusiastic observer. In August, the new Declaration of the Rights of Man and of the Citizen is published by the National Assembly. Word spreads through the city's squares and meeting points. He sees King Louis XVI himself speak to the people from the balcony at the Tuileries Palace, no longer a young man but imposing nevertheless, in the prime of life. The King speaks warmly of the new constitution, the very symbol of the old accepting the new. During the next few months, the city appears to have stabilized under the new order. But he senses its fragility and bides his time. He stays for the rest of the year. And the next.

Johannes Balk knows that hate requires fear just as a fire needs fuel, and he feels the fear growing around him. Maybe it is this more than anything else that makes Paris feel like the home Birdsong never became for him. Here he is not exceptional: everyone is afraid; most people are as full of hate as him – and, among them, Johannes feels superior. They have only just begun to acquaint themselves with emotions he has harboured for as long as he can remember. Although belief in the power of the people grows stronger at the expense of the King, anxiety spreads among the ranks of the revolutionaries. Many see enemies in every shadow, both in and outside the city's walls. Marat the agitator writes caustic pamphlets advocating drastic measures: a purge of the blight of the Jews for the good of the many. It is now said that the end will justify the means.

For the first time in his life, the young man feels that he is a part of something he understands, surrounded by people like himself. He senses a colossal death approaching, unseen by the masses, biding its time. He awaits it with great anticipation, eager to find out which forms it will take.

———•———

In December ninety-one, he is awakened by a commotion in the stairwell. Men in the home-made uniforms of the National Guard, reflecting the colours of the new flag, kick in his door. He has been informed against. Who the sneak was, he never discovers. Someone seeking favours from the Jacobins? Maybe his banker, or his landlord? As a foreign nobleman, he is an easy target of suspicion. They say he is a spy. He is brought to the Abbey of Saint-Germain-des-Prés, quite near his own lodgings, where they tell him he will be interrogated.

No such interrogations ever take place. He is placed in a cell in the dungeon of the military prison, deep down under the old Benedictine monastery. There is no window or light of any kind. At first, he waits patiently and prepares his defence as best he can. A guard brings bread and water, sometimes other morsels, without ever showing his face. A bowl is shoved through an opening at the bottom of the door and no one responds to any questions. He is left there to rot. Perhaps the hierarchy among the revolutionaries has shifted, so that the order for his arrest has been forgotten. The cell is completely black. He can't see his hand in front of his face. In time, he becomes uncertain if his eyes are open or closed, or where his body ends and the darkness begins. He can only sit still in the dark.

He becomes aware of the fact that he is not alone. Things that cannot exist there become visible. The father he believed to be dead comes to visit him. When he fumbles his way over to the stretcher to sleep, his mother – who has patiently been waiting for him – crawls over to him and reaches out to claw his face. He defends himself by giving back as good as he gets. In this way time goes by, with no means for him to measure it.

⎯⎯•⎯⎯

He is awakened from his state of slumbering wakefulness by terrible sounds that he soon realizes are human voices raised in anger. His door is slammed open, and in comes a light so strong he is forced to cover his face with his hands. Random fists grab him and lift his body. He is carried out into the grounds in front of the church where hundreds of people have gathered. The sans-culottes, the revolutionary mob and the National Guard are all gathered, and the prisoners of Saint-Germain are all dragged out into the open.

He sees the large crowd swaying. Here and there, heads stick up out of the mass, only to sink back down to the level of the others with a thud. At first he is confused by what he is seeing; then he realizes that they are trampling each of the prisoners to death. A dozen men at a time get up on top of a single victim, holding on to each other's shoulders and waists for balance, and then bounce by bending and straightening their knees. Soon the prisoner's body gives way. The chest bursts with a bang, the skull is trampled flat with such force that the eyeballs shoot across the cobble-stones. Under all of them is a bloody mess where no one can tell any longer which body part was attached where.

More and more people are crowding into the yard, until panic breaks out and the men who have carried the young man out are obliged to let go of him in order to fend the others off. He crawls between the forest of battling legs until he reaches a fence. He sees a gap between two boards – impossibly narrow – and then, to his surprise, realizes that his body is thin enough to pass through.

In this way, he regains his freedom. On the other side, there is no longer anything that separates him from the other paupers who flock around the church. He washes himself clean down by the Seine. He doesn't recognize his own reflection. In time he hears that a rumour had spread about the number of imprisoned foreigners having grown large enough to threaten the Commune itself, and that the enraged mob was emboldened to take matters into its own hands. Saint-Germain-des-Prés is only one of many prisons where such scenes are played out.

During his imprisonment, the death that he has for so long been waiting for has come to Paris. On his way through the city, he sees bodies piled up higher than his hand can reach. They have been massacred in their thousands. Chaos reigns. On the other side of the river he sees drunk men force a woman up onto a pile of corpses, to dance and sing in praise of the republic, and when she refuses, the bayonets pierce her body. It is now September 1792, and the autumn leaves are everywhere. A few days earlier, the King was forced to flee the Tuileries when the palace was stormed, but he has now been captured, along with his family. On the streets, people are singing 'Ça Ira', a melody he knows well from the first year of the revolution, but it has different lyrics now. They used to sing about justice for the oppressed. Now the song is about hanging aristocrats from the lamp posts. All men have to wear the revolution's tricoloured cockade on their hats, the colours that were supposed to symbolize liberty, fraternity and equality. His way out of the city takes him to the eight-sided square he once knew as Place Louis XV and in the middle of which a strange object now stands, placed next to the plinth on which the King's father was once depicted sitting astride a horse. It is the first guillotine he sees. No executioner can be expected to manage all the beheadings that the revolution demands, so someone has invented a machine for it. He claps his hands and laughs so vigorously that cracks appear all over his dry lips.

He wanders north, barefoot. No one bothers him. His appearance is alarming and he possesses nothing of value. In Flanders, he finds some fellow Swedes whom he convinces of his family background, and from whom he can borrow some money in return for a payment three times the amount. Then he makes his way home to Rostock, where he can buy himself a berth on a ship to Karlskrona. At the end of the year, he returns to his native land after years of absence, though he appears to have aged far more than this.

———— • ————

Balk returns to the light. His eyes appear unseeing, as if his gaze is turned inward to his memories to pull a lost image from the past.

'It was then I met Daniel Devall. I was looking for a ride to Stockholm to take me back to Birdsong, the only home that remained to me. At the roadside inn where I was looking for a driver, there he was. He had bought a place in the same sleigh and on our journey, we began to converse. You know yourself how slow and uncomfortable the hours are as the horses toil. You never saw him in life, Mr Winge. I am sorry that the remains you recovered from Larder Lake did not manage to do him justice. He had a glow about him, as if his soul were shining from the inside and made him into a lantern to light the world for others. His eyes were wide and a clear blue, slightly tilted in a face that had perfectly symmetrical features. He had a glint in his eye that was at once roguish and innocent, bold and modest at the same time, like that of a blessed child no parent could ever bring themselves to discipline. He wore his golden hair long when we met, tied at the neck with a silk ribbon but, as time wore on, often worn loose around the shoulders. When he smiled, he had two milk-white rows of teeth. The upper ones were completely straight, and in the lower row he had a tooth that was slightly askew, as if his creator had been worried about taking perfection to excess. His body was slender and finely formed, dressed in beautiful clothes tailored

364

to flatter his proportions. He had the hands of a virtuoso, with long slender fingers. Even his scent was appealing: a discreet suggestion of a flowering meadow, at a time when others drench themselves in perfume to cover their stink.

'The hours simply flew by, to the point I would have wished them to last longer. Daniel was charming and quick-witted, a superb conversationalist and easy-going. He sat very close to me and when I told him something that amused him, he burst into laughter and laid his hand on my knee as if he could not stop himself.'

He pauses and pours himself some more water.

'You have to understand, Mr Winge, that I have never had a friend. My loneliness was far greater than that. I cannot recall anyone ever paying me any attention or asking me a question out of pure curiosity. That's why I was so poorly prepared for Daniel Devall. I was . . . vulnerable.'

He drinks of the cold water until it is all gone.

'When we reached our destination, Devall offered to be my guide in Stockholm for the next couple of days. The journey had worn me out and I needed to rest. He was familiar with the city that I had only seen very briefly and where I would otherwise quickly have become lost in the maelstrom of bustling life. I saw no reason not to accept his offer.'

He nods to himself.

'Let me tell you about one of the evenings in particular, Mr Winge. There was a masked ball that night, although it was less than a year since the King had been murdered at just such an event. The men appeared to take pleasure in this element of incongruity; they were not of the kind to mourn for King Gustav. They all wore masks, but their clothes betrayed their noble birth and wealth. Neither I nor Duvall belonged to these circles, but after Daniel managed to procure each of us a mask, no one noticed that we were strangers, not least because of the amount of wine that flowed. As evening became night, the gentlemen went on to other establishments. We were pulled along, and in this way arrived at a house that was set apart from the others, by the water-side where only the grain cargo boats go. A dark-skinned servant greeted us, and soon we found ourselves in ornate rooms.

'Horrors awaited us there, Mr Winge. I had been drinking and when I first saw some masks that I had not noticed earlier, I was astounded at how lifelike they were. There were distorted faces with bulging growths, heads that had been twisted into strange shapes, costumes to transform their wearers into cripples and grotesque figures. But soon I realized that these poor wretches were not wearing masks at all. This was their true form and they belonged to the house for the entertainment and distraction of the gentlemen. After a while, women arrived, dressed only in veils over their naked bodies, and soon the men loosened their belts and let their clothes fall to the ground. Before long the room was a slithering mass, with men and women copulating in all manner of ways. The deformed cripples provided any service that was required of them. This scene revolted me and when I pulled the mask from my face, Devall could read the expression on my face. "I thought . . . your father . . ." he said to me, and the extent of what he meant did not strike me until much later. We left. I saw no reason to postpone my departure any longer and made the necessary preparations. I asked Daniel to accompany me to Birdsong as I had no servants and his requirements were not great.'

'What happened after that, Johannes? Did you find his correspondence?'

'I knew that he wrote letters, Mr Winge. But I did not find that strange. It took me a while to figure out who he was writing to and why. The letters to Liljensparre he wrote in code – as you must surely know – but he wrote them first in plain text and used a key to translate them into the code. He must have opened the masonry stove in his bedroom without first checking if there were still embers in there. It was a cool evening and I opened it later to make sure there would be enough heat until the morning. There was a piece of paper crumpled in the ashes. His original copy. I could not keep myself from reading it.'

'And what were your conclusions?'

'Daniel Devall was a fortune hunter, Mr Winge. He wanted nothing more than to find favour with Police Chief Liljensparre and thereby further his interests. I imagine that someone had told him about my impending arrival in Karlskrona, perhaps from one of the Swedes I met in Flanders. His assignment as informant was to survey the harbour and carefully observe any suspect persons who came from France to spread the revolution in the north. He assumed I was a Jacobin who had taken part in the revolt and who was now returning home to spread the same message. That's why he came with me to Birdsong. He was hoping that I would confide in him my plans to overthrow the monarchy, and that he would win the honour of having uncovered the plot.'

'What did you do after you read the letter?'

'My thoughts went to my mother. How she pulled the limbs from her crane flies in place of my father. And what was Devall if not a crane fly that had bumbled into my house? Was he not deserving of the same fate? It took me many hours to ponder how such a thing could be accomplished. My mother had laid her prey on the windowsill and left them there to languish. I needed a windowsill large enough for Daniel Devall. Then I recollected Keyser House, where we had found ourselves among naked half-men and grotesque figures, and only now did I realize that the visit had been deliberate. I remember the words Devall had uttered by mistake, and I realized their meaning. He had led me there as he knew my father, who must have been a regular guest at the house. Devall guessed that I shared the same tendencies. In his mind, he must have imagined that the Honourable Gustav

Adolf Balk had taken his firstborn son to Stockholm to introduce him to the appetites of the flesh that appeal to the gentlemen of his class. I cannot with words describe how much this thought disgusts me. And so I found it fitting to let him end his days at Keyser House, associating with people like my father. In their circles, Daniel Devall would be welcome, such as I would shape him.'

He squints up at the slit of light near the ceiling, which is growing fainter.

'I hardly need to tell you the rest, Mr Winge. All you do not know now are some practical details. I had to take myself to Stockholm for these arrangements, and had to be assured that Daniel would not leave Birdsong before my return. My first stop was to that board of trustees who thought me long dead. I asked for a lump sum payment against the promise that I would never darken their threshold again. Inquiries led me to the Jew, Dülitz, whose services I could now afford. Through him I found the surgeon's apprentice, Kristofer Blix, and purchased both his debts and his life. Magnus was the only one of the residents of Birdsong who was there when I returned from France. He was a half-feral hunting dog who remembered enough of my smell to associate me with being fed. He allowed himself to be chained in the shed and I did not disappoint him.'

Winge allows the silence to settle before he speaks.

'You know that Blix wrote down everything that he had done, witness accounts that allowed us to track you down. What happened to Kristofer when he had played out his role?'

'Blix was afraid of his own shadow and prepared to do anything to save his own skin. After he had completed everything I asked of him, I let him run off into the woods.'

'And if you are now prepared to confess to everything, why did you wait until we found you, Johannes? Why did you not come to me directly?'

'I lacked evidence for my crimes, Mr Winge, and it is of great importance to me that my confession not be refuted. I read in the *Extra Post* that you had taken on the case of the Larder corpse and felt secure in the knowledge that you would find me and bind me to what I had done.'

A sense of unease causes Winge to hesitate before raising the question he has been waiting to ask.

'Why are you doing this now, Johannes? What is your goal?'

Johannes Balk looks straight into his eyes. His pupils, large and black in the dim light, seem to Winge to be two deep wells without end, containing only a raging emptiness.

'I have seen the world now, Mr Winge. Humans are lying vermin, a pack of bloodthirsty wolves who want nothing more than to tear each other to pieces in their struggle for power. The enslaved are no better than their masters, only weaker. The innocent only retain their blamelessness due to their lack of ability. Before Paris became a bloodbath, everyone spoke of equality, liberty and brotherhood, of human rights, and now those same voices are heard here. I saw the declaration of human rights bound in the tanned hides of men who had been flayed once the guillotine had separated their heads from their bodies. Here, the burghers and farmers also stand ready to rise up against the nobility, their ancient oppressors. Do you remember, Mr Winge, how a noble officer at the beginning of the year raised his hand against a merchant and the City Guard had to drive the agitated mob from the gates of the Castle itself? Revolution hung in the air then. It does so still. I, the final descendant of one the kingdom's most prominent houses, firstborn son of a member of the Council of the Realm, will step forward in the lower courts and confess in detail what I have done to Daniel Devall, a common man of the people. You yourself will prove my guilt beyond a shadow of a doubt. And the people will rise up in vengeance. Before you lay me under the sword, I will tip the scales of revolution. In Paris, the streets flow with blood as we speak. The blade of the guillotine has to be sharpened several times a day in order to manage its load. I wish the same for Stockholm. The gutters will run red. The fewer of us who survive, the better. Let the City-between-the-Bridges choke on corpses. Let the graveyards be flooded. Let only the ravens remain.'

He chuckles.

'And then there is you, Mr Winge. In a world of wolves, you are the exception. A man of a better kind, born to the wrong time. You uphold justice and reason when others simply wish to better themselves. I read your name in the *Extra Post* and, when I understood who you were, all became clear to me. Providence has brought you to the place where my journey ends. You are famous for always allowing the accused to tell their side. And tell it, I will. That which must come to pass afterwards will be as much your doing as mine.'

55

WHEN CECIL WINGE wakes on Tuesday morning after a couple of hours of sleep, the room is chilly. His bed clothes feel heavy. Still groggy with sleep, he wonders at first who has laid an unfamiliar blanket over him, dark maroon rather than his own white one. When full consciousness returns, he realizes that he is mistaken. The blanket is red with blood. Where it has had time to dry, it has hardened into a dark shell. During the night, he has started to cough and not been able to stop. There is a red crust on his chin and throat. His skin is so pale it is almost transparent. How much has he lost?

His fingers are as white as bone when he holds them up in front of him. They lack feeling, as do his legs. He stumbles out of bed on unsteady feet, crushes the ice that has formed in his pitcher of water and pours it into the bowl. The rest he drinks straight out of the pitcher and he is horrified by the loss of fluids that his thirst bears witness to. It takes time to scrub everything clean. His skin stings. When he is ready, he dresses as quickly as his weakness allows, walks down into the kitchen and sends a son of one of the maids to fetch him a carriage to bear him back to the City-between-the-Bridges and to Mickel Cardell.

———•———

Steam from freshly brewed coffee rises up towards the beams in the ceiling of the Small Exchange. It is early morning. Inquisitive early birds mingle with the hungover and regretful, who are having an invigorating mug before they head off through the labyrinth of alleys to report to work. Even though he is late for their meeting, Cecil Winge finds himself the first to arrive. He waits without complaining, lost in thought, until Cardell's imposing figure darkens the entrance. He stamps the snow from his shoes and shakes himself like a wet dog.

'You'll have to excuse me. I ran into our dear friend Blom just now, who was staggering from building to building up on Blackfriar's Lane. He was so incoherent, my conscience didn't let me leave him be. I dragged him to his office at the Indebetou where he can sleep off the worst of it without freezing to death.'

'And what was he celebrating?'

'I think it was more like the opposite. It wasn't easy to tell from his slurring, but I think he received a letter yesterday about Ullholm being on his way from the western parts with his whole retinue, ready to take up his new position as police chief and move into Norlin's old rooms. He is expected tomorrow. Blom may have his quirks but somewhere deep inside there's a decent man in hiding. He doesn't look forward to working for a crook, hence the drunkenness. How about you? What have you discovered?'

'Johannes Balk has told me a story about how a monster is created. I have seen it before, Jean Michael, but rarely with more clarity, how every perpetrator begins as a victim. But we are not yet done. There are details in his story that don't add up. I must confirm my suspicions before I see him again.'

Mickel Cardell weighs his wooden fist in his hand and sees before him all the blows he has dealt and the devastation he has wrought. He knows better than anyone that Winge speaks the truth.

'Jean Michael, there is something I must ask of you.'

'You know you only have to ask.'

'I need more time before Ullholm arrives. At least one day.'

Cardell scratches his forehead and looks confused.

'What is it that you're afraid will happen when Ullholm becomes police chief?'

'I am guessing he will choose the path of least resistance and relieve me from all the authority Norlin gave me, declare my investigation closed, and set Balk free just as soon as he becomes aware of Balk's existence. That must not happen. He is far too dangerous.'

'But surely not even the police chief's authority is unlimited? Why don't you make sure Balk is brought to the courts immediately? Ullholm can hardly put a stop to a trial without looking like a despot.'

Winge's look back at Cardell is filled with respect.

'I would like to understand his motives completely before I add his name to the register of arrests and in the records of the lower courts. Only after this do I want to decide how best to pursue the trial. Therefore, Jean Michael, I need one more day. If you can do this for me then we still have hope.'

'Hope? Of what?'

'I will not keep anything from you but I don't have a moment to lose. For now, I have to ask you for patience.'

'And how exactly do you think that a wayward watchman should stop the incoming police chief of Stockholm?'

'I have no answer for you, Jean Michael, and neither can I offer any help to you with this task. All of my resources will be directed to my current duties. There is nothing left of me.'

Cardell scratches his head and makes a face. Then he sits without saying anything. He taps repeatedly with his hand on the table, the rhythm of an unheard military march. Only after a full minute does he raise his head and meet Winge's gaze again.

'If that's what you need, you'll have it. One day.'

He turns on the bench and waves his wooden arm in the air.

'Girl! Remove these coffee mugs and get me some brandy. Mickel Cardell needs something to help him think and the hurry is great.'

Winge leaves him and sets off through the alleys towards the Scorched Plot, crouched in the wind. He presses the handkerchief to his mouth while trying to keep his breaths shallow and calm. Slowly he regains control over his body and rubs his face with a handful of snow before crossing the square.

56

THERE'S A BEGGAR at the corner of Priest's Street whom Anna Stina has walked past many times on her way up the hill to Old Square and its market. He usually sits on two pieces of wood that he has bound together into a stool, and in front of him on his lap he displays the disfigurement that is his livelihood. Both his hands are deformed, to such an extent that people who walk by either stop and stare or move over to the gutter rather than get too close.

It is not an injury caused by fire. It is as if something has turned his flesh into wax and formed it into strange new shapes and left him to set in this way. The tissue on his fingers looks as if it has melted and run off, and left his fingertips without nails and a layer of skin barely thick enough to cover the bone. On his palms and the back of his hands, there are odd patterns, hollows and bulges. The skin is colourless and almost as smooth as that of a newborn.

It is to him she turns with her question, and she finds he does not sit there all the time. She has to wait and tries to stamp the cold from her body when it becomes hard to bear. Finally he appears with a small sign under his arm and his hands wrapped in cloth. She gives him time to set up his pitch and sit down, as he gently unwinds the cloth to expose his lacerated hands to the gaze of others and to the falling snow. Her breath quickens as she sees they are just as she remembers. She walks closer and holds out the bread she has saved from her own breakfast. He blinks in bewilderment at this generosity, and is even more astonished when he sees who the giver is.

'God bless you, my child, but what have I done to deserve such a gift?'

'I want to hear what happened to your hands.'

He smiles, almost relieved.

'That is a story I have told many times and for less than this. Have you been down to Klara Lake, my girl?'

She nods.

'Then you may have smelled a certain smell, one that comes neither from the rot in the water or from the dreck on land. There is a manufactory there where I was apprenticed. They make soap, both the kind that the poor folk scrub with for their Christmas bath and the kind that is used in the morning toilette of noblewomen. The craft is the same. The difference is in the exclusivity of the scents. But before the scenting there is a stench, and that comes from the animal cadavers. You melt them to render the fat. It is mixed with other ingredients and left to solidify, and before you can count to ten, the soap has turned clear and is ready to be used. I was a young and eager disciple and I became too enthusiastic when I was going to mix the potash with lime. The dose became too strong. I spilled the white powder over both my hands, and at the same time as I dipped them in water to clean myself, I heard my master call out his warning. It was too late. It was as if I had put my hands in boiling oil. Ash burns in water, you see, and it consumes everything in its way. That's how I became like you see me today. They took pity on me and let me work with a broom since then but I'm not as good at working as I was before and what I make isn't enough to live on.'

Anna Stina lets the words sink in as she thinks.

'How did it feel?'

He laughs.

'It felt as a foretaste of the hell to which I am surely on my way, little girl.'

When he sees that she is not satisfied, he continues in a more serious tone.

'I have never experienced anything worse. When my master took a bit of woollen cloth and brushed off the ash that had become a bubbling mess, it felt as if my skin was being peeled from my hands. He sent for lemons because he said their juice would ease my suffering, and maybe he was right but the pain stayed for days and it felt like I was squeezing hot coals with all my might.'

He spits at the memory and when he looks up his good mood is evaporated.

'Well, was there anything else? Now that I remember it all, I don't think the bread is any kind of fair payment.'

'Can you make the ash again? The same kind that burned you? I'll pay for it.'

It doesn't take them more than a half an hour to leave the City-between-the-Bridges. Maybe it is an illusion caused by the terrain, but it looks to Anna Stina as if the building by the shore of Klara Lake is leaning out over the water, as if the marshy land on which it was built will no longer carry its weight. They have to wait for the sun to go down and the work to stop. The labourers abandon the workshop one after another or in small groups and slip-slide over the ice. She can hear how the man with the deformed hands counts them all under his breath to make sure that everyone has gone home. He looks around anxiously before he signs for her to follow him.

They walk around the exterior of the building towards land and slide down the beach to the ice that is there. On the lake side, the house is supported on stilts tall enough to allow someone who is bent over to crawl in underneath. The beggar makes his way over to the planks above and swears quietly when his feet slip again and again below him. But he finds the hole he is looking for, large enough to admit a hand and forearm to pull a latch back. Under the trapdoor is a pile of frozen rubbish, and Anna Stina assumes that this is opened every morning when the floor is swept clean, and the dross deposited into the lake. Her companion asks for silence with a gesture as he props open the door slightly and looks up, his free hand over his mouth so the vapour from his exhalation won't betray him. He stands for a long time before he pulls himself up onto the floor. Anna Stina waits for a sign before she follows him up.

57

CARDELL WINDMILLS HIS healthy arm to pump blood into his frozen fingertips and he jumps in place to keep warm. He has been waiting for more than half an hour in the yard outside the low house. The maid, who has refused to let an unknown man pass the threshold – let alone someone like Cardell – has forced him to wait outside until her mistress is ready. When he asks for something warm to keep the cold at bay, she snorts loudly and slams the door in his face. He is thoroughly sick of waiting. Each time he looks up at the Katarina parish clock – which he can bring into view above the ridge of the tiled roof by putting one boot on the chopping block and balancing on top of it – he is convinced the clockwork has frozen and that the hands no longer move. Finally the door opens again and the same sullen maid's round face appears in the gap.

'You can step into the hall now and have a cup of warm beer, if you like. My mistress will see you soon.'

The thought of something warm is enough for Cardell to banish any thoughts of vengeance. He brushes the snow from his shoulders and stamps his boots carefully before he steps inside. The house smells of newly baked bread. Once his coat and scarf have been hung up, he feels the heat of the stove start to thaw his stiff shirt and he sighs in gratitude.

The mistress of the house waits beyond the kitchen in a poorly illuminated room. Widow Fröman is still dressed in black from

379

the hem of her dress to her cap, although it has been many years since her husband passed on. She must be nearing sixty. He has the impression that the couple remained childless and that lack of family has made the grief for her departed husband a fixture of the house. Despite the modest dimensions of the chamber, the widow makes a formidable impression where she sits close to the fire. Her back is as straight as a poker. In her flinty face, Cardell sees no hint of self-pity, only a measured dignity, an expression that tells a hurtful world that she is ready and able to answer in kind. Cardell finds his neck, that hardly bent an inch for his officers in the artillery, here tilt towards the floorboards as of its own accord. He clears his throat.

'Good day.'

He has the feeling that Mrs Fröman scrutinizes him from head to toe without even moving her gaze, and that she reads off him everything she needs to know. She allows a few moments to pass before she replies.

'They tell me your name is Cardell and that you are a watchman. What matters you have to discuss with me go beyond my powers of imagination, and the fact that my life rarely presents me with surprises is the only reason that you are here right now and have not been shown the door. So, what do you want?'

Cardell feels his ears - recently so cold - suddenly glow with heat, and he squirms uncomfortably. He realizes that he has been wrong about the old woman's firm gaze. She is blind. As his own eyes grow accustomed to the dark, he sees that hers are covered with a milky membrane. He shivers involuntarily and tries to find the right words.

'I'm sorry to arrive unannounced, and let me express my humblest condolences for your husband's all too hasty departure . . .'

She silences him by raising her hand.

'Hush, watchman. Magpies do best when they croak, not when they try to sing like nightingales. Arne Fröman, pastor in Katarina parish, may he rest in peace, has been gone many a year, even if his corpse was surely so soaked in brandy that any worm daring to dig itself within a foot of his coffin must have died on the spot. That I still feel grief says more about myself than about our blessed pastor. Come now, watchman, you'd do best to stop pussyfooting around and get right to it.'

Cardell nods before he remembers she can't see. He searches for courage inside himself and is surprised to find it there.

'You live awfully modestly here, it seems to me, in view of Pastor Fröman's prominence.'

He feels a measure of satisfaction when he sees that she flinches a little at the words before she regains her self-control. He hurries on.

'Tell me, do you perhaps recognize the name of Ullholm? Magnus is the first name.'

He feels something shift in the room, as palpable as an icy draught from a newly cracked pane. Every dry hint of sarcasm is gone when she answers.

'Yes. I remember Magnus Ullholm.'

'I've been told that Ullholm fled to Norway with the church's widows' fund some years ago. Perhaps this included money that could have been helpful to you, Mrs Fröman, after your husband's demise.'

Cardell wonders if it is possible for someone who is already sitting still to sit even stiller, but observes that if anyone is capable of such a thing, it is Mrs Fröman.

'There's no need to remind me who Ullholm is or what he did. I know it all too well.'

'Surely there are others in the same situation as you, Mrs Fröman, who also remember Ullholm's name. They probably have children and grandchildren who have been denied a secure childhood because of what he did. I imagine that you would know their names, all of them.'

'I imagine I would.'

'Tell me, Mrs Fröman, since you spent so many years as the wife of a God-fearing man, do you recall the expression, "An eye for an eye and a tooth for a tooth"?'

Mrs Fröman pulls her lips back to reveal a row of sharp teeth. It takes him a moment to realize that she is smiling.

58

NORTHERN SQUARE IS deserted and covered in a blanket of snow. In its centre stands the statue of Gustav Adolf, as yet incomplete and still concealed under frozen wrappings, awaiting an unveiling that has already been two years delayed. It is said that it will be the first equestrian statue in the realm. Winge stops in front of it and studies the shapeless form, a ghostly silhouette that looms threateningly above the square as if it belonged to the reaper that Johannes Balk wants to let loose in the City-between-the-Bridges. On Winge's right hand is Princess Sofia Albertina's palace and, on the left, the Opera. Each building is the other's mirror image, one lit by the pale morning light, the other still in shadow. He lingers a little while longer, his gaze flitting between the two, before he turns around and walks through the gaol gate. When he has reached the correct door and had it unlocked for him, Winge is forced to steady himself against the doorpost before stepping over the threshold. The cell is not Johannes Balk's.

This cell is only a few doors down and cannot be differentiated from Balk's in any way except for its occupant, who pulls back as the door is unlocked and Winge enters.

'Dear Lord, what is wrong with you? You look like a phantom, a living skeleton. You frighten me. Is this death itself come for me?'

'You have nothing to fear from me. Quite the opposite. My name is Cecil Winge and I am with the police. That is, in a way, although it is not by their authority that I seek you out at this time.'

'I've seen you before. Your pale face has passed outside my door. Each time I thought it was a skull floating past.'

'May I sit down? My legs are not as steady as they once were.'

The man, who has crawled up onto his cot in the far corner of the room, shrugs. Winge sits down on the stool, which is exactly like the one next to Balk's bed. He takes a closer look at the condemned man. A normal man with an ordinary face, now starting to be obscured by a day-old beard. He wears a simple linen shirt, soiled by the days spent in the cell, and worn leather breeches untied at the knee. He has wrapped his blanket and a brown jacket around him. Winge waits until he has caught his breath before he speaks again.

'Your name is Lorentz Johansson. Isn't that so?'

'I make no secret of it.'

'Your profession?'

'I used to make barrels.'

'Tomorrow the cart will come and take you to the gallows at Hammarby.'

The man sighs and shudders.

'Yes, that is so. Master Höss will cut my head off. The best I can hope for is that he is sober enough to sharpen the blade tonight, and sound enough to hit the target with his first blow come dawn.'

'Has the pastor been here?'

'Yes, he was early. He was dressed in his finery, the devil. You don't have to be any smarter than me to realize he was on his way to more enjoyable things on a Friday evening. He could hardly consign my sinner's soul to the hereafter fast enough before he had slipped out the door again. I heard him humming as he passed under my window on his way towards the Royal Garden.'

'Would you like to tell me how you came to be here?'

'What could I say that's not common knowledge?'

'I would like to hear it in your own words, if you please.'

Johansson shrugs his shoulders again.

'By all means. My story is as short as it is sad, and the hours are passing by slowly enough as it is. I killed my wife, Mr Winge. That's all there is to it. Our marriage became less happy with every passing year, I'd drunk a few that night, and we started in on the same old quarrels that had plagued us forever. And then I lost it.'

'Did you have any children?'

'None that saw more than their first year.'

Winge nods thoughtfully.

'I am of the opinion that there are murderers and then there are murderers, Lorentz Johansson. What do you have to say about that?'

'I don't know what you mean.'

'I think that a person who commits a crime in a given situation doesn't necessarily do so in another. Would you have killed your wife if she had been an unknown person that you had never met before?'

'Why would I? And if she had had more sense to marry a better man she would still be alive and I free as a bird.'

'Do you regret what you did?'

Johansson thinks about it.

'She was a hateful woman, Mr Winge, always quarrelling and fighting. I grew to detest her over the years. But I loved her too. The fact that I regret it doesn't change anything. I'll pay for what I've done between the block and Master Höss's dull steel and that's all there's to it. If my death could give her her life back, I'd be happy, but such is not the way of things.'

Winge gazes at Lorentz Johansson for a long time.

'Were you good at making barrels, Lorentz Johansson?'

'Among the best. A mere year from becoming a burgher, perhaps less.'

'And if you could choose between celibacy and death, which would you choose?'

59

THE SOAP MANUFACTORY is quiet and still, and the darkness is filled with a stench not quite like putrefaction, more sharp and cloying. Anna Stina feels the uneasy atmosphere that so easily settles on places that are accustomed to life and movement but that have suddenly been abandoned. Slowly her eyes grow used to the dark, and the beggar moves with ease past barrels and water butts. The wooden walls are simply constructed and so poorly patched that Anna Stina glimpses the last red glow of the setting sun through the cracks behind her. She can hear him moving among the shadows and sees him now and again. She follows him through the rooms to a storage area filled with flasks, where he stops. He selects one, then another, and carries both to a stained table where he finds a funnel and a small bottle. He reaches for some rough leather gloves hanging on a hook, pulls them over his hands and removes powder from both of the flasks. He seals the bottle and turns around.

'You've seen my hands and heard my story. I don't need to remind you how dangerous the powder is. Treat this as carefully as if it was Satan himself that had let himself be bottled.'

He holds the bottle out to her but pulls it back as she reaches for it.

'What about my payment?'

Anna Stina reaches down to the lining of her skirt for the piece of cloth in which she has wrapped all of the coins she has earned in tips from the customers at the Scapegrace. Slowly she unfurls the small package in her left palm so that he will see the whole sum. He sighs and shakes his head.

'That's not much. D'you know how many logs are needed to burn even a pound of wood into ash? The labour required of the log drivers, the crews and those of us who drag the logs up here and chop it ready for the ovens? This is not enough money to compensate for that work.'

'I have this as well.'

Anna Stina holds out a bottle, filled with strong brandy from what the customers have left at the bottom of their cups. The beggar laughs.

'I'm not one to turn down a good drink but given what I could get for what you want to buy, I could buy many bottles of what you're offering.'

He stops to think. She can't see his face clearly enough to discern what thoughts are going through his head.

'What's it you want it for, anyway?'

She hesitates, tired of lies and of pretending, and doesn't see what she has to lose by telling him the truth.

'I am going to change my face so that no one will recognize me anymore.'

She feels him startle and it takes him a moment to speak.

'But my girl, why would you do that?'

'It's a long story and it's my business. It's enough for you to know that it is a matter of life and death.'

Not just my own, she thinks. He starts to walk back and forth across the floor. His breathing has quickened and he rubs his mangled hands together. Finally he stops and turns to her again.

'You're beautiful, my girl. It goes against nature to see such beauty go to waste, and with my help. What you have isn't enough to pay me for what I have to offer. Let me show your beauty the appreciation it deserves one last time and then we'll call it even.

There are piles of sackcloth here and it isn't much, but it will do as our bed for the night.'

Anna Stina freezes. Her silence makes the beggar uncomfortable and shifts his weight from foot to foot. She senses the shame that is not quite strong enough to overcome his lust.

'I'm not really that kind of man, you understand, but the circumstances . . .'

'I didn't know that there was any other kind.'

She holds out her hand.

'Will you at least give me my goods first, before I give you mine?'

He shrugs and hands her the flask. She weighs it in her hands, a paltry weight to conceal such atrocious power. She loosens the cork and sniffs but there is no smell. She nods, and their agreement is sealed. The beggar starts to pull sacks out onto the floor to prepare their bed for the night as she stands still. When he is satisfied, he shows her with a gesture that all is ready and invites her to lie down. She shakes her head.

'You go first, I'll be on top.'

He answers her with a leering smile and loosens his breeches as he lies back against the floor where the sackcloth receives him, wrenches off his jacket and pulls the shirt over his head. His body is starved and worn under the filth. He raises his deformed hands to welcome her in an embrace when she turns the bottle upside down and shakes the powder over him. His surprise quickly turns to anger and then into a mocking laugh.

'Didn't I tell you that the powder has to have liquid in order do damage, you stupid little whore? The only thing you've done is drive my price up even higher.'

She pulls the stopper out of her bottle of brandy and pours it out over him and immediately the room fills with the smell of scalded flesh. A stinging white smoke rises from him as the skin on his chest, stomach and face bubble and contort into fantastical new shapes. She doesn't know if he can still hear her whisper over the sounds of his own screams, but she says it anyway.

'Let that be a foretaste of the hell to which you are surely on your way.'

She leaves him and takes the same way back as she has come. She shakes the small bottle of powder to make sure there is enough left.

60

BEHIND THE SCAPEGRACE, the inner yard is deserted. The snow that has just fallen is still white and not yellow, as it will be soon once the line to the outhouse becomes longer than necessity permits. The uppermost layer rustles softly as Anna Stina gathers it in a bowl and then melts it by the stove. When she pours the water over the powder, the mixture seethes for a while in her bowl and fills the room with a strange smell but then settles down. It is not easy to understand how the liquid can possess such power without in some way giving an indication thereof.

She fetches a piece of meat from the kitchen, a small strip cut from a dried ham in the ceiling. She drops it into the bowl, and it does not disappoint. The piece starts to hiss like a cat and from all sides the strip of meat is attacked by invisible teeth and claws that pull and tear, consuming it without betraying where it has gone. It smokes and bubbles and when the smoke clears up it is as if nothing has happened. The meat is gone without a trace.

Still Anna Stina hesitates. She leans forward and from an upside-down world on the other side of the surface of the liquid, another girl looks back at her, exactly like herself. Anna Stina's breath ruffles the surface and distorts the reflection. She closes her eyes and draws a deep breath.

———◆———

The cold air tears at his throat and nose, but Mickel Cardell is happy to have exchanged it for Widow Fröman's musty room. The meeting went better than he could have hoped. All has now been set in motion. Hearing of Magnus Ullholm and the news of his return to Stockholm seemed to have lifted years from her and the spark of life lit by old grudges has spurred her to bloodthirsty vigour. Cardell had hardly left the house before maids and errand boys were running past him across the icy snow, as relieved as he was himself to have escaped Mrs Fröman's unseeing gaze. He needed some brandy to wash the widow out of his eyes, and he makes a stop by the square before reaching the Lock. He sits there for an hour or so until he decides to see if the City-between-the-Bridges has anything better to offer. While he reviews his selection of pubs, he remembers some unfinished business, takes a left on Ironmonger's Square and steers his course to the Scapegrace.

Cardell sees the recognition in Karl Tulip's eyes immediately as he comes up to meet him with his hands raised in an apologetic gesture. Cardell scratches himself under the brim of his hat and makes a sour face.

'Should I assume Miss Lovisa Ulrika is still otherwise occupied?'

Tulip nods.

'Yes, that is how it is and I can only extend my regrets. Could I tempt you with a drink to temper the disappointment?'

Something is different and Cardell narrows his eyes.

'I see customers starting to arrive and if the girl is helping you with the work I don't understand why she would be elsewhere?'

'She . . . Lovisa isn't feeling well, she came home with a fever of some kind and I haven't had the heart to get her from her room.'

'Oh, so is she home now, is she? Maybe I'll have better luck than you.'

Cardell starts to walk towards the stairs behind the counter.

'Are you out of your mind, man? You can't invite yourself in where you aren't wanted. And you're drunk too, I can smell it from here. Go off with you before I send for the constable to have you sober up in a cell.'

Cardell pushes him aside as easily as if he had been a swarm of gnats.

'Out of my way, damn it.'

———•—•———

Anna Stina hears the commotion on the stairs, listens to Karl Tulip's fruitless objections and realizes that her indecision has caused the moment of opportunity to slip out of her hands. It is lost now, the opportunity she has been striving for and had within reach. She wants to scream but all that comes across her lips is a whimper. She lifts the bowl with shaking hands and places herself behind the closed door, ready to throw the entire contents over the watchman as soon as he crosses the threshold.

———•—•———

Mickel Cardell has senses that he himself doesn't know exactly how he has acquired, abilities of a kind that must have come from his years in the shadow of death. Through his mist of intoxication, he senses an approaching danger, sees a shadow in the corner and instinctively ducks with his wooden arm in front of his face. The bowl shatters against it. He hears the hissing of the cloth and wood and from sheer instinct he tears the fabric from his body quickly enough to rip the seams apart. The vapours cause his eyes to tear up. He doesn't feel any pain, believes himself to be unhurt, and as he stands there blinking in bewilderment over what just happened, a slender figure slips out under his outstretched right arm and down the stairs. Cardell knocks Tulip out of the way for the second time, in hot pursuit.

———•—•———

Anna Stina doesn't know why but she turns to the left instead of the right, into the kitchen where the tiny window cannot offer her a way out. Here there is only escape of the other kind. She waits for him in the far corner of the room and he doesn't keep her waiting long.

———•———

Cardell rounds the corner and sees in her face an expression he knows only too well. He remembers it from the war. There were those for whom hope became too painful when the odds seemed impossible. Instead they threw themselves willingly at death. Maybe they experienced in their final moments a sliver of satisfaction, the feeling of having regained control over their fate. All it cost them was their lives. The girl is holding a knife with both hands. She doesn't listen to him as he calls out. Cardell sees her turn the point to her throat, close her eyes and push as hard as she can against her unprotected skin.

61

'Y OU HAVE COME much later today. It is already evening. And you look so pale, Mr Winge.'

'I have been sleeping poorly of late.'

'The last thing I wish is to jeopardize your health. Would you like to call for a blanket and some coffee from the guard?'

Winge waves this away and, with some effort, sits down on the stool in the cell with Johannes Balk.

'I have achieved three things since we last saw each other, Johannes. The first of these confirmed that you have not told me the entire truth.'

Balk's eyes narrow but he remains silent as he awaits the rest.

'There were a few details in your story that rang false to my ears. As you yourself mentioned it was only after having become aware of my name that you realized what effect your confession could have. The crime was already a fait accompli. Devall was mutilated and dead. This left me to search for another reason why you treated him in the manner that you did, and my instinct tells me the motive is personal and that suffering must have been the objective. The seed to such hate must have been sown in other emotions.'

Balk's voice is a hiss when he replies.

'What does it matter? What is done is done.'

Winge shakes his head.

'It has always been my ambition to understand the crimes that come under my scrutiny. What I have heard since our last

394

meeting makes me think that I now understand you more clearly, Johannes. I set off for the Scorched Plot with my questions, and it just so happened that I eventually found a driver who remembered driving two young men from Karlskrona to Stockholm last spring. His story differed from yours in small but essential ways. You did not share a ride on equal terms, Johannes. You yourself paid for the both of you. The driver told me that what he heard of your conversation quickly became more intimate than one would have expected from two new acquaintances, and that when he reached Stockholm and you got off, he saw how Daniel took your hand in his and held it as you walked away.'

Balk has chosen to close his eyes rather than meet Winge's gaze.

'I believe that your upbringing tempered you, Johannes. Like the hands that spend all day in their craft become calloused, I think your childhood caused your entire being to develop a hardened skin. I also believe that Daniel Devall changed all that. I think that you became for a short while something other than the monster you describe so vividly, and that it was just this that sealed Daniel Devall's fate.'

Johannes Balk does not say anything.

'There is also something else, Johannes, and I wonder if you are aware of it or not. When you talk about Daniel Devall, you don't stammer.'

Balk turns towards him.

'What is it you are trying to say?'

'Was it love, Johannes? Did you love him?'

'Would that surprise you? If a monster were to find such things hidden inside himself, although so much of his life had gone by?'

'No. Not at all.'

'Have you ever loved another person, Mr Winge?'

'Yes.'

'Perhaps you can then understand how love must feel for the one who never even knew such things existed. I am not a special

395

person, not like you; the world has never found a reason to show me any affection. I have lived a life without finding a single reason not to answer humanity with the same repugnance it has shown to me – until, that is, I thought that Daniel had offered me one.'

He pauses.

'Daniel was so easy-going, so amiable. The smallest little thing could coax laughter from him. To me he was as some alien spirit, descended from a higher sphere to bless us simple humans. Sometimes, when we were speaking in confidence, he would take my hand and, as if it were the most natural thing in the world, keep it tenderly between his own, sometimes holding it against his chest so that I could feel his heart beating.'

Balk's mouth has become twisted in a grimace. He turns away as if to seek solace in the shadows.

'We travelled from Stockholm to Birdsong as the trees were in bloom. The house was dilapidated. It had been boarded up by the trustees who had not wasted any time in helping themselves to my inheritance at the same moment the notices of me stopped coming from France. But it was as if nature itself were welcoming us home with wreaths of leaves and bunches of fragrant flowers. In the pantry there were still some things to serve as sustenance, and the bushes were overflowing with berries. Daniel Devall and I spent all of our time together, always in the best of moods. For a time.'

'Until you found his letter.'

'Yes. It turned out all had been a ruse to gain my trust and help his own interests. If I had confirmed any of his suspicions, he would immediately have sold me to Liljensparre.'

Balk draws a deep breath and Winge shivers at his self-control in the face of the pain of his memories. Balk opens his eyes and turns back to Winge.

'You are a clever man and it was foolish of me to think that I could have kept anything from you. Now you know my secret. I kept it quiet out of shame. Not for the love, but shame at how easily I was deceived. But my intentions remain the same and when you let me speak at the trial, Stockholm will get itself a bloodbath that will cause the first to pale in comparison. This changes nothing.'

'I mentioned three things that I accomplished since we last saw each other. Perhaps the second of them could do just that.'

Winge searches in his jacket pocket and takes out a thin bunch of papers. He unfolds them and holds them out to Balk, who lets them hang in the air between them, suspicion drawn on his features.

'What is this?'

'After having talked to the driver, I returned to the Indebetou, to the same room where my friend and I recently found the letters that led us to Birdsong, written by Daniel Devall but never before opened. I wanted to know their contents and it took me many hours to grasp the method of his code. But I was eventually successful.'

'I already know his wild fantasies about Jacobin conspiracies. What difference would this letter make?'

'First and foremost, the date. The letter you found in the ashes at Birdsong was not the last one he wrote. The last letter to leave Birdsong was the one I read last night.'

A shadow passes over Johannes Balk's face, and a shudder as if someone had just walked over his grave.

'There is no talk of conspiracies here. Daniel Devall is submitting his resignation. He writes that you are innocent of all you have been suspected of. He writes that he has found love and that it is reciprocated. Here is the letter that he wrote, with its key and its draft. Read it yourself.'

A bone white hand reaches out and lifts the papers from Winge's hand so carefully as if the slightest touch were enough to cause them to disintegrate into dust and ash. In the darkness of the cell, Johannes Balk's tears run down over the trembling pages and turn the ink into black streaks. Winge listens for the sounds of a soul being torn to pieces but the sobs are all he can hear. He turns away and lets the time pass before he begins to speak again.

'Happiness could have been yours, Johannes, if only you had the patience to ascertain the truth. You loved Daniel. And he you. It was an innocent life that met its end in such a terrible way. There are others like him, Johannes, among the people you say you hate so much and whose destruction you seek, all as deserving of life and happiness as Daniel Devall was. Which brings us to the third thing. I have a proposal for you.'

62

ANNA STINA KNAPP is surprised that death doesn't feel like
anything at all, when she opens her eyes and finds herself
still alive. Both of her arms are still locked and shaking as they try
to press the knife to her throat but Cardell – quicker than his
large body would suggest – has wrapped his right hand around
the blade and is gripping it so hard the knuckles whiten. He is
panting with the exertion but can't wrest the knife from her grip.
His voice emerges from behind teeth clenched with effort.

'Would you please drop it, for God's sake. I mean you no harm.
I've come to talk about Kristofer Blix.'

She lets go when all strength drains from her trembling muscles.
Cardell lets the knife fall to the ground and closes his fist to
staunch the blood.

———•———

He tells his story while she is washing his hand and wrapping rags
around the wound. She tells him hers. Cardell listens while his
heart twists in his chest.

'My God, my girl, never have I been so glad that I abandoned
the life of a watchman.'

He spits over his shoulder.

'What about Kristofer Blix? He deceived you before he took his
own life. Are you angry with him still?'

Anna Stina shakes her head.

'I was at first. He had promised to help me get rid of the child that had been made against my will, and I thought that was what he wanted more than anything. When I started to drink his decoctions, the child was quiet and unmoving. Now I feel it every day. It seemed to me to be an impossible thing to be able to love a child and hate its father, but I know better now. Each time my mind wanders, I find my hands resting on my stomach to search out its heartbeat. He saved its life, as well as my own. Now I feel only gratitude, and regret that he is not here for me to thank.'

Cardell nods thoughtfully.

'You're talking about things I know next to nothing about, but I'm happy that Blix was able to achieve something at the end of a life filled with such tragedy. I never met him myself but what he wrote affected me and, without him, my friend and I would have exerted ourselves in vain. We owe him our thanks as well.'

'What brings you here today? What's your business with me? He may have been my husband in name, but I know nothing more about Kristofer Blix than what I have told you. He was a stranger who did me a good turn, contrary to my own wish.'

'I come with a belated wedding gift. Blix was swindled of a considerable sum of money in a game of cards, which was the beginning of his bad luck. I happened to cross paths with one of the gamblers, and after having delivered a punishment I found suitable, I also saw a possibility to collect the debt. Blix wanted to make a future possible for you and your child, and as far as I'm concerned, these coins belong to you.'

Cardell lifts the purse out of his jacket pocket and hopes that Kristofer Blix – wherever he is, whether in heaven or hell – can see him at this moment and know that the debt he and Winge owe has been repaid. He places the purse on the table in front of her, heavy enough to set the wood vibrating. She opens it with unsteady fingers and gasps. Cardell has to smile.

'There's one hundred dalers and a little more. It should give the unborn the best start in life one could imagine. The money will be your security. The watchmen could come here and make accusations against a helpless girl, but not against a wealthy widow. Stop dressing like a servant and show that you are of different kind than you were. That is the best defence you can give yourself and your child.'

While the blood drips from his cut hand, Mickel Cardell feels how another wound, both older and deeper, closes within him. When Johan Hjelm's drowning next haunts him in his dreams, when he feels the *Ingeborg*'s anchor weighing on the arm that he lost, when terror claws its way up his throat and deprives him of breath, then the memory of the girl's face at this moment will be the consolation he needs. And Anna Stina Knapp, who once swore to herself that she would never cry again, feels tears streaming down her face.

'Will you come again?'

Cardell bites his lower lip as he considers his answer.

'That depends on whether you intend to throw some witches' brew over me when I walk in next time, and how much your father charges for his brandy. But first I must see to one or two other matters.'

63

I T IS AFTERNOON when Mickel Cardell glances in through the
crowds at Cellar Hamburg and catches sight of Cecil Winge
on his chair under a window covered with frost, emaciated as
never before and as pale as the snow outside, holding his handkerchief over his mouth. Outside, the cold cuts through flesh and
bone, but inside a fire is crackling in the hearth. The heat is
increased by the fact that every inch of the place is packed. Cardell
holds his wooden arm in front of him and makes his way over to
the table. With a sigh, he sinks down across from Winge, relieved
to take the weight off his legs. Cardell notes with a wide smile that
Winge already has a glass on the table in front of him, and waves
for some hot punch himself. Cardell is in high spirits.

'Quite a crowd here today, but I guess it should be expected.
They've just beheaded a wife-murderer on the hill, and people
come here to have a lucky drink from the murderer's glass. I heard
them talking at the door. They said no one had seen Mårten Höss
quite as drunk as he was today, and that he can hardly be expected
to remain at his post after the mess he made of the poor bastard
on the block. I don't understand why you wanted to meet at the
Hamburg, of all places. Do you know this is the very place I was
sitting the night that I fished Karl Johan out of the lake? That
feels like an eternity ago now.'

Cardell blows on the warm drink and then downs it with such
gusto that he has to make a pause in his commentary. He is

smiling from ear to ear, so broadly that his chewing tobacco is in danger of falling out.

'You should have been there. Widow Fröman rounded up some twenty widows, their grown children and many grandchildren, all at one time or another driven to the brink of ruin by our soon-to-be police chief's handling of the widows' pension fund. We loaded them all onto a cart and drove across the ice to Oakenhill on the Hessian Islet, where Blom said that Ullholm had planned to spend his last night before going through customs. You know that I have been to war but I swear that I've never seen a more blood-thirsty crew. We set off in the dead of night so we could arrive before anyone was up and when Magnus Ullholm – ugly as a toad, I might add – came out of the front door ready to leave, they had already frightened the horses away and stripped the wheels off the carriage. They let him come halfway across the yard before he realized anything was amiss. I'll be damned if it wasn't Mrs Fröman herself who sniffed out the dungheap and realized it wasn't frozen. She hit him straight in the face with her first salvo, taking his wig off – never mind her blindness. He was dressed for the occasion, I must say, with an ermine fur collar and a watch on his thigh. But he managed to set off at a sprint I would not have guessed him capable of – now covered in dung from head to toe – and secured himself behind the inn door by a hair's breadth. But there were no escape routes. The women and their children made a ring around the whole house and didn't let a soul in or out. The siege lasted long into the night before anyone managed to get out a message and alert the City Guard. And so I can proudly declare my mission completed. Well, were you able to do what you had hoped with your extra day?'

'Yes, Jean Michael, thank you for everything you have done. I could have expected no more.'

'Are your conversations over?'

'Yes.'

403

Cardell leans back and rubs the sleep out of his eyes.

'And a broken heart is the answer to our mystery?'

'It is the oldest of all motives. Johannes was right in what he first told me. He was raised to become a monster and become one he did. But love will heal hate, and in Daniel Devall's company he regained his humanity. Until it dawned on him that the love was a lie, and then the monster returned, worse than ever.'

They sit silent for a while. Winge is the one who speaks first.

'What will you do now, Jean Michael?'

'There are still some loose threads to gather up, enough to keep me occupied until 1794. I have a bone to pick with Madame Sachs, if I am able to find her. There are others that I would also like to have a word with. I should not be surprised if that slave driver Dülitz should be awoken one night by the sound of wood on wood. And if the spirit should move me, the Order of the Eumenides would prove a reasonable challenge for the one who managed to put a stick in the wheel of the police chief himself.'

He empties his refilled glass.

'That is, as long as I don't allow myself to be distracted by the brandy. There is a pub that I've found that I think I will like and where my credit is good. Name of the Scapegrace. How about you? How will the trial against Balk proceed?'

Winge doesn't answer. Cardell notes with concern how shallow and rapid his breaths are, how his cheeks have sunk and made a hollow on either side of his face, how his eyes have retreated into his skull and how something about him has changed. He feels a cold shiver run down his back.

'You're different. It's not your illness. Something has happened. Something is wrong.'

Winge's voice is so low that Cardell has to lean in to catch what he is saying.

'When I think back upon my life, Jean Michael, I see a braided cord of cause and effect. The ideals to which I adhered in my

404

youth steered my actions when I fell ill and wanted to ease my wife's suffering. To ease my own, I went to Norlin and asked him for work. He did me a service, and when he asked me for a favour in return, I could not refuse. Then we met, you and I, over Karl Johan's dead body, and we began to walk the path we have followed all the way to where we are now.'

He stifles a cough. Cardell leans across the table.

'What have you done?'

'Life is like two roads heading in opposite directions. One follows emotion, the other reason, and the latter has been mine. Johannes knew my name and reputation, and assumed that I would continue along the path of reason without discrimination, as I have always done. I am certain that he would have been successful in his efforts if I had not decided to break the pattern that I have followed my entire life.'

Cardell shakes his head helplessly before this stream of words.

'Tell me what you have done.'

'I showed Johannes the letter from Daniel Devall that we found among Liljensparre's correspondence, in which Devall resigned from his duties and expressed his love. Johannes killed an innocent man. The monster found that it had a conscience, that it deserved to be punished and that the thoughts which had caused it to want to doom our entire race lacked foundation. I offered him an arrangement that was in my power to realize. In the cell next to Balk, there was a prisoner by the name of Lorentz Johansson, sentenced for killing his wife and scheduled to be brought to the gallows this morning. Balk's own name was nowhere in the arrest ledgers, as you know, something I made sure of when we brought him to Kastenhof. Yesterday evening, I offered Johannes the place on the block that should have been Lorentz Johansson's. And he accepted. I pawned my pocket watch and these last few coins that I own I gave to the guard to help me and to swear him to silence. When the executioner's cart came, we put Johannes Balk in it and sent him to his death in Johansson's place.'

'But Devall's letter was written in code. How could you decipher its contents?'

'I couldn't.'

Cardell has to lean back to get some air. Winge goes on.

'I used the time you gave me to construct a key that made Daniel Devall's letter say what Johannes needed to read to accept my offer. It was not easy, Jean Michael, and it cost me a great deal, but I managed it. All I then had to do was mark the letter with a later date. I'm no great forger, but that detail was too insignificant for Johannes to notice any difference in handwriting.'

Cecil Winge slowly pushes a glass across the table, filled to the brim with brandy.

'The glass before you is the same one that Johannes was offered this morning on his way to his execution, the final drink that is given to each prisoner headed beyond the city walls. He emptied it, not ten steps from where we are sitting now. I was here, and he saw me in the crowd, and when our eyes met, I found only gratitude there. With my lie, I had shown him that the world was not the hell that he had hated so. He trusted me and could not know that in reality I had just proved that the depravity of our species is a rule without exception. I took his life, Jean Michael, with my papers, as surely as if I had used them to separate his head from his body. He gave me a final glance across his shoulder as the cart rolled on towards the Sconce Tollgate and then I lost sight of him. Mrs Norström carved the name on the glass with a nail. Now it bears the date and the name Johansson, even though the real Johansson is sitting on a wagon headed to Norway, there to help in the breweries under his mother's maiden name. This glass belongs to Johannes Balk. And now I ask you, Jean Michael, if you would drink to my health one last time?'

Cardell sits silently for a while before he stretches out his hand, wrapped in rags, across the table. It trembles as he picks up the small beaker with its sloppy writing and downs its contents. The liquid stings his throat and turns his exhalation into a hiss as Winge watches him.

'You asked me earlier about the child, if it is mine or the corporal's. I still don't know, but I hope with all my heart that it is his.'

Winge stands up, leaning heavily against the back of the chair, and begins to make his way to the door. He is not halfway before Cardell calls out to him in a voice strained near to breaking.

'You told me once of how you stood before an abyss and how you found comfort in a flame you cupped in your hands. Will there be only darkness now?'

Cecil Winge smiles in return, a smile filled with sorrow but free of remorse, where victory and defeat both share a place. Night starts to fall, settling over Stockholm, one of the last of this year. It rises above the batteries that stand guard against the sea, climbs up the palace walls and onto the spires of the church towers. Night reaches over the waves towards the Quayside and the City-between-the-Bridges, past Polhem's Lock and beyond. Out of the alleys of the city, shadows rise in answer.

The coughing fits now strike Cecil Winge ever more frequently as the hours go by. He can no longer hold them in check and sees no reason to do so. When he smiles back at Mickel Cardell in the light of the fire, his teeth are all stained red.

From Byron, Austen and Darwin

to some of the most acclaimed and original contemporary writing, John Murray takes pride in bringing you powerful, prizewinning, absorbing and provocative books that will entertain you today and become the classics of tomorrow.

We put a lot of time and passion into what we publish and how we publish it, and we'd like to hear what you think.

Be part of John Murray – share your views with us at:

www.johnmurray.co.uk

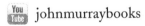 johnmurraybooks

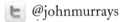 @johnmurrays

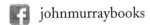 johnmurraybooks